# THE STORY OF
# A MODERN WOMAN

# THE STORY OF
# A MODERN WOMAN

## Ella Hepworth Dixon

*edited by Steve Farmer*

broadview literary texts

**National Library of Canada Cataloguing in Publication**

Dixon, Ella Hepworth
  The story of a modern woman / Ella Hepworth Dixon ; edited by Steve Farmer.

(Broadview literary texts)
Includes bibliographical references.
ISBN 1-55111-380-5

  I. Farmer, Steve.   II. Title.   III. Series.

PR6007.I98S76 2004        823'.8        C2003-905845-X

Broadview Press Ltd. is an independent, international publishing house, incorporated in 1985. Broadview believes in shared ownership, both with its employees and with the general public; since the year 2000 Broadview shares have traded publicly on the Toronto Venture Exchange under the symbol BDP.

We welcome comments and suggestions regarding any aspect of our publications –
please feel free to contact us at the addresses below or at broadview@broadviewpress.com.

*North America*
Post Office Box 1243, Peterborough, Ontario, Canada K9J 7H5
3576 California Road, Orchard Park, NY, USA 14127
Tel: (705) 743-8990; Fax: (705) 743-8353;
e-mail: customerservice@broadviewpress.com

*UK, Ireland, and continental Europe*
Plymbridge Distributors Ltd.
Estover Road
Plymouth  PL6 7PY  UK  Tel: (01752) 202301; Fax: (01752) 202333
e-mail: orders@plymbridge.com

*Australia and New Zealand*
UNIREPS, University of New South Wales
Sydney, NSW, 2052
Tel: 61 2 9664 0099; Fax: 61 2 9664 5420
email: info.press@unsw.edu.au

www.broadviewpress.com

This book is printed on 100% post-consumer recycled, ancient forest friendly paper.

Series Editor: Professor L.W. Conolly
Advisory editor for this volume: Michel W. Pharand
Typesetting and assembly: True to Type Inc., Mississauga, Canada.

PRINTED IN CANADA

# Contents

# Acknowledgments

I would like to thank Diana Day and Stephanie Farmer for reading this novel with me and for giving me helpful advice as I prepared this edition.

Ella Hepworth Dixon, *circa* 1888 (from her autobiography, *As I Knew Them*, 1930).

# Introduction

This edition of Ella Hepworth Dixon's *The Story of a Modern Woman* makes accessible to many a work whose austere and sober beauty led Victorian scholar John Sutherland to call it "the greatest unread novel of female struggle of the century."[1] Sutherland's statement speaks in part to the fact that most *fin de siècle* novels of female struggle, known then and now as New Woman novels, are very difficult to find today. They are either long out of print and long forgotten by all but literary historians, or they are available only in very limited numbers from very small presses. This misfortune exists, in part at least, because many mistakenly look upon the issues examined within these novels to be dated, unique to the 1880s and 1890s, and thus no longer relevant to modern readers. What these would-be readers fail to understand, though, is that these novels offer much more than *tableaux* of a certain social, political, and literary period in England's history. They also do far more than examine the problems within the patriarchal social system in England at the end of the nineteenth century, or question some of the day's troubling marriage and property laws. These stories—and there are many that deserve re-publication—offer universal and timeless truths as they document the constant and difficult struggles of all women always to live life unfettered by cant and blind tradition.

## The Concept of The New Woman and the New Woman Debate in Nineteenth-Century England

At one point late in Ella Hepworth Dixon's 1894 novel *The Story of a Modern Woman*, an anxious Alison Ives exacts a promise from her steady and loving companion, Mary Erle:

> Promise me that you will never, never do anything to hurt another woman.... I don't suppose for an instant you ever would. But there come times in our lives when we can do a great deal of good, or an incalculable amount of harm. If women only used their power in the right way! If we were only united we could lead the world. But we're not. (164)

---

1  *The Stanford Companion to Victorian Fiction* (Stanford: Stanford UP, 1989) 2.

Mary answers her friend slowly and deliberately, with words that Hepworth Dixon would later point to as the "keynote of the book," as her "plea for a kind of moral and social trades-unionism among women":[1]

> [O]ur time is dawning—at last. All we modern women are going to help each other, not to hinder. And there's a great deal to do——. (164)

The uncertain tone of this exchange, with its conflicting hints of melancholy resignation and hopefulness, goes some distance toward representing the ambivalent tone of the novel as a whole. *The Story of a Modern Woman* is a powerful, somber novel of both promise and defeat. It explores the courageous resolve of a woman to live her difficult life with a quiet but expectant dignity, but at the same time it follows her slow and painful journey toward the stark realization that she is out of place in the world into which she has been thrust by cruel circumstance.

This overriding conflict in the novel also illustrates the varying and contradictory attitudes expressed in the contemporary discussions surrounding the *fin de siècle* New Woman phenomenon, of which Hepworth Dixon's novel is a part. The New Woman was a potent phrase first used by novelist Sarah Grand in her 1894 article "The New Aspect of the Woman Question"[2] and thereafter quickly adopted by the British periodical press as a rather baggy catchall reference to anything or anyone "feminist."[3] Arising initially out

---

1  Hepworth Dixon's statement appears in "The Book of the Month: The Novel of the Modern Woman," a review by W.T. Stead for *Review of Reviews* 10 (1894): 64-74. [See Appendix A.] In her 1930 autobiography, *As I Knew Them: Sketches of People I Have Met on the Way*, Hepworth Dixon credits Stead's essay for much of her novel's success.

2  Sarah Grand (Frances Elizabeth McFall, 1854-1943) published this article in the March 1894 number of the *North American Review*, a monthly published initially in Boston and later, from the late 1870s until its demise in 1940, in New York. It may seem odd that "New Woman," a phrase most often associated with British fiction, was coined in an American journal, but the *North American Review* at the time was often a vehicle for British writers.

3  In her 1996 work *British Women Fiction Writers of the 1890s*, Carolyn Christensen Nelson suggests that "the words 'feminist' and 'feminism' with their present meanings entered the vocabulary during the 1890s and were employed by critics, usually pejoratively, in their reviews of the New Woman fiction during this decade" (1-2).

of the "Woman Question" debates then raging about suffrage, occupation, marriage, and maternity, the New Woman possessed, to use the label Sally Ledger employs in her 1997 study *The New Woman: Fiction and Feminism at the fin de siècle*, a "multiple identity." To the Victorians who wrote about the phenomenon, the New Woman was "variously, a feminist activist, a social reformer, a popular novelist, a suffragette playwright, a woman poet; she was also often a fictional construct, a discursive response to the activities of the late nineteenth-century women's movement" (Ledger 1).[1]

As the Victorians wrote quite a lot about the New Woman, her identity also depended on which of the various London journals happened to be weighing in on the issue at any given time during the last decade of the nineteenth century. Many literary and cultural reviews routinely attempted to define, explain, describe, characterize, categorize, praise, or condemn the idea of the New Woman as it was being developed and shaped by a number of recently published novels which were, as one reviewer observed, "written by a woman about women from the standpoint of Woman."[2] Conservative journals regularly castigated the New Woman and New Woman fiction, reproving those writers whom *Fortnightly Review* commentator Janet Hogarth labeled "Literary Degenerates,"[3] decrying what poet and critic Edmund Gosse called "the decay of literary tastes,"[4] and denouncing what staunch Tory traditionalists hoped would be a short-lived feminist uprising. At the same time, these journals attempted to re-affirm the patriarchal social norm, praising the "Old Woman" of Victorian England, the woman whose duty early in life, according to poet Charles Kingsley, was to "Be good, sweet maid, and let who will

---

1  Ledger, whose study is certainly one of the most important full-length assessments of the New Woman phenomenon and New Woman fiction, even suggests that the "New Woman, as a concept was, from its inception, riddled with contradictions" (Ledger 16).

2  This often-used description comes from W.T. Stead's review of several New Woman novels, "The Book of the Month: The Novel of the Modern Woman," *Review of Reviews* 10 (1894): 64.

3  This was the title of Hogarth's rant about the decline of literature, published in the April 1, 1895 number of *Fortnightly Review*.

4  English scholar and poet Sir Edmund Gosse (1849-1928) used this claim as the heading of his section of a co-authored article titled "Degeneration and Evolution," which appeared in *The North American Review* 161 (July 1895): 109-18.

be clever,"[1] and whose only callings later on were marriage and maternity.

Such conservative publications as *Nineteenth Century* and *Blackwood's*, and others with the same or a similar political slant, tended to portray the New Woman in any number of unflattering ways, often under such derogatory headings as "Modern Mannish Maidens," "Wild Women," the "Anti-Marriage League," and the "always manly" Novissima.[2] They also likened the debate to a pitched battle in an all-out war, regularly discussing the women's movement in military terms, referring often to "revolts," "regiments" of women, "anti-marriage brigades," "battalions of revolutionaries," and "social insurgents." This foundation-shaking crusade was, after all, a deadly serious matter.

Articles appeared describing the New Woman as a sexual revolutionary incapable of love and intent on undermining the sanctity of marriage and maternity. Writers in *Cornhill* condemned this "Novissima," arguing bluntly, "She proves nothing. She has tried to prove that woman's mission is something higher than the bearing of children and the bringing them up. But she has failed" (Scott and Hill 368).[3] Another critic of the New Woman, Ella Winston, used her 1896 *Forum* article, "Foibles of the New Woman," to denounce

---

1   See English novelist and poet Charles Kingsley's (1819-75) poem "A Farewell" (1858).

2   These labels come from journal articles of the day. "Modern Mannish Maidens" is the title of an unsigned article from February 1890 number of *Blackwood's*; "Wild Women" is an epithet used by Eliza Lynn Linton in three anti-women's rights articles—"The Wild Women as Politicians," "The Wild Women as Social Insurgents," and "Partisans of the Wild Women"—that appeared in *Nineteenth Century* between July 1891 and March 1892; the "Anti-Marriage League" was the title of Margaret Oliphant's condemnatory review of Hardy's *Jude the Obscure* (1895) and Grant Allen's *The Woman Who Did* (1895) in the January 1896 number of *Blackwood's*; and "Novissima" is the name given to the New Woman by H.S. Scott and E. Hall in their "Character Note: The New Woman," an article in the October 1894 number of *Cornhill*. See Appendix D for excerpts from some of these articles.

3   Unlike the notoriously conservative journals that regularly bombarded their readers with vicious assaults on the notion of the New Woman, *Cornhill* was considered to be one of the more enlightened middle-class literary journals of the day. Even *Cornhill*, though, would occasionally strike out against women's rights, as shown by "Character Note: The New Woman," an extended and sarcastic caricature of the New Woman.

women who attempted to subvert "the Creator's design for the reproduction and maintenance of the race" (Winston 192) by shirking their maternal responsibilities. She claimed that women who condemn marriage and motherhood ignore "the silent testimony of countless happy wives" (Winston 187), concluding, "When we read of women assembling together, parading streets, and entering saloons ... it is but natural to ask, What are the children of such mothers doing in the meantime?" (Winston 192). Others saw those women who promoted a life outside the bonds of marriage as provocateurs, political activist Frederic Harrison condemning the "specious agitation" that "must ultimately degrade them, sterilize them, unsex them." Harrison then reveals what he believes to be the true duty of all women: "The glory of woman is to be tender, loving, pure, inspiring in her home; it is to raise the moral tone of every household....."[1]

Some fearful adversaries saw in the New Woman an athletic, cigar-smoking gender invert and pseudo–intellectual decadent incapable of understanding either the limitations of women or the inner workings of the man she apparently aspired to emulate.[2] The novelist Eliza Lynn Linton, certainly one of the most vocal and acerbic opponents of women's rights, used her 1892 article "The Partisans of the Wild Women" to rail against the "woman who smokes in public and where she is forbidden, who dresses in knickerbockers or a boy's suit, who trails about in tigerskins, who flouts conventional decencies and offends against all the canons of good taste"(Linton 460). And one writer for *Blackwood's* spends much of his article, "Modern Mannish Maidens," bemoaning the fact that too many

---

1   In other political matters, Frederic Harrison (1831-1923) was a radical liberal, fighting in particular on behalf of trade unions. The "Woman Question" apparently was a different matter. The article from which this passage was taken is titled "The Emancipation of Women" and appeared in *Fortnightly Review* 50 (1 October 1891): 437-52.

2   These broadly painted character traits offered a prototypical view of what would eventually become the adopted stereotype of lesbianism. The notion of lesbian sexuality, though, had not yet become a part of the discourse of the period. The term "lesbian" as a reference to female sexuality was not used until late in the 1890s. And since sex for a woman was understood to be solely a procreative activity, the possibility of female same-sex sexual relations was never considered. Sexologist Havelock Ellis offers an early discussion of lesbianism in his 1897 study *Sexual Inversion*, in which he divided lesbians into two broad categories: inverts, women genetically pre-disposed to lesbian sexuality, and perverts, women who choose to be attracted to other women.

women had begun to take an interest in physical sports such as rowing, bicycling, or lawn tennis. He sneers at what he calls "tennis-y" girls and then laments the passing of the "female form":

> One cannot expect all Eve's daughters to be fashioned alike, but there is a type of them one sometimes meets at garden-parties that may be known at a glance,—hard, wooden-looking, muscular, from whose figures the softness and roundness which nature usually associates with womanhood seem to have been played out. It is probably that any violent physical exercise of this kind, habitually overdone, may bring the female form to this masculine and uncomely aspect, or at least intensify any tendency that way where it may already exist.[1]

Still other articles represented the New Woman as a capricious creature recklessly insisting on enfranchisement which, once gained, would lead to an involvement in the political arena that would inevitably bring down the British government. The novelist Ouida (Marie Louise de la Ramée), in her essay "The New Woman," a doomsday commentary full of stereotypes, spelled out the perceived political dangers as she saw them:

> Woman in public life would exaggerate the failings of men, and would not have even their few excellencies. Their legislation would be, as that of men is too often, the offspring of panic and prejudice; and she would not put on the drag of common-sense as man frequently does in public assemblies. There would be little to hope from her humanity, nothing from her liberality; for when she is frightened she is more ferocious than he, and when she has power more merciless. (Ouida 614)

Eliza Lynn Linton went even further, using a trilogy of "Wild Women" articles to characterize this new type of woman and those who supported her positions as people whose vocal opposition to longstanding British cultural proprieties exposed them as traitors fully capable of selling state secrets to enemies of the Empire. In "The Partisans of the Wild Women," she writes:

---

1  See "Modern Mannish Maidens" in *Blackwood's* 147 (February 1890): 252-64.

In politics, in morals, in taste, they are equally examples of what to avoid. Whatever tells against the dignity and integrity of our empire they advocate. They eulogise and uphold the pronounced enemies of our country. They would give the keys of our foreign possessions into the hands of Russia or of France; they brand patriotism as jingoism; and they teach all who listen to them to break the laws, to despise our national institutions, to ridicule our national traditions, to dishonour our national flag. (Linton 458)

Such remarkably malicious portraits, frequently penned by women and truly astonishing to read today, clashed, of course, with those that appeared in the more forward-thinking and liberal journals of the time. And though the conservative journals cried foul more frequently and more epithetically, some of the more enlightened magazines occasionally offered readers fervent defenses of the character of the New Woman as it was being shaped by the fiction of the day. Proponents saw in her a beacon of truth and hope, someone who would finally expose and correct the innumerable inequalities to which women had long been subjected, someone who could inspire crucial and much needed social, cultural, and political reforms for which English women had long been fighting. They insisted that a new day had begun to dawn for women, that they were, as Sarah Grand put it in her article "The New Aspect of the Woman Question," "awaking from their long apathy" (Grand 271) to realize a potential for themselves beyond the limitations of forced matrimony and maternity, and to raise their voices collectively in an effort to bring about long-needed change. Grand wrote of this new awareness: "[T]he new woman ... has been sitting apart in silent contemplation all these years, thinking and thinking, until at last she solved the problem and proclaimed for herself what was wrong with Home-is-the-Woman's-Sphere, and prescribed the remedy" (Grand 271). Later in the article, she spells out the commitment of the women's movement: "The man of the future will be better, while the woman will be stronger and wiser. To bring this about is the whole aim and object of the present struggle" (Grand 272). And finally, she levels an angry charge at those she sees to be accountable for the miseries of women: "Let him who is responsible for the economic position which forces women down be punished for the consequence ... " (Grand 276). Such statements as these, which seem both a rallying cry to all disenfranchised women and a potent warning to others that dramatic change was soon to sweep the country, depict the New Woman as a powerful figure whose strength of character and intelligence allow her to thrive despite a thousand outdated traditions that exist to hold her down.

Alongside Grand, Mona Caird, another popular novelist of the day, also frequently used the periodical publications as a megaphone for the women's rights movement. In an 1892 article titled "A Defence of the So-Called 'Wild Women'," she answers Eliza Lynn Linton's charges and paints what would soon be labeled the New Woman as someone struggling nobly for basic freedoms. She spends most of her essay beseeching women to insist on change: "The demand that all women shall conform to a certain model of excellence, that they shall be debarred from following the promptings of their powers and instincts, whatsoever be the pretext for the restriction ... ought to be resisted as all attacks on liberty ought to be resisted" (Caird 817). In her best-known essay, "Marriage," Caird portrays the New Woman as someone strong enough to realize "the obvious right ... to *possess herself* body and soul, to give or withhold herself body and soul" (198, Caird's emphasis). For Caird, the New Woman was wise enough and now ready to see the institution of marriage as "a vexatious failure," and she was strong enough to defy this "worst ... form of woman-purchase" (Caird 197). The New Woman, then, to those English advocates of women's rights in the 1890s, often appears within journal discussions as a bold, vital, and even rebellious figure, someone who felt herself to be newly liberated, independent of men, who saw herself as a strong person focused on women's rights.

These various assessments suggest that the New Woman was to the Victorians a difficult concept to define, that she was, as Ann Ardis suggests in her 1990 study *New Women, New Novels: Feminism and Early Modernism*, "many things to many people" (Ardis 10).[1] But in addition to the extended nineteenth-century discussions, modern literary critics and feminist historians have recently added to the discussion, using what Ledger calls "rather more loosely applied" definitions to re-shape and re-characterize the New Woman (Ledger 1).[2]

---

1   Ann Ardis's *New Woman, New Novels* (New Brunswick, NJ: Rutgers UP, 1990) is another of a handful of landmark studies of the English New Woman.

2   It was not until the last quarter of the twentieth century that literary critics and historians began to explore in any depth the New Woman movement. A.R. Cunningham's essay "The 'New Woman Fiction' of the 1890s," *Victorian Studies* 17 (December 1973): 177-86 offers one of the

They tend to push her into the twentieth century and study her as some sort of prototypical anticipation of the feminist and modernist movements—"the new woman was nothing if not modern" (Ledger 150)—in twentieth-century British culture and literature; they create for her a legacy as literary and cultural godparent to any number of twentieth-century feminist activists, writers, and thinkers. Ledger notes this problematic modern re-contextualization, suggesting that though "[t]he New Woman was very much a fin-de-siècle phenomenon ... [l]ate twentieth-century feminist literary history has constructed a genealogy of first- and second-generation New Women: the first living and writing in the 1880s and 1890s, the second in the 1920s and 1930s" (Ledger 1).

This last part of Ledger's claim exposes a thread common to all of these assessments and re-assessments of the New Woman. Whether of the nineteenth or the twentieth century, and no matter how far they range or how politicized they become, these various discussions exist because of the literature of the period. The fiction is at the heart of the matter. Ardis worries that the conservative periodical press of the late nineteenth century neutralized the power of the feminist political drive for enfranchisement by effectively limiting the New Woman debate to a discussion of fiction, thereby marginalizing literature and relegating the New Woman novel "to the margin of that margin" (Ardis 13). One must realize, though, that fiction at the time played a tremendously important role in shaping public opinion. Many novelists of the day felt responsible for the social and cultural education of a vast and growing reading public and believed that their works could, in fact, effect social and political change.

In other words, a discussion of the New Woman should focus, when all is said and done, on the fiction of the period. Today's readers need not possess a complete historical, political, or cultural understanding of the *fin de siècle* New Woman phenomenon to be able to see emerging within much of the fiction of the period patterns that help to define the genre, that help one to appreciate that these novels offer, more than anything else, a clear and penetrating

---

first twentieth-century definitions of the New Woman, dividing the genre into two groups: the "purity" school and the "neurotic" school. Elaine Showalter was the first scholar to offer an extended study of the New Woman novelists and New Woman fiction in her 1977 study *A Literature of Their Own: British Women Novelists from Brontë to Lessing* (Princeton, NJ: Princeton UP, 1993).

examination of the universal struggles for equality—on any number of levels—faced by British women of the nineteenth century.

## Characteristics of the New Woman Novel

In her 1993 study *The Woman Reader: 1837-1914*, Kate Flint outlined some of the patterns that emerge as common features in many of the better known novels of the last decade of the nineteenth century:

> [The New Woman novel's] plotting is rarely complex in the sense of involving the reader in concealment and suspense: it is not predicated upon the reading process gratifying a desire for clarification and resolution. Its preferred form is the *Bildungsroman*, and it shares a certain number of characteristics with nineteenth-century women's autobiography. Frequently, it privileges childhood, both as a nostalgic realm which cannot be recaptured, and as a recognized site of gendered injustices. More noticeably, it presents life as process, stressing the value of continuity, even endurance, and of adhering to often painfully learnt principles: principles which are self-generated and rationally arrived at, rather than being imposed by dominant social beliefs. (Flint 294-95)

As it addresses characteristics of the New Woman as a literary concept, Flint's catalogue also reveals a sharp distinction between the New Woman of the late-century periodical discussions and the New Woman of the novels of the day. Far from being the potent social anomaly feared by conservative writers, or the vibrant instrument for sweeping social change depicted in some progressive articles, the New Woman as a fictional creation appears as a noble but fatigued figure struggling against overwhelming odds to find her place, ultimately compelled merely to survive in a male-dominated social and political world. She is a young woman attempting, for the first time—though often failing—to resist the horrors of sexual subservience to which she had long been shackled by her society's antiquated marriage laws and sexual conventions. Moreover, she is someone who recognizes the scope of her intellect but at the same time becomes sadly aware that its potential will be wasted by a society's insistence that her sole purpose for being is maternity. And finally, she is often a lonely and alien figure laboring in the bleak urban landscape of London—a place of few opportunities for single women—a figure further alienated by statistics that show she is among the "superfluous" or "odd" single women who outnumber single men in England by hundreds of thousands at the end of the century.[1]

The New Woman novel as a sub-genre emerged in the late 1880s and early 1890s with the appearance of a cluster of works that shared quite a few of these structural and thematic characteristics. Popular—and in some circles notorious—women novelists such as Sarah Grand, Mona Caird, Emma Frances Brook, George Egerton (Mary Chavelita Bright), and Ménie Muriel Dowie, among others,[2] generated works of fiction that in one way or another trace a woman's difficult and often painful path to self discovery. Even a glance at just a few of their better known works reveals parallels and patterns common among much of the fiction of the day.

Perhaps the best known New Woman novelist of the last decade of the nineteenth century was Sarah Grand, in large part because of her notorious trio of interrelated novels—*Ideala*, *The Heavenly Twins*, and *The Beth Book*—published over ten years between 1888 and 1897. These novels, all bestsellers, possess various and strikingly autobiographical depictions of her own failed marriage to a tyrannous older man. Grand's main figures are all noble, suffering women compelled by circumstance and propriety to marry men of questionable character and with whom they are not in love. Defiantly polemical, these books scrutinize the sexual double standard of the age, portraying main female figures as women devastated as they slowly come to see the vast social and cultural inequities that exist between genders. Ideala, the title character of Grand's 1888 novel, realizes through the actions of her adulterous husband that

---

1 The 1891 census counted 900,000 more unmarried women than men. Other sources place the figure as high as one million.

2 The blurred boundaries of the label "New Woman" suggest that any number of writers in the last decades of the nineteenth century could be categorized as writers of New Woman fiction, or at least as writers who occasionally produced what seems to be New Woman fiction. Often, in fact, male novelists appear among the category. George Meredith's novel *Diana of the Crossways* (1885), if not a New Woman novel *per se*, certainly explores the "Woman Question" of the day. Thomas Hardy's *Tess of the D'Urbervilles* (1892) and *Jude the Obscure* (1895) both possess many of the characteristics of New Woman fiction written by women. George Gissing's *The Odd Women* (1893) explores the grim fate of single women in London along the same lines as Hepworth Dixon's novel.

men wish to keep women in a degraded, subservient state. Evadne Frayling, Edith Beale, and Angelica Hamilton-Wells, all major figures from the three loosely related parts of *The Heavenly Twins* (1893), also suffer as they learn from life's experiences that their society's demands for sexual purity in women simply do not apply to men. Trapped in a marriage to the disreputable Colonel Colquhoun, Evadne is driven to attempt suicide, and Edith dies of the syphilis she has contracted from her unfaithful husband. Only Angelica survives intact, though not without first witnessing the freedom of her twin brother's life while experiencing the constraints placed on her own. The third novel of the set, *The Beth Book* (1897), traces the life of Elizabeth Caldwell Maclure from childhood through a lamentable marriage to a sadistic adulterer and vivisectionist, a man who works at a hospital where prostitutes are forcibly subjected to examinations for venereal disease.[1] Beth suffers mightily, though she does manage to use the painful experiences to become, by the end of her tale, an outspoken advocate for women's rights.

Mona Caird, another best selling novelist of the 1890s, also used her fiction to tell the stories of noble and long-suffering women who battle against—but eventually capitulate in one way or another—the tyrannies of the English marriage system. Viola Sedley, the heroine of Caird's *The Wing of Azrael* (1889), agonizes under the cruelties of her sadistic husband. She ultimately stabs him to death before hurling herself over a cliff. And in her popular novel *The Daughters of Danaus* (1894), Caird's heroine, the Scottish-born Hadria Fullerton, attempts to discover herself within various relationships in England and on the continent. Her attempts are in vain, though, for she drifts into various oppressive associations with men before returning to her family, effectively beaten down by their attempts to shame her for having left them to pursue her own happiness.

---

1  These forced examinations were a reality. The Contagious Diseases Acts of the 1860s, which held women primarily responsible for the spread of venereal diseases in England, allowed for the forcible incarceration and treatment, in prison-like hospital wards, of prostitutes even suspected of suffering from syphilis. Though the main Act of 1864 was repealed in 1886, many at the time still believed that syphilis could be spread only to men by women with the disease, and this element of the Victorian sexual double standard became fair game for some of the bolder New Woman novelists.

Emma Frances Brooke, George Egerton, and Ménie Muriel Dowie were three other New Woman novelists almost as popular as Grand and Caird were at the time. Brooke's *A Superfluous Woman* (1894) is certainly among the grimmer New Woman stories of the decade. Her heroine, Jessamine Halliday, attempts to reject the stifling, destructive life of London society by fleeing to Scotland, where she falls in love with the noble farmer Colin Macgillvray. But the relationship fails and Jessamine returns to London and marries the hateful Lord Heriot, a man she despises but by whom she bears three children—an idiot daughter, a deformed son, and a stillborn baby—before dying mad of syphilis. Egerton's *Keynotes*, a brief series of sketches first published in 1893, though not so starkly melodramatic as Brooke's novel, offers its own examinations of women at the mercy of a society that ignores injustices within the institution of marriage. Two stories in the collection, "Under Northern Sky" and "An Empty Frame," depict a woman's attempt to escape from a loveless marriage into a world of fantasy. Egerton, who herself suffered at the hands of abusive and alcoholic husbands, used her fiction to depict marriage to such a man as a trap from which most women cannot escape. And Dowie's *Gallia* (1895), which shocked readers with its frank discussions of extra-marital sex and procreative choices based on the theories of eugenics rather than love, offers an extended view of the many difficulties faced by Gallia Hamesthwaite, an Oxford-educated and strong-willed woman out of step with and misunderstood by society. The radical Gallia chooses as her mate the young Mark Gurdon—even though she loves someone else—because she believes such a match would produce more physically and intellectually suitable offspring. In an attempt to demonstrate the substance of Gallia's modern views of society, Dowie paints her in stark contrast to the many other women of the novel, all types representing various incarnations of the Victorian "Old Woman"; but despite her brave modernity, Gallia nevertheless seems finally compelled by social pressures to embrace the institutions of marriage and maternity.

Again, then, within all of these works, and many others, lie stories in which women brave the daunting injustices and prejudices of their world, but in which they are also more often than not frustrated by the pressures placed upon them by the caddish, brutish men in their lives. Each is a story of growth, education, and awareness for the main female characters, but the awareness gained is ultimately a grim and disheartening one. Each shows a woman coming of age but coming also to realize that women are burdened by social propriety and forced into lives with very few choices.

## *The Story of a Modern Woman* and the New Woman Novel

*The Story of a Modern Woman*, Ella Hepworth Dixon's only novel, shares with many works published at the time, several of the same characteristics.[1] The story is, as Hepworth Dixon herself claimed, "a somewhat gloomy study of the struggles of a girl alone in the world and earning her own living."[2] And like the others, it sets out to delineate the inequities of an anachronistic patriarchal social system, to document the plight of women in a world run by essentially thoughtless, if not dishonest men unwilling to relinquish any authority. It traces the life of Mary Erle, ostensibly the title character, from her London childhood through her awakening to the hardships of life as a single, self-supporting woman in a culture where such women are not valued. And Mary's story, like these others, is in many ways measured out by the various betrayals she suffers at the hands of the men in her life. It is also, as were many of

---

1　Hepworth Dixon wrote a substantial number of short stories, most of which she published in two collections: *My Flirtations* (1893), under the ironic pseudonym Margaret Wynman, and *One Doubtful Hour* (1904). The two collections also share many of the same themes explored in *The Story of a Modern Woman*, in particular the idea that women, trapped by a society that offers up marriage as the only option, are eventually forced to barter away their emotional and intellectual well-being. *My Flirtations*, narrated by Margaret ("Peggy") Wynman, is a series of thirteen short sketches, one for each of Peggy's thirteen suitors. Though the tone initially is relatively light, the stories become darker as the narrator is pulled inevitably toward the bonds of marriage. *One Doubtful Hour* contains ten stories that had initially appeared in the late nineteenth century in the journals *The World*, *The Pall Mall Magazine*, *Lady's Pictorial*, *Ladies' Field*, and *The Yellow Book*. The collection's title story sets the melancholy tone as it tells the story of Effie Lauder, a single woman who believes she has no prospects but marriage, but who also fears that she is probably too old to attract a suitor. At a local ball, she makes a desperate and ultimately humiliating bid for the attention of the eligible Colonel Simpson, and after he shuns her advances, she returns to her shabby apartment, turns on the gas, and kills herself.

2　This assessment appears in Hepworth Dixon's autobiography, *As I Knew Them: Sketches of People I Have Met on the Way* (London: Hutchinson, 1930) 136.

its counterparts, a novel grounded in autobiography, for many of its scenes offer a rather straightforward recounting of events in Hepworth Dixon's life.[1] The novel's power and uniqueness, though, derives not from any sense that it is part of a collective, or from any general, broad-brush treatment of familiar Victorian "Woman Question" issues, but from Hepworth Dixon's meticulous attention to all shades of realistic detail as she establishes atmosphere, and from her magnificent braiding of this atmosphere with setting, character, and theme.

### Mary Erle's London

Hepworth Dixon hems her reader in with detail, a strategy that creates an oppressive, stifling atmosphere that hangs heavily over the story from beginning to end. Hers is a very close novel, nearly all the action—what little action there is—taking place within the dismal, gloomy urban landscape of London, and more often than not within various dark, cramped, and suffocating apartments and offices within the central city. The detailed descriptions of these various places, relentlessly crowding in upon the reader as they do, create a very real sensation of claustrophobia. It is in many respects clearly symbolic of the plight of the nineteenth-century Englishwoman as someone cornered by the cant of tradition and prevented at every turn from achieving even modest gains.

This closeness, this claustrophobia, begins with the novel's opening sentence, which juxtaposes the brightness of the day out of doors with the literally funereal atmosphere of the Erle home, with its "sickly, yellow twilight" created by "blinds ... scrupulously drawn down" (43). Mary Erle's father has just died, and as his body lies in his room at the top of a "narrow London staircase," the "strange,

---

1   *As I Knew Them*, published two years before Hepworth Dixon's death, recounts some details of childhood and early womanhood that echo several of the episodes in Mary Erle's life. Hepworth Dixon, like Mary, was born into a family that embraced reading and education; her father, William Hepworth Dixon, was a famed editor of the *Athenæum* between 1853 and 1869. Like Mary, Hepworth Dixon attended school in Germany as a child before a serious illness forced her to return to England. And like Professor Erle, Hepworth Dixon's father died suddenly when Ella was a young woman in her early twenties, leaving her more or less to fend for herself. She did so, as does Mary Erle, by becoming a journalist and fiction writer. Ella Hepworth Dixon never married.

unmistakable odour of death, mixed with the voluptuous scent of waxen hot-house flowers, hung, night and day ... " (45). Even out of doors, at the Highgate funeral later in the week, the atmosphere is crushing: "the sun grew hotter and hotter overhead" and "the perfume of the pink hawthorn became almost oppressive" (47). That the story opens with a death and a funeral is quite telling.

From the high ground of the cemetery, Mary Erle looks out over the vast panorama of London stretched out below her.[1] From this distance, she sees only the domes, the spires, the tree-tops; she cannot get a real sense from here of the immense crush of humanity below her, saying to her younger brother, Jim, excitedly but with some trepidation, "there's London! We're going to make it listen to us, you and I. We're not going to be afraid of it—just because it's big, and brutal, and strong" (48). London, then, becomes from the outset one of the story's central symbols. It is for Mary a living being, a powerful entity capable of listening, but certainly more likely, she learns, unwilling to cooperate. It may offer great opportunities for some, but for most it remains a cruel master. The power of London as a symbol of brooding, brutal force remains palpable throughout the novel, right through to the final chapter, in which Mary returns after many years to Highgate cemetery and once again looks out over the city.

That is not to say that the London of *The Story of a Modern Woman* is a grotesque and surreal Dickensian landscape of hidden dangers and caricaturistic criminals. Nor is it the abyss of utter hopelessness that it represents in George Gissing's grim novel *The Odd Women* (1893), wherein the reader sees the city claim the lives and souls of one Madden sister after another. And the symbolism certainly is not as extreme as that which Richard Jefferies employs in his extraordinary novel *After London* (1885), a story set in the distant future, after some sort of environmental affliction—"the event"—has reduced London to "a vast stagnant swamp, which no man dare enter, since death would be his inevitable fate" (Jefferies 68).[2]

At the same time, though, Mary Erle's London is certainly not the vibrant, bustling city that Henry James could write about so lovingly, a city that put him "in a state of deep delight" each time he visited, a city he "took possession of." James may have embraced

---

1 London in the last decades of the nineteenth century was the largest city in the world, a vast metropolis of over six million people.
2 Richard Jefferies, *After London; or, Wild England* (London: Cassell, 1885).

the might of London and reveled in the freedom it offered him, writing in his journal simply that "it is the right place to be,"[1] but for a single woman trying to make her way by herself, the city offered few advantages. She would almost certainly feel constricted by limited opportunities.[2]

Such is Mary's London, both limited and limiting; it consists, for the most part, of a few plain, rather shabby rooms within the gloomy central city, a city she rarely leaves for a taste of the world outside.[3] It is a lonely place, the narrator notes, one that offers "hundreds of acquaintance and but few intimate friends" (69), and ultimately, it poses for Mary very real physical dangers, of which her doctor bluntly warns her: "You live too much in London. There is too much strain on your nervous system" (143). Ironically, on the one occasion that Mary ventures outside of London, when she is sent to school in Germany as a young woman of sixteen, disaster strikes. She is overcome by a severe illness, nearly dies, and is sent home to England to recover. It is as if London, the same London that drains her of her strength, demands that she remain within its pull.

Throughout the novel, Hepworth Dixon supplies ample and detailed evidence of the choking narrowness of life for Mary Erle. The apartments into which Mary moves after the death of her father are dreary and confining. Her bedroom, which she finds herself comparing unfavorably with the pretty little room she slept in as a child, looks out on her "grimy back-yard" and contains not much more than "a small iron bed with starved-looking pillows" and walls "covered with a paper on which apples of a dingy yellow

---

1 James expressed his satisfaction with London in his journal in 1881. For more on his views of the city, see *The Complete Notebooks of Henry James*, ed. Leon Edel and Lyall Powers (New York: Oxford UP, 1987).

2 The huge metropolis presented only difficulties for most single women. Decent employment opportunities were limited, almost non-existent for women, and decent housing was expensive outside of the slums of London's East End. Near the turn of the century there were upwards of one million more women in England than men—thus the phrases "odd women" or "superfluous women"—and many of these women drifted into London's East End from rural counties, only to end up competing with one another for a hard-scrabble existence.

3 To get a sense of just how small Mary's world is, see Appendix B, an 1883 map of London keyed to show locations of importance in the novel.

sprawled, in endless repetition, on a dull green ground" (96).[1] Her furniture was "old, shabby, and pretentious," and Hepworth Dixon amplifies Mary's loneliness with the slow ticking of her "gilt clock with the hovering cupid" (97–8). Cupid certainly offers a harsh and fitting irony here. At one point, Mary rather plaintively tells an acquaintance who has asked about this dwelling, "I hope that I will not have to stay there long. What I should like would be a little house somewhere in a suburb. A little house with a garden" (131). It is a dream she never realizes.

These are the same dismal apartments where on one occasion Mary sits alone for an evening, awaiting the return of her lover, Vincent Hemming, from overseas. As she waits—Vincent, of course, does not appear—Mary again endures the oppressive isolation that has become her life:

> It was very hot; stuffy with the damp, vitiated air of a London night verging on August. Few people passed. Bulstrode Street is a quiet thoroughfare. Once, about eight o'clock, cab-wheels were audible. Mary shrank into the farthest corner of the room, clasping her little hands tight, and listening for the sound of the door-bell and that well-known step on the stair. But neither came. (118)

Outside of her rooms, whenever Mary travels about the city itself, the atmosphere remains stifling. More often than not she is accompanied on her journeys by a dense London fog, torrents of rain, and "the clatter and roar of the street" (107). And her destinations themselves almost always serve to shade even further the gloomy landscape of the novel.

Early in the story, as soon as Mary realizes she must provide for herself, her father having left her with nothing but her own resourcefulness, she attempts to become an artist, attending the Central London School of Art in the hope of gaining admission to the Royal Academy. As she ventures to the school for the first time, fittingly on a "raw December day," she finds it in "a dreary by-street near Portland Road; a small thoroughfare of sinister aspect, in which the houses seemed to be frowning at each other's dubious appearance" (84–5). These frowning houses serve to emphasize

---

1   This image recalls Charlotte Perkins Gilman's "The Yellow Wall-paper" (1892), another story of confinement and restriction.

Mary's growing isolation: "The white blinds—now grey with age and dirt—seemed always drawn; no one ever seemed to emerge from those faded, bespattered front doors" (84). In fact, the street itself seems to shrink her world, eerily closing off all opportunity to her: "It was a dreary, mysterious street, of which, when Mary thought of it, she invariably saw the two ends swallowed up in a dingy, yellowish fog" (84).

The Strand, home to the Fleet Street journals where Mary hopes to sell her writing, appears to her "so dreary, so cheaply vicious" (145). The editors' offices, always at the tops of dark, narrow staircases, sit guarded by melancholy men and hissing gas-fires; they are practically empty cells, imprisoned themselves by the "encrusted grime of the windowpanes" and the "tall brick houses of the opposite side of the Strand" (108). And the Whitechapel Hospital that Mary tours with her friend Alison offers further images of imprisonment, with its windows "giving on a grimy back garden, a garden whose sodden grass plot was closed in by high brown brick walls, and over which hung a heavy, fog-laden sky, etched with sooty branches" (149).

Even those places that *should* offer Mary some relief from the monotony of her life, some sense of community, instead tend only to lower the ceiling. The modish new theater, where Mary attends the production of a current comedy, is described in suffocating terms as "one compact mass of human beings" (137). And the afternoon kettledrums, the drawing-room teas, the art showings, and the elaborate dinners that Mary frequents as she prepares to write her society articles for *The Fan* magazine, often turn for her into uncomfortably stifling affairs that feature little more than the "conventional voices of the men, the foolish, fixed smiles of the women all around ... " (156).

The suffocating crush of the cityscape, then, clearly helps to establish and maintain Hepworth Dixon's theme of oppression and subjugation. Many New Woman novels told essentially urban tales, stories wherein a woman either struggles with her anonymous life in the city or is an outsider drawn inexorably to it, more often than not to be destroyed by it. *The Story of a Modern Woman* is certainly no exception, Hepworth Dixon creating, with many images of a grim and indifferent city, a very powerful symbol of the anonymous toil which was the fate of many single women at the time. But she also weaves precise and very real characters into this rich fabric and extends her novel's theme well beyond its lowering urban setting.

## The Men in Mary Erle's Life

For most of the novel Mary remains confined and limited at every turn by the various men in her life. Her father, who has just died as the novel opens, may have seemed a protector to Mary during her childhood, but his was ultimately a false security; his failure to provide her with any substantial inheritance serves to imprison Mary in a lifelong struggle to survive in a working world in which most young, single women are treated with scorn. Her aggravatingly carefree and careless younger brother, Jimmie, whose profligate spending habits create constant worry for Mary, also restricts her, chaining her to a life controlled by mounting debt: "Brothers are so expensive—they want such a lot of neckties" (130), she sighs at one point.

The novel's central male figure is Vincent Hemming, who also severely limits Mary's potential. He is the lover who secures from Mary a pledge to wait for him while he travels the world for a year, and who then abandons her to marry a coarse and vulgar woman whose father can aid him in his attempts to advance in politics. As he draws from her the promise of constancy and love, "[h]is hands, which held her two wrists as they stood there gazing at each other, felt like links of iron" (82). And Hepworth Dixon, not content with this dramatic penal metaphor, makes certain a moment later that her reader does not overlook the dark power behind the promise: "In that one supreme moment Mary Erle tasted for the first time, in all its intensity, the helplessness of woman, the inborn feeling of subjection to a stronger will, inherited through generations of submissive feminine intelligences" (82). Mary, in essence, realizes that Hemming now owns her, regardless of his actions in the future. He has confined her to a social and cultural purgatory of sorts, and they both know it: "The nerve no longer ticked in his forehead, the muscles of his mouth relaxed; there was already something of triumph in his look" (81). Much later in the story, when as a married man he asks Mary to flee England with him as his mistress, he is certainly less in control of his emotions and Mary's, yet he nevertheless maintains possession of her, for because of him, Mary will never take another lover.

Despite his penchant for melodrama, however, Hemming is much more than the stereotypical two-dimensional cad of lesser fiction. His is a painstakingly constructed character, one significant enough to Hepworth Dixon's story that on at least two occasions she suddenly, and for a prolonged period, shifts the point of view away from Mary to focus on Vincent's life. These portraits reveal a desperately unhappy man who chooses to relinquish his sense of moral responsibility, preferring instead to allow himself to be borne along by the tide of life in hopes that good things will come to him. There is a clear irony in the fact that a man's conventional successes—a career, a wife, children—can come to him without real effort. And Hepworth Dixon furthers the irony by having these ostensible successes only make Hemming more miserable, eventually driving him to debauchery. Just as Mary's pledge binds her to this man for a lifetime, Vincent himself, as well as the wife he betrays, becomes ensnared by the unnatural conventions of marriage.

Hepworth Dixon also uses her novel's minor male figures to delineate Mary's stasis and intensify the story's larger themes. When Mary's good friend Perry Jackson, the up-and-coming Royal Academician, surprises her with a marriage proposal, his motives are noble: "He would like to have saved her from the struggle of the woman who works, the fret and the fever, the dreary fight for existence" (136). At the same time, though, the proposal takes on the air of a business deal; it seems as if he is attempting to acquire Mary—as if she were one of his pieces of art—by marrying her. That she must refuse him because she believes herself still bound spiritually to the unfaithful Vincent Hemming serves only to accentuate her paralysis.

Dunlop Strange, the dashing doctor and a "favourite with women in society" (92), comes as close as any character to being the story's villain. Of all the novel's carefully drawn male characters, Strange also comes closest to stereotype. He does not so much restrict Mary as he represents all those men who callously abuse their authority for personal gain. In this light, his actions parallel those of Vincent Hemming. A seemingly caring young doctor, and the fiancé of Mary's good friend, Alison Ives, Strange is revealed ultimately to be a predator of sorts, a man who in his past casually ruined a young girl, abandoned her, and later, as she confronted him from her deathbed, denied any knowledge of her past. So, as she does with Vincent Hemming, Hepworth Dixon uses Strange to underscore her outrage with the moral and sexual double standard in late-century Victorian England.

The ostentatious and cynical society figure Mr. Beaufort Flower—modeled, some say, after Hepworth Dixon's acquaintance and occasional employer, Oscar Wilde[1]—represents, along with his equally sardonic friend and new editor of the *Comet*, Mr. Bosanquet-Barry, those disagreeable men who make a game of attempting to control others, women in particular, simply for the pleasure of the subjugation. Though he appears on only a few occasions in the novel, each time he does, this fashionable young man indulges in his "favourite modern amusement of whispering malicious things of one's host or hostess behind their backs" (95). Beaufy, though he may seem to be ostensibly a comic figure, exploits his acquaintances with his destructive gossip. His nasty musings tend to cast people, Mary among them, in trite dramatic roles that allow him to become a cynical and manipulative stage manager of sorts.

In addition to all of her personal acquaintances, Mary's editors, those men to whose journals Mary contributes her rather shapeless fiction, also are very much in control of her. They callously censor her writing, reprimand her for bringing realism into her stories, and demand that her work conform. Hepworth Dixon's argument here is two-pronged. In addition to showing that Mary is once again bound and limited by the men in her lives, she uses these scenes to speak out strongly for the necessity of artistic freedom and to argue against the rigid restrictions placed on writers by such puritanical and self-declared censors as the circulating lending-library baron Charles Edward Mudie.[2]

On one occasion, Mary finds that she has run afoul of her edi-

---

1 Oscar Wilde, for whose *Woman's World* magazine Hepworth Dixon wrote, finds his way into the novel in various incarnations, in part as Bosanquet-Barry, the new editor of the *Comet*, in part as the pale young Beaufort Flower, and in part as the supercilious editor of *The Fan*, a journal to which Mary contributes her "society" pieces.

2 Mudie (1818-90), the puritanical and stubbornly censorious owner of "Mudie's Circulating Library," the largest subscription library in the world, held the English publishing industry in a stranglehold for the last half of the nineteenth century. Because his volume business could make or break a publishing house, and because he frequently refused to carry novels that contained material he felt to be morally offensive or indecent, his role as self-imposed literary censor caused much friction among novel writers of the day. Mudie's presence is apparent in the editor's insistence that Mary's work be light enough to gain easy entrance to all English households. For more on the Victorian censorship debate, see Appendix F, which contains excerpts from published articles by George Moore, Walter Besant, Eliza Lynn Linton, and Thomas Hardy.

tor's rules and regulations when he barks at her about her latest offerings: "I can't put that sort of thing in my paper. The public won't stand it, my dear girl. They want thoroughly healthy reading" (146). He goes on to explain his philosophy, telling Mary, "I should suggest a thoroughly happy ending. The public like happy endings. The novelists are getting so morbid. It's all these French and Russian writers that have done it. It's really difficult now to get a thoroughly breezy book with a wedding at the end" (147). At one point, as a threatening afterthought of sorts, he warns her, "if you take my advice, Miss Erle, and cultivate your talents in the right way, you will be able to make a—a—comfortable income" (147).

On another occasion, Mary explains to her friend Perry Jackson that she has contracted to write a novel but has been told that it must follow very particular and rigid guidelines, that it must be a "three-volume novel on the old lines—a dying man in a hospital and a forged will in the first volume; a ball and a picnic in the second; and an elopement, which must, of course, be prevented at the last moment by the opportune death of the wife, or the husband— I forget which it is to be—in the last" (130). The broad humor here does not disguise the fact that these editors, aside from controlling her purse-strings, control Mary. In some ways these men own her, for if she does not write the insipid trash that they say "must be fit to go into every parsonage in England" (146), she will not be able to support herself and her brother. Compounding the cynicism of these scenes are the constant shouts, heard in the streets outside the offices, of the newspaper boys hawking their papers with news of the latest salacious society scandal.

## The Women in Mary Erle's Life

The women of the story also help to sharpen the focus of Hepworth Dixon's theme of oppression. Though there are only a very few female characters, each makes an impact on Mary that helps to define her as a woman. Alison Ives, the most important woman in Mary's life, serves in many ways as a foil in the story. The differences between her and Mary are many and apparent, yet the two women are bound to one another as sisters in their struggle to survive. One of the most intricately drawn figures in the novel, and certainly one of the most fascinating, Alison is in many ways the novel's title character; at one point the narrator even labels her an "eminently modern young woman" (70), quickly adding, though—clearly aware of the poison of stereotype—that "she never smoked, was ignorant of billiard cues and guns, and hated playing the man" (70).

Alison, in a way, appears in the novel as Hepworth Dixon's mouthpiece, giving a frank voice to strong sentiments that otherwise might remain unsaid. Though the story is certainly Mary Erle's, Alison, far more so than her best friend, lives the life of a modern woman, of a strong woman who attempts actively to throw off the social and cultural bonds to which her sex has restricted her. In short, she is a woman who acts, and her actions, always charitable, stem from "her real desire to be in sympathy with her own sex" (70). She attempts to help the poverty-stricken women of London's East End, first by taking up residence among them in an effort to offer assistance, and later by adopting them, after a fashion, one at a time, removing them from the wretched slums, educating them, and finding them employment and a better life outside the misery of Mile End Road. Alison's charity is not the "telescopic philanthropy" of Dickens's Mrs. Jellyby, though she is pained by the notion that some people believe she has simply "taken up slumming," or what they call condescendingly "district visiting." After describing for Mary in detail the unpleasant circumstances surrounding the fall of Evelina, a pitiful young girl left alone in the city with a child to care for, Alison says gravely and with the strength of experience in her support, "My dear, these London idyls are not pretty" (75).

Regardless of her great strength and vitality of character, however, Alison is not immune to suffering. Her personal agony comes when she discovers to her horror that her fiancé, Dr. Dunlop Strange, has in his past ruined a young girl, driven her in despair to attempt suicide, and abandoned her on her sickbed. In fact—and the irony is clear here—Dunlop Strange becomes in large part responsible for Alison's demise as well, for she herself contracts consumption from this dying young girl while attempting to comfort her during the final stages of the illness. There is, of course, an even greater and overriding irony that serves Hepworth Dixon quite well. Alison, the one constant voice of strength and compassion for Mary, the person upon whom Mary depends for happiness—even the "house seemed blank and empty" (76) when Alison was not present—is, after all, no stronger than any others. Mary gives voice to this solemn realization as she sits by Alison's sickbed, thinking to herself that "Death, the great destroyer, had an irony which is all his own. Beautiful, noble, helpful lives were crushed, destroyed, annihilated" (172).

Aside from Alison, the other female characters in the novel are in many ways types designed to intensify Hepworth Dixon's assertions that women, regardless of social or class background, are bound together by a common suffering. There is Evelina, the young unwed mother looked after by Alison, a girl who ran from her employer to escape his sexual assaults and who later bore the child of a young man incapable of caring for her. And there is Number Twenty-Seven, the nameless woman whose life is destroyed after she is seduced and then deserted by Dunlop Strange. Mary and Alison, though their stories are perhaps a bit less sensational than these, clearly have much in common with Evelina and Number Twenty-Seven. Mary, much like these other women, is victimized by Vincent Hemming and a culture that allows men to control women, to come, in fact, very close to owning them. And Alison, of course, very much like the wretched and pathetic Number Twenty-Seven before her, also becomes a statistic, another casualty of Dunlop Strange's crass heartlessness.

Lady Jane Ives, Alison's 65-year-old mother, and even high society's Lady Blaythewaite, whose ugly and scandalous divorce trial lurks in the background throughout the novel, offer two more broad representations of women limited by their culture's sense of propriety and social expectation. Though at the other end of the social and economic spectrum from these other women, they nevertheless share what Mary calls "the burden of sex" (172). Alison's mother, Lady Jane, is the "Old Woman" of the Victorian age, a woman imprisoned by the past and by worn tradition. She is an anachronism, someone who "disliked new fashions in her house," who "had arranged the rooms on her marriage some forty years ago, and it had not occurred to her to change them" (89). Secure in the sameness of her life, and at odds with her daughter's puzzling tendency toward helping the poor, Lady Jane wants simply to hold afternoon Kettledrums, "At Homes," and dinner parties where she might talk of her long-past flirtations, where fashionable people might see and be seen by other fashionable people. She has, in other words, given herself over to the cant of popular sentiment that suggests women should remain tethered, voluntarily or otherwise, by blind tradition.

Complementing Lady Jane is Lady Blaythewaite, a shadowy figure in the novel, a society woman married to wealth but engaged through much of the story in rather sensational divorce proceedings. The details of Lady Blaythewaite's life are daily shouted out to the masses by street vendors trying to sell a newspaper: "Spesh-shul!

Extry Spesh-hul! Fifth Edition! Sir Horace Blaythewaite in the box! Revolting details! The great divorce case!" (148). Suffering under the harsh glare of a society eager to tear at her for any perceived marital indiscretions, she is sentenced by each day's headlines. The messy trial finally becomes a powerful metaphor for the rottenness of a system that makes public a woman's private pain: "The Blaythewaite scandal hung, like a pestilence, over England. Like some foul miasma, it poisoned everything" (145).

## A Final Ambivalence

The conflicts that resonate among the meticulously drawn characters serve Hepworth Dixon well as she attempts with this novel to throw light on the difficult contest being waged not necessarily between women and men but between women and a culture grounded in the distant past; between women and woefully outdated laws, customs, and traditions; between women and the unpalatable human tendency to resist change, even when change would clearly rectify glaring flaws and usher in a new age of enlightenment. But beyond these frictions in theme, setting, and character, this austere, darkly powerful novel of struggle and paralysis offers one last conflict for its readers, for the book can appear to them in at least a couple of different lights. Kate Flint, in her 1993 study *The Woman Reader: 1847-1914*, urges readers to see it and other New Woman novels in a hopeful light, as affirmations of the dawn of a new age: "Even if such novelists did not reward such efforts with fairy-tale happy endings, thus emphasizing the struggles ahead, these fictions served, potentially, as confirmation of the fact that independently minded women readers were not without others who thought and felt along the same lines" (Flint 297).[1] Their importance, Flint claims, lies *not* with the fact that most of these novels, *The Story of a Modern Woman* in particular, fail to celebrate "the triumph of the independent woman," but that they "offered images of articulacy and efforts at self-determination" (Flint 296-97). Flint is right: *The Story of a Modern Woman*, as a representative of the New Woman novel, speaks eloquently and clearly to the quiet suffering endured by women in *fin de siècle* England. At the same time, though, Hepworth Dixon has made it extremely difficult for her readers, her contemporaries as well as those who

---

1   Kate Flint, *The Woman Reader: 1847-1914* (Oxford: Clarendon, 1993).

come to her story more than a hundred years after its publication, to see through the darkness to this light. More than anything else, the novel offers a stark and grim assessment of women's struggles at the end of the nineteenth century.

It is not by accident that the novel ends with Mary Erle's return to Highgate Cemetery, where she once again looks out over the vastness of London. This time, however, many years and many cruel disappointments having passed since her first visit, she no longer sees a city that will listen to her when she speaks, but only an "inexorable, triumphant London" (192).[1] And this time she stands alone, without companionship. The light of the city behind her silhouette illuminates the reader's dilemma: to believe that Mary will continue her fight may offer some trace of hope, but to see that she has found life itself to be nothing more than a dreary battle fought in lonely isolation seems only to offer despair.

---

1 Hepworth Dixon uses the word "inexorable" seven times over the course of her novel, further emphasizing the inflexibility of Mary's life.

# Ella Hepworth Dixon: A Brief Chronology

1855    Ella Hepworth Dixon is born in London, the seventh of eight children and youngest of three daughters, to William Hepworth Dixon and Marian MacMahon Dixon.

1860s    Hepworth Dixon spends her childhood in her Regent's Park home surrounded by a loving family that stresses the importance of literature and the arts. Her father's position as editor of the *Athenæum* brings into the family home many great writers, artists, travelers, and thinkers, among them Geraldine Jewsbury, Lord Bulwer Lytton, T.H. Huxley, Sir Richard Burton, E.M. Ward, and Sir John Everett Millais.

1870s    Hepworth Dixon receives a remarkably complete formal education, studying languages and philosophy in Heidelberg, painting in Paris, and music at the London School of Music.

1879    Hepworth Dixon's father dies in London.

1880s    Hepworth Dixon turns to journalism, writing and publishing various sketches, essays, and reviews in English newspapers and journals.

1888    Hepworth Dixon accepts Oscar Wilde's invitation to become the editor of his new journal, *Woman's World*.

1890    Hepworth Dixon publishes her first fiction, "A Literary Lover," in *Woman's World*.

1892    Hepworth Dixon's *My Flirtations*, a connected series of short stories, is published in volume form by Chatto & Windus.

1894    *The Story of a Modern Woman*, Hepworth Dixon's only novel, is published to positive reviews in May by Heinemann in London and Cassell in New York.

1895    Hepworth Dixon accepts the editorship of a newly established journal, *The Englishwoman*.

1896    Hepworth Dixon resigns her editorship of *The Englishwoman*, in part because she finds the journal to be too tamely middle-class for her tastes. She continues to publish short fiction in various English journals.

1904    *One Doubtful Hour and Other Side-lights on the Feminine Temperament*, a connected series of ten short stories, is published.

1905   Her interests turning to theater, Hepworth Dixon collabo-
       rates on a play with her friend H.G. Wells.
1908   Hepworth Dixon's play *The Toyshop of the Heart*, is per-
       formed—a one-time charity production—in London.
1920s  After the war, Hepworth Dixon spends much of her time
       traveling on the continent, dividing her time among what
       had become a remarkably vast circle of prominent friends,
       among them Max Beerbohm, Bernard Shaw, H.G. Wells,
       and William Butler Yeats.
1930   Hepworth Dixon publishes her autobiographical remem-
       brances, *As I Knew Them: Sketches of People I Have Met on
       the Way*.
1932   Ella Hepworth Dixon dies on January 12 at the age of
       seventy-six.

# A Note on the Text

*The Story of a Modern Woman* was published in May 1894 by Heine-mann publishers in London and Cassell publishers in New York. For the text of this edition I have used Cassell's 1894 first edition. Subsequent editions of the novel appeared with many minor editorial changes and corrections, along with at least two major alterations: Chapter III, "Wonderings," in this edition was removed from later editions; and Chapter XXIV, "The Woman in the Glass," the final chapter in this edition, was divided into two chapters in later editions. I have silently corrected typographical errors and occasional inconsistencies in punctuation that appeared in Cassell's first edition.

An asterisk (★) in the text indicates a location in London that can be found on the map in Appendix B.

# THE STORY OF
# A MODERN WOMAN

The Novel's Table of Contents

# CHAPTER I
## AN END AND A BEGINNING

GLARING spring sunshine and a piercing east wind rioted out of doors, and here and there overflowing flower baskets made startling patches of colour against the vague blue-grey of the streets, but indoors, in the tall London house, there was only a sickly, yellow twilight, for the orange-toned blinds were scrupulously drawn down. There was awe in the passages, and hushed tones even in the kitchen, as if the dead could hear! Some wreaths and crosses of wax-like exotic flowers lay on the hall table, filling the passage with their sensuous odour. Friends calling to inquire had left them there, but they had not yet been taken up—up to that awful room where a marble figure, a figure which was strangely unlike Professor Erle—lay stretched, in an enduring silence, on the bed.

Downstairs, in the little study giving on a meagre London yard, a girl was bending over a desk. "*You will, I know, be grieved to hear that my dear father passed suddenly away the night before last,*" she wrote, while a great nerve in her forehead went tick, tick, tick. The visitors who came all day long, leaving bits of pasteboard,[1] spoke in low, inquisitive tones. When the bell rang, there were veiled whispers at the hall-door. "So terrible—so sudden!" Mary could hear them inquire how she was keeping up? And Elizabeth's answer: "Miss Erle is as well as could be expected." The trite, worn-out, foolish sentence almost made her laugh. All the stock phrases of condolence, all the mental trappings of woe, seemed to be ready-made for the "sad occasion," like the crape skirts and cloaks which had been forwarded immediately from the mourning establishment in Regent Street.[2]★ "Yes, I am

---

1  The Victorians were adept at mourning; pasteboards, in this case, amounted to business cards, or visitor cards, left by those who had stopped by the home to pay their respects.
2  Regent Street was the fashionable shopping district in London through the century. [Refer to Appendix B: 1883 Map of London for street names and landmarks (noted with ★) mentioned throughout the novel.] The geography of the novel is very interesting in that by looking at the map, one is instantly struck by how very small and close Mary Erle's world really is. Aside from a childhood journey to the continent, she rarely ventures more than a few blocks from her residence in the central city. Over the course of her story, Hepworth Dixon reinforces the claustrophobic atmosphere of Mary's life in London with various images of dark and narrow streets, low skies, and small, musty, airless rooms. See the Introduction for more on London as a symbol of oppression.

as well as could be expected," she thought, "and father is dead. Father is dead."

And all the long afternoon she went mechanically on writing, "*I am sure you will be sorry when I tell you that my dear father—*" on paper bordered with black an inch deep. How he would have disliked that foolish ostentation of mourning; it was contrary to the spirit of his life. "To-morrow," she said to herself, "I must send for some note paper with a narrower edge." These letters were to be sent abroad. The English newspapers had sufficiently announced the death, for Professor Erle was perhaps the best-known man of science of the day.

In the little back-room they had to light the lamp early, there was so much to do, so many details to arrange. The ceremony was to be as simple as might be; above all, no paid priest would stand at the grave to give hearty thanks that the great thinker had been delivered out of the miseries of this sinful world. The sinful world would have as its spokesman another famous professor, who had asked to be allowed to say a few words. Then there were the newspapers. There was the brisk, smartly dressed young gentleman who came to do a leader for a daily paper, who had a wandering, observant eye and a leather note-book, and who proceeded to make a number of notes in shorthand, asking innumerable questions as his omnivorous glance travelled rapidly round the study. Another reporter—a small, apologetic man with greyish hair and a timid cough—asked to see the house for the *Evening Planet*.[1] He begged of Elizabeth on the hall steps to tell him if the Professor had said anything—anything particular, which would work up as a leader, just at the last? "Oh! sir," said Elizabeth, "didn't you know? Master didn't say anything. He just died in his sleep."

The daughter went about her tasks with a sense of detachment, of intense aloofness. "I wonder if I really feel it?" she thought, "and why I have never cried? I should like to, but it is impossible; I shall never, never cry again." It was as if Death, with his cruel, searing wings had cauterised her very soul. Sometimes she pictured herself in her long crepe veil at the funeral, and heard in imagination her friends murmuring pitying words, as they all followed the coffin up

---

1   Some of the periodicals mentioned in the novel—here the *Evening Planet* and elsewhere *The Fan*, the *Comet*, *Illustrations*, and the *Easel*—are fictional. Others referred to—the *Fortnightly*, the *Contemporary*, *The Observer*, *The Graphic*—were real.

the Highgate slope.[1]* Alison Ives, of course, would be with her. She would stay by her, perhaps, and hold her hand. And probably Vincent Hemming would be near. Yes, he, too, would be there.

At dinner-time she had to sit down to table alone. She was hungry, and she ate hardly knowing what was on her plate. Nothing happened as it does in tales and romances. In innumerable novels she had read how the heroine, in a house of mourning, lies on the bed for days and steadily refuses to eat. As for Mary, a demon of unrest possessed her during that horrible week, and it was as if she could not eat nourishing food enough. She never stopped arranging, writing, adding up accounts. It was useless to try and read. Did she but take up a book, that dominant image in her mind—the image of a dear face turned to marble, with the cold, triumphant smile of eternity on its lips—shut out the sense of the words as her eyes travelled down the page.

And the strange, unmistakable odour of death, mixed with the scent of waxen hot-house flowers, hung, night and day, about the staircase.

Toward the end of the week, there was more noise and bustle, and at last had come the morning when the house swarmed with undertakers' men, and Mary and her young brother Jim, who had arrived from Winchester,[2] sat with a few old friends in the dining-room, waiting for the signal to go. There was the shuffling of men's feet, as they staggered down the narrow London staircase with their heavy burden, and then someone had made the girl swallow some sal volatile, and she was pushed gently into the first mourning carriage, along with Jim. They had made the boy drink some of the sal volatile too, and they both felt strangely elated and highly strung. There were only those two now, and Mary felt warmly drawn to Jimmie, as they sat side by side in their new black clothes, the two chief personages in the ceremony of to-day. She even pretended not to hear when, some gutter urchins making complicated cartwheels as their contribution to the imposing procession, Jim, boy-like, gave way to a furtive giggle.

---

1　Highgate Cemetery, located on the southern slope of Highgate Hill, was consecrated in 1839. William Hepworth Dixon, the novelist's father, was buried there in 1879. Among the writers and thinkers buried there are Mrs. Henry Wood, George Eliot, Karl Marx, Christina Rossetti, and Herbert Spencer.

2　The county seat of Hampshire, Winchester, where Jim attends school, lies about fifty miles southwest of London, just north of Southampton.

The drive to Highgate seemed interminable, but at last, when the long procession crept slowly up the hill, it was in a kind of stupor that the girl saw and heard what happened. There was, she remembered afterward, a long line of people, habited in black, awaiting them in silence inside the cemetery gate; a tolling bell, neighing horses, and a penetrating scent of early lilac. Sunlight on the paths, on the shining marble tombs, on the humble little mounds covered in plush-like grass; then a moving mass of black, a yawning hole, the creaking of ropes, and the mellifluous voice of the eminent professor, speaking his oration over the upturned clay.

"England, I may say the world, is mourning to-day for her illustrious son"—how the people pressed round the yawning gap, and pushed against the guelder rose-tree overhead, so that the flowers fell in a minute white shower on to the oaken coffin below—"England is mourning for her illustrious son. Not that her tears will flow in vain, for those tears will moisten and fructify the precious tree of Truth; a tree which is evermore putting forth fresh branches and new fruits which are indispensable to the physical and moral evolution of humanity."

In a neighbouring laburnum-bush, a thrush was swelling its brown throat with a joyous morning song. Athwart the pale sky dappled with fleecy clouds, the lilac bushes were burgeoning with waxen pinkish blossoms. The very air throbbed with coming life.

"Nature," continued the orator, in his measured, lecture-room tones, "Nature, who works in inexorable ways, has taken to herself a life full of arduous toil, of epoch-making achievement, of immeasurable possibilities, but to what end, and for what purpose, is not given to us, who stand to-day with full hearts and yearning eyes around his last resting place, to know."

The sun was warm overhead, the scent of the pink may was strong in the nostrils; a joyous twittering in an adjacent bush told of mating birds, of new life in the nests, of Nature rioting in an insolent triumph.

The orator paused for an instant, coughed, and felt in his breast pocket for his notes. He was anxious, above all things, that the reporters should not print a garbled version of his speech. Round the open grave pressed the devotees of science, the followers of the religion of humanity; grey-skinned, anxious-looking men and women, with lined foreheads and hair prematurely tinged with grey; large heads with bulging foreheads, thin throats and sloping shoulders; the women with nervous, over-worked faces, the men with the pathetic, unrestful features of those who are sustained in a life of self-denial by their ethical sense alone. The ceremony of to-day was a great moral demonstration. All classes who think were represented. Side by side stood a white-haired Radical countess in simple half-mourning and the spare form of a Socialist working woman, with red, ungloved wrists and an inspired look on her worn face. There, with her mother, Lady Jane, was Alison Ives. Lady Jane, who was impressionable, was already exhibiting a pocket-handkerchief, and not far off, Mary caught for one instant the brown, wistful eyes of Vincent Hemming.

The sun grew hotter and hotter overhead. One or two of the mourners began putting up umbrellas. The perfume of pink hawthorn became almost oppressive; an early butterfly lighted on a baby's grave planted with sweet-smelling flowers. A light breeze fluttered through a laburnum-bush which hung over a neighbouring marble tomb, a large, opulent marble tomb, on which was cut in glittering gilt letters: "OF SUCH IS THE KINGDOM OF HEAVEN."[1] And everywhere there was the whiteness of graves. In ridges, in waves, in mounds, they stuck, tooth-like, from the fecund earth. They shone, in gleaming, distant lines, up to the ridge of the hill; they crowded in serried battalions, down to the cemetery gates.

The speaker was concluding his speech. "For though to isolated men," he said, raising his voice so that all who were on the edge of the crowd should hear, "it may be given here and there to scale the loftiest heights—aye, and ever new peaks rising upon peaks in the great undiscovered country which we call the realm of science; there, too, the finite touches the infinite, and must recognise what of tentativeness, what of inconclusiveness belongs to mere human effort. Here, on a sudden, the dark, impenetrable curtain, which none may draw aside, envelops us; here we know not whether all ends with this our last prison house, or if to us may be opened out yet further cycles of aspiring activity."

In the silence which followed there was heard one long, sweet, penetrating bird-call.

One of the chief mourners, the boy Jimmie, was sobbing loudly when the professor's voice stopped, and with something gripping at her throat, the sister led him away. She reproached herself with having brought him; the young, she thought, should not know what sorrow is. The two spare, black-clad figures stepped aside up the hill.

---

1   Matthew 19:14.

Out yonder, at their feet, the dun colour of the buildings lost in the murkiness of the horizon line, London was spread out. Here and there a dome, a spire loomed out of the dim bluish-grey panorama. A warm haze hung over the great city; here and there a faint fringe of tree-tops told of a placid park; now and again the shrill whistle of an engine, blown northward by the wind, spoke of the bustle of journeys, of the turmoil of railway stations, of part-ings, of arrivals, of the change and travail of human life, of the strangers who come, of the failures who must go.

"Jim," said the girl suddenly, taking the boy by the arm, "there's London! We're going to make it listen to us, you and I. We're not going to be afraid of it—just because it's big, and brutal, and strong."

"N—no, dearest," said the boy, turning up a pretty, sensitive face, and a pink nose all smeared with tears. "Of course not."

The black crowd yonder was swaying, separating, and disinte-grating itself into separate sable dots, which were now seen descending the paths to the cemetery-gate. And slowly, they, too, stepped down the grand path.

They came home to a house that was empty and orderly again; a house in which *his* door stood open, the pale light of a spring afternoon filling the desolate room. The blinds were pulled up, and downstairs, in the kitchen, the servants had begun to talk and laugh.

Toward dusk Jimmie got engrossed in a new book of adven-tures, but the girl, restless still, wandered about the house in her black gown looking at everything with strange eyes. Something terrible, unforeseen, had happened which altered her whole life. Toward the boy poring over the picture-book she felt much of a mother's feelings; it behooved her to look after him now that his father was gone. How long the time seemed—would the inter-minable day never end? There must be lots for her to do. And cast-ing about in her mind, she remembered that this was the day on which she always gave out the groceries from her store cupboard; there was the seamstress to pay, too, who was altering a black dress for her upstairs. So Mary dragged herself down to the kitchens and presently to the top of the house. It would be nice of her, she thought, to go in and speak to the woman who was sewing alone. It was sad for a young woman to be alone.

The pale, pinkish light of a spring evening fell on a drab-com-plexioned girl, whose fat hand moved, as she sewed, with the reg-ularity of a machine. Now the needle was thrust in the fold of black stuff, and the light fell on her ill-cut nails; now the hand was aloft, in the semi-obscurity; it was all tame, monotonous, and regular as a clock. She was a docile, humble, uncomplaining creature, who suggested inevitably some patient domestic animal. Her features, rubbed out and effaced with generations of servility, spoke of the small mendacities of the women of the lower classes, of the women who live on ministering to the caprices of the well-to-do. To-day it would seem she had assumed an appropriately dolorous expression.

It sometimes soothed Mary to stitch. Taking up a strip of black merino, she began to hem.

The seamstress's hand continued to move with docile regularity, and, as Mary looked at her, she was curiously reminded of many women she had seen: ladies, mothers of large families, who sat and sewed with just such an expression of unquestioning resignation. The clicking sound of the needle, the swish of the drawn-out thread, the heavy breathing of the workwoman, all added to the impression. Yes, they too were content to exist subserviently, depending always on someone else, using the old feminine stratagems, the well-worn feminine subterfuges, to gain their end. The woman who sews is eternally the same.

The light began to fail now; very soon it would be dark. Mary threw down her work with an impatient gesture, and, in the grey twilight, an immense pity seized her for the patient figure bending, near the window, over her foolish strips of flounces.

It was not so much a woman, but The Woman at her monotonous toil.

## CHAPTER II
## A CHILD

THE life of Mary Erle, like that of many another woman in the end of the nineteenth century, had been more or less in the nature of an experiment. Born too late for the simple days of the fifties, when all it behooved a young woman to do was to mind her account-book, read her Tennyson, show a proper enthusiasm for fancy-work stitches, and finally, with many blushes, accept the hand of the first young man who desired to pay taxes and to fulfil the duties of a loyal British subject (and the young man, it must be remembered, in the middle of this century, actually did both), Mary was yet too soon for the time when parents begin to take their responsibilities seriously, and when the girl is sometimes as carefully prepared, as thoroughly equipped, as her brother for the fight of life. A garden full of flowers, a house full of books, scraps of travel: these things were her education. Out of the years she could pick scenes and figures which typified her bringing-up.

There was the plain, self-contained, and not too clean baby. A child who was always grubbing in a garden, for it lived then in a house in St. John's Wood;[1]★ a child who was devoted to animals and insects, who was on intimate terms with the many-legged wood-lice, which curled themselves up with all haste into complete balls when she touched them; a child for whom snails and black-beetles had no terrors, and who had much to say to the fat, hairy caterpillars which hung about the pear-tree.

There was a huge, fluffy black cat, too, which represented, perhaps, the child's primitive idea of a deity; for, though she adored it, the adoration was leavened with a wholesome awe, a feeling which was not unconnected with certain unmerited chastisements in the shape of scratches on her fat, bare legs. More often, to be sure, the black cat was amiable, and even allowed itself to be carried up to bed, with its hind legs straying out helplessly from under the child's arm, to be presently concealed with all haste and caution under the white sheets and blankets, from whence its sharp-pointed ears and fat black cheeks arose with the most exquisitely mirth-provoking effect. With what inscrutable amber eyes did the black cat gaze for hours into hers: how it imposed on her babyish imagination with its self-contained, majestic manners, its air of detachment from the vain shows of the world! The man with the kind smile, whom the child called "father," used to laugh at her adoration, tell her she was a little Egyptian, and called the cat "Pasht." She thought it a funny name, and not being altogether sure the black cat would approve of it, generally addressed it as "you." And the cat would sit on long summer afternoons on the grass under the pear-tree, or on foggy autumn days on a stool by the fireside, with paws neatly tucked away, its neck-ruff fluffed out, purring benignly in response to her confidences. Indeed, in looking back, the first tragedy of the child's life was the death of the black cat. It lay, one sultry July day, under a laurel bush in the garden, with glazed eyes which gave no signs of life. All morning and all afternoon the child sat there and fanned the flies away, until her idol was stiff, and then a hole was hastily

1  In the mid and late nineteenth century, the St. John's Wood area, north-east of the city center, still possessed a pastoral, idyllic beauty that made it a place sought out by artists, authors, and scientists.

dug, and the black cat was thrust out of sight. And never any more, in the warm summer afternoons, did a soft, furry thing go sailing, tail in air, over the close-cropped lawn; nor, on winter evenings, was a rhythmical purring to be heard hard by the tall fender which guarded the nursery fire. It was the first great void; the first heart-ache had come.

A strange, indolent, not too clean child, whose little hands were usually thrust beneath her pinafore when anyone spoke to her; for surely she could not be always washing herself, and to be on really intimate terms with insects and things, one cannot, like grown-up people, be always thinking of one's nails. She usually, too, concealed a small piece of putty about her person—an unpardonable sin, this, in the eyes of mother and nurse—for putty is useful in a thousand ways, and is, besides, so thrillingly delicious to feel surreptitiously in the recesses of one's pocket. At this time the child held the whole race of dolls in high scorn. They were a foolish, over-dressed, uninteresting tribe, with manifestly absurd cheeks and eye-lashes, and with a simper which was as artificial as that of the ladies in chignons and flounces who came to call at the house in St. John's Wood. She, on her part, was all for the violent delights of miniature guns and real gunpowder, the toilsome construction of fleets of wooden boats with the aid of a blunt knife and a plank of wood: fleets which were set a-sail, with flying pennants, on the cistern hard by the kitchen. There were boy neighbours who aided and abetted her in these delights, and great naval battles would come off between the Dutch and English fleets in the kitchen cistern, in which sometimes Van Tromp and sometimes Blake emerged victorious.[1] The child, perhaps, did not take her patrio-

---

1  Maarten Tromp (1597-1653) was a Dutch Admiral who won control of the English Channel by defeating the British fleet, under admiral Robert Blake (1599-1657), in an engagement off Dungeness in May 1652. Tromp died during another battle with Blake and the British in July 1653, the last major conflict of the first Dutch War. Hepworth Dixon would have learned all about Tromp and Blake from her father's *Life of Robert Blake* (1852), a popular biography; in her memoirs, *As I Knew Them* (1930), she recalls childhood naval battles similar to those Mary describes here: "[M]y soul was in the Navy, especially in old-time sailing ships, which I cut with my own hands, making the masts and sewing the sails. These men-o-war were duly launched in a rather unavailable cistern, and naval actions ensued, in which an elder brother insisted on being Robert Blake, while I had to be Van Tromp—when he was beaten" (15).

tism seriously, as the boys did; she was content to be Van Tromp, since they insisted on being Blake and Monk. All that was of vital importance was that a fight of some sort should come off.

The mother sank early out of ken. First they said that she was poorly, and had gone to Italy, and then they said that she was very ill, and afterward that she was in heaven; so that for a long time the child used to think vaguely, as she sat in the summer-house with pursed-up lips and knitted brows, notching and slicing at her ships, that Italy and heaven were perhaps the same place. Nurse said that her mummy was an angel now; but, in all the picture-books, angels had long, smooth hair, wore a kind of night-gown, and had enormous, folding wings. The child could not picture her mother looking like that; she always remembered her in many flounces, with a head-ache; and certainly, no, certainly, mummy never had any wings out of her back.

The child could recollect that, some little time before her mother went to Italy, they took her upstairs one day and showed her a baby, with a red, crinkled face, lying in an over-trimmed cradle. She did not care for babies, she would rather have had a nice, new, fluffy kitten to replace the old black cat; but when they told her it was a little brother, of course that altered matters. She was sorry her brother should be so small, so fretful, and so red in the face; she would rather have had him the same size as herself, so that he could have been Van Tromp for once, and she the victorious Blake; but still, any sort or size of brother was better than none. Although, in a year or so, the baby developed into something suspiciously like a doll, with his fat, pink cheeks, his round, china-blue eyes, his dump of a nose, and his entire absence of chin, still, he was far more entertaining than that simpering and foolish tribe. Baby Jim's pink toes could kick; his little fist, with the creases of fat at the wrist, could hit out; there were warlike possibilities in him. In a word, Baby Jim was alive.

At ten years old the girl began to have strange fits of vanity. There were little shoes and frocks which she held in high favour, and others which nothing would induce her to put on. To wear a pinafore, now, was a bitter humiliation, and about this period she had the most definite theories about the dressing of hair. The discussion on coiffures usually took place in her bath, when a small, slippery person covered in soap-suds was to be heard arguing with her nurse—an argument which was not unusually enforced by physical violence—on the superior attractions of crimped to curled locks. At ten years old she was of opinion a person was grown up, or at least as old as any one should be. Why, big, tall men, with long beards and spectacles, who came to see her father, would bend down and ask her gravely if she would be their little wife? The child had been to more than one wedding, and she was aware that a wife was a person who began by wearing a beautiful white satin train, with white flowers and a veil; a person who was as imposing as that angel which nurse said her mother had become, although she had not, of course, any wings. The child was not sure whether she would best like to be a bride or an angel. The latter, it was true, had the additional attraction of a golden halo; but she thought, probably, that matters might be compromised, and that she could be a wife and have a halo too.

The scene shifts now, for they had moved to another quarter of London, and the change made a vast difference in the child's tastes and habits. There was no cropped lawn, where the pear-tree made long shadows on summer afternoons, where she had a personal interest in a plot of ground of her own, and at least a bowing acquaintance with a whole host of fussy bumble-bees, gay yellow butterflies, furry caterpillars, and lazy snails. There was no summer-house in which ship-building could be carried on, and no convenient cistern in which to sail one's fleet. The firing off of toy guns was erased from the list of possible amusements. The house was a tall one, in a street in town, and rural delights were represented by a square yard at the back, which was haunted by stray, attenuated cats, and in which grew a solitary, stunted sycamore. But, on the other hand, there was the new fascination of book-shelves, which ran all over the new house, so that the child had but to mount a chair and reach out a small hand, and, lo! romance and battles, laughter and tears, were all to be enjoyed at her will. She had only to pick out her volume. It was a revelation in the possibilities of life.

Looking back now, it must be owned that she led an odd life. The man with the kind smile was fond of his little daughter, but he was always at work, either at experiments in his laboratory or bending over his desk in the study. Nothing happened in the way of experience as it does to other children. One night her father took her to the theatre for the first time. A famous actress, an old friend, was giving *Antony and Cleopatra*, and they went first behind the scenes. They walked across a bare, lofty, cavern-like place, with dusty wooden boards, which sloped upwards, and the child was lifted up to peep through a little hole in a red velvet curtain, and through it she saw a large horseshoe with quantities of people chattering as they waited. There was a great deal of tawdry gilt, and many gas chandeliers, and the people, especially at the top of the horseshoe, stamped with their feet and whistled. She did not care much for the play, when they presently took their places in a box close to the stage. There was a stout lady in long amber draperies, who kept throwing her arms round a tired-looking man with a brown face and a suit of gilt armour. The child was more amused when, between the acts, they went behind the scenes again to see the famous actress in her dressing-room. Unfortunately, the stout lady looked fatter than ever when seen close, but there were so many amusing things about—a wig with long plaits, several serpent bracelets, a diadem, and a beautiful golden girdle set with emeralds as big as pheasants' eggs. There was a middle-aged gentleman, too, who sat at his ease in a shabby armchair, and drank some pinkish, sparkling wine out of a low, round glass. Someone said that he was the editor of a great paper. The child had never seen an editor; she was glad to see one, because she had always thought they were quite different from other people. She liked to see him laugh, and whisper in a familiar, condescending way to the stout lady, and yet keep on drinking the pink wine out of the round glass.

The child was incorrigibly idle. A mild, nondescript, unimaginative governess and a fat, bald Frenchman who came once a week to instruct her in the Gallic tongue did nothing to take away the inherent unattractiveness of "lessons." She could read, and that was enough. The child read all day long. She lay concealed among the footstools under the long dining-room table, poring over *The Ancient Mariner*[1]—her favourite poem—or thrilled with the lurid emotion of *Wuthering Heights*.[2] A little later *Villette*[3] became her cherished book; a well-thumbed copy, long ago bereft of its cover, stands on the girl's shelf to-day. Poor drab, patient, self-contained Miss Snow! How the child's heart ached for you in your bare, dis-

---

1  Samuel Taylor Coleridge's most famous poem, *The Rime of the Ancient Mariner* (1798), seems to suggest Mary's yearning for adventure, which her life allows her to experience only vicariously.

2  Emily Brontë's 1848 novel offers another indication that Mary lives adventure through her reading.

3  Charlotte Brontë's 1853 autobiographical novel *Villette* is the story of Lucy Snow and her love for the dominating professor Paul Emanuel. Here Mary Erle recalls the end of the novel, in which Lucy refuses to tell the reader whether Paul has been drowned at sea returning to her from the West Indies.

mal, Belgian schoolroom, when Dr. John grew fickle; how she rejoiced when you found your ugly, be-spectacled Fate; how choky she felt at the throat when she read those last pessimistic, despairing words—words full of the sound and fury of angry seas and moaning winds. Why, poor patient hypochondriacal soul, were you destined never to be happy? And all these people were real to the child, much more real than the people she saw when she went out to tea-parties in her best frock and sash. They were as real as the little Tin Soldier and the little Sea-maiden of Hans Christian Andersen,[1] types of humanity which will last as long as there are tender little human hearts to be touched.

And, later on, there is the rather plain girl of fourteen, with somewhat inscrutable eyes, and a seriousness which would have been portentous were it not laughable. Gone, for the time being, were her fits of high spirits and her wild gaiety; lost, the love of battle, and even the love of books about battles. The girl had much to occupy her mind. She began to understand something of life now. It was no longer a kind of coloured picture-book, made to catch the eye and amuse an idle half-hour. The pictures meant a great deal more than that. There were dreadful things, sad things, horrible things behind. Things that the girl could only guess at, but which were there, she was sure, all the same. The world, she could see from her books and newspapers, was full of injustice.

There was the great wrong which had been done some eighteen hundred years ago, when the most beautiful life that was ever lived had come to a shameful end, when the pale Socialist of Nazareth was thrown to the howling populace just as a bone is thrown to a pack of snarling dogs. The girl was always reading that moving, touching story; the Old Testament, with its revengeful, ferocious Deity, did not appeal to her at all. The poignant tragedy enacted at Jerusalem ate into her heart, and this child of fourteen felt herself burdened with the reproach which that senseless crime had left on humanity for well-nigh two thousand years.

Yes, those were serious days. At fourteen one has to make up one's mind on a great many subjects. There are the questions of marriage, of maternity, of education. The girl had learned French by now, and the chance fingering of a small, last-century volume,

---

1   The stories of the tin soldier, in "The Steadfast Tin Soldier" (1838), and the sea-maid, from "Little Claus and Big Claus" (1835), are two of Danish storyteller Hans Christian Andersen's (1805-75) poignant tales for children.

under the somewhat fantastic and insecure guidance of Jean-Jacques Rousseau,[1] made her approach those supremely feminine subjects. She imbibed, indeed, the Swiss philosopher's diatribes on virtue before she had comprehended what civilised mankind stigmatises as vice. *Émile: ou, de l'éducation* was wearily, conscientiously toiled through for the sake of posterity. *Le Contrat Social* was a work which it behooved a person of fourteen, a person who wished to understand the scheme of civilisation, to know.

Strange, anxious days, passed in the twilight of ignorance, groping among the vain shadows with which man in his wisdom has elected to surround the future mothers of the race. It was not, of course, till years afterward, that Mary became conscious of the fine irony of the fact that man, the superior intelligence, should take his future companion, shut her within four walls, fill that dimly lighted interior with images of facts and emotions which do not exist, and then, pushing her suddenly into the blinding glare of real life, should be amazed when he finds that his exquisite care of her ethical sense has stultified her brain.

The little girl was reading *David Copperfield*[2] when she descended one day, with knitted brows, to the room where her governess was laboriously copying in water-colours a lithographed bunch of roses.

"What is a fallen woman really, Miss Brown?" demanded the girl, with her tense look. "Dickens says that little Em'ly is a fallen woman, because she goes to Italy with that Mr. Steerforth. Was Mr. Steerforth a fallen man, too?"

The little girl, it was evident, with all her reading, had yet a great deal to learn. She had yet to apprehend the hard-and-fast rules by which civilised man sets to work to cast stones at his neighbour—and more especially at his female neighbour.

When, at sixteen, the girl—still burdened with doubts—had to pack her trunks for a sojourn in Germany, she packed among the books which she was to take, her New Testament, and the *Men and*

---

1 Rousseau (1712-78) was the French philosopher whose controversial novel *Émile: ou, de l'éducation* (1762) and essay *Du Contrat Social* (1762) outline his idea of the *volonté générale*, or general will, inspired the leaders of the French Revolution.

2 Charles Dickens's (1812-70) novel *David Copperfield* (1849-50) exposes a puzzled and naïve young Mary to the intricacies of the sexual double standard of the age.

*Women* of Robert Browning.[1] When she returned, a year later, she had some difficulty to find room for her Testament, for her favourite volumes of Darwin and Renan[2] took up so much space, and from the virile optimism of Browning she could not now afford to part.

## CHAPTER III
## WONDERINGS[3]

THE scene shifts to a garden in a German town. Over yonder, across the swirling, rushing river, lie the bare, barrack-like university buildings, the narrow streets vandyked with gables, the noisy drinking-shops and the green-canopied *anlage*;[4] while over the mediæval bridge come and go, all day long, a procession of students, dogs, school-children, market-women and burghers of all sorts and conditions, sweltering under the fierce summer sun.

But here, in the professor's garden, it is placid enough; in the vine-trellised *laubgang*[5] it is always cool and shady. There is the arbour to sit in, after twelve o'clock dinner, where the sultry afternoon can be dreamed away till coffee-time with an open book on one's knee. The rest of the house-hold have probably gone to bed again, for in Germany, where one rises at six, the weakness of the flesh is apt to manifest itself after a Teutonic midday meal, and sleep becomes imperative unless one has secured the "Buch der Lieder" from the top book-shelf in the study, and Heine's "cynical smile"

---

1 Browning (1812–89) published *Men and Women*, a two-volume collection of fifty-one poems, in 1851. The set includes some of his most impressive dramatic dialogues from the middle period of his career, among them "Fra Lippo Lippi," "Bishop Blougram's Apology," and "Andrea del Sarto."

2 Charles Darwin (1809–82) was the English naturalist whose landmark works *The Origin of Species* (1859) and *The Descent of Man* (1871) shook the foundations of Christianity. Ernest Renan (1823–92) was a French naturalist/philosopher best known for his controversial *Life of Jesus* (1863).

3 This chapter does not appear in subsequent editions of the novel, though it offers important indications of Mary Erle's early exposure to radical German and French philosophers and novelists and their influence on her life in England.

4 A small park or enclosure.

5 An aisle or corridor of greenery or foliage.

is illuminating the placid German landscape for the first time.[1] Other days it would be the "Wahlverwandtschaften" or, "Wilhelm Meister,"[2] or the red-hot, palpitating *novellen* of Paul Heyse.[3] Was the worthy Frau Professorin asleep, or looking after the Sauerkraut fermenting in tubs in the cellar, or seeing to the pressing of the little white wine, which grew primarily in small bunches of green grapes, overhead in the *laubgang*? The Frau Professorin led a busy life. So long as the English professor's daughter was reading German, what did it matter much what she read? The good little woman had a nice eye for the baking of a cake or the stewing of cherries to be served with tomorrow's roast veal, but with all that poring over books she had no patience. When one had secured a distinguished husband like the Herr Professor—she always alluded to him by this title—and produced several boys and girls who all wore spectacles, and gave promise of the highest intellectual attainments, a German female citizen had sure fulfilled her mission?

In her own opinion, she, the Frau Professorin, had every intellectual attainment. When she was a young girl, she had learned by heart portions of Schiller's plays,[4] and could have recited to you, had you suffered it, the whole of "Hermann und Dorothea."[5] Goethe's domestically didactic idyl embodied all the virtues as well as all the emotions which were permissible to the German girl of the mid-century. When the Frau Professorin was formally betrothed, on that well-remembered-and-never-to-be-forgotten night when she wore a wreath of real myrtle on her smooth blond hair, together with a comfortable gown of brown linsey-woolsey,[6]

---

1   Heinrich Heine (1797-1856) was a German writer whose first collection of poetry, *Buch der Lieder* (1827), or *The Book of Songs*, outlined his tempestuous and unrequited love for his cousin.

2   Two novels, the first published in 1809, the other in 1795-96, by the great German Romantic poet, philosopher, playwright, and novelist, Johann Wolfgang von Goethe (1749-1832).

3   Heyse (1830-1914) was a German novelist whose idealized stories cut against the grain of the school of literary naturalism that dominated Europe in the late nineteenth century.

4   Friedrich von Schiller (1759-1805) was a German dramatist whose greatest play, the tragedy *Wallenstein* (1798-99), examines the rise and fall of the general of the armies of the Holy Roman Empire during the Thirty Years' War.

5   Goethe published this poem, his response to the French Revolution, in 1798.

6   A coarse fabric of cotton or linen woven with wool.

and sat, with her plump hand clasped by her betrothed, on the state sofa in the drawing-room at home, where the stove had been lighted expressly for the occasion and wax candles were actually placed on the piano—on that never-to-be-forgotten-and-dearly-cherished evening, her father had presented her with a framed line-engraving of the famous pair of German lovers. And the English professor's daughter might see them now, for they hung on one side of the tall white porcelain stove, in the best drawing-room upstairs. Hermann, with luxuriant locks, and tenderly solicitous of his beloved's safety; Dorothea, with her amazingly solid ankles, forever descending those steps with that docile, cow-like expression of subserviency. This picture the Frau Professorin intended to hand on to Ottilie, her eldest, when that damsel should have been fortunate enough to secure the hand of one of the many hard-working *privat-docenten*,[1] over yonder in the town.

But Ottilie, who was rising eighteen, and extremely short-sighted, would have none of it. Fräulein Ottilie insisted not only on smoking cigarettes, but on reading Strauss and Schopenhauer.[2] She announced herself a determined agnostic, and, indeed, a succession of South German cook-maids had summarily "given notice," because the fräulein, when she went to the kitchen to make the pastry, persisted in stating her views on the apostolic legend of the Annunciation. These heated arguments, it must be owned, had a disastrous effect on Fräulein Ottilie's pies, while they wholly failed in the desired effect of convincing the round-cheeked Bavarian peasant girls. But if the young lady's cakes left something to be desired, there was no fault to be found with her logic; a faculty which she probably inherited from her father, a not undistinguished German scientist. He has long since slipped away into the brumous Teutonic Walhalla, but the recollection of his personality is strangely clear. Tall, spare, and pale, with keen grey eyes shining behind ample spectacles, he was the kindest, the most lovable of men. Of guile he had not a trace. Year out, year in, he toiled at his laboratory, at his books, at his university lectures, keeping up a close and uninterrupted correspondence with Professor Erle, whose cult like his own was a simple and an all-embracing one—to wit, worship of Truth.

---

1 Student lecturers or tutors at the university.
2 David Strauss (1808-74) was a German philosopher and historian of religion who, influenced by Hegel, regarded the Christian mythology as a human invention. Arthur Schopenhauer (1788-1860) was another German philosopher influenced by Goethe and also Hegel.

The simple, German home life pleased the motherless English girl. It was like returning to primeval Saxon ways. The thrift, the frugality, the delight in simple little pleasures—a luncheon of black bread and coarse cheese in some tiny inn among the mountains, when she had walked in the pine-scented air since early morning, singing *volk-slieder*[1] in chorus, or arguing on the old, old problems as they stepped along—all delighted the girl who had been accustomed to a far more elaborate scheme of life. On dark, velvety summer nights, when the very air caressed them like a beloved hand, they would sit out on the terrace overhanging the river and watch the students slip down stream in their torch-laden boats, singing sturdily in unison:

*"Bleib du in ewigen Leben*
*Mein guter Kamarad!"*[2]

Over yonder, across the black river, twinkled the lights of the town. There were the lecture-rooms where young Germany toiled and moiled; the taverns where they hiccoughed eternal friendship over their endless mugs of beer; the mysterious holes and corners where they fought their duels and slashed at each other's cheek-bones and foreheads, or made boisterous love to stout, frowsy damsels of equivocal renown. It was the first decade after the great war.[3] Young Germany was full of the lust of life, of the bravado of a supreme victory. Henceforward the Teuton, armed to the teeth, was to regenerate an effete Europe; nay, even to become the great coloniser.

And at home at the villa, Fräulein Ottilie, who was addicted to the surreptitious perusal of the romances of Georges Sand (MM. Zola and de Goncourt had not been invented as yet, so far as the "young person" was concerned),[4] was also given to discoursing on

---

1  A folksong.
2  May you live forever, my good friend!
3  The Franco-Prussian war of 1870-71, in which Germany, in little more than six months, pummeled the French, captured Emperor Napoleon III, captured Paris, and claimed the Alsace and Lorraine regions that were to become the bitterly disputed areas in World War I and World War II. The war signaled the rise of German military might.
4  George Sand, pseudonym for Amandine-Aurore-Lucile Dudevant (1804-76), was a French novelist known for her early tales of passion and her later *romans rustiques*, or regionalist pieces. Émile Zola (1840-1902) and the de Goncourt brothers Edmond (1822-96) and Jules (1830-70), who wrote and published novels as one until Jules's death were French novelists of the naturalist school.

love as she puffed at her cigarettes in the nightingale-haunted woods at the back of the garden. Love, she said, was like certain diseases, such as scarlatina, the measles, chicken-pox: one might escape it in one's youth, but so much the worse for you if you caught it when you were middle-aged. One caught it, and once infected, one sometimes gave it to the object of one's affection; more often one did not. Then came unhappiness, an aggravation of the malady, and in cases of weak will, even death. On the other hand, the best treatment was something like that since practiced by M. Pasteur.[1] To be dosed with the beloved object was an almost certain means of cure, and marriage was, in nine cases out of ten, the only infallible remedy. The English girl, listening with pricked ears to the words that fell between Fräulein Ottilie's neat rings of smoke, said little, but marvelled exceedingly. She never talked of love. It was an almost sacred subject, something intangible, far-off, priceless; a thing which she might grasp some day, or which she might never see or hold within her hands in her long journey from the cradle to the grave.

At the end of the year, in the burning, stifling summer-heat, there came a strange listlessness over the young girl. She crept about the garden, looking at the familiar potato plots and the green grapes in the *laubgang* with leaden eyes. One day, she was too tired to get up, and later on, when Fräulein Ottilie insisted on reading aloud a burning love-scene from *Indiana*,[2] she thanked her with a smile. She had suddenly become deaf. The doctor who was called in looked grave. At night, grinning skeletons gibbered in the four corners of the room, while it was an absolute certainty that a thing which made a noise was concealed in a room cupboard where her dresses hung. It was an eternity till the next morning, when the doctor came again, and then all at once, everyone seemed much concerned, and late in the evening a nurse in cap and apron appeared, and the girl, lying prone on the bed with her leaden head and aloofness from all that were up and stirring, caught the words of the doctor:

---

1 Although Louis Pasteur (1822-95), French chemist and the founder of microbiology, was not the first to explore the benefits of vaccinating by deliberately introducing the disease into a patient—that distinction belongs to English scientist Edward Jenner (1749-1843)—he *did* devote much of his career to disease prevention. Here the narrator is having fun with the "science" of love.

2 George Sand's first novel without collaboration, *Indiana* (1832) is a passionate work exploring the fate of women trapped in loveless marriages.

"Yes, typhoid fever. And rather a ticklish case."

Then came æons of tossing nights and restless days, the burning nights of mid-Europe, where no fresh breeze from the sea ever penetrates, and where the mosquitoes whizz, and the open window lets in the sultry air and the sound of a tolling church bell. Days of fierce, sultry heat which could not be kept out, and when a students' *fête*, with its firing cannon, gave exquisite torture to the fever patient. But the cannon were only fired through one endless day, while there were other forms of torture which went on and on. There came a dreadful hour when double bags of ice were laid on her head and chest, and when she laid on her back, struggling heroically for each breath that seemed likely to be her last. The girl was perfectly conscious now; she could see the anxious eyes of Herr Professor behind his gleaming spectacles, the set mouths and the searching glances of the two doctors who were bending over the bed.

"Is father there?" asked the girl suddenly.

"No, dear child. Shall we send for him?" said the Herr Professor.

The girl nodded. And so it was all over! She must be very, very ill, or in that thrifty German household they would never dream of telegraphing to London to insist on the hurried journey. It was all over, and somehow it did not matter. The bed was so uncomfortable, and how that swarm of mosquitoes buzzed round her head! All day, all night, the *schnarken*[1] went on buzzing. And there were flies, too. Ugh, how she hated flies! Years ago, when the black cat lay ill under the laurel bush in the garden, she herself had sat there all day and fanned away the flies. And so was it over? Well, she was not afraid. One could die even if one were only a girl, and, now, at any rate, it was impossible to rest. Life—Death? They were perhaps only phrases. The main thing was that the bed on which she lay was like a newly ploughed turnip field; she ached all over, and there were tons of lead on her forehead. Too weak to turn over, she lay on her back, until a new nurse came, who touched her gently and turned her on one side. Ah, that was better, to be with one's face to the wall.

"Perhaps, if I am lucky," she thought, "father's dear head will come round that door before—" The girl lay a long time, gazing

---

1   *Schnarken*, or *schnarchen*, means literally "to snore"; in this case the narrator refers to the sound of the bothersome mosquitoes.

with dull eyes at the foolish pattern of the wall paper—little bunches of pink roses on stiff diamonds of an ugly grey.

And then, one morning, a dear, kind, well-remembered face did come round the door, and in another minute a pair of strong arms was lifting her up in bed. The traveller had arrived from London.

After that, all went well. The worst was over, and now the healing process was to begin. Ten days later, the invalid was carried down, wrapped in shawls, and placed in a basket chair in the *laubgang*, where the warm summer sunshine only filtered through a canopy of vine-leaves. As often happens in cases of typhoid fever, the girl, as she recovered, found herself, mentally, a child again. She was hungry, ravenously hungry; she whimpered when the doctor came and forbade her anything more solid than broth or jelly. She wanted so much to get well and strong!

Out yonder, over the whirling, hurrying river, lay the busy little town, with its university buildings, its green *anlage*, its shops. Across the old bridge, with its quaint spans, she could watch once more that ever-moving procession of townsfolk hurrying to and fro. How good to breathe the pure, open air, to hear the young voices on the river, to watch the grapes ripening in the *laubgang* overhead. It was Life, glorious, sunshiny, palpitating Life. She wanted to know it, to seize it, to make sure that she had lived. Henceforward, she was sure she would never care much for books. Why, they were but the vain reflections of someone else's life—that one desirable thing which one must make haste to seize, before the dark curtain falls which shuts us out for ever from the beautiful things we see and touch and hear.

## CHAPTER IV
## A YOUNG GIRL

LOOKING back, across the vague, misty years, the egotism, the ferocious egotism, of the young girl appears well-nigh incredible. At eighteen, she, with her fluffy hair and her white shoulders, is the most important thing in her little world. There is the day she first discovers she has a throat with fine lines; the secret delight with which she hears an artist tell her that the movements of her body are graceful. Does black, or blue, or white become her best? It is never too late, and she is never too tired when she comes back from a ball, to light all the candles again in her bedroom and examine herself critically, anxiously, in the glass. There is a little pink spot of excitement on each cheek; her hair is ruffled. She looks pretty, she has been happy to-night. Some one—no matter who—has told her she looks charming.

There is the desire of the young girl to coquet, to play with, to torture, when she first learns the all-powerful influence which she possesses by the primitive fact of her sex. With all the arrogance which belongs to personal purity, she stands on her little pedestal and looks down on mankind with a somewhat condescending smile. She is—and she feels it instinctively—a thing apart, a kind of forced plant, a product of civilisation. At present, the ball-room, with its artificial atmosphere, its fleeting devotions, its graceful mockery of real life, is the scene of her little triumphs. The eyes of all men—young and old alike—follow the girl approvingly, wistfully, as she ascends the staircase, her full heart beating against her slim satin bodice, the clear, peachlike cheeks pink with excitement, her swimming eyes raised invitingly to some favourite partner, or dropped as she passes a man she wishes to avoid. At the door her slender white arms and shoulders disappear in a circle of black coats; the programme is scrawled all over;[1] she notes exultantly that one or two men are scowling at each other, and that she has no dance to give someone who has joined the group too late. It is the woman's first taste of power.

There is, too, the *joie de vivre*, the delight of the young animal at play, the imperious will-to-live of a being in perfect health. The girl must dance till her feet ache horribly, the room swings round, and the pink dawn comes creeping in behind the drawn blinds; but still she must go on till that music stops, the swaying, voluptuous, heartrending music which draws her feet round and round. The violins, with their *navrant*[2] tones, the human, dolorous strains of the cornets, the brilliant, metallic, artificial sounds of the piano, all act powerfully on the young girl's nervous system. Then comes the stifling crowded supper-room, with its indigestible food and sweet champagne; the young men who move nearer and look at her with strange eyes, after they have eaten and drunk. It is all new and intoxicating, and a little frightening; but it is life, or the nearest approach to it that a young girl, gently nurtured and carefully looked after, can know.

Admiration, at this period, is the very breath of her nostrils. No

---

1 Young women at formal cotillions held dance cards, programs that allowed them to schedule and keep track of their dancing partners for the evening.
2 Distressing or upsetting.

matter from whom, no matter when or where. A smile, seen like a flash, on a face in a passing hansom;[1] the ill-bred pertinacity of a raised lorgnette[2] at a theatre; the dubious gaze of men about town, leaning against ball-room doors—nothing offends her. It is simply incense burnt at the feet of her youth.

But at last, out of the vague crowd of black coats and wistful eyes, the first lover emerges. It is a little difficult to recall his face, after all these years. Looking back dispassionately, he seems to have been very like all the others, only that he made her suffer, while the others, perhaps, suffered a little for her sake. There were the horrible half-hours of torture when she waited, in some crowded party, for his sleek head and his somewhat foolish smile to appear in the doorway; the blank, empty days when there was no letter; the shamefully sweet, the incredible surrender to the first tentative embrace, a surrender which tortured her night and day, and then the joy, the supreme joy of knowing, for certain, that he cared.

It is all a little remote, now, but the beautiful secret was hugged like a very treasure. He was young, he was poor, there were diffi-culties of every sort to contend with, and finally there was a part-ing one warm, windy night in November. It was a Sunday, about seven o'clock, and through the window, which was ajar in the drawing-room where they stood, came the sound of a tolling bell. It was only a neighbouring church summoning pious folk to evening service, but it sounded like a knell. It was a well-nigh hopeless affair, and all that they could do was to promise to write to each other. For some weeks the girl watched, in the column of the shipping intelligence, the eastward progress of a Peninsular and Oriental steamer on its way to Australia, and after that, on Monday mornings, when the mail comes in, she would stand, with her heart in her mouth, and her hand on the knob of the dining-room door, afraid to go in and find that no foreign envelope lay beside her plate. For some months, to be sure, the letters pretty nearly always lay there, but gradually they got rarer and rarer, and one day she told herself finally that she need not expect any more. Torture is not made more bearable by being slowly applied. During the months in which those letters from Australia grew rarer, the girl understood for the first time the helplessness, the intolerable bur-den which society has laid on her sex. All things must be endured

1  A two-wheeled carriage for hire with the driver's seat above and behind.
2  A pair of opera glasses with a short handle.

with a polite smile. Had she been a boy, she was aware that she might have made an effort to break the maddening silence; have stifled her sorrow with dissipation, with travel, or hard work. As it was, the trivial round of civilised feminine existence made her, in those days, almost an automaton. One looks back, with wonder, at the courage of the girl. To find a smile with which to face her father at the dinner table; to take a sisterly interest in Jim's exploits at school; to show due surprise each time her brother announced the arrival of a new batch of rabbits; and a partisan's joy in the licking which Smith minor had administered to Jones major—these were the immediate duties which lay before her.

Not feeling strong just now, the girl gave up going to balls; they reminded her too much of that episode which she wished to forget; and now the prospect that opened out before her was a vista of years full of scientific *soirées* where one walked down long sparsely peopled rooms and looked through microscopes at things which wriggled and squirmed. Sometimes the girl felt strangely like one of those much-observed bacilli; the daughter of a scientist, she knew well enough that her little troubles had about as much importance as theirs in relation to the vast universe. Yet there she was, fixed down under her little glass case, while the world kept a coldly observant eye upon her. Ah, the torture of the young—the young who are always unhappy, and whose little lives are continually coming to a full stop, with chapters that cease bluntly, brutally, without reason and without explanation!

That she was thrown aside, dropped overboard, as it were, in the terrific battle for existence mattered nothing to the young girl. Having no self-pity, she never questioned the justice of the blow that had been dealt her. Afterward, in the years to come, she might wonder why she should have been made to suffer so. But not then. One's first sorrow is a very precious thing. In those far-off days, she would gladly have sacrificed everything—even life itself—for the young man who forgot to write, and whose face, with its rather foolish smile, it is so difficult to recall exactly as it was.

About this time, when she began to work at the Central London School of Art,[1] father and daughter became great friends. On

---

1   This fictional school is representative of any number of urban, state-supported public art institutes existing at the time in London.

the days when he went to lecture at the London University,[1]★ she would either walk with him, or go to fetch him on those afternoons when he was coming straight home to tea instead of making his way to the Athenæum Club.[2]★ With her chin in the air, looking straight before her, she stepped along, in the half-dark, with a royal scorn for the well-dressed loafers who find their pleasure in accosting ladies in the street. She was twenty-one, and a woman now; it behooved her to be able to take care of herself. And, after all, they were perhaps more easily disposed of than some of the men who took her in to dinner, men who had tired eyes and a dubious smile, and who were fond of starting doubtful topics with a sidelong, tentative glance.

They went out a great deal to dinner, father and daughter, so that she early learnt the ways of the world, or at least the ways of the world which gives and goes to dinner-parties. There were always nice men, famous men, interesting men, at the parties at home in Harley Street.[3]★ The girl smiled again a good deal in those days, scrupulously hiding what she thought was a dried-up little heart. How well she always remembered the last time they had gone out together. She could recollect driving with her father in a hansom, and their talk on the way to the Foreign Office.[4] His last book but one had but lately appeared, and was now being scratched and bespluttered assiduously by clerical pens, while it was received with rapture by the large class which like their advanced thinking done for them and turned out in fat print with ample margins once in every third year. All the way up the crowded staircase there is a great display of teeth, of tiaras, of stars and orders, and shining bald heads. The wife of the Foreign Secretary is delighted to see the professor, though no one in that eminently aristocratic gathering "insists" on anything, and most people are content to exchange two fingers, two words, and two smiles,

---

1 Now located in Malet Street just south of Euston Station, London University, founded in 1826, was in the last half of the century located to the south, near Piccadilly Circus, in the Burlington Gardens buildings, which now house the Museum of Mankind.

2 One of London's most elite social clubs, the Athenæum Club was founded in 1824 and moved to its Pall Mall location in 1830.

3 Known by the last third of the century as a gathering place for scientists and medical specialists, Harley Street is a natural place for Mary's father to take his family to live.

4 The office responsible for England's foreign affairs and overseas relations.

one at greeting and one at passing on. His Excellency the German Ambassador detains the father and daughter, for he has just heard that the Emperor intends to bestow on the English professor the Order of the Crown, for his distinguished services to the progress of modern thought. The two move on, and are caught up in other small circles, where they hear agreeable commonplaces, in an atmosphere where everything is taken for granted, and in which smooth phrases and smooth faces abound—faces which have inherited, for hundreds of years, the art of expressing nothing in a polite way. It is all suave and artificial and decorous. No epigrams make themselves conspicuous in the well-bred chatter, and one great lady, exhibiting a superfluity of bare flesh, raises a tortoise-shell lorgnette when someone—who can it be?—is heard to laugh outright. A famous guardsman has several charming things to say, and the girl finds her chatter received with flattering attention by the handsome man with the garter, who is at once a viceroy[1] and the most suave of diplomats. Surely, when one looks back, the girl's eyes are bright again that night; her blond hair is full of electricity; she has regained, though with a curious little composed manner, something of the roundness, the joyousness, of nineteen. Life is a compromise, and must not be taken too seriously. It is absurd to be much in earnest, and it bores people. So much the girl has learned.

She works now regularly with her father, acting as his amanuensis when his eyes are tired, or verifying facts in the library. It is better, far better, more satisfactory in every way, than leading an ordinary "young lady's" existence. Jimmie, the little brother, has grown into a boy with charming, insinuating manners, who is curiously un-British in his demonstrativeness. His sister, he says, is the most charming of girls. He announces that he is always going to live with her. Nothing shall separate them. His whole life, he declares, with his arms round her neck, is to be devoted to his dearest Mary.

Yes, the pictures which rise up of the home life are pleasant; those are happy, but entirely irresponsible years. There is plenty of travel, and the practical kind of culture that comes of travel. And more and more father and daughter are drawn together.

And then came that spring when the father was hard at work. The two rarely left the study now, except for a short walk after din-

---

1   The Order of the Garter indicates the highest order of knighthood; a viceroy was the governor of a country, province, or colony, ruling as a representative of the Queen.

ner, for the professor's book absorbed him. Not feeling quite himself, he was anxious—terribly anxious—to get it done. After this they would go abroad and get a long holiday. He wanted to go to Zermatt.[1] At the Riffel Alp he would get the air and exercise he craved. No, he was not quite himself; he felt overstrained, nervous; he had a continual headache. It was, perhaps, he said, a touch of bile.

But one evening, just before dinner, the book was actually done. He bent over the girl at the desk, kissed her crisp hair, and wrote at the bottom of the page, in his own cramped hand, these words: "The End."

And so it was, indeed.

The next morning, when the servant went up to call him, the professor had been dead some hours. The doctors spoke of a clot of blood in the brain, of overwork, and overstrain.

And in the tall, darkened house in Harley Street, the child who had played, the girl who had danced, died too.

## CHAPTER V
## ALISON

AS sometimes happens with busy people in London, the Erles had hundreds of acquaintances and but few intimate friends. A friendship is costly, in point of time, and Mary found, when one chapter of her life was done that spring morning, that there were two people only that she must imperatively see. A man and a woman—Vincent Hemming and Alison Ives. How their features stood out among the crowd of vague faces, which belonged to that other life. Alison Ives especially, with her handsome, clever face, looking like a Reynolds,[2] with her superb air, and her huge hat tied under the chin. With that grave sweetness which endears to us the Siddons in the National Gallery,[3]*

---

1  A resort village near the Matterhorn in the Swiss Alps.
2  Sir Joshua Reynolds (1723-92) is among the most important of English portrait painters. Among those who sat for him were Oliver Goldsmith, Laurence Sterne, Edmund Burke, Edward Gibbon, and Mrs. Sarah Kemble Siddons.
3  Sarah Kemble Siddons (1755-1831) was an English actress, the most distinguished member of the famed Kemble family. Her portrait was painted by Gainsborough and Reynolds. The National Gallery, founded in 1824 by George IV, is one of the world's premier art museums. It has been at Trafalgar Square since 1838.

she yet had the look of a thinker—modernised by a slightly bored expression—and a little distinguished way which at once made other women in her vicinity look dowdy or vulgar. Her clothes always seemed to suit her as its feathers do a bird. There are women who look like an *édition de luxe* of a poor book; Alison Ives suggested that of a classic.

It had been her habit for a couple of years past to sit at the feet of Professor Erle; she constantly announced, laughing, that he was the only man she ever wanted to marry, only that he was firm, and would not permit it. Besides, it was no good trying to compete with her mother, Lady Jane, who was sixty-five and irresistible. Women of sixty-five, she said, were nowadays the only people who inspired a great passion. She supposed her turn would come—a quarter of a century hence. But, all the same, the daughter was much admired in "the world"; but "the world" as understood by her mother, Lady Jane, by no means entirely satisfied this eminent-ly modern young woman. It was whispered that she had serious views, though it was certain that she was pretty enough to please a Prime Minister and clever enough to entertain a guardsman, if she found herself next to either at dinner. Alison did not mind which, she said; in fact, after a long day in the East End,[1] when she was tired, she rather preferred the guardsman, who would be content to talk of polo ponies, whereas, when a young woman is put next to a Premier, it behooves her to look, at any rate, very brilliant indeed. Though she never smoked, was ignorant of billiard-cues and guns, and hated playing the man, Mary had heard Alison mur-mur something like an oath—but only when they were alone. It was a habit which she had picked up in Paris, when she was work-ing in a sculptor's studio; and she always declared that "*dame*" and "*sapristi*," being in a foreign tongue, were notoriously less effica-cious and by inference more pardonable, than swearing in the ver-nacular. For the rest, with the best heart in the world, she had a somewhat caustic tongue, could interpret Chopin like an artist, and always had her hair exquisitely dressed.

What attracted people at once was her intense womanliness, her utter absence of snobbery, her real desire to be in sympathy with her own sex. Like all exceptional people, she had her moods, and sometimes, for months together, she was heard of only as forming

---

1 The East End of London was, at the time, synonymous with slums and poverty.

one of a party in this or that great country house, while at other times she would come to town and study fitfully, or devote herself to the task of helping young girls. Once, in the middle of the season, she took a lodging in a by-street in the Mile End Road,[1]* but she only stayed seven weeks, and when she appeared again, the expression on her face was sadder than before. "Of course one ought to *know* what it is like," she said, when Mary asked her why she had left so soon. "It's an experience—but a terrible one. It's not only the drunkenness, the down-at-heel vice, the astounding absence of any thrift or forethought, and the incredible repetition of one solitary adjective; but it seems to me that when one or two of us go and live down there we absolutely do no permanent good at all. The thing will be to bring the East End here—one by one, of course, just as we go there."

Alison kept her word. This spring had found her ensconced in a workman's flat in the Mayfair district,* with one small servant whom she had rescued in Whitechapel.[2]* "But it's as much for myself as her," explained Alison, laughing. She hated to be thought philanthropic. "All we women are so incredibly dependent on other people. It's absurd that we don't know how to do anything useful. I shall keep my flat, and go to it now and again, when I am tired of shooting parties. It will be a little home for my East End girls, whom I intend to train. I daresay I shall be disappointed in them, but that's inevitable with all experiments. Anyway, it will probably do me more good than it will them. The only real slavery nowadays is the slavery of luxury. We are all getting so pampered that we can't exist without it. People do the most incredible things. I have known a woman stay with a husband whom she loathed, and whom it was an outrage to live with, simply because she couldn't do her own hair. I'm going to get our cook at Ives Court to teach me how to broil a mutton chop, though I daresay she's too grand for that; and I shall go and watch the laundry-maid at her work."

---

1  By the nineteenth century, Mile End was a quietly respectable area of East London with many who worked in the city's nearby industrial area. Mile End Road, one of the main roads into the city from the east, cuts through the southern part of Mile End.
2  Positioned along the main route into the city from Essex and the east, Whitechapel—best known perhaps as the locale of all the Jack the Ripper murders of 1888—at the end of the century was a bitterly poor slum district, home to most of England's eastern European immigrant population.

"And your hands, you lunatic?" Mary had exclaimed. "I think I see you with red knuckles!"

"Oh," said Alison, laughing, "I shall tell that little manicure just out of Bond Street★ to come twice a week. There's that new stuff, 'Eau des Orchidées'; it's wonderful. Don't imagine I'm going to give up the only old-fashioned quality we modern women have got—our vanity. It's the only thing that makes us still bearable."

This was the young woman who was shown into the study by Elizabeth one morning a few days after the funeral at Highgate. Mary was bending over a desk, busy with her father's proofs, when she came in. The elder girl's beautiful brown eyes were suspiciously shiny; it had evidently cost her an effort to come into the study which she knew so well. The two girls wrung each other's hands silently. But after the first kiss, in which she said everything that she dared not put in words, Alison, with her ready tact, began talking business at once.

The younger girl announced her plans frankly. There was just enough money for her to live meagrely, quietly on for the next few years, while she tried her luck at art. Mary had always meant to paint some day, when her whole time should be at her own disposal. Why, she had always drawn ever since she was a child, and the sense of colour was almost an emotion to her. Yes, to paint was a long-cherished ambition, mused over on long, drowsy afternoons in the reading-room of the British Museum,★ nursed during the days when she had remained bending over a desk in her father's study, patiently inscribing what the professor dictated as he walked up and down the little room. As for Jimmie, he was to remain at Winchester, and, if he could succeed in winning a scholarship, was to go to Oxford as the father had wished. By living carefully this could be managed.

"No woman ever made a great artist yet," said Alison, shrugging her shoulders, "but if you don't mind being third-rate, of course go in and try. I suppose it'll mean South Kensington,★ the Royal Academy,[1]★ and then—portraits of babies in pastel or cottage gardens for the rest of your life."

---

1   South Kensington is a reference to the Royal College of Art on Exhibition Road near what is now the Victoria and Albert Museum. The Royal Academy, founded by George III in 1768 as an art school, moved to its present location, Burlington House, Piccadilly, in the mid-1850s. It is best known, perhaps, for its annual summer exhibitions, which have been held every year for more than two centuries.

"Oh, don't."

"Never mind, my dear girl. You must work at something. Try the British Art School.[1] Has Vincent Hemming been?" she added, rather inconsequently.

"Yes, he has called. Two or three times, Elizabeth says, but I haven't seen anyone," said Mary, remembering with a little shudder the inquisitive voices at the door.

"I don't see why," said Alison thoughtfully, "you shouldn't take a flat in the same building with me. Of course there are little drawbacks. The ladies use a limited, if somewhat virulent, vocabulary, and now and again one has to step over an elderly gentleman who lives just below, and who comes home tired, and sometimes goes to sleep on the stairs. But one gets accustomed to that."

"I think, on the whole," said Mary, smiling, "I'll take some rooms near, and furnish them. There's Jimmie, you see."

"Where is the boy, by the bye?"

"Oh, the poor boy, I let him go—the day—the day after. He was very good; he said that nothing would induce him to leave me, and sat, poor child, for at least an hour with his arms round my neck, crying. Then another note came from Smith minor—the boy who keeps so many lop-eared rabbits, you remember—asking him to go and spend a week with them in the country."

"And then," said Alison quietly, "ah! I can see Jimmie saying he shouldn't dream of going, and then, when that was settled, wandering round the room, asking if you were not perhaps going out of town yourself? 'It would look rather rude if he refused, as they—the Smiths—knew he wouldn't have any other engagement,' I can hear Jimmie urging. And about seven o'clock an epistle was indited to say that he would be very pleased to go, and the next morning Jimmie went off in a four-wheel cab, looking quite cheerful."

Mary smiled in spite of herself.

"Poor boy," she said softly, in an extenuating voice, "he can't bear anything sad!"

"So much," said Alison after a pause, "for brothers."

"We've got," answered the other, "fortunately or unfortunately, to depend upon ourselves in all the crises of life. I've got lots to do: lawyers to see, these proofs to correct, and to make arrangements for my own future."

---

1  Again fictionalizing here, Dixon points out that there were many institutes available for anyone, talented or not, interested in pursuing the arts.

"Only that? She refuses herself nothing," said Alison. "I am modestly contented with arranging for Evelina's future. Evelina is my last girl. As for my own, I leave it to Providence."

"You can afford to," replied Mary, "but we have it on the authority of a proverb that Heaven is not above taking assistance from mortals in this respect."

"Mary, you're trying to be cynical, and it doesn't suit you. I want to tell you about Evelina," she went on nervously, afraid every minute that one or other of them might break down. "That is my new girl," she continued, settling down on the fender-stool. "Her name is actually Evelina—isn't it preposterous? I should like to call her Polly, only I don't believe in changing poor people's names to suit your own fancy, as if they were cats or canaries. Well, Evelina's baby—"

"Oh, there is a baby?"

"Why, of course. A poor waxen little thing that screams all day long. I've put it out to nurse in a *crêche* that a friend of mine has started in Kentish Town.[1]★ And now I'm trying to cultivate a sense of humour in Evelina."

"It will be difficult, won't it?" said Mary, trying hard to take an interest.

"Never mind. It's what women ought to cultivate above all other things, especially the poorer classes. With a keen sense of the ridiculous, they would never fall in love at all; and as to improvident marriages, they wouldn't exist. If you could see the baby's father!—a pudding-faced boy, who helps in a tiny cheesemonger's shop down there. She 'walked out' with him for two years. He is now nearly nineteen. It is all very well to smile, but it is terrible— for the woman. In the evening, when she has done her work, she lights the lamp in my little sitting-room (everything is quite simple, you know; only I've got a few books, and the tiny Corot[2] from my den at Ives Court, and the Rossetti drawings),[3] and then I read

1  By the late nineteenth century, Kentish Town, to the north of the city center, was a grimy working-class district given over to railway development. The *crêche* is a foundling hospital, or in this case, a day nursery.

2  Jean-Baptiste Camille Corot (1796-1875) was a French painter noted for his sketches of Italian landscapes.

3  Dante Gabriel Rossetti (1828-82) was the English painter and poet who, along with William Holman Hunt and John Everett Millais, helped found the Pre-Raphaelite Brotherhood in reaction against what they saw to be the unimaginative work of the Royal Academy.

aloud while she knits. I read comic things—Dickens, Mark Twain, and so on; and when the poor girl laughs, I feel that I have scored one. She isn't much more than a child, you know, and she has such a good heart. I think she likes to talk to me; she tells me her little story."

"A story," repeated Mary; "she *has* a story then?"

"Oh! a common one enough down there," answered Alison. "She drifted into the East End from Essex,[1] about three years ago, and is a country girl who got a place as drudge-of-all-work in a family of ten, in the Mile End Road. Her master was pleased to make love to her when his wife and the eight children had gone for the day to Southend; Evelina ran out of the house, leaving her box behind, and never dared to go back. My dear, these London idyls are not pretty. She is, however, beginning to show a faint sense of the ridiculous. I believe I shall make a sensible person of Evelina."

Mary raised her head, for she had been listening mechanically, with her eyes fixed on the ink-spots on her father's desk, the desk on which his hand had so often rested. But it was impossible not to feel cheered by Alison's whimsical yet energetic personality. She looked so bright, so alert, so capable, as she stood there, in her pretty black gown and her rakish hat, a little askew with the wind.

"By the bye, did I tell you the adventure I had on my visit to the Blaythewaites? My dear, it was only by the intervention of Providence that I didn't have to dine the first night in my tailor-gown. Of course, I went down third-class—"

"That's because you are saving for Evelina's baby, I suppose," interrupted Mary.

"And so," went on Alison, taking no notice of the interruption, "and so the footman never thought of looking for me there. They all drove off without me, and my basket trunk, with my favourite white gown in it, got taken off with some other people to another place about five miles off. However, it was got back in time, and when I told my little story at dinner to Sir Horace, he was immensely amused, though I'm sure Lady Blaythewaite thought I was graduating for a lunatic asylum. People who don't know me well always do."

---

1   Such a scenario as this was typical during the Industrial Revolution. Poor country farmers from Essex, a rural county to the east of London, drifted into east side slums of the city hoping for a better life. Lacking money, often they became trapped there, falling prey to any number of big-city problems.

"Did you tell Sir Horace Blaythewaite about the workman's flat—and Evelina?" said Mary, laughing. Alison was already at the door, tying on her hat firmly.

"You know I never talk about that," she said, flushing up. "Why, it would look like a pose—as if I thought myself better than other people. And I couldn't bear any one to say that I had 'taken up slumming.' You know how I detest the whole attitude of the upper and middle classes toward the poor. Lifting the lids of people's saucepans and routing under their beds for fluff are not to my taste. Why, district visiting is nothing less than a gross breach of manners—a little worse than electioneering, if that's possible. I'm just going up," she said, giving a rakish twist to her velvet hat-strings, "to the *crèche* in Kentish Town to see Evelina's baby. I'm going on the top of one of those charming trams. I told Worth when I was in Paris that I always went on the tops of omnibuses, and he designed me this little frock on purpose. It's pretty, isn't it, but a little too *ingénue* for me? It smacks of the Comédie Française.[1] I think I see Reichemberg[2] in it," said Alison, doubtfully smoothing down the folds of her loose bodice. "Now you've got to promise to come and dine with me in Portman Square.* We shall have the house to ourselves. Good-bye. Eight o'clock!"

"Nonsense! It's very sweet of you, but I can't possibly go," cried Mary down the passage.

In another instant she was gone, and the house seemed blank and empty again. But trying not to think of her sorrow, Mary went steadily on with the proofs.

*a supporter of feminism??*

## CHAPTER VI
## MARY'S LOVER

MR. VINCENT HEMMING was looked upon by the professor, by Jimmie, by the servants, and indeed by everybody except Mary herself, as her especial property. He was, in fact, one of the few

---

1  Established in 1680 by Louis XIV, the Comédie Française was France's "official," state-protected theater company. The revolution of 1789 swept away the company's corporate privileges, and by mid-century it had fallen out of favor with the play-going public, having gained a reputation for being rather behind the times.

2  Suzanne Angélique Charlotte Reichemberg (1853-?) was a French comedic actress who performed in the Comédie Française theater company.

intimate visitors who came when he liked to the Harley Street house. He had become part of her grown-up life, having first appeared about a year after that Sunday night parting, when the world had seemed very empty indeed. His little air of deference was eminently attractive to a young girl who fancied that she had done forever with emotion. As for Jimmie, he adored him, though Jimmie generally adored new acquaintances—for the space of about six weeks.

Hemming's father had been a politician of some note, who had held office once, and Vincent had pre-eminently the manners of one burdened with state secrets; and his little reserves, a certain air of caution, of discretion, all belonged to those early experiences when his father was alive. To be sure, he had charming, rather old-fashioned manners, affected the speech of the mid-century, and was carried away by none of the modern crazes or fads. A well-shaped forehead—of the showy intellectual type—wavy hair, already threaded with grey, a short, pointed beard, and eyes of an innocent, penetrating brown, made up a personality which appealed at once to dowagers and young girls. At table, he looked very well, although his shoulders were inclined to slope slightly; but when he stood up you saw that he had not the eminently British habit of planting himself firmly, squarely, and self-assertively on his feet. For the rest, he had a small property which brought him in about three hundred a year, and, though already grey, was still spoken of by his elders as a "promising young man."

Though a Conservative, he believed in the higher education, even the enfranchisement of women.[1] It was a subject on which he was persuasively eloquent. It was quite pretty, ladies always thought, to hear him talk of his dreams, his sacrifices; and an occasional article which he succeeded in getting inserted on his favourite subject in the *Fortnightly* or the *Contemporary*, was laboriously written in studied English, and with a convincing, patriotic pen. He had a great deal to say on the future of the race, and of the necessity of maintaining a high ethical standard, and he always waxed exceedingly wroth over the literary excesses of MM. Zola and de Goncourt, and thanked heaven, so to speak, that those emi-

---

1 Many women fought for much of the century to be afforded the basic rights of citizenship, especially voting rights, which they were denied until 1918. The electoral Reform Bills of 1837, 1867, and 1884 each granted enfranchisement to a larger portion of British citizenry, but each of these bills ignored the rights of women.

nent pioneers of Realism did not belong to the Anglo-Saxon family. "We are passing," he announced one day, when he was calling on Lady Jane Ives, "through one of the reconstructive periods of the world's history. Art, under such conditions, is necessarily tentative, rarely complete."

"Yes," said Alison dryly, "and building, you see, always makes a mess. The smoking lime, the dirty puddles, the unpleasant odour of baking bricks are inevitable." But Lady Jane, who had knocked about the most depraved society in Europe for half a century, and who clung with amiable tenacity to her illusions, always agreed with Mr. Hemming. Lady Jane, who was a connoisseur in such things, said that he was one of the few modern young men whom she could endure in her drawing-room for more than twenty minutes.

A day or two after Alison's visit Mr. Vincent Hemming appeared, looking charmingly correct and sympathetic, in a black-and-white spotted tie and a band round his hat. He had gauged to a nicety his degree of intimacy with the great man who was gone.

It was a day when outlines were clearly cut, and colours glaring; everything looked crisp, hard, decided, inevitable. The rooms wore the unsettled, desolate look of a house that is soon to be empty. One or two favourite pictures had already been lifted down from off the wall, leaving a patch of clean paper visible; one book-case was already a dark void; the volumes were piled on the floor ready to be packed. Most of the library was to be sold, and Mary now stood on a ladder, running a regretful eye along the next case of beloved volumes, when Vincent Hemming came in.

"My poor child," he said, in his sympathetic voice, "why wouldn't you let me see you before?"

"I've been very busy," said Mary, getting down from the ladder, and putting out a dusty hand. "There was so much to do. Father's lawyer has been here constantly, and I had to think of everything, you see—of Jimmie, and all that."

"What are you going to do?" he asked, after a little pause, during which his eye had travelled round the dismantled walls and cavernous shelves of the once cosy drawing-room.

"Of course we can't stay in this big house," she explained; "I've taken some lodgings in Bulstrode Street,* near the Central London School of Art."

"By yourself, my dear child?"

"I suppose so, for the present," she answered, knocking two volumes together in a determined manner, to get the dust from the edges. Her mouth had got those little obstinate tucks at the corners now, which he knew so well. "Aunt Julia—mother's sister, you know—has written, offering me a home. But she is very High Church, and lives at Bournemouth[1] in one of those dreadful little gabled villas."

"And of course you prefer an artistic life in London." He was relieved, distinctly relieved, when Mary announced her intention of adopting art as a profession. Painting, especially in water colours, he considered an eminently ladylike occupation; it was, indeed, associated in his imagination with certain drawings of Welsh mountains and torrents, executed by his mother with the prim technique of the forties, which now adorned his chambers in the Temple.[2]*

"That's so brave—and so like you," said Vincent, as his eye wandered round the room again. The tone of his voice was vague: he was evidently considering something which took up all his attention.

"It isn't brave at all," she said simply. "It's an absolute physical necessity. I should go mad if I sat down to think. It all seems so cruel, so terrible, so unjust. He was only fifty-three, and there was so much work for him still to do. He used to say that an ordinary long life could not suffice—"

"The death of Professor Erle is a national disaster," replied Vincent, "and is not to be gauged all at once."

There was a long silence, during which all that this loss meant to each of these two passed through their minds. They had moved to the window now, through which a light breeze fluttered in. The tall, brownish-grey houses were spruced up for the season with clean blinds and boxes of daisies and spiraea. A couple of blond girls in pink cotton made a gay splash of colour against the grey-toned street as they walked buoyantly along. A hansom was drawing up at the pale-green door yonder, and out of it sprang a young man in a glossy hat, a gardenia, and patent leather boots. Just opposite

---

1 To be High Church means to belong to that section of the Church of England distinguished by its "high" conception of Church authority, by its stressing the historical links with Catholic Christianity. Bournemouth lies on the southern coast of England, west of Southampton.

2 Originally occupied by the Knights Templar, who protected pilgrims as they journeyed to the Holy Land, the Temple, near the Thames just south of the Lincoln's Inn, was later occupied by the Inner Temple and Middle Temple—two of the four Inns of Court, those London institutions which accommodated barristers and their offices. Pip, we recall, had chambers in the Temple in Dickens's *Great Expectations*.

some workmen were stretching a red-and-white awning for an evening party. The outward aspect of affairs was unchanged.

"I feel," said Mary, gazing at the striped awning which the men had now succeeded in propping, "as if I had done with *that* world for always. And now I want to do something, to live. Oh, Mr. Hemming," she added, with one of her comic little frowns, "I don't want to be a 'young lady'! Do you really think that because I am a woman that I must sit by and fold my hands and wait?"

"You are very modern in one thing, dear child; you have the modern craze for work."

"It probably saves some of us from the madhouse."

"Ah, but you will marry one of these days, and then where will your work be?" replied Vincent, smiling a little fatuously.

Mary turned from the window abruptly.

"Let us go carefully over the books," she said, with a brusqueness which she sometimes affected. "Help me to choose," she continued, mounting the steps and beginning to hand down the volumes. "I want that Lamb and the Heine, the Goethe and the Jean Paul Richter. Here, catch the *Phædo*, and put it with the Marcus Aurelius and that little Epictetus over there on the cabinet."[1]

"My poor child, you will no doubt require such consolation as the philosophers can afford," said Vincent Hemming, in his somewhat pompous way.

"Here's *Pippa Passes*, and Musset's *Proverbes*, and my special Shelley, and the *Anatomy of Melancholy*.[2] Yes, yes, all those."

---

1 "Lamb" is a volume by Charles Lamb (1775-1834), one of the great English essayists of the nineteenth century; Heine and Goethe we have already met; Jean Paul Richter (1763-1825) was a German novelist who combined idealism with "Sturm und Drang"—the "Storm and Stress"of a work that depicted an impulsive man struggling against convention—in his best known novels *Hesperus* (1795) and *Titan* (1803); *Phædo* is one of Plato's dialogues; Marcus Aurelius (121-180 AD) was the Roman emperor/ philosopher whose *Meditations* (167 AD) Mary is probably asking for; and Epictetus (55-135 AD) was a Greek stoic philosopher whose *Discourses* Mary must want. All of these works, those listed earlier in the novel, and those listed below, attest to Mary's passion for learning and knowledge.

2 *Pippa Passes* (1841) is Robert Browning's (1812-89) verse drama; Alfred de Musset (1810-57) was a French poet, dramatist, and novelist whose *Proverbes* are comedies based on proverbs; Shelley is Percy Bysshe Shelley (1792-1822); *Anatomy of Melancholy* (1621) is English clergyman Robert Burton's (1577-1640) oddly masterful treatise that attempts an exhaustive explanation of what Burton calls the "inbred malady" of Melancholy.

Some colour had come into the girl's cheeks as she sat on the top of the ladder and dropped the books into his arms, covering him, as she did so, with a light cloud of dust; but she looked pathetically delicate in her close-fitting sombre gown, which threw up the pallor of her throat, the mauvish tinge of her lips, the dark rings round her eyes. Vincent Hemming, whatever he had meant to do when he entered the dismantled drawing-room, was fairly carried away by the spectacle of Mary's childish face and busy, nervous little hands rearranging her destiny in her own decided fashion. It touched him, and at the same time irritated him, producing the feeling that, as a man, he was bound to interfere.

One step nearer now, and the course of a life-time would be changed.

"Mary, dear child," he said suddenly, in an imploring tone, while they were both startled by the loudness of his voice, "do you think you—care for me a little?"

The girl turned to look at him. His penetrating brown eyes were actually suffused with tears; a nerve was ticking visibly in his forehead. It all seemed far-off, improbable, impossible. Vincent Hemming, her old friend, had turned into this imploring, visibly suffering man. Mary burst into a hysterical little laugh.

"But you—you don't care for me, do you? You're only saying that because you think I'm lonely—that I want someone to take care of me—aren't you?" she asked hurriedly. "Why, we've known each other so long," she added, seeing that he was still silent. He had flipped the dust from his face and coat with easy tact, and stood, smiling up at her, close by her side.

"I don't know," continued the girl doubtfully, slowly twisting one of the buttons of his frock coat. She had come down several steps of the ladder, so that her eyes were on a level with his. The nerve no longer ticked in his forehead, the muscles of his mouth relaxed; there was already something of triumph in his look.

"Don't smile, dear," she said very gravely. "I can't bear you to look at me like that. Do you—really—want me?"

"Dear heart, I have always wanted you," said a changed, thick voice in her ear, and in the next instant two arms encircled her, and two lips were crushed against hers. For the first minute a consciousness of sorrow overwhelmed her. For good, for evil, the girl knew that she was giving herself up to this man, whom a minute ago she had looked upon with the cool eye and discriminating judgment of mere friendship. All the tragic potentialities of a woman's life, the uncertainties and sorrows of her who gives her happiness into another's keeping, flashed before her.

Why, why must it be? Only a minute ago and she had been ready to face the world alone, to be herself, to express herself, to work out her own destiny. And now it was all changed. Something held her against her will. The demands of the flesh clamoured louder than those of the spirit. This man—a minute ago her friend, and now, in this infinitesimal atom of time, her lover, who stood before her with red, flushed face, and looked with longing eyes into hers—this man had already communicated his trouble to her. His hands, which held her two wrists as they stood there gazing at each other, felt like links of iron.

In that one supreme moment Mary Erle tasted for the first time, in all its intensity, the helplessness of woman, the inborn feeling of subjection to a stronger will, inherited through generations of submissive feminine intelligences.

"I can't, oh, I can't," she said. "Don't ask me now. You don't— you can't understand how I feel. And I don't know you like that. I've always thought of you as a friend," she protested, drawing herself away with her fine smile. "Besides, it's dreadful to be—love-making—when father—"

"I don't ask you to think of it just now, my darling," said Vincent. "I—I—the fact is, I have much to do, and many plans ahead myself. I—I—haven't the right to tie you definitely, Mary. I am thinking seriously of taking that trip to India and Australia of which I told you."

"You're—going—away?" she exclaimed blankly. Already the inexorable chain which nature forges bound her to this man.

"Yes, to collect materials for my book on the Woman Question.[1] I might come home by way of Canada, and if so, the thing would take me the best part of a year. Then, when I come home,

---

1  Victorian England was preoccupied with what was called the "Woman Question," a vocal debate—carried on for decades in all manner of newspapers and journals, as well as in churches, even Parliament—over a woman's role in society. Numerous philosophers, educators, literary and religious figures, and politicians spent most of the nineteenth century trying in one way or another to define "Woman," her "sphere," her "mission." The resulting debates helped to spur the Women's Rights movements of the last third of the century and to begin the push for women's suffrage. The discussions also played a crucial role in fueling the New Woman fiction of the 1880s and 1890s.

I shall have my book to do; and I hope, if the present Government keeps in, to get a legal appointment. So you see, little one, you will have ample time to think about it, as well as to perfect your artistic studies," he added, with a touch of his old-fashioned manner. He was sitting down on the sofa now, and looked already his quiet, well-bred, rather deferential self again.

An hour later Vincent got up reluctantly to go. "I have to dine with a member of the Government at a quarter to eight," he explained. "My new article must be finished before I start, and I'm thinking of starting quite soon."

"Are you?" said Mary sorrowfully, turning to the window and gazing down the street.

It was so different now. She belonged to this man who was going away. Why had he spoken? Could it not be as it was? A few yards out a piano-organ was rattling out a cheap German valse. The sun was off the houses now, and the street wore its familiar, dingy look. Vincent searched among the disarranged furniture and the piles of books for his hat.

Mary followed him to the door. She wanted to say something nice, but she could think of nothing. Just at parting, he took her in his arms again, and brushed her downcast lids with his lips. During that embrace she thought of nothing except that she was sure that she had always cared for him. "Dear," he muttered, "I'm afraid that if I go away I shall leave the best part of myself with you."

When he had gone, she stooped about again among the rows of books, sorting them mechanically, without thinking much what she was doing. Little clouds of dust rose in the twilight room. The tall, grim houses shut out all that remained of a daffodil-tinted sky. Tired and unstrung, the girl threw herself on to the sofa where she and Vincent Hemming had sat. Presently, to her surprise, she was conscious that two large, salt tears were coursing their way down her dusty cheeks.

## CHAPTER VII
## THE CENTRAL LONDON SCHOOL OF ART

THE Central London School of Art, though backed by all the majesty of state support, was, at the first blush, a somewhat disillusionising place to the youthful aspirant for fame. To the over-nice, to be sure, it lacked an art "atmosphere," except such a material one as is generated by ancient paint-tubes, oily rags, furtively munched sandwiches, and the presence of a preponderance of people to whom the daily tub is possibly not of vital importance.

Outwardly, the Art School was only No. 55, in a dreary by-street near Portland Road;* a small thoroughfare of sinister aspect, in which all the houses seemed to be frowning at each other's dubious appearance. The white blinds—now grey with age and dirt—seemed always drawn; no one ever seemed to emerge from those faded, bespattered front doors. It was a dreary, *louche*,[1] mysterious street, of which, when Mary thought of it, she invariably saw the two ends swallowed up in a dingy, yellowish fog.

Inside this temple of the fine arts consisted of one long room with a glass roof, divided, toward one end, by a dingy serge curtain of bronze green. The walls, too, were tinted a dubious olive colour, throwing up the plaster Venus of Milo, the Laocoön, and the torso of the Theseus. There, too, was the Apollo Belvedere, with its slightly supercilious air, the frowning Moses of Michael Angelo, and the simpering Clytie, with startling distinctness.[2] A small *écorché*[3] stood on a shelf, and all around, looking like the frozen remains of some monster operating-theatre, were eerie-looking arms, legs, feet, and hands cut off above the wrist.

Here, too, were the candidates for the Royal Academy, all laboriously stippling the Laocoön with twists of bread and stumps; a process in which they had been engaged for some six months past; while in the other division of the room was posed a child dressed like an Italian contadina, surrounded by easels on every side. It was

---

1 Shady or shadowy.

2 Laocoön was the Trojan priest who, along with his sons, was killed by two serpents for having warned his people against the Trojan horse. The marble statue of the father and sons battling the serpents sits in the Pio Clementino Museum, Vatican. Theseus was a hero of Attica who slew the Minotaur and conquered the Amazons and married their queen. The best known image of Theseus is a bronze of him slaying the Minotaur. The marble Roman copy of the original Greek "Apollo Belvedere" sits in the Pio Clementino Museum, Vatican. The Moses of Michael Angelo was commissioned by Pope Julius II in 1505. It was finished by the master's students in 1545 and sits at the Church of St. Peter in Chains as the centerpiece of a tableau for the Pope's unfinished tomb. Clytie was a waternymph in love with Apollo, who paid her no attention. She sat all day and watched the sun pass through the sky until she rooted to the ground and her face turned into a flower.

3 French for "skinned," *écorché* was a model of the human body without the skin. The artist could use it to study the arrangement of human muscles and bones before creating an image of the body.

the afternoon on which the model sat. Painting from the life was carried on at the Central London School of Art in those days on but two afternoons a week; it was looked upon as a kind of frivolous extra which should not be allowed to occupy the mind of the serious student to the detriment of the stippled Laocoön.

It was a raw December day, but inside the fumes of a charcoal stove made the students' heads feel queer. They were an odd-looking collection of people, who were gathered there that winter afternoon in the falling light. The young women were of the lower middle class; daughters of retail shopkeepers, who dressed, as became their future career, in weird gowns of orange or green serge, cut rather low about the throat, and who were further beautified by strings of amber or Venetian glass beads, while some, on gala days, had been known to appear in gowns adorned with iridescent beetles' wings, a trimming which is sacred to the lady artist the wide world over. And though perhaps their hair left, like their speech, something to be desired, on the whole the girls were less objectionable than the boy students, whose linen was not irreproachable, and who used to disappear in groups of five or six during the sitting, to return to their places presently bringing with them a suspicious odour of bitter beer and inexpensive tobacco. An English art-school has none of the boisterous, contagious hilarity of a French *atelier*.[1] Decent silence reigned, broken only by the hoarse, repressed chuckles of a couple of boys as they exchanged a whispered witticism, or the rare, high-pitched, but almost inaudible titter of a student with ringlets as she bent over her easel.

Mary Erle, with her neat hair and her well made black dress, looked like a little princess as she sat, with a slight frown and tight-shut lips, among the outer ring of easels. She wore the same expression as of old, in the summerhouse in St. John's Wood, when she sat alone notching and slicing at her wooden fleet. And indeed, the girl was as much alone now, in this studio full of human beings, as in the silence of the leafy garden. Vincent had gone on his travels—had been gone, indeed, for nearly six months, and all that she had to remind her of that unexpected demonstration in the Harley Street drawing-room, was a crumpled letter with an Indian postmark which she carried about in her pocket. Yes, she was alone, for had she spoken to the boys, she was sure they would have tried to be jocose; and she dreaded the confidences of the young ladies,

---

1 Workshop or artist's studio.

some of whom had prosperous flirtations, carried on in neighbouring pastry-cooks' shops, or in the rooms of Burlington House with the "advanced" male students. Indeed, the only person she ever spoke to was an old student who had been through the Academy schools, and who now came occasionally to the Central London to work from the draped model, his studio on Haverstock Hill★ being just now in the hands of workmen.

Mr. Perry Jackson was an under-sized, drab-faced young man of about thirty, who gave the casual spectator the impression that he was a grown-up London gutter boy. But in truth he had had no such dramatic beginnings. His parents, the well-to-do proprietors of a small upholsterer's shop in the Hampstead Road, had given him a fair education, and were proud of having turned their only child into an "artist and a gentleman." To Mary, Mr. Jackson was so frankly, so completely himself, representing such a completely unknown, unguessed-at type, that he ended by amusing her. He had a charming Cockney good-humour which was eminently attractive, and he never disappeared now, since he had struck up a sort of acquaintance with Mary, to come back redolent of beer and smoke. Already he had had one or two clever, flashy pictures just above the line at the Royal Academy. He had, to be sure, a fatal facility for drawing pretty faces. His black and white work in *Illustrations* was already much admired at the railway stations.

How well Mary remembered the day she had begun her Laocoön, for the Royal Academy competition. It would take, with its infinitely minute stippling, six months to complete.

"I'd advise you to look sharp and begin, Miss Erle," said Mr. Jackson, who, though rather abashed by his neighbour's manners, was inclined to be friendly. "That serpent'll take you every day of six weeks, let alone the figure. They're awfully down on a fellow, I can tell you, at the Academy, if the shading ain't quite up to the mark. Anybody can correct the drawing for you, don't you see, but you've got to do that blessed stippling yerself."

"Thanks. I think I will begin at once," said Mary.

"Right you are. Take this place, Miss Erle, there's a better light," suggested Mr. Jackson, who was good-nature itself. "Let me fix your easel. There. You may use the plumb-line as much as you like," continued the young man, his small, pale eyes twinkling with vivacity; "and old Sanderson, he'll correct your outline for you. I ought to know something about it," he added with sudden candour. "Why, I went up for the R.A. three times myself."

There were two or three girls, besides herself, who were competing for the Academy, and several men, one of whom was verging on fifty years of age, and whose hair and unkempt beard were already turned grey. A legend current in the school related that this person had been competing for the Royal Academy Schools ever since he was eighteen years old. There was Miss Simpkins, a strapping young woman with a large, vague face, which somehow suggested a muffin, and who carried a small edition of *Modern Painters*[1] about in a leather hand-bag, together with a pocket-comb, a hand-mirror, some ham sandwiches, and a selection of different kinds of chalk. There was a pale girl with red ringlets, whom Mary remembered as the daughter of a confectioner in St. John's Wood, a girl who affected peacock-blue velveteen, and was understood to be intermittently in love with Mr. Jackson. These were Mary's companions for six months behind the dingy serge curtain.

On the December day in question, the glass door opened, and a small, pale man, wearing a frock coat and a narrow black necktie, and having the appearance and manner of an attorney's head clerk, stood bending over the first easel. Mr. Sanderson, the head-master, was a person who rarely committed himself to a definite opinion, and especially to an adverse one. He wished, above all things, to be well with the students, so that his usual criticism took the form of:

"Going on ve-r-y nicely, Miss Simpkins. Perhaps, on the whole, you might look to the movement of that head. Yes, just so. The arms, now, should you say they were just a little out of drawing? And the right leg, eh? perhaps, too, it might be as well to reconsider the position of the torso. Coming on nicely, Miss Simpkins."

And Miss Simpkins, a lady whose devotion to the doctrines of Mr. Ruskin was perhaps more remarkable than her artistic skill, settled her amber necklace and continued to paint.

At the next easel was heard, "Ah, a very ambitious view of the model, Mr. Jackson. It might be perhaps as well to reconsider the position of the figure. Just as well, on the whole, for the artist not to hamper himself with unnecessary difficulties. Very good, very good. In quite a promising condition, Mr. Jackson."

At the Central London, it will be seen, everything worked smoothly. The advent of the head-master was the signal for gener-

---

1 English artist and critic John Ruskin's (1819-1900) monumental encyclopedic investigation of beauty and art, a work he published in five volumes between 1843 and 1860.

al amenities. Every daub, every ill-drawn head, and every smeared, smooth drapery received its meed of praise. There were no tears, such as water the upward path of the student in a Parisian *atelier*; there were no ambitions, no heart-burnings, no rivalries. No one at the Central London had ever been known to have a theory to express, or, if he had, it remained locked in his own breast.

It had already begun to dawn upon Mary that the whole thing was a foolish pretence at work. Slipping from her seat, she dropped back to the easel on which stood her drawing of the Laocoön, a drawing which was beginning to assume, as it was destined to do, the appearance of a dotted engraving.

She was standing, somewhat desponding and disheartened, before this thing which had cost her so much toil, and on the success of which so much depended, when the door burst open, and there appeared a radiant vision of velvet and sables, and of an audacious hat which only Alison Ives in one of her "worldly" fits could have invented.

"*Nom de Dieu!*" cried that young lady, descending on Mary and forcibly removing her drawing board; "am I to stand by and see you become a British female artist? You've got to come to a tea—a tea at home in Portman Square. We're driving straight back. Mother's out there in the carriage. Come on."

"I can't," said Mary. "I told you I couldn't. I'm not going out, and I ought to work for another hour. The thing goes in, in a fortnight."

"Pooh," said Alison, as she found the girl's hat and cloak, and bundled her unceremoniously into the carriage; "the whole thing is a farce."

"But I believe these schools are excellent things for—for the kind of persons whom dear Mary describes so amusingly," put in Lady Jane.

"Nonsense, mother," said Alison. "You've never been inside one. The whole thing is impossible. Schools of cooking, and not schools of art, are what we want," shouted Alison as they rattled over the stones. "You may leave your painter genius to find his way to the front, whereas boiled potatoes are a daily necessity. Go and talk," continued the girl, with a smile, "about your stippled gladiators and Laocoöns in a serious French studio, where they *work*. Why, they would laugh in your face."

"I think I should like to go to work in Paris," said Mary with a sigh. A place where they disapproved of the Laocoön as an exercise in art seemed to her to open out a vista of delightful possibilities.

# CHAPTER VIII
## A KETTLEDRUM[1] AT LADY JANE'S

LADY JANE IVES was always to be found in Portman Square at five, but to-day she had sent out cards, so that an hour later the lofty, gaunt rooms, with their faded crimson carpets, their flowery chintzes, and their many mirrors, were dotted with little groups. Lady Jane disliked new fashions in her house, and the general effect, in an over-luxurious age, was somewhat cheerless. The stiff, hard Guardis[2] on the walls, in which tin gondoliers were propelling iron gondolas on a leaden *lagoon*, with a background of grey zinc palaces, were but faintly visible by the tentative light of the circle of candles in the quivering lustre chandelier. Between the starched lace curtains stood monster Chinese vases, swollen like vases seen in an uneasy dream. The buhl cabinets had chilly marble tops; the rosewood tables held vast photograph albums. Lady Jane had arranged the rooms on her marriage some forty years ago, and it had not occurred to her to change them.

Parliament had just opened; people were back in town. Here and there a man's black coat was visible. There was a subdued murmur of talk. People were slipping out quietly under cover of someone else's arrival, dropping the perfunctory smile which they had exhibited for ten minutes under the lustre chandelier, as they made their way quickly out into the portico, where a small army of grooms, with faces as drab and unemotional as their overcoats, hung about the steps.

"I've just come from the Ambassador of all the Russias," drawled a pretty woman to Lady Jane, as she stood, in the swaggering attitude which she affected on entering a drawing-room, just at the door.

"My dear, you shouldn't encourage those barbarians," declared her hostess, "it's so shockingly radical to approve of foreign tyrannies." Alison was pouring out tea in the gaunt back drawing-room. It was noticeable that most of the men had collected round the tea-table. "I won't have my friends fed at a sort of sublimated coffee-stall in the dining-room," announced Lady Jane. "It's a young

---

1  A punning name for an afternoon tea party, on a smaller scale than the regular "Drum," which was an evening party.

2  A reference to a painting by Francesco Guardi (1712–93), a Venetian artist best known today for his views of Venice.

woman's mission to make tea for her friends. Alison, remember Lady Blaythewaite doesn't like sugar."

"*Vous versez le thé avec une grâce parfaite*,"[1] sighed a sentimental attaché of vague Slav nationality, who was famous for turning compliments out of the most unlikely materials.

And Mary Erle, in her black clothes, sat on one side and looked at the little comedy with impartial eyes. It seemed so long since she had been in society; she supposed she was out of touch with the world. Vanity Fair,[2] since she had left it for so many months, seemed curiously foolish. Close to her the pretty woman, who stood sipping her tea amid an admiring circle of black coats, had already got on to one of her favourite topics.

"I tell my maid I must have my tub hot," she announced in a penetrating voice, and with the air of one who is accustomed to have her least brilliant observations received with attention—"hot, and in front of a huge fire. I like to take my time. Lots of scrubby towels, and a masseuse afterward, if you like; but no beastly cold water for me."

The eyes of the complimentary Slav waxed brilliant as he gazed admiringly at Lady Blaythewaite.

"Ugh!" objected a perfectly dressed young man, whose every sense, one could see at a glance, was satisfied, and who gave to the casual spectator the impression, from the parting of his beautifully cared-for hair to the pointed toes of his shiny boots, he was elaborately, exquisitely new and clean. "All very well for ladies," he said deliberately, "but how on earth is a feller to feel fit in the mornin', if he don't have a cold tub, what? I gave my man a rare old rowing this morning. What do you think the brute did——"

But to make room for two new arrivals, the exquisitely clean young man was obliged to step into the background, and the rest of his story was lost to every one but the pretty woman. After these two had thrashed out the engrossing subject of their tub, the word "Plumpton" was bandied about, and afterward the name of the latest three-act farce. The exquisitely clean young man, it transpired, was a great theatre-goer; in fact, he admitted that he went so often

---

1  You pour the tea with perfect grace.
2  Vanity Fair, in John Bunyan's (1628–88) *The Pilgrim's Progress* (1678–84), was a fair established by Beelzebub, Apollyon, and Legion in the town of Vanity. It lasted all year round and boasted all sorts of sins and evils. Evidently, Mary does not think much of the socializing that she has missed since her father's death.

that it was impossible to recollect the name of the house, the play, or the actors.

"I don't remember the name of the piece, don't you know," he confided, "but we saw it the night before last at the Criterion[1]—I think it must have been the Criterion, because we dined in the restaurant first—and the feller I liked awfully, don't you know, was the one who played the feller who kicks out the Johnnie in the third act. Awfully good, what?"

"Oh, yes. Awfully good—wasn't he? We all thought him a dear," said the pretty woman in a bored tone. She had had enough of what she called intellectual conversation.

"What have you done with that charming Mr. Hemming, my dear?" demanded Lady Jane in a stage whisper, descending on Mary and leading her out of her corner by the arm. And, not waiting for an answer, she went on, "You've sent him off to India, you naughty child, and he may die of the cholera or heat-apoplexy, and then you'll be sorry. Poor fellow, he looked so terribly cut up. He came to see me just before he went. His father was an old flame of mine. But the men were more enterprising when I was young. They didn't take 'no' for an answer."

"But, dear Lady Jane," whispered Mary, "I didn't give 'no' for an answer." All this was said while a lady with sloping shoulders and dyed black hair was performing a rather deliberate solo on the harp.

But her hostess, whose eyes were turned towards the door, did not apparently grasp the import of Mary's words. Lady Jane was very fond of Professor Erle's daughter—the professor had always been one of the familiar faces at her Sunday dinners—but she was a somewhat indifferent listener, and just now she had not only to thank the fair harpist—but a new arrival was claiming her attention.

"Ah! there is my dear doctor," exclaimed Lady Jane with much vivacity. "How good of you," she said, with more enthusiasm than she had yet exhibited, "to find time to come and see an old woman."

The man addressed was a striking figure enough; he had moreover that imposing air which endears itself to the feminine imagi-

---

1 Opened in 1874 as an annex of Spiers and Pond's restaurant in Piccadilly Circus, the Criterion was one of the first theaters to be built entirely underground.

nation. Dr. Dunlop Strange was a favourite with women in society. His speciality was nervous disease. He had done a great deal of useful work, and had made one important discovery which had gained him the Fellowship of the Royal Society, and was understood to be about to receive a baronetcy. Mary remembered his face. She had met him out often in the old days: at *soirées* at the Royal Society, at the dinner-tables of the celebrated or the merely smart.

He was a man of forty-five, a little under the medium size, with a perpetual upright pucker just between his eyes; those eyes, the girl noticed, spoilt his face; they were small and somewhat shifty, but as he usually wore a pince-nez this peculiarity was not noticeable. He looked tired, but not at all bored.

The doctor was understood to be devoted to Alison, and, for once, Alison seemed pleased. Though she was good looking and moved in a somewhat go-ahead set, she had never been known to have an ordinary flirtation. She used to say that she supposed that she should have to marry some day—the later the better—because it was absurd to suppose that old maids had any influence on people's lives; and Power, to put it plainly, was what the modern woman craved. She supposed, in that respect, that she wasn't any better than the rest of her sex. Lady Jane was delighted; asked the doctor constantly to dinner, and insisted on his assisting at one of the Happy Afternoons for Pauper Lunatics. And Dr. Strange went; as indeed he would have gone anywhere, just now, to meet Alison.

"By the bye," she said, giving him a cup of tea and pretending not to notice that his eyes were devouring every detail of her handsome personality, "I want you particularly to know Mary Erle—Professor Erle's daughter, you know. Of course you've met her, but I want you to know her. She's one of my few friends."

Alison seemed in high spirits since Dr. Dunlop Strange's arrival.

"Here's Mr. Bosanquet-Barry," she whispered, as a beautiful young man with Parma violets in his coat appeared in the doorway, closely followed by a pale-faced boy with tired eyelids and an exaggerated button-hole; "one of mother's young friends. He's the new editor of the *Comet*."[1]

---

1  Oscar Wilde—whom Dixon knew and for whose magazine, *Woman's World*, she wrote—finds his way into this novel in part as Bosanquet-Barry, the "new editor" mentioned here; in part as Bosanquet-Barry's pale young companion, Beaufort Flower; and in part as the supercilious editor of *The Fan*, a man Mary meets a bit later in the novel.

"The editor," repeated Mary incredulously, emerging from a conversation with Dr. Strange, which she had carried on with difficulty, seeing that his eyes were fixed on Alison all the time. "The editor of the *Comet*! Why, he looks a mere boy."

"My dear, he's seven-and-twenty. Besides, that's the new idea in journalism. You pluck your editor nice and hot from Oxford—someone who has none of the old hackneyed Fleet Street ideas."*

"This one," observed Mary thoughtfully, "doesn't look as if he had any ideas at all."

"Oh! but then he's devoted to the Primrose League.[1] Mother makes a perfect fool of him. He goes to her Happy Afternoons. I hear all the smart set are in love with him—if that's any recommendation. Mary, you must be introduced. You'll have to know these people, if you're going to be an artist."

On closer inspection Mr. Bosanquet-Barry turned out to have a somewhat *faux air* of youth. The effect of extreme juvenility was produced by his fair skin, his dazzlingly white teeth, and his piercingly blue eyes. He entertained Mary, as he got her a cup of tea, with a spirited account of a visit to a minor music-hall, which he and the pale-faced boy had arranged the night before for Lady Blaythewaite.

"It all went all right," said Mr. Bosanquet-Barry confidentially, "until the last. Lady Blaythewaite swore she'd never enjoyed anything so much in her life. Can't say I did, as I had to talk to the girl she brought with her, who was ugly as sin. However, I had to leave 'em a minute at the door to see after the carriage, and then some beastly cad spoke to her."

"How very unpleasant," said Mary, who felt she was expected to sympathise with this lady's adventures in a London music-hall.

"Oh," chuckled Mr. Bosanquet-Barry, with a laugh which was not quite pretty. "I don't believe she minded—I shouldn't wonder if she rather liked it. At any rate, she shouldn't wear such outrageous clothes. I wonder Sir Horace——"

"Oh, Sir Horace doesn't care," interrupted the pale-faced boy, whose name, it transpired, was Beaufort Flower, though everyone

1 The Primrose League is a Conservative organization founded in 1883 by Lord Randolph Churchill to promote their ideals of Tory democracy. The name commemorates Benjamin Disraeli (1804-81), the conservative prime minister of England in 1868 and again between 1874 and 1880, the primrose having been his favorite flower.

seemed to address as "Beaufy"; "oh, Sir Horace doesn't care, he don't pay for them, you know."

And with a display of all his white teeth at once, the editor of the *Comet*, who with all his boyishness had picked up the editor's air of not meaning to allow anyone to detain him, bowed abruptly and was now seen pressing the hands of several ladies of quality as he steered his way toward the door.

"He is an odious youth," said Alison calmly. "I'm not responsible, you know, for all mother's 'boys.' Sometimes he comes and stops for hours. They talk scandal all the time, and, Heaven preserve us! the scandal of the fifties—about women who are grandmothers, or in their graves. Don't you think it a depraved taste, Dr. Strange?" continued the girl.

"Perhaps," he answered with a smile, "he's going to write a book of reminiscences. You begin collecting at about twenty, and you keep your scandal, well-corked and in a dry place, till you are about eighty. Then you publish, with additions."

"I dare say," laughed Alison, "that scandal doesn't 'keep' any better than other things. A little venom has to be added."

"Scandal," put in the pretty woman, emerging suddenly from a flirtation with the sentimental Slav, "is only interesting about one's contemporaries."

"Dear me, what an interesting woman Lady Blaythewaite must be," whispered Mr. Beaufort Flower into the ear of a solemn man with a heavy jaw, who was well-connected, and who was understood to write essays in Addisonian English.[1]

"Ah!" ejaculated the solemn man, with a thoughtful glance at the pretty woman.

"My only objection to immoral people," chattered the boy, gazing at her with weary, half-closed eyes, "is that they're generally so shockingly censorious."

"No one else's conduct, I suppose," rejoined the solemn man deliberately, "comes up to their high ethical standard."

"My heavens!" exclaimed the pretty woman, who had heard part of the answer, "they've begun to talk of ethical standards. I mustn't keep the roans any longer. Good-bye, all you people, good-bye."

---

1  Essayist Joseph Addison (1672-1719) was a distinguished classical scholar whose prose was described by Dr. Johnson as "the model of the middle style; on grave subjects not formal, on light occasions not groveling."

And sweeping away among her rustling silk petticoats the complimentary Slav, Lady Blaythewaite's tiny head and wide shoulders were seen descending the staircase.

There was a pause. Most of the people were leaving. From the open hall door came the click of closing carriage doors, the word "Home" pronounced in the official voice of the unemotional grooms, and the sound of departing wheels. Dr. Dunlop Strange was bending toward Alison, talking earnestly.

"Charmin' rooms," said the pale-faced boy vaguely, terrified at finding himself alone with Mary, whom he took for his especial aversion, a *débutante*. His eye ran round the rather bare walls, the fluted steel fenders, the marble mantelpieces topped by their huge mirrors. "So nice and old-fashioned, aren't they? Should you say early Victorian now, or late William the Fourth?"

But Mary was not to be drawn. The favourite modern amusement of whispering malicious things of one's host or hostess behind their backs had never appealed to her. And much to his surprise the fair girl in mourning evinced no further desire for his society, but with one of those little manœuvres which only women of the world know how to execute without offence, she had joined Alison and the doctor.

"Good gracious!" he said to himself as he tripped downstairs to his brougham. "How pert! I don't believe she's a *débutante* after all."

## CHAPTER IX
## MARY TRIES TO LIVE HER LIFE

ONE night, about a fortnight later, Mary walked home to her lodgings in Bulstrode Street more than usually weary with stippling the Laocoön. Somehow she felt hipped;[1] she would have liked to creep back, just for once, to the book-lined drawing-room in Harley Street, with its indefinable air of perfect taste and perfect comfort; the little tea-table near the fire, with its silver kettle, its dainty china, the hot cakes which cook used to make so well. And always, when he was at home, a well-known step would be heard ascending the stair, and the professor would come in, Mary remembered, with his keen eyes and his dear, thin face, and stand with his back to the fire while he sipped his tea and teased his "little girl."

---

1   To feel melancholy, low-spirited, to be suffering the blues. It may be an abbreviation of hypochondria.

But instead she entered the narrow passage of a house in Bulstrode Street, of which the varnished marble paper, as well as the grained staircase and stiff patterned oilcloth were worn and stained with age, and ascended to her own domain, consisting of two rooms, communicating by a large, creaky, grained folding-door. In the little bedroom, giving on a grimy back-yard, there was a small iron bed with starved-looking pillows, a washing apparatus of which every article, by a strange chance, was of a different pattern, two chairs, and a chest of drawers in imitation grained wood, with white china handles. On the walls, covered with a paper on which apples of a dingy yellow sprawled, in endless repetition, on a dull green ground, were several framed texts. A yacht in full sail, on the bluest of lithograph-seas, was accompanied by the words, "Search the Scriptures," while opposite, encased in an Oxford oak frame,[1] a stout, highly-coloured kingfisher emerging from a colony of bulrushes, faced the text, "Come unto Me, all ye that are heavy-laden."[2] These pictorial aids to piety were the only ornaments of the bedroom, and Mary often smiled when she thought of the delicate silver-point drawings that hung on the pink walls at home. She thought, too, of the things that used to strike her as she read, and which she would write out and pin up in her pretty luxurious bedroom. The scraps of poetry in various tongues which she would scribble hastily on the back of some young man's visiting card and then pin up, with a slender gilt tack, on to her door; especially those lines of James Thomson's,[3] which, about a year after her first heartache, when all had ended in disappointment, it had given her such ironical pleasure to nail up in her bedroom, to the bewilderment of the new housemaid:

The old three hundred sixty-five
Dull days to every year alive;

★ ★ ★ ★ ★

---

1  According to the *OED*, an Oxford frame is "a picture-frame the sides of which cross each other and project some distance at the corners."
2  Matthew 11:28.
3  Scottish poet and essayist James Thomson (1834–82) is best known for his dark, despairing poem "The City of Dreadful Night" (1880), which presents readers with a haunting look at his bouts with despair and alcoholism. These lines come from his long poem *Vane's Story* (1880).

Old toil, old care, old worthless treasures,
Old gnawing sorrows, swindling pleasures,
The cards were shuffled to and fro,
The hands may vary somewhat so,
The dirty pack's the same we know,
Played with long thousand years ago;
Played with and lost with still by Man—
Fate marked them ere the game began.

Ah, she could afford to be pessimistic in those days! As Mary took off her hat and threw her cloak on the narrow bed, hastening her toilet for the evening because of the bitter cold of the room, she repeated these lines softly to herself; oddly enough, they evoked an image of that pretty bygone bedroom, of a tent-bed with gay draperies, a fire blazing against a background of Dutch tiles, on which blue ships in full sail were scudding over stiff curly waves, of soft mats of white fur on which it was a joy to tread with bare feet. "No, I can't afford to be pessimistic, now," thought the girl, as she pushed open the door and went into the other room. The fire was nearly out, but two gas-burners, which had been lighted by the maid of all work, and left on at full tap, had already loaded the air with the fumes of gas. It was now a quarter past six; she could not ask for tea, although her throat burned and her head ached. No, she must wait for dinner—her modest little dinner which was served, with variations as to punctuality, about seven o'clock.

She threw herself on the hard sofa, and her eyes travelled round the room. The furniture was old, shabby, and pretentious, and she had an idea that there were cheap Landseer engravings[1] on the wall, but Mary had made up her mind never to look at the pictures; otherwise, she said, she would have had to change her lodgings at once, and that she did not wish to do, as the landlady was an old servant of theirs, and would look after her better than a stranger. After all, it would do well enough as a make-shift. It was best, she thought, not to accept invitations from friends, but to begin to live her own life. And days like to-day, when she was

---

1 Thomas Landseer (1795-1880), elder brother of the more famous animal artist Sir Edwin Henry Landseer, was in his own right an eminent engraver. He often exhibited his copper engravings at the Royal Academy in the 1850s and 1860s.

weary and disheartened, Mary found it necessary to repeat this phrase in her mind: "To live her own life." And yet it was all dispiriting enough. Art and artists, as exemplified in the "Central London," were but doubtfully alluring; Mary wondered if anywhere else she might find the "art" atmosphere of which she had read so much. But anyhow her Academy drawing was done; it had gone in with a dozen others, and to-morrow she would know if she had succeeded.

She lay like a log on the hard sofa, while the gilt clock with the hovering cupid slowly ticked out three-quarters of an hour. On the mantelpiece a long photograph of Alison, in a smart evening gown exhibiting a good deal of a fine arm and shoulder, was supported by a large one of Vincent Hemming, with his grave and *posé* expression, and wearing an orchid in his button-hole.

At last came dinner, heralded by an odour of boiled potatoes and frizzling meat. But the girl was too tired to eat the badly cooked food; she pushed away the steak, which was tough and hard, and tried to drink some of the small bottle of stout, which was flat, with a strange flavour. Mary rebuked herself for these fantasies of the appetite; it behooved a young woman who wished to make her way in the world and compete with men to indulge in no such over-niceties. But a very feminine backache overcame her, and presently the maid of all work, in creaking boots, removed with much clattering the dishes, and Mary was left alone with the firelight for a companion.

The photographs of her two friends looked down on her from the mantelpiece: Alison, with her sweet expression and her distinguished *mondaine* air; Vincent Hemming, with his intellectual forehead, his impotent mouth, and the slight frown which he sometimes affected. What a long time it seemed since they had said good-bye at Tilbury,★ when the great P.&O. steamer had been swallowed up in the greyness of the wide river and tearful sky. Yes, a long time; but he had grown more to her in his absence than he had ever been, even at the last, for Mary was of the order of women who idealise the absent. Oddly enough, Vincent, pacing the deck of the *Sutlej* in his flapping ulster[1] and his soft felt hat (he was not one of those people who look their best in travelling costume), had seemed more of a stranger than the man whose letters, arriving by the Indian mail, lay beside her plate every Monday

---

1   From Ulster, Ireland, this was a heavy, loose, long overcoat.

morning. She remembered with a smile how fussy he had been about his luggage, and how humiliated she had felt when, man-like, Vincent Hemming had insisted on a last embrace, and, draw-ing the girl into his cabin, had shut the door in the face of the steward. She had dwelt a great deal on those last moments. He had seemed so passionately attached to her; the whole affair, though it had been obliged to remain vague, had become a solemn fact in her existence.

A letter from Vincent had arrived that morning; Mary felt in her pocket for the thin, crackling envelope bearing the post-mark "Calcutta." It was a peculiarity of Hemming's that one, and some-times two, pages of his letters were indited in a flowing hand, while the rest of the paper was covered with uncertain upright hiero-glyphics, which took all the reader's patience and good-will to decipher.

"My dear Mary" [it began]: "My delightful roamings have been brought to a standstill in this ancient and historic spot, one so emi-nently suited to the special studies which I desire, in furtherance of my scheme, to make. You will, I am sure, be delighted to hear that on all hands I have had every civility and courtesy extended to me from officials of every class, and that my father's name alone has been a sufficient introduction for me in those circles in which it is most desirable for the purpose I have in hand to move.

"You will also, my dear Mary, be rejoiced to hear that my health has vastly improved since my departure from England; the fact alone that I anticipate with pleasure the advent of breakfast will give you a fair idea of my improved state of health, and I think I may say that, considering the somewhat trying nature of the cli-matic conditions, my appearance has wonderfully improved. But enough of myself. I need not say that I am delighted to hear that you are bravely and earnestly attacking those art studies, which, with due application, will ensure your fame, and possibly wealth, and which will, my dearest girl, be no mean factor in our (possi-ble) future happiness."

Mary sighed as she let the letter drop, and gazed thoughtfully into the fire. It was here that the flowing persuasive handwriting terminated abruptly, and that the upright uncertain characters began.

"Had I" (it went on) "no dreams, no aspirations for the amelio-ration of the English race—were I, in short, a man to whom per-sonal happiness is paramount—I might have spoken more deci-sively in relation to a possible future together before I left England.

But I am paying you no mean compliment, my dear Mary, when I tell you that I have every confidence that in you, as in myself, questions of vast importance rise superior to mere selfish considerations, and that in you, above all women, I have a sympathetic sharer alike of my ambitions, dreams, and hopes. It is above all in studying the marvellous system of government of a vast aggregation of human beings of divers nationalities, of such widely-differing ethical standards as this great Indian Empire—" and here the handwriting changed again to the slanting style and meandered on over three crisp pages which the girl let fall on her lap. Somehow she would not reconcile this lover, with his old-fashioned phrases and copybook platitudes, with the Vincent Hemming who had held her in his arms in the cabin of the *Sutlej*, crushing the breath out of her body in the supreme moment of farewell. Of the fine irony which results from the clash of human passion and human ambition she had not, as yet, a conception. It is to be feared that Mary, with all her somewhat worldly training, was, as far as her affections were concerned, astonishingly naïve. She was only a girl after all.

And so, in the dim light of the dreary apartments, Mary sat and dreamed her little dream. Lonely, tired, discouraged, she clung to the thought of their marriage with curious tenacity. She was haunted incessantly by a vision of tender brown eyes, of a caressing hand, one of a sympathetic voice; of a pretty interior with books, and pictures, and soft lamplight; of a man's head uplifted from a desk, while she held her latest picture up for her husband to see. He was not a judge of pictures, she remembered with a smile; he would probably think her modest attempts first-rate. . . . They would live a charming, simple, intellectual life; knowing the people that are worth knowing, content with modest surroundings, but with everything in perfect taste. After all, Vincent and she together would have enough to live quietly on; if she succeeded in her art, he might even yet realise his ambition and enter on a political career. What, indeed, might not the years bring forth? However dismal things seemed now, there was Hope—that will-o'-the-wisp of the young—beckoning her from the dim valleys of the future.

Mary took up the letter again, and bending down to the fire, reread one or two affectionate phrases at the last. Then she put it carefully into a locked case which contained some twenty epistles in thin envelopes, turned out the gas, and went into her chilly bedroom, where, in the process of brushing out her fluffy blond hair for the night, she told herself valiantly that she was a lucky little person.

## CHAPTER X
## NEW HOPES

THE next day—the day which was to decide her fate with the Academy schools—revealed itself shrouded with fog. By the light of one gas-burner Mary tried to eat some breakfast, but the doubtful allurements of the boiled eggs which usually awaited her appealed to her to-day in vain. She had slept badly and risen late; it was now half-past ten. Already, at the art school, in the grimy little office, the names of the successful candidates would be nailed up. No, she could not eat; she must know. It meant so much to her, so much more she thought than to any of the others. It meant independence, a profession, a happy union. How many hoped-for marriages she had seen fail among professional people just for the want of a mere hundred or so a year. If she were good enough for the Academy schools, she felt that there was a future before her. She saw herself, in imagination, working, earning, helping.

Putting on her coat and hat she was soon outside in the fog, and threading her away along the streets to the School of Art. Underfoot was a layer of greasy mud. In the little shops a bleared gaslight made an orange patch in the all-pervading greyness. At the fruiterers' the mounds of golden oranges, crimson apples, and scarlet tomatoes flamed with startling assurance against the blurred, brownish-grey of the houses, the pavement, the very atmosphere. She was curiously alive, now, to effects of colour, to "values"; everywhere the girl saw a possible picture. If she had passed, Mary made up her mind she would telegraph to Vincent. It would be an extravagance, but it would make him so happy. Mary pictured her lover reading that charming message from over the seas, as he sat in an Indian verandah in a white flannel suit, with a hazy background of punkahs and date palms.

Afterward when she thought of that day, she remembered that the hall of the art school was full of students all talking at once. At the sight of the girl's expectant face someone called out goodnaturedly, "I say, you're in, Miss Erle. I'm sure I saw your name on the list. It's in the office, pinned up over the mantelpiece."

Mary slid into the little room without a word. Yes, there was the list of successful probationers, written in Mr. Sanderson's careful hand on a slip of note paper, and pinned up with a brass drawing pin over the mantelpiece. Her eye ran hastily along the list—

"Simpkins, Dorothy Muriel; Smith, Mary Gwendolen; Walsh, Joseph Frederick; Billington, George Francis; Thomson, Pamela Evelyn; Beadle, Reginald Forsyth." That was all. She read it again to make sure, repeating to herself, mechanically, the Dorothys, Pamelas, and Gwendolens of the back-shop. No, there was no possible mistake. The name of Mary Erle was not there.

And so it was all over! Never, she felt, should she have the courage to spend another six months labouring and stippling over another Laocoön. She sat down in a corner. Her disappointment had affected her physically, her feet were icy cold; she felt, without being hungry, as if she had nothing inside her, while the voices of people talking around sounded strange and far away.

But presently she roused herself and went through the big room to collect some things she had left. Only Mr. Perry Jackson met her behind the olive-green curtain: Mr. Jackson, who, although the workmen were now out of his studio, was curiously often to be seen at the school. He glanced at Mary and instantly read the disappointment in her face. Though young, he was, after all, a Londoner, and had the Cockney's intuitive knowledge of the world. He even went so far as to congratulate Miss Erle in having failed to attain the desired standard of excellence. He had, as he admitted with pleasing candour, only got his own drawing admitted, in the years gone by, "by the skin of its teeth." As for himself, he had mainly attended the classes (and this was said with something very like a wink) to make friends with the Royal Academicians. "They're all right when you know 'em, but you've got to know 'em first," quoted the rising artist. "There's old Jack Madder, who always does Wardour Street pictures;[1] he's not half a bad old chap, and thinks no end of me. He's on the Hanging Committee next year. I go and ask his advice. I'm going to do a big thing for next year's Academy, and I'll eat my hat if it isn't on the line!"

"I hope so, I'm sure," replied Mary, smiling. "When are you going to begin?"

"At once. I've got an idea that's bound to fetch the public."

"Indeed?" replied Mary, amused at his naïve optimism.

"I shall call it 'The Time of Roses.' What do you think of that? Neat, eh? Nothing but girls, and nothing but roses. Lord, you can't

---

1  In the nineteenth century, Wardour Street, near Trafalgar Square, was known as an antique-sellers district with a dubious reputation, a place populated by dishonest dealers and confidence men.

give the public enough of either of them. It likes 'em, because they both 'go off' so soon," added Mr. Jackson, charmed with his own perspicacity. "It'll be an eight-footer, if it's an inch, and if it isn't 'on the line' next May——"

"I dare say it will be an immense success," said Mary quietly, as she thought of bygone Private Views, and of the canvases which had become "the picture of the year."

"Now, for the Grosvenor,"[1]★ continued Mr. Jackson—"after my 'Time of Roses' they'll be spry enough with their invitations to exhibit there—I shall do a girl in a graveyard. Bless you, people are 'death' on cemeteries. Black dress—limp black hat, hangin' on her arm—black circles round the eyes. And there you are, don't you know."

Mary laughed. There was not much doubt about the fact that Mr. Perry Jackson was destined to get on. He had a certain facility in painting; in the summer time he worked at vast canvases, out of doors, in the country, painting with large square brushes, in the approved modern manner.

"Oh! I say, Miss Erle," said Perry, detaining the girl with a look as she stood putting her painting things together. There was something of despair in the way in which Mary was folding up her easel, and arranging her chalks and paint-brushes in the long tin box, and with his quick sympathy the young man wished to assuage her sickening disappointment.

"Just look here," he continued, pulling from a cardboard portfolio an Indian-ink drawing of a beautiful young woman in a ball-dress reading a love-letter. "Old 'Stick in the Mud,' he says he'd like this drawing for *Illustrations*, only he must have a short story or some verses to go with it. Now, you're so clever, and literary, and read so many books, can't you knock me off something to print with it?"

Mary, who had never heard of this primitive method of producing imaginative literature, stared in blank astonishment at Mr. Perry Jackson. Her eye caught his knobby hands, his stubbly hair, his knowing, anæmic, town-bred face, and then the picture of the exquisite woman robed in tulle, which he held in his hand. And then she smiled.

---

1  The Grosvenor Gallery was founded in 1877 by Sir Coutts Lindsay and his wife, Lady Blanche Lindsay, to serve as an alternative to the Royal Academy.

"Oh, yes. Why not?" she found herself saying eagerly. "I will try, if you like. I think I could do quite a short story. And I can only—fail," she added a little bitterly, as her mind ran back over the months she had spent in that odious room, herding with hulking boys, who smelt of stale tobacco, with young ladies who tossed their heads archly and whispered anecdotes of "fellows" whom they met in pastry-cooks' shops, or in the sculpture galleries of the British Museum.

"That's right. Knew you could," rejoined Perry, repacking the drawing. "It'll be time enough if I have it in a week. I'm doing a story for *Illustrations* now. Blessed," he added, with a comic twinkle, pushing back his shock head of hair, "if I didn't make an ass of myself yesterday. Last week old 'Stick-in-the-Mud,' he asked me if I'd do some pictures for a story. 'Oh!' I said, 'I'm game,' I said; 'who's it by?' And he says: 'By Waklyn.' Well, I never heard of him—did you, Miss Erle?"

"I know the name," said Mary.

"Well, presently comes the MS., and I read it through, and it was pretty tough work, I can tell you, what with not being type-written, and I not feeling quite fit that day, havin' taken the chair at our smoking concert the night before. However, a few days later comes a stiff kind of a letter from this Waklyn, saying I must call at once, that evening, at his house, out Notting Hill way.★ So off I go, in my carriage and pair (the red-and-gold one, don't you know), and presently I find the house. Well, the servant girl, she showed me up a passage covered all over with autotypes, framed alike in white. Crikey! thought I, here's 'High Art.' There's nothing good enough for this chap but Rossetti, and Burne-Jones, and Watts.[1] And in the drawing-room it was just the same——"

"Ah, I know who you mean," said Mary, smiling.

"Well, blessed if I knew!" rejoined Mr. Jackson. "And so this Mr. Waklyn comes in. 'Oh, good evening,' says he, without any more ceremony than that. 'Have you brought the rough sketches for my story?' 'No,' I said, 'I haven't,' I said, just imitating his off-hand manner, 'because you wouldn't have understood 'em if I 'ad'."

"But didn't you know," said Mary, "that Mr. Waklyn is the art critic of four or five London papers?"

---

1   Sir Edward Burne-Jones (1833-98) was an English painter and decorator; he was a friend of William Morris and a member of the Pre-Raphaelite Brotherhood. George Frederic Watts (1817-1904) was an English painter and sculptor who studied at the Royal Academy. His works were influenced by the Italian Renaissance and by Greek sculpture.

"Nary a bit. Well, he laughed—a sort of thin, superior laugh it was—but he didn't say anything; and so I got out all right. But I felt a precious fool when I heard who he was."

"Let us hope," said Mary, who remembered the great art critic at dinner parties, exhibiting his culture with an ineffable air, "let us hope Mr. Waklyn isn't vindictive."

Perry looked uneasy.

"I say," he suggested, genially, "why shouldn't you turn art critic, Miss Erle, and slate us all round? Old Ruskin, he's made a good thing out of it!"

A wan white light was beginning to creep in at the windows. A wind, blowing up the Essex flats, had swept away the fog. A chilly, surprised-looking ray of sunlight lay tentatively on the grimy Art-School floor. How the aspect of things had changed when Mary stepped into the street again! Although it was out of her way, she made up her mind she would walk in the flower-garden of the Regent's Park★ a little, and go home by Portland Place. She wanted to avoid the fried-fish shops, the malodorous liquor vaults which beset her path on the short cut to her lodgings. Besides, there was the story to be thought out.... Why, now she had really something to do; something for a newspaper for which she was to be paid.... Pacing the trim, neat paths of the flower-garden Mary tried to think of a plot. The people who haunt the parks on fine mornings were there as usual, but to-day they seized her imagination. Strange types, such as are only to found in the heart of great cities; people with vague, impotent faces, waiting eternally for destiny, while they sat idly by the numbed, gloveless hands folded on their knees; a young woman, with restless eyes and a hard mouth, keeping a rendezvous with a lover who had not yet appeared; one or two foreigners, out of elbows and out of work; a nurse or two with a swarm of children from the surrounding Georgian terraces, racing and squealing and looking like white rabbits with their pink noses and creamy furs. Erect and military, the figure of a park-keeper, in his gilt buttons and his peaked cap, gave an official air to the trim paths, the avenue of bare trees—every blackened twig etched against the delicious blue-grey of the distant landscape to the stiff, last century pots and vases—just now filled only with black mould, but in a month or two to be ablaze with gorgeous tulips or golden daffodils.

As she paced briskly up and down the central path, Mary tried hard to concentrate her mind on a plot—a plot in which was to figure a young lady in a tulle ball-dress, reading a three-cornered note. But she could think of nothing. It was all a blank. What had girls in ball-dresses got to do with life; with life as it swirled and rushed by her, with its remorseless laws, its unceasing activities. But yet she might think of something. The scene of her story must be laid at a ball; that, as Mr. Perry Jackson would have said, was sure to "fetch the public." Surely, surely she could invent a love-story. Over yonder was the girl with the hard mouth still pacing up and down alone. Mary felt drawn toward her; she would have liked to have gone up and said something kind.

"If that tawdry looking girl would write down her story," thought Mary, as she passed her, "we should have another masterpiece! It is because they suffer so that women have written supremely good fiction."

By-and-by the nurses began to put by their tatting and gather their chattering, swooping broods together. Perambulators were pushed forward on the creaking gravel, and little white boots and gaiters were seen trotting in the direction of the shining, columned terraces. One or two of the occupants of corner-seats rose up silently and slouched away. A shabby looking foreigner produced something edible from a newspaper and began to munch. A clock on a neighbouring church struck one. The girl with the hard mouth was still glancing from right to left in search of someone who did not come, and Mary could see her desponding back as she loitered, for an instant, at the tall iron gates. A minute later someone dressed like a gentleman had joined her, and she could see their two backs sauntering down the Broad Walk toward the Zoological Gardens.★

"I am glad he has come," thought Mary, who had the true feminine interest in a love affair, "but it's one o'clock and time I got home and set to work."

## CHAPTER XI
## IN GRUB STREET

IT was a bright morning in March, with scudding, woolly clouds, showing patches of vivid blue. Sunshine brightened the huge gilt letters over the newspaper offices; the crowded, brightly coloured omnibuses, the hansoms laden with portmanteaux on their way to Waterloo Station,★ the flaxen hair and beflowered hats of the little actresses hurrying along to rehearsal. An ever-moving procession of people poured like a torrent up and down the street; journalists, country folk, office boys, actors, betting men, loafers—all the curious, shifting world of the Strand★ was jogging elbows on the pavement.

Mary stepped along with a certain sense of adventure. She had to see the editor of *Illustrations*, but she had no idea of the whereabouts of that popular weekly journal. She had in her pocket, too, a letter of introduction to *The Fan*. For her first attempt at fiction had actually appeared in print, and she was curiously anxious to go on. For the first few hours, when she had sat staring helplessly at the sheets of white paper which she had torn into loose pages, neatly folding down an inch border for corrections, she had imagined that the thing was impossible. Nothing came. There seemed no reason, in the eternal fitness of things, why the hero should be dark and faithful or blond and fickle, or if the scene should be laid in the country, in town, or abroad. And there was the illustration, too, for which the story was to be written, and Mary, before she began, had grown to loathe the simpering young lady in tulle, eternally reading her love-letter.... But at last, after hours of torment, an idea came, and then the girl wrote steadily on, with the easy facility of the amateur.... And in the end she was delighted with her work. Her heroine was a beautiful young girl, with grey eyes and a large mouth, whose eighteen years sat lightly, even giddily, upon her. In one of her numerous freaks she dresses up in a cap and apron and waits on the hero, a dashing cavalry officer, who has come down to her brother's cottage at Maidenhead for the first time, and is enamoured at once of the amateur parlour-maid. Subsequently the hussar departs to India for six years, but after the well-known manner of cavalry officers he remains immaculately faithful to the fair one of the cap and apron, and meeting her again at a ball in London, offers her an undamaged heart. The little note of Mr. Perry Jackson's picture was an offer of marriage from a wealthy baronet, which the damsel in tulle is considering in the conservatory by herself, when the faithful but impecunious hussar unexpectedly appears in the nick of time.

She had not an idea that her story was like everybody else's story—her way of telling it like that of hundreds of third-rate authors of fiction whom she had read.

After the clatter and roar of the street, the staircase which led to the editor's room at the office of *Illustrations* seemed curiously dark and silent. The bare wooden treads were black with age and dirt, and were lighted only by a wan light, which flickered through a frosted-glass door, on which was printed, in gilt letters the word *Illustrations*, the first letter having become effaced in the course of years. Underneath was to be read, in black italics: "*Editor's Room. Private.*"

It was some little time before Mary was able to overcome the scruples of the office boy, a young gentleman whom she found dallying in an ante-room, pensively whistling a sprightly air which was just then much in favour, while he leisurely perused sundry inexpensive comic journals; but at length she succeeded in persuading him to take in her card. And presently a door was flung open, and Mary found herself in a small room giving on Fleet Street, fronting a tall man with a large melancholy face, who was bending over a desk. With some trepidation she remembered that the tall melancholy man, according to Mr. Perry Jackson, had the reputation of being able to get people out of his office quicker than any other editor in London.

"Professor Erle's daughter, I believe?" said the editor severely, without looking up from the proofs he was correcting.

"Yes."

"Ah! We were able to make use of your story, though it was not quite up to the mark."

"I'm sorry—" began Mary.

"The name, of course," went on the editor, without noticing the interruption, "the name counts for *something*. Your late father's name carries weight with a *certain* section of the public. And then, with practice, you may do somewhat better. With practice you may be able to write stories which other young ladies like to read."

And with not a suspicion of the ambiguity of his compliment, the editor rummaged in his desk for some missing object.

Mary's heart fell. Was her story as bad as all that, she wondered? She was quite aware that, from a literary point of view, such praise was worse than blame.

In the pause which followed she had leisure to look round furtively. And so this was the office of a big weekly newspaper? The walls, once painted a kind of pea green, were dim with soot, and adorned only with a map of London on a roller; on the floor was stretched a grimy, threadbare carpet. A bluish gas-fire hissed in a narrow, black mantelpiece, and through the encrusted grime of the window-panes appeared the tall brick houses of the opposite side of the Strand. A long procession of omnibuses rattled by continually, and she could see the tops of the hats of those who sat on the outside. The sole furniture of the room consisted of a bureau with pigeon-holes, and three chairs covered in cracked maroon-coloured leather, whose legs partook of that especial curliness which was in high fashion in 1860.

Meanwhile the editor had found his cheque-book, and tearing out a leaf, wrote: "*Pay to Miss Erle two pounds two shillings for contributions during the month of January.*"

Mary took the cheque with a heightened colour and a beating heart. It was the first money she had ever earned. This was the beginning.

A tinkling of the electric bell was heard, and the office boy put in his head.

"A gentleman to see you, sir."

"What for?"

"Drorings, sir."

"Show him in."

Mary rose.

"Wait a minute, Miss Erle."

A long, shambling youth, whose face seemed swollen with the toothache, shuffled in, carrying a portfolio of sketches.

Not a word passed. It was a strange little scene. The shambling youth stood nervously twisting his shabby pot-hat in his fingers as the editor rapidly ran his eye over the drawings.

"Thanks," he said, retying the strings and handing back the portfolio over the desk. "No use to us. Good morning. Top handle," and he waved his pen toward the door. In another instant the aspiring artist was gone.

"Terrible waste of time," muttered the large, melancholy man. "Hundreds of them a week."

"Poor boy," said Mary, who had seen his disappointed face.

"Pooh," rejoined the editor, frowning; "what we want are well-known names; the public likes a name," and apparently with an eye to that section of it which had sat at the feet of Professor Erle, he added abruptly, "We will consider anything else you may care to submit to us, Miss Erle."

"Oh, thank you," said Mary, "I should like to try again," and treading on air she made her way out, followed by the now admiring glance of the office boy, who was not accustomed to see people detained in the editorial sanctum so long.

The girl was inordinately proud of her cheque for two guineas. How much better, after all, than stippling eternally at the Discobolus[1]—for it was the Discobolus this time, with which she was to try her fate at the Academy schools—in the dubious atmosphere

---

1  Myron, a fifth-century Greek sculptor, was noted for his athletes in action. His "Discobolus," or "the discus thrower," is his most famous work.

of the art school. The story had taken four days to write. There were 365 days in a year, so that by writing a story or an article every four days she could earn something like two hundred pounds a year! And what lots of papers there were. Fleet Street was full of them. They lurked up alleys and in quaint little squares at the back. Here they were: *The Daily Telegram, The Observer, The Graphic, Black and White.* Why should she not walk in and demand some work to do? The idea was fearfully alluring. She passed a poster of *Illustrations*, with the name of her story in bright blue print, and Mary stood still and read it over and over again with a quickened pulse, until she was pushed aside by the tide of human beings eddying along the street. But at present, she recollected, she had to find *The Fan.*

After many inquiries, Mary found that the office was located in a huge building in one of the queer little squares out of Fleet Street, and that it was only one of many magazines and newspapers published by the same firm.

It proved to be a little world in itself, this vast bee-hive, for the printing, publishing, and editing of some dozen magazines and journals were all carried on on the premises. There was a deafening whirr of machinery which reminded the girl vaguely of international exhibitions and at every turn she saw an editor's room, with the name of the journal printed in fat, assertive black type. She was wafted down long corridors of frosted glass—frosted glass, it seemed to Mary, was inseparately connected with journalism—until she was shown into a small room containing a bare mahogany table, three chairs, and a framed lithograph of a young person in pink muslin ogling the spectator over a diaphanous fan.

"The editor," said the man in a kind of commissionaire's uniform, who accompanied her, "the editor is engaged on business, but will you kindly wait?"

And Mary waited. In the next room, she could hear, in a muffled way, the voices of that functionary and his visitor. The business, it would seem, on which they were engaged was of a somewhat hilarious nature, for frequent guffaws of laughter reached her, and there was an unmistakable odour of cigarettes. Ten minutes, fifteen minutes, twenty minutes, went slowly by. The murmur of voices, the baritone laughter in the next room continued to be audible. At last, when Mary had finally made up her mind to go, the door was flung open and a young man with a high colour stumbled out.

"Ta-ta, old chap. Thanks, awfully. See you at the club to-night," and, bestowing on Mary a prolonged stare, he disappeared down the long glass corridor.

"Will you please come in?" said a rather affected voice, and Mary, walking into the editorial sanctum, found herself opposite a well-dressed, supercilious looking young man of thirty, a man who curiously resembled all the young men whom she used to see in the park on fine mornings. Searching her memory, she wondered vaguely where she had seen him before. Why, surely he, or his twin brother, figured on all the advertisements of fur-lined overcoats which adorned the outside sheets of the weekly newspapers.

Something like a blush darkened his smooth cheeks as Mary entered, and the editor of *The Fan* raised a pious prayer to the gods that this apparently inexperienced girl had not heard the conversation which had been going on for the last twenty minutes.

"I am sorry to have kept you," he said lamely, glancing for the first time at the card and letter, which had been waiting at his elbow on the table, "but you've no idea what a fool that man is. He never told me that a lady was waiting to see me."

"I dare say," replied Mary a little stiffly, "that you are dreadfully busy."

"Oh, as to that, of course, we're frightfully 'rushed'—especially just now, at the middle of the month. We come out, you see, on the 23rd. I'm most anxious, you see, to make *The Fan* a success. I want it to be quite the smartest thing out, and a real authority on dress and fashion. As to the dress part, I'm not afraid of that. I do it all myself."

"Indeed?" said Mary, to whom the young man who spends his life describing petticoats was as yet an unknown entity. She felt vaguely uncomfortable as the supercilious editor's eye dwelt upon her, not feeling sure that he would approve of the shape of her sleeves, and being morally certain that he was by this time aware that her gown was not lined with silk.

"I came," said Mary, "to ask—to ask if you thought there was anything I could do for *The Fan*."

The supercilious editor pursed up his lips, and looked at Mary's sleeves. Her name, it was obvious, carried no sort of weight in the office of *The Fan* magazine.

"The fact is, we are inundated with stuff which isn't any good to us. We are refusing stuff every day. What we *want* wouldn't be in your line, I'm afraid. The only thing I really think of starting," he announced, standing on the hearthrug and twisting a neat moustache, "is a really good society article. Only about smart people, don't you know. We don't want what the other ladies' papers have got: 'Mrs. Townley Tompkins gave a most successful ball at her beautiful house in Lancaster Gate, or Cromwell Road, or any of those God-forsaken places. Lady Jane Ives, Lady Blaythewaite—those are the sort of people. Really smart, don't you know, and the *vieille souche*[1] as well. Now, I should have liked a smartly written account of Lady Jane Ives's party the other day. Of course I knew lots of people there, but they haven't got the *cacoëthes scribendi*,[2] don't you know."

"I think I could do you that, if you thought it interesting enough," said Mary, "as I happened to be there."

"Oh, you were there?" said the editor, with rising respect in his tone; and for the first time looking at the girl with any interest, he added: "It's possible we might arrange something; in fact, we might begin something this month. We might manage an article for the next number—something smart, you know, and just a wee bit malicious. We'll call the thing 'Behind My Fan,' and that'll give plenty of scope. Don't be afraid, Miss Erle. Any gossip that hasn't got into the papers, you know.

"Lady Jane Ives, now, must be a very interesting acquaintance," went on the editor, in deferential tones, "quite one of the women of the day. I wonder if you could get her to be interviewed for *The Fan?*" he added, visibly brightening.

"I'll ask her," said Mary, smiling. "But I ought to tell you that I am not going out much this season."

"Oh! that don't matter," said the editor hopefully. "What we want is somebody who really knows *the set*. Little bits of gossip, don't you know, that the 'lady journalist' can't possibly get hold of. And you'll have all the society weeklies to help you. Do you care to try?"

"I think I will."

"We can do with three columns a month. The firm pays a guinea a column. When may I have the pleasure of seeing your first article? It would appear next month if you let us have it by the 20th. Thanks, awfully. Good-day."

And the stuffy, jolting omnibus conveyed back to Bulstrode Street a young woman who was conscious neither of hunger, fatigue, nor rattling stones. This was a beginning! Her pocket, in

---

1  Old stock.
2  Passion for writing.

which lay the cheque for two pounds two shillings, had suddenly acquired a special importance. She had earned that money herself; it was the output of her brain. Secretly she would like to telegraph to Vincent, who was now in New Zealand, but she felt the impulse was a silly one. She would write by the next mail.

## CHAPTER XII
### THE WOMAN WAITS

"SAPRISTI!" said Alison, "he's come back, you say? I think I shall insist on the marriage coming off at once."

"No, you won't," answered Mary, reddening, "because we've got to earn enough between us to set up house."

"Pooh," rejoined the other girl. "I'm in the vein for weddings. I had an interview yesterday with Evelina's baby's papa. Don't stare, you idiot. I've been arranging a match."

It was a sultry day at the end of July, and the two girls sat in the dingy lodgings in Bulstrode Street. Vincent Hemming had telegraphed from Liverpool; he was to be in London that afternoon.

"Alison! you don't mean to say you———"

"Certainly. I found the young man open to reason, especially when he comprehended that I might be likely to give Evelina a small *dot*,[1] though it took some time to overcome his moral scruples."

"His moral scruples!" ejaculated Mary.

"My dear, you must know that the average man is, in theory, enamoured of virtue, but in practice his devotion usually takes the form of insisting on that of his female belongings———"

"A vicarious offering to the gods," said Mary, "which it is to be hoped is sometimes efficacious."

"It's astonishing," said the elder woman thoughtfully, "what a lot of human nature one sees down there in Whitechapel."

"More, I daresay, than in Mayfair."

"The wedding," observed Alison, "will come off in the autumn—I shall give the bride away. You may come and look on if you like."

"Poor little Evelina," said Mary abstractedly.

"Poor!" laughed Alison. "What do you think the girl asked for

---

1  Dowry.

when I told her she might choose a wedding present? A white silk dress! She knew, she said, where she could get one, second-hand, for twelve and sixpence, but what she held out for most was a white tulle veil and a wreath of orange blossoms."

"The veil and the orange blossoms are quite pathetic," murmured Mary, getting up and pushing the window wide open. There was a long silence, during which a large bumble-bee swayed in and buzzed ponderously round the little room.

"You ought now," said Alison, jumping up, "to be getting into your most becoming dress, and a proper frame of mind in which to receive so estimable a young man——"

"Oh, don't go. It's so dreadful to wait all alone. He can't be in London till four o'clock, so I don't imagine I shall see him till six or seven, or perhaps not till after dinner."

"Ah," said the elder woman thoughtfully, "then you had better come with me. I'm going to take a lot of poor girls over the National Gallery at three o'clock."

"Oh, I can't. It's too far. And he might come while I was out."

"And considering," laughed Alison, "that you intend spending the rest of your natural existence with Mr. Hemming, that would be nothing short of a calamity."

"You are an unsympathetic demon, and you can be off to your East End young women," said Mary peevishly.

"Pooh," said Alison calmly, "I shall stay till the last moment, and give you the benefit of my mature advice. It's wonderful," she added, snatching up her big Gainsborough hat[1] and putting it on at an extraordinary angle, "how kind I am to young people. I believe I've been making a mistake all this time. I ought to have been the mother of six boys—for Heaven forbid that I should bring another woman into the world."

"You would have been bored to death with them," said Mary.

"Nonsense! Depend upon it, I should have been a pattern parent. All we people make the mistake of doing everything more or less badly. Here are you," she continued, taking up with an impatient gesture a small book bound in red calico, which was lying on the table, "reading a ninepenny translation of 'Epictetus,' when I'll be bound you can't make a pudding properly without it 'catching'—or whatever the cook calls it."

---

1  A high-crowned, big-brimmed hat decorated with feathers and ribbons.

"I know I can't; but it's eccentric—to say the least of it," rejoined Mary, "for a young woman like you to want to make puddings at all."

"I suppose it is an affectation," said Alison candidly, fastening her velvet strings firmly with a diamond scorpion, "but it's so much more amusing than going to balls. Oh, those old club-hacks who go out to exercise their livers, and the boys who dance till they stream with perspiration, because they want to make acquaintances—in society."

"It's doubtfully alluring—the London ball of to-day," assented Mary, "but why go?"

"I don't," said Alison; "it's what I remember out of the dim past. Well, good-bye, I'm off to explain Mantegna[1] to my girls. I only hope they won't *all* come in ostrich feathers. Your most becoming gown, and your most angelic manners, please. *C'est le moment suprême*, remember."

After she had gone, she put her head in at the door to say:

"That baby of Evelina's makes my joy. You never saw such a dumpling, and it doesn't cry now. I have it to spend the day at the flat, and it crawls all over me, and sticks its fat little fists in my eye."

When the street door had finally closed, Mary felt horribly restless. She put on her hat and went out. Secretly, she would have liked to go to Euston★ to meet her lover, but he had said nothing about it, and she thought it best to wait. So she walked to the Regent's Park, and there, in the trim flower-garden, where the avenue of chestnuts was making long shadows on the neatly swept paths, Mary sat down and waited. It was high midsummer now; there was a velvety smoothness on the trim lawns, the green light filtered through a canopy of broad chestnut leaves, and the beds were odorous with heliotrope, purple with pansies, and aglow with rosy geraniums. Four o'clock! Now perhaps the train was thundering into Euston Station.★ Vincent Hemming was getting out of his compartment, collecting his manifold baggage, hailing a cab. London was the richer for one important person; London contained her lover! How charming the Park looked to-day; the faces of the people who passed seemed radiant. Oh, if she could only do a picture of that moving, buoyant, crowd; the umbrageous trees on either hand, the deftly planted flower-beds, the great vases with geraniums frothing over their sides, the distant, white-columned

---

1 Andrea Mantegna (1431?–1506) was an Italian painter and engraver.

terraces, the delicate blue-grey of far-off trees. Yes, he was driving now to his rooms at St. James', passing, actually rolling on London streets, in a London cab, not so very far from where she sat. It seemed incredible, and yet it was true. The only drawback to her happiness was Jimmie; for her brother was back for the holidays, and even a most affectionate sister can do without a little brother's company on occasions. Jimmie, to be sure, was unaware of the engagement, and he would be sure to be there when Vincent came. Mary could not picture the scene with a third person. Not that she cared, of course, but they would naturally have a great deal to say to each other, Vincent and she. She would have to tell him how hard she had worked for the Academy schools, and how the Discobolus, painfully, laboriously stippled, had gone on in its way to judgment. She would have to tell him, too, of her beginnings at journalism, of how she worked in the evenings, and all day on Sundays, at her stories and on her monthly article for *The Fan*. It was not difficult, she had found, to catch the pert, omniscient air of those who purvey social gossip, and in this case, at any rate, the writer had a personal knowledge of the things chronicled. Lady Jane told her of everything that went on in society. Without her stories she could make thirty-six pounds a year. The girl was very proud of those thirty-six pounds.

Twenty past four now. If the express had been punctual, Vincent might almost be at his chambers by this. Very soon she must go home. Supposing he came, and she was out? She got up, her heart thumping at the thought, and began to walk rapidly up the Broad Walk. Everything, to-day, seemed etched on her brain; the delicate arrangement of mauves and lilacs in the distant flower-beds; the foolish faces of the nurses bent over a penny novelette as they pushed forward their perambulators; the vague loafers who haunt the parks in summer time. Yes, and there was the girl again, the girl with the hard mouth, whom she had seen that winter morning, waiting, poor soul, for *her* lover. How the face was changed! She sat on a green bench now, her shabby boots stuck hopeless out. Her hair was untidy. In her hat was a dirty pink bow. Her dark stuff gown was frayed at the edge. The woman in her was dead; she was past the stage of caring about her appearance. Despair was written on her face. "Poor girl," thought Mary, "she is waiting, too, for someone. But he will not come to-day; she didn't expect it, really, when she came out." No, he had not come, and in her glittering eyes one read the fact that in all human probability he never

*—she's awaiting Vincent's return

would. The girl with the hard mouth waited a long time, but finally she disappeared down the Broad Walk.

And now, suddenly, Mary began to hurry. It was quarter to five! She wanted to buy some flowers, too; lots of flowers, to disguise the terrible ugliness of those lodgings. At a florist's she bought an armful of roses, peonies, and tiger-lilies; and then she almost ran home to Bulstrode Street. There were the flowers to arrange, and she would like to change her gown. Vincent didn't like black, she remembered; she would wear the little grey dress she had just had made, and stick some roses in her belt. At home, in the drawing-room, the *milieu* in which she was so soon to receive her lover was not enticing. The tea-cups—common thick-lipped earthenware—were laid out on a battered tin tray; a small glass jug contained a bluish white fluid, and a moulded glass basin was filled with dubious looking lumps of sugar. And to complete the picture Jimmie had apparently taken a seat for the afternoon at the table, and only raised his head from a story-book to clamour for his tea.

"Presently, dear, presently," said Mary, hastily filling all the available bowls and vases with flowers. What could she do with the boy? she wondered, as she ran into her bedroom, put on the grey gown, and pinned some roses at her waist.

"I say, dearest," said Jimmie, banging at the door, "aren't we ever going to have tea? Or are you waiting for old Hemming?"

"Oh, no," said Mary faintly, still pondering what she could do with her young brother. "Tell them to bring up the tea."

It was past six now; he probably would come after dinner. That would be very nice—they would have a beautiful long evening to themselves. The rooms, too, did not look quite so dreadful at night. She had bought a small copper lamp, with a rose-coloured shade, in expectation of Vincent's arrival so that those dreadful milky glass gas-globes would not have to be lighted. And then she had an idea. It was an extravagance which she would not have permitted herself, but then——

"Jimmie!" she called out, as she stood at the looking-glass, her hands trembling as she tried to fasten the over-blown roses at her waist, while one by one the petals fell away and left a bare stalk.

"Yes, dearest."

"Would you like, for a treat, to go to the theatre to-night? There's that new piece at Drury Lane with the real railway-engine in it,[1]* and you might go with Smith major, you know." She opened a drawer and took out an old purse where she kept her spare money. Yes, there was just enough left out of her last cheque to send the two boys to the theatre. "Here's ten shillings, and mind you're back at half-past eleven."

And Jimmie was nothing loath. He insisted, however, on having fried eggs and bacon with his tea, and Mary resolved, when the sitting-room was finally saturated with the odour of fried fat, that she would say she was "not at home" if Vincent called. But at last the room was aired, and the house quiet again. Jimmie had finally disappeared.

The twilight of a summer evening settled on the dingy room. Mary paced the floor, after crowding all her flowers on to the centre table, and opening the two windows wide to let in the sultry evening air. When she neared the window she listened intently for the sound of cab-wheels, or for that of on-coming footsteps. Yes, there were footsteps—footsteps coming to the door. There was an agitated ring of the bell, and someone hurrying up the stairs. Mary got up from her chair, and stood with tightly clasped hands, looking vaguely down at the faded true-lovers' knots which meandered with foolish reiteration over the carpet. The door opened. It was Jimmie.

"Oh, I say, dearest, I quite forgot the ten shillings you gave me! Where can I have left it?" And then a hunt began for the missing money. Presently it was found, and Jimmie had gone for the evening.

It was very hot; stuffy with the damp, vitiated air of a London night verging on August. Few people passed. Bulstrode Street is a quiet thoroughfare. Once, about eight o'clock, cab-wheels were audible. Mary shrank into the farthest corner of the room, clasping her little hands tight, and listening for the sound of the door-bell and that well-known step on the stair.

But neither came. The cab drove on, having emptied its fare two doors off. It was nine o'clock now.

---

1 Victorian theater often attempted to lure audiences with extravagant stage machinery. J.O. Bailey writes of lavish theatrical productions that employed "mists (made of gauze), agitated seas, waterfalls, raging fires ... snow storms, fire engines, and railroad engines" (*British Plays of the Nineteenth Century* [New York: Odyssey, 1976] 6). W.S. Gilbert remarked caustically that "every play which contains a house on fire, a sinking steamer, a railway accident, and a dance in a casino, will ... succeed in spite of itself" (qtd. in Bailey, 7).

"I am so lonely, so tired," thought the girl. "I wish he would come. I want to talk to someone who cares for me, to get my little share of happiness. I am so tired of drawing the Discobolus, of writing for *The Fan*. I wonder if any man alive really knows how dreadful it is to be a woman, and to have to sit down, and fold your hands and wait?"

Half-past nine now. Still he might come. He would have dined at his club in all probability, and he would come on after exchanging gossip with the men he would meet. Mary lighted the copper lamp now, and placed the pink shade over it. How pretty the flowers looked! Only the roses at her belt were faded. She went into the next room and pinned in a fresh bunch. A quarter to ten! He would hardly come now; he always had a nice eye to the proprieties. But his cab might have broken down; he might have been detained at the club. The march up and down the room continued. Mary never knew how much she walked that night. The long, empty hours seemed interminable. But at last, in the still, sultry air, she could hear Big Ben strike eleven. Oh, eleven! Then it was all over. She might as well take off the pretty grey dress, unpin the bunch of roses.

At half-past eleven Jimmie returned, full of the delights of the play.

"Oh, I say, dearest, are you sitting up? I'm so jolly hungry, darling! Can't you get me something to eat? It was so sweet and dear of you to send me to the theatre. But, I say, where's old Hemming? Hasn't he been?"

"I haven't seen anything of him," said Mary. "I suppose he was too tired to come to-night."

And though she went to bed soon after, she lay with her eyes wide open, until the grey dawn began to creep in behind the dingy white blind. Oddly enough, the face of the girl she had seen twice in the Regent's Park rose up again and again. And yet what had they in common?

CHAPTER XIII
THE MAN RETURNS

HEMMING was there now, sitting on the hard sofa opposite, very bronzed since she had last seen him, but studiously correct in his London clothes and his frothy white tie.

At the first instant, when she had gone into the drawing-room to meet him, they had stared at each other as if they were strangers.

Then Vincent Hemming had advanced to meet her with his unemotional smile, holding in his hand a new, shiny hat, and a minute later it seemed natural enough to both of them that her blond head should be resting on the young man's shoulder, and that he should be murmuring vague phrases which for once had nothing to do with the enfranchisement of the women of the Anglo-Saxon race.

Like all people who have been separated for a long time, they found little or nothing to say.

"And did you have a good passage across the Atlantic," asked Mary, when she had made him sit on the hard little sofa, and she had taken a stiff, high chair some little way off, and was looking at him with all her eyes. Was this neatly turned-out young man, in his tightly buttoned dog-skin gloves, the lover with whom she had corresponded all these months and months? She felt strangely shy in the midst of her happiness.

"Fairly good. Yes. I may say it was a tolerably agreeable experience. There were some pleasant people on board. And I was not troubled with sea-sickness."

"I'm glad you came back by the Canadian Pacific. And you went to Ottawa—and Niagara," added Mary vaguely, as people always talk of places and countries they have never seen. "And what is Niagara like?"

"Niagara," said Hemming, with a certain solemnity, "Niagara is something like London. The great falls, you know, are not beautiful; neither is London. But they are, like London, a unique, a terrifying spectacle. The roar, the immensity, the sense of a great power for ever driving forward; all these things are identical. Some day Niagara will have dried up, retreated, become a mere dribble among waterfalls. Some day London will be a handful of ruins."

"What an unpleasant idea!" said Mary, laughing; "what dreadful things you always think of!" And then, with a pretty, frank outburst, she crossed to the sofa, knelt down on the floor, and, putting her two hands on his shoulders, she shook him gently.

"Why didn't you come yesterday," she whispered. "You old silly, you stopped and talked to somebody at the club, I suppose?"

But Vincent did not hear. He had gathered her up in his arms, the little, pale face, on which overwork had already told, the charming, childish mouth, with its curved upper lip, the ruffled fair hair. There was a long silence.

Presently Hemming sighed. Mary had almost forgotten her disappointment of yesterday in the emotion of to-day. Men were like that, she thought. The horror of waiting, waiting, and waiting did not occur to them. They never had to do it; how could they know?

"Dear, aren't you glad you're back?" she asked, raising her head a little so that the brown eyes and the grey eyes met.

"Of course, of course," he muttered, glancing vaguely round the room; "but there are so many things to be thought of."

"Is that," said Mary, gently disengaging herself from his arms, "is that—why you didn't come yesterday?"

"My dear child, I had a thousand things to think of. I was obliged to see the Colonial Secretary on my arrival in London. I had a confidential message of the highest importance from the Governor-General of Canada."

Vincent Hemming had assumed his most official manner—a manner that Mary had always instinctively disliked.

"Ah!" she said, looking down at her belt, where the roses had dropped off one by one yesterday, "I see."

"And afterward some friends—some rather important people with whom I crossed over—insisted on my joining them at the theatre. And for reasons which I need not go into now, I thought it better to go."

"And did you amuse yourself? Was it a good piece?" said the girl frigidly. "I should not like to think you had been bored—the first night of your homecoming."

He looked at her in slight surprise. It was so rarely she said anything sarcastic.

"What's the matter with you, little one? You look fatigued. I am afraid this sultry weather is too much for you; you must go away. We must get the roses back to those pale cheeks," he said in his old-fashioned way.

"Oh, I can't go away. I'm hard at work. You don't know how hard I've worked. I didn't mind, you know. It was all for you, so that we—we—" She almost broke down, covering her face with her bloodless, nervous hands.

"You are unstrung, overwrought," said Hemming, in his kind voice—a voice which always meant twice as much as he intended to say. He touched her wrist tentatively. "Don't, little woman, don't."

"Oh, it's nothing. I'm—I'm a little over-tired. I didn't sleep last night. Please don't bother about me; perhaps it's the weather. You see I don't remember," she added, "ever being in London so late in the summer. Yes, I daresay it's that."

"No doubt the sultriness of the weather may have a good deal to do with your indisposition. Poor little Mary! You must try a change of air."

"I don't know where," said Mary, with a little shrug. "If I went to Aunt Julia's at Bournemouth, I should have to sleep in a bedroom hung with framed photographs of tombs and talk to ritualistic curates—"

"But Lady Jane Ives? She will be sure to want you at Ives Court."

"They're going to Aix on Monday, and later on the house will be full. It would mean many more frocks and much higher spirits than I've got just now. But we'll go down and have long days in the country together, won't we?" she asked wistfully, twisting with two white fingers one of the buttons on his coat. "There's the river—the river at Goring or Marlowe, Vincent, so cool, and green, and quiet on a weekday! Or the Surrey Hills, places that are mauve with heather and pine-woods, beautiful, solemn pine-woods— don't you remember—like the place where we went the day before you sailed? We'll go there again, won't we?"

"Y—es, I hope so, if possible," said Hemming; "but for the next week or two I am afraid I shall be a good deal engaged."

There was a silence which Mary, as hostess, did her best to break. She did not look at him in the eyes any more during his visit. It was almost as if he had struck her. There was a sort of ball in her throat. Her cheeks had got hot; there was colour enough in them now, and her hands shook as she poured out the tea which the maid of all work had brought in. But she must not look as if she cared. A woman—especially in her own house—should always smile. It was on that acquiescent feminine smile that the whole fabric of civilisation rested. And for the next half-hour, as Vincent Hemming discoursed of the unusual opportunities he had enjoyed in Calcutta, in Sydney, and in Ottawa of studying the different systems of government which obtained in various parts of the British Empire, Mary was a model hostess.

And soon, too, he was gone. Afterward, she remembered, he had spoken of seeing her again very soon, as he kissed her cheek at the door—of taking her and Jimmie to the theatre. And then his close-cropped, greyish hair, the back of his shining collar, and his well-cut frock coat, were seen descending the dingy staircase.

And that was all. The meeting for which she had longed with all the ardour of a frank, loyal, and direct nature had come and was over. She went into the little dreary bedroom and threw herself on the narrow bed. No tears came. She lay blankly staring at the blue and green kingfisher, with the text in large German letters, "Come unto Me, all ye that are heavy laden, and I will give you rest." She wondered, vaguely, what connection there was between a kingfisher and that exquisite, musical phrase. And then she remembered how her Aunt Julia, from the chaste seclusion of her gabled Bournemouth villa, had once written her a long letter foreshadowing, with the perverse joy of the righteous, the day when her niece Mary would infallibly need the consolations of religion. Her Aunt Julia had spoken of her as "hardened." Well, that exactly described her state of mind. Mary felt not only hardened, but petrified. What did it mean? He was here, was he not; the man who had just left her? All her thoughts turned naturally to him; she was incapable now of comprehending a life which they were not to share together. She was perfectly aware of his little poses, his not altogether amiable peculiarities, but she had got to the stage when they made no difference. A French wit has it that "*C'est le ridicule qui tue*"[1]—an aphorism which may be true of politics, fashions, or art, but which, alack! does not apply to the vagaries of human passion.

Vincent Hemming, once outside the door, felt in his breast-pocket for his cigar case, carefully chose a promising cigar, and thrust it firmly between his teeth while he stopped in a doorway to strike a match. His sensations that afternoon were mixed. It had been, he reminded himself, delightful to see little Mary again. If only he had not been so imprudent as to speak before he went away. And yet what could he do? Curiously enough, the girl appealed to the sensual side of his nature. Her slight, thin shoulders, her long, delicate throat, the rather pathetic curve of her jaw, belonged to the type of beauty he preferred. The nervous energy, which was her special characteristic, touched while it troubled him. As on the day that he asked her about the future, he always, whatever she announced her intention of doing, felt constrained to interfere. He admired her pluck, her perseverance, her dogged determination to get on, her fine appreciation of all that was best in literature and art. "She's a little girl in a thousand," he said to himself, "and not at all likely to make unpleasantness if things become impossible. Not that one would dream of doing anything but the 'straight thing' by her; but she's young—she may see someone she likes better. By Jove! she ought to make a really good

---

1   It is ridicule that kills.

match." And in his modesty Mr. Hemming allowed himself to caress this idea. He pictured her, in many diamonds, at the head of a long dinner-table—a table scintillating with silver and crimson with roses, with a vague, undefined husband at the other end. And he, Vincent, sat by her side, and she—his little Mary—looked at him, as he talked, with her emotional eyes, and murmured pretty sympathetic phrases with her deliciously curved lips. "Who knows?" he muttered, throwing away the end of his cigar; "odder things have happened."

And then he went over his year of travel as he strolled down Regent Street on his way to call at the Métropole.[1]★ Everything, from the very beginning, had gone off smoothly. He had enjoyed it from first to last. His letters of introduction—he had had excellent letters, he reminded himself—had brought him in touch with all the important men in India and the colonies. He had ample material for a book. The thing, it was true, had been somewhat overdone, but then he was sure of his style; the book would not be written after the manner of the globe-trotting M.P. And yet, by the time the volumes were out, he, too, would be among England's legislators. It was typical of Hemming that he always thought of the hedgerow member of parliament as a "legislator." He had quite made up his mind about that. Marriage might well be postponed a year or two, but for a man to have any real influence on politics, he must be in the House. As luck would have it, the member for Northborough was known to be seriously ill, a lingering illness which must terminate fatally, and the party were already making arrangements for contesting the seat. He had reason to know that his candidature would be highly appreciated by the Conservatives. All that was wanted were funds. And it was then that his mind ran back to his meeting with his new friends. He had found them first, Mr., Mrs., and Miss Violet Higgins, of Northborough, Lancashire, engaged in a protracted quarrel with the black porter in a train bound New York-wards from Niagara. The Higgins family had wished to have the windows of the long compartment opened, but the black porter, having no personal objection to tropical heat, had insisted on shutting every aperture. Finally, Vincent had effected a compromise, and the perspiring mayor and mayoress of Northborough had been, he thought, somewhat unduly thankful. The

1   The Métropole, a lavish hotel built in the mid-1880s, stood on Northumberland Avenue near Charing Cross.

daughter, a young lady with beady eyes, a high colour, and a complete absence of chin, had watched him all the rest of the journey with extreme interest. He had not liked her appearance or her manners; her clothes were trimmed all over with gold braid, and she looked unnecessarily conscious on being addressed; but this first aversion had worn off during the seven days on the steamer, for they met again on the wharf at New York, in the rush and bustle of embarkation.

The father, a manufacturer of the staunchest Tory principles, took a curious fancy to the young man. Vincent remembered how impressed the Mayor of Northborough had been when he found out that this was "young Hemming," the son of the late Cabinet Minister. How confidential he had got, exercising with him on the summer nights. How easily the parents had surrendered Miss Violet to his care, did that young lady evince a desire to pace the hurricane deck. Their wealth was abundant, but not ostentatious, like that of the Chicago pork-packers' wives and daughters who graced the steamer with their presence. Violet was their only child, and Elijah Higgins took occasion, one night when the smoking-room was empty, save for a select party of San Franciscans who were playing poker and emitting fantastic oaths in the midst of a cloud of smoke in a distant corner, to mention that he was prepared to settle a considerable fortune on his daughter if she chose a husband of whom he approved. Yes, old Higgins was inclined to be friendly. He had offered to be president of his committee should he think of standing for Northborough; he had talked of heading a subscription to defray Vincent's election expenses. He thought, on the whole, he should accept their invitation to run up north and look around him at his future constituents. One couldn't put things in motion too soon. He crossed Trafalgar Square, and stepped down Northumberland Avenue to the Métropole. Miss Violet had had a headache, the night before, at the theatre; it would only be civil to go and ask how she was. He had an idea they expected him, and so, it transpired, they did. They not only expected him, but they expected him to stop to dinner.

The next day Mary received a note from Vincent, to the effect that he was running up north on parliamentary business, but that he hoped to see her very soon. The postscript was typical of the man: "I rejoice to think that you are continuing your literary and artistic studies with your usual courage and energy. Only I implore you to consider your health, mental and physical. You tell me you are writing stories now—love stories, I presume. Remember that work which entails a drain on both the imagination and the feelings is more exhausting than you perhaps imagine."

A month later Vincent was still at Northborough, and Mary, whose drawing for the Academy had again been refused, was working, all through the dog-days, at her new profession of journalist.

## CHAPTER XIV
## THE APOTHEOSIS OF PERRY JACKSON

IT was a bright October morning, and the light of midday fell searchingly on the pictures in their garish new frames. Scotch mountain streams, eastern bazaars, young ladies reading love-letters, fishermen mending nets, ran promiscuously up the walls to the very cornice, or modestly hung on a level with the boots of the spectator. Everywhere was the obvious, the threadbare, the *banal*; everywhere there was a frank appeal to the Philistinism of the picture-buying public. It was press day at the galleries of the Society of United Artists—the Benighted Artists, as they were called at a certain club consecrated to the fine arts—so that, for once, there was a sprinkling of people moving about the polished parquet floor. Indeed, in a distant room there was even a small crowd; but that, it transpired, was due to the fact that a buffet spread with a boiled ham, a magnificent display of Bath buns, and several decanters of fiery looking sherry, presided over by a young lady with arch manners and pendant earrings, had been provided to seduce the austere journalist. Sounds of hilarity, as well as whiffs of tobacco smoke, frequently penetrated to the large room where Mary Erle was taking notes. Shaggy-looking men, with wide-awake hats and Inverness capes of dubious freshness,[1] strolled in twos out of the luncheon room, lit a cigar, took a seat on the red velvet divan in the middle of the room, making incongruous figures enough as they rested under the fronds of a giant palm, and fell to talking Fleet Street, until one or the other, producing a watch, hastily rose and shuffled downstairs. These curious proceedings on the part of a certain portion of the "press" aroused some astonishment in Mary. The scene was as new to her as the work;

---

1 A wide-awake was a felt hat with a low crown and wide brim, punningly named because it never had a nap. An Inverness was a loose rain cape first popularized in Inverness, Scotland.

for she had only taken the art critic's place on the *Comet* during the temporary illness of that functionary.

So she walked slowly, conscientiously round the room, stopping at every picture that she could possibly mention in her article, and stopping, too, before pictures she would have to mention whether she liked them or no. Yonder was a yellow and blue "Rome from the Pincian Hill," by a man with whom, she remembered, her editor constantly dined; she would have to say something vaguely civil about that canvas; while close beside it was a portrait of Mr. Bosanquet-Barry himself, by a lady more celebrated for her charms than her talent. She must find, of course, some phrase which might encourage the fair artist to go on painting editors' portraits. Marking with a pencil the titles of these works of art, she absolved her conscience by making some elaborate notes about a clever little picture by an unknown man, which was hanging near the floor, an effect of the Strand on a rainy day. Mary had to kneel on the floor to see it, and as she rose, her eyes were on a level with a tolerably large canvas, hung in the place of honour. The scene represented Trafalgar Square by moonlight, with a young woman of superhuman beauty wrapped in a threadbare shawl, huddled in the shadow of one of the lions. In a passing brougham was seen the profile of another girl, painted, bedizened, supercilious.

"*Two Sisters*, by Perry Jackson, A.R.A.," said Mary, consulting the catalogue. "I thought so."

"How do you do, Miss Erle?" said a voice—a voice which she had not heard for many months, and, turning, she saw that the painter of the picture was taking off his hat, and blushing a bright pink as he advanced to meet her. She noticed, with amused surprise, that he was dressed in the height of the fashion, and wore a pink carnation in his buttonhole. His shock head, too, was closely cropped now, but as there was still no trace of hair on his face, he had as of old the look of a grown-up London street-boy.

"If this isn't a sight for sore eyes!" declared Perry gallantly. "Why I haven't seen you, to speak to, for quite a year. Not since the old days at the Central London."

"No," said Mary, "and you have become famous since then! I must congratulate you on your election to the Royal Academy."

"Oh, it don't mean much—except in the £.s.d. line,[1] you

---

1  Perry Jackson refers here to his income, his "pounds, shillings, and pence."

know," said Perry, apologetically. "But I told you I'd do it, didn't I? You remember 'The Time of Roses'? That was what did the trick, the girls and the roses. Agnew bought it, sold thousands of engravings—especially in Australia. Australia, you know, is like England—only more so. And in America, too. I'm told that in America they give away an autogravure of that picture with every pound of Scourer's Soap and every bottle of Parkins' Pain-killer."

"America is a wonderful country," said Mary gravely.

"Of course," continued Perry, "you've seen my big picture in the Academy. Sold for two thousand pounds, at the Private View. That's what got me my election," continued the new Associate confidentially, "all rot about encouraging talent. What fetches the public is a long price. I hope," he added wistfully, "that you'll come and see my studio. I'm down Kensington way now—all among the Royal Academicians."

"I shall certainly come," said Mary, "and bring Jimmie. Do you remember Jimmie, who used to fetch me sometimes at the School of Art? He is a big boy, thinking of Oxford."

"Of course. Delighted. When will you come?" continued Mr. Jackson, with an unmistakable show of eagerness. "I'm in old Madder's house, the big red one with the white balconies. He couldn't keep it up, poor old fellow. Would go on doing historical pictures: 'John Knox preaching before Mary, Queen of Scots,' 'The Last Appeal of Monmouth,' and all that sort of thing; and the public won't have him at any price."[1]

"Those things were in fashion," replied Mary, "when he was young. There is something pathetic in his clinging to them, like one or two old ladies in society, who still wear the ringlets and berthas of 1850."

"Well, it may be pathetic," said Perry, staring in a somewhat bewildered way, "but, anyhow, it don't pay. Poor old Madder was glad to get rid of the house as it stands; so I took it just as it was:

---

1 John Knox (1505-72) was a Calvinist Reformer who attempted to get Mary, Queen of Scots, to convert from Roman Catholicism. She reportedly said of him, "I fear the prayers of John Knox more than all the assembled armies of Europe." James, Duke of Monmouth (1649-85), the illegitimate son of Charles II, attempted to raise a rebel army and claim the crown. The rebellion was crushed and Monmouth executed. His last appeal, made to his executioner, was said to have been: "Do not hack me as you did my Lord Russell." Perry Jackson comments here on the maudlin nature of Madder's choice of subjects.

tapestries, Venetian overmantels, suits of armour, and all the rest of it."

"And do your—your people live with you?" said Mary vaguely, remembering the old couple in the Hampstead Road upholsterer's shop.

"Oh, no! They wouldn't care about it, you know. The old people like to come and walk round the house. There's the Venetian drawing-room, now; that rather takes their fancy."

"It's rather a responsibility, isn't it, setting up such a big establishment?"

"Bless you," whispered the new Associate confidentially, "it's all for show! I live in a little room at the back; couldn't be bothered to sit down and eat my mutton chop in that great big gold and amber dining-room. Oh, no! Not for this infant. But it fetches the public, no end. Why, I've had any amount of tip-top swells there already. They come in and say, 'What a *perfectly* beautiful house, Mr. Jackson. What *exquisite* taste! Where *did* you get that cabinet? I wonder now, if I were to ask *very* prettily, if you could find time to paint my portrait?'"

"I see," said Mary thoughtfully, "that you thoroughly understand your public."

A loud guffaw of laughter burst from the inner room. One of the United Artists, emboldened by several glasses of the dubious looking sherry, was playfully disengaging the arch young lady's earring from a stray lock of hair. A female journalist, who wore a waterproof and a pince-nez, emerged hastily, with a superior expression, through the doorway, and in the general hilarity which followed this little scene several more glasses of sherry were hastily poured out and a quantity of fresh cigars were lit. Artists and critics were seen exchanging cards, and an atmosphere of extreme sociability hung about the galleries. An old man with a white beard, who had painted the interior of Cologne cathedral for forty years, was leading affectionately by the arm the young gentleman who did the galleries for the *Easel*, toward the room where his latest contribution to the fine arts hung. A little group of critics had collected round Perry Jackson's canvas. It was easy to see that they considered it the picture of the exhibition. A vague official crossed the room and, bending down, whispered confidentially:

"May I suggest your taking some slight refreshment? It is all in the next room."

"Thank you," said Mary, in her stiffest manner. "I lunched before I came out."

There was an awkward pause, which Perry Jackson hastened to break.

"And you—what are you doing now, Miss Erle? I've seen your stories in *Illustrations*—though I haven't much time for reading myself. Why, you must be making 'a pile'."

"My income varies," said Mary, smiling a little pathetically. "It sometimes exceeds thirty-six pounds a year."

"Great Scott!" ejaculated Perry, "I'm glad I don't write."

"One writes for the fun of it, I suppose," said Mary. "Why—I've even written a novel!"

"Oh! When was it published?" asked the young man.

"It hasn't been published," answer the girl. "It has been several journeys to various publishers, but I don't think I ever expected it to be really published. You see it was 'observed.' It was a bit of real life. It had twenty-seven years of actual experience in it."

He looked at her surprised. So she was twenty-seven; as old as himself. Somehow, he could hardly tell why, the thought was disagreeable to him.

"And you've done nothing with the book?" he asked quickly.

"No. It was too sad, 'too painful,' all the publishers said. It wouldn't have pleased the British public. But I have been given a commission to do a three-volume novel on the old lines[1]—a dying man in a hospital and a forged will in the first volume; a ball and a picnic in the second; and an elopement, which must, of course, be prevented at the last moment by the opportune death of the wife, or the husband—I forget which it is to be—in the last."

"I dare say it will be ripping good," said Perry optimistically.

"I am quite sure it will be dreadful," said Mary; "but then I can't afford to say no. I've got a big brother going to Oxford in a year or two. And grown-up brothers are so expensive. They want such a lot of neckties. And I dare say it doesn't matter much what one writes. It will all be forgotten soon enough. I used to have my little ideas about what was artistic and so on; but then, as you say, one *must* think of the public," she added, rather dismally, as her eye ran along the walls covered with smooth views of Rome, of the Thames at Wargrave, impossible fisher-girls, and treacly sunsets. She was sur-

---

1 Through much of the last two-thirds of the nineteenth century, virtually all fiction was published in three volume editions, called "three deckers," and many publishers came to expect a certain plot pattern from writers, something akin to that suggested here by Mr. Perry Jackson.

prised at herself for talking so openly to this young man whom she had not seen for so long; but there was a fund of frankness and kindliness under Mr. Perry Jackson's somewhat unattractive manners which was difficult to resist. He was so perfectly candid himself that few people were ever anything but frank in return.

"Why, of course you must," replied the new Associate, resting a complacent eye on his own canvas, which stood out in all its meretricious cleverness from the ruck of commonplaces around. After all, Mary thought, there were points in the picture—the moonlight was broadly painted, there was real movement in the passing coupé, and the girl's face inside, lit up by the carriage lamps, was cleverly indicated.

"By the bye," said Mary, as she put up her note-book, "I suppose you've heard from *Illustrations*? They're going to have an article on you and your work, on your election to the Academy, you know. And I think they rather want me to do it."

"I wish you would, Miss Erle," said Perry, blushing. "You know pretty well all about me, don't you? And I'll show you all the work I've got now at my place, and—and will——"

"In that case," said Mary, "I shall pay a state visit to your studio, and I shall be highly critical, so don't attempt to disarm me with sherry and Bath buns."

"You looked then," cried Perry, "just like you used to when you first came to the Central London, with a funny little twinkle in the tail of your eye."

"Did I?" laughed Mary. "I don't feel like it. I believe I'm about a hundred," she added, gathering up her note-book and parasol.

"May I—I should like to see you home?" said Perry gallantly, as they descended the stairs together. "Where did you say you lived?"

"In the same place, in Bulstrode Street. But I hope I shall not have to stay there long. What I should like would be a little house somewhere in a suburb. A little house with a garden," she added, as they passed out into the street, and her thoughts flew back to Vincent Hemming.

And in the empty galleries the rays of an autumn sunset touched the threadbare "Romes" and "Wargraves" and "Cornish Fisher-scenes" with its delicate golden fingers. One by one the pressmen and the lady journalists had slipped away. The odour of tobacco was evaporating. Even the buffet was deserted, save for one elderly gentleman, who, as he stood talking to the presiding nymph as she washed up the glasses, leaned with one elbow on the table and regarded the empty decanters with a fixed smile.

"IT'S the deuce of a wet day, dearest," murmured Jimmie, strolling into the little room where Mary was writing. "Must you really go out?"

"Yes, dear. Don't bother. I must go directly I have done this article for *Illustrations*," answered the girl, with the irritated look of a person who is interrupted in the middle of a train of thought—thought which was to be paid for at the rate of threepence a line.

"But you really don't look the thing, darling. You really should see Danby. By the bye, does Sarah know I'm down? or is there any breakfast about?" added Jimmie, with his newly acquired drawl. He had grown up into a curiously pretty young man, who already wore his clothes with a charming air. It was characteristic of him that he addressed his sister with as much politeness as any of his rather numerous loves. Everybody agreed that Jimmie Erle was a delightful boy. Laudatory adjectives abounded when his name was mentioned. Just now, lounging in his cricketing blazer against the mantelpiece, he looked the picture of airy and irresponsible youth.

"As it's half-past-eleven," said Mary, laughing, blotting her MSS., and thrusting it in an envelope, "Sarah may have some vague idea that you might be putting in an appearance soon."

"Dear, you're not cross with me?"

"No, boy. Sleep as long as you can. I daresay you have to get up very early at school."

"Oh, yes, sometimes," said Jimmie vaguely. But Mary had crossed into her tiny bedroom now, and was rapidly doing up her hair, and putting on a waterproof. As she left the flat there was a brief vision of Jimmie helping himself to a third serving of marmalade. The morning paper was at his elbow, and there was a suggestive-looking box of cigarettes on the chimney-piece.

"I think," said Mary to herself as she clattered down the bare stone staircase in her flapping waterproof, "that Jimmie will always be comfortable and happy. He will never have to go out on a wet day."

In the Underground Railway it was at any rate dry, and Mary could rest her back, tired with bending over a desk since nine o'clock. For a long time she had felt wretchedly weak. The strain of writing was intense; there were whole mornings which she spent staring at a sheet of white paper on her desk. The only ideas she had came at night, when she ought to have been asleep, and after hours of insomnia she would get up and go to her desk with every nerve in her body quivering. Mary told herself severely as the train rattled on its way to Kensington, that she could not afford to break down now. She wanted so much to retain her position on *The Fan* magazine; if she gave it up for a month there would be a dozen women ready to snatch it from her. Then, too, she was getting on with her three-volume novel, which was to appear in *Illustrations*, and there was the Perry Jackson article for the same paper, over which she had taken a deal of trouble, and to finish which she was on her way to the new Associate's house. And she smiled as she thought how amused Vincent would be to hear that she had met Perry Jackson again, and to learn that she had been chosen to write an article in *Illustrations* on "The Time of Roses," and the beautiful house and studio in which the artist was now installed. And with the clarity of mental vision which is one of the first signs of ripened powers, Mary contrasted the two men. Perry with his ridiculous manners, his good heart, his stubborn determination to get on, and his curiously keen knowledge of the public; Vincent with his smooth, charming phrases, his good looks, his vacillating nature.

It was pouring rain as Mary stepped out of Kensington High Street Station. A heavy, pinkish sky lowered overhead, and the trees of Holland House[1]★ took a strange metallic hue in the changing stormy light. The end of the road was swallowed up in mist and rain, and on the streaming pavement, which reflected everything like a mirror, she could see a vision of her own umbrella hurrying along through the storm. By the time she rang the bell of Mr. Perry Jackson's imposing house her feet were soaked through.

The door was opened by an elderly person in a bonnet profusely trimmed with lilies of the valley, a lady whose dark stuff gown and bibulous eyes contrasted strangely enough with the spacious white hall with its Persian tiles, its soft, flame-coloured carpets, and its vases of delicate peach-tinted rhododendrons. And the lilies of the valley, with a confidential, if somewhat mysterious air, shuffled along the discreet, silent passages, and after a tentative knock at the door, ushered Mary into the studio.

---

1 Kensington High Street Station was an underground railway station opened in 1868 by the Metropolitan Railway; Holland House, owned by the Holland family, was the social center for liberal politicians and literary figures in the nineteenth century.

The subject of her article was at work on a large canvas when she was shown in. In the vast studio, with its vista of polished boards, its golden ceiling, and its tapestry hung walls, the artist made a somewhat insignificant figure, as he stood on a step-ladder and reached up to put in a piece of background. The gorgeous colouring of the great silent room accentuated the paleness of his features. With his profile outlined against an alcove of golden mosaics, he looked more than ever like a grown-up London street boy, who had found his way, by mistake, into some oriental palace fashioned by superhuman hands. The wan, veiled light of a rainy day crept through the great north window, and on a small outer studio of glass—destined for out-of-door effects—the rain pattered monotonously. Palms and azaleas in giant pots repeated the enchanting note of green which was visible through the glass walls of the outer studio.

The huge canvas at which he was at work represented a convent garden in the grey crepuscule of a summer evening. The pale pensive faces of young nuns, faces of unnatural loveliness, with haunting eyes and flower-like mouths, shadowed by wide blue headdresses, were seen bending over beds of tall white lilies, while here and there a transparent hand was stretched to gather the passionless, immaculate flowers. This picture, destined for next year's Academy, was to be called "The Hour of Lilies." Mary was startled when she looked at it. Only a short time ago she had suggested the subject to him. He must have set to work at once, leaving everything else. The picture was already blocked in.

"Oh, I say, this *is* good of you," cried Perry, blushing crimson.

Mary observed, with some annoyance, that he had lately taken to blushing at her advent. It was ridiculous, for they had to see each other so often about the article that they had become like old friends. And she always thought of him, moreover, as the Perry Jackson of the Central London School of Art—a little man with a shock head, whose parents, moreover, sold cheap dining-room suites in the Hampstead Road.

"That thing must be all at the office not later than to-morrow morning," said Mary, sinking into the nearest chair and surveying her damp boots with solicitude.

"And a fine mess they've made with that process-block of 'The Time of Roses,'" said Perry, indignantly. "I'm blessed if you'd know they were roses. Why, they might be—artichokes—or anything else."

"Well, we can't help that now," said Mary doggedly. "What I

want to-day is just the last touches for my article—something to make the thing literary, with a meaning, you see. I should be glad to know, for instance," continued Mary, glancing round the walls with a slight smile, "if you have a Message?"

"What's that?" asked Perry, putting a flat high light on the golden hair of a novice.

"I have never," said Mary, abstractedly, "been quite able to ascertain. But nowadays most people—writers, painters, and so on—are supposed to have a Message to deliver to their contemporaries. And I thought," she continued encouragingly, glancing at the canvasses around, at the feminine faces with haunting eyes and flower-like mouths, "I thought perhaps you meant to insist, in your art, on the cult of beauty, the pagan love of form, the delight, so to speak, in a physically perfect existence?"

Perry whistled thoughtfully.

"Well," he said, after a pause, "I never thought about it like that. But you can put it in that way if you like. I don't mind what you say about me," he said, magnanimously; and then, with engaging candour, he added: "All I want to do is to make the thing pay."

"But, dear Mr. Jackson, it evidently does pay," urged Mary, laughing; "here you are, 'arrived,' with poor Mr. Madder's beautiful house and studio all to yourself."

"Yes," said Perry, looking at her curiously, with a side-ways glance, "all to myself. There was a lady here yesterday," he continued with a short laugh, "who came to interview me for an evening paper, and what do you think she asked me? If I was married—or going to get married."

"And are you?" asked Mary, in a politely interested tone; but something in his look made her drop her eyes, and she turned away, asking two or three embarrassed questions about a distant canvas on the wall.

There was an awkward pause. Outside the rain poured with a sibilant sound on the roof of the glass studio, and the great trees drooped, soaked and soddened with wet. It had grown dark in the big room. Perry had thrown down his palette, and was standing gazing at her with a nervous, agitated look. Mary began to walk round the studio, the drips from her waterproof making tiny pools of wet on the polished parquet floor and on the eastern rugs.

"I really ought to go," she said nervously, looking down; "your room is much too gorgeous for a damp journalist."

He hurried forward imploringly, his sharp face whiter than ever with emotion, and for years after she could not forget the painful scene which followed. She remembered how she had been intensely conscious of her damp boots, and of the little spots of water which her dripping waterproof made on the polished floor, while Mr. Perry Jackson, who in moments of intense excitement, had an occasional difficulty with his aspirates, proffered her his name and fortune, and the undisturbed possession of the Venetian drawing-room, the amber and gold dining-room, and a Japanese boudoir on the first floor.

In the pause that followed there was no sound but that of the pitiless rain hissing on the outer studio roof. Mary stood with her eyes fixed on the polished boards. How could he have misunderstood her so—what could she say to soften it? Didn't he know? Didn't he understand that it was impossible? Well, she must say something. A strange misgiving forbade her to mention the name of Hemming, so she spoke of vague things, of Jimmie, and of her profession.

"Is—is—there anyone else that you care for?" stammered Perry forlornly, just as she was going.

"Yes," she said, but she did not meet his eyes, and as the word left her lips a sharp foreboding seized her.

In silence Perry Jackson clasped her hand at the door. Each felt that the parting was more or less final.

"Then you'll speak about that process-block to the editor?" said Perry awkwardly, just at the last, as she was crossing his threshold.

"Oh, yes, of course. No doubt it can be touched up as you suggest. And that about your ideal in art will make the article much stronger," she said in a loud, would-be cheerful voice.

Each of these two young people was already thinking of their work. He saw her out, and watched the slim figure, in its grey waterproof, disappear down the street in the rain and mist. He would like to have saved her from the struggle of the woman who works, the fret and the fever, the dreary fight for existence. As he turned back down the clear white passages, with their soft, glowing carpets, their masses of transparent flowers, the sumptuousness of his home struck him for the first time as ludicrously incongruous.

He strode back into his studio, and began searching among his portfolios for the sketch of a girl's head which he wanted for the new picture. As evening fell, he was still working.

## CHAPTER XVI
## A COMEDY IN REAL LIFE

THE first act was over, the curtain was down again. A buzzing sound was heard all over the theatre. Men were standing up in the stalls, raking the house with their opera-glasses; the critics were seen exchanging significant looks and portentous monosyllables; while here and there was visible the profile of a pretty woman craning her neck to be seen speaking to some distant celebrity. The house, viewed from above, was one compact mass of human beings, the clear, pale dresses of the women making gay patches among the rows of black coats, white shirt fronts, and slightly bald heads of the men.

It was the first night of a new comedy at a modish theatre. In the private boxes the little canvas doors opened continually, revealing a glimpse of the begilded corridor darkened by the figure of a man in evening dress. In some of the boxes, notably that of Lady Jane Ives, the door opened almost with the regularity of a machine, while a small procession of young gentlemen sidled in and out.

"All mother's 'boys' will be here before the evening's over," whispered Alison to Mary. "I don't know whether our brains will hold out." But Alison, for one, made no effort to entertain them, for hardly had the curtain fallen when Dr. Dunlop Strange, who was in the stalls, had taken the chair behind her, and had begun telling her of a new medical discovery in which she was interested.

For the moment Mr. Bosanquet-Barry and Mr. Beaufort Flower were the other occupants of the back chairs.

"Dr. Strange, you've got to personally conduct us over the Whitechapel Hospital," said Alison, turning her beautiful, intelligent eyes upon him. "Miss Erle wants to write a chapter about a hospital, and you can explain the internal arrangements to her."

"When will you come?" said the doctor eagerly.

"Oh, arrange it with Mary," said Alison, laughing. "These young women who write are always so busy. At present I'm one of the unemployed."

"Dear Lady Jane," objected Mr. Flower, "you're not going to allow them to go over to one of those nasty hospitals. Why, you don't know what they will catch, and I'm told the language of the patients is quite ornamental," he added with a titter.

"Allow them!" ejaculated Lady Jane. "My dear Beaufy, if you had a grown-up daughter, you'd find that you were 'allowed' to do things or not as *she* chose. That's why I'm so young," said the old woman with a fat laugh. "It's because I go with the times. And as for that child Mary, I can't refuse her anything. You see Alison and I both wanted to marry her poor dear father. He was the most delightful creature that ever lived."

Mary, in her little white frock, was looking radiant. The morning papers had announced the results of the by-election, and Vincent Hemming's name headed the poll with a majority of forty-seven votes. In a day or two—perhaps even now—he would be in town; he would have time for her. They would have leisure, perhaps, to see a great deal of each other once more. She had become accustomed by now to a certain vagueness about the future. But just to know that he was happy and successful was enough for the moment.

"Why are you looking so pretty to-night?" whispered Beaufy to Mary, to whom he had taken a perverse fancy because she generally snubbed him. He prided himself on being allowed to say impertinent things to ladies.

"I never look pretty," said Mary calmly.

"No? That's true. I've seen you," he added with engaging candour, "look positively ugly. And other times, you know, you become radiantly lovely."

Meanwhile Lady Jane, showing a good deal of plump shoulder and bland bosom, in a gown of excruciating red, was gently tapping Mr. Bosanquet-Barry with a carved ivory fan, as he leaned over her chair.

"Tell me who's here, you shocking creature," she gurgled. "You know I can't see. And what are you young men there for except to tell us the news?"

"Oh, yes. Everybody's here. Lots of people have come up to town on purpose. No end of smart people in the stalls. And who do you think is down there in the omnibus box? Lady Blaythewaite, of all people. *C'est crâne, hein?*[1] Three days before she has to appear in the divorce court. They say," he added, dropping his voice so that only Lady Jane could hear, "they say it will be a *cause célèbre*. She brings the case, of course, but she won't get it. They're betting on it at the clubs."

"I see she's got that old woman, what's-her-name, who's so very proper, in the box," said Lady Jane, as she surveyed the coming heroine of the divorce court exhaustively with her tortoise-shell

---

1  It is bold, eh?

lorgnette. "How *clever!*" she continued in an approving tone. "White muslin, and not a jewel. I was so fond of her poor mother. She was one of the first women who smoked—I mean before people. She was a sort of Mrs. Norton. Lord Houghton used to say she was one of the few women in society that he could ask to his literary breakfasts. Her daughter hasn't inherited her wits."

"No, or she wouldn't have committed the fatal error of being found out," murmured Mr. Bosanquet-Barry, and then he added, showing all his dazzling teeth in a fatuous smile:

"Lady Blay's a charming woman, mind you, when she lets you know her, and by Jove, she's becoming the smartest of the smart! I assure you, she's quite irresistible."

"Ah, because she doesn't care about anybody," rejoined Lady Jane dryly, letting her glass travel on to the next box. "I see all you young men are quite *épris*,"[1] replied Lady Jane, in her well-bred, indifferent tone. "Do you see much of her?"

"One's supposed to be able to find her at five. But very often she's out."

"Yes," put in Mr. Flower, in his waspish voice, "she says it's so effective to be out occasionally. Isn't it malicious of her?"

"My dear boy, Lady Blaythewaite is quite good lookin' enough to do these things. Who are those curious looking persons in the next box?"

"Aren't they quite too delicious for words?" cried that young gentleman with some animation. "They're my discovery. There's a man—a political man—in the stalls who knows. It's the mayor of Northborough, the mayoress of Northborough, and the heiress apparent. They're as rich—well, as rich as Americans. Their name is Higgins. Aren't they nice? I never saw a provincial mayor before. I wonder if he is red all over, like his face? I'm sure he wears his chains of office under his clothes. Look at the mayoress' gown, dear Lady Jane. Do you see it has a small V at the throat, and *tight* elbow sleeves, and you may swear it's high at the back! And the daughter—*qu'elle est fagotée, mon Dieu*,[2] and with diamonds put in all the wrong places. It is a relief to look at Lady Blay, who's got hardly anything on at all."

And so these were the Higgins; Vincent's friends, whom he had picked up in America, and who had got him returned to Parlia-

---

1  Smitten.
2  My God, she's dressed like a scarecrow.

ment. Mary gave one swift, comprehensive glance at the daughter, taking in her underbred face, with its beady eyes and fretful mouth, her over-trimmed, provincial clothes, and her uneasy attitude. She remembered Hemming's fastidious tastes, and then she decided, with a little throb of feminine exultation, that she had nothing to dread from Miss Violet Higgins.

"Does anybody know what the play is about?" asked the girl in a relieved voice, in which there was even a note of happiness. "It seems to me to be rubbish."

"Oh, I simply *love* these old-fashioned pieces, where all the poor young men turn out to be baronets, and all the women marry their first loves. They're so adorably untrue to life, don't you know," opined Beaufy. "One *wants* that sort of thing in a pessimistic age. Of course Ibsenism[1] and that sort of thing amuses me, but I don't really care for it."

"But that's very ungrateful of you," said Alison, turning suddenly round. Dr. Dunlop Strange had caught sight of Lady Blaythewaite in the box opposite, and his eyes seemed rivetted on her insolent, superb beauty. Somehow the fact annoyed her. Alison did not like Lady Blaythewaite.

The curtain drew up on the second act, revealing a rose-clambered cottage and a sundial. The play proceeded after the manner of love-stories which are enacted to lime light. Two sets of lovers, one arch, one sentimental, wandered through a wicket gate in rotation, though during the scene between the arch lovers—in which a watering pot and some artificial geraniums played a prominent part—it was noticeable that some of the habitual theatre-goers began a mumbled conversation. It was unmistakable, however, that the interest of the dress circle was aroused when a rising moon illuminated the embrace of the sentimental lovers, during which the ominous figure of an adventuress was seen hovering behind a hedge.

The door of the Higgins's box down below opened, and there was visible the figure of a youngish man against the pale gold of

---

1   Norwegian playwright Henrik Ibsen's (1828-1906) dramas were introduced to the London stage in the late 1880s and immediately caused a stir. His realistic depictions of the dark side of the middle class in *A Doll's House* (1879) and *Ghosts* (1881) caused an outcry from British literary traditionalists, who denounced the plays as "morbid" and condemned those who attended their performances.

the corridor. Mary could not see his face, which was black against the light. But in another instant the man, after shaking hands all round, had slipped into the chair behind the younger lady, and his face was now illuminated by the glare of the footlights. Miss Higgins began to fan herself violently with a jerky movement, and fidgeted about in her chair. Mary's eyes were riveted on the face of the newcomer. Just where she sat he could not see her. It was Vincent Hemming.

Then she turned her eyes away—as if ashamed—and kept them fixed upon the stage. The sentimental lovers were now swearing eternal fidelity, moving their arms like puppets pulled by wires. Were they the real puppets, Mary wondered, or she, Vincent, and Miss Higgins, and the Blaythewaites, each pulled this way and that by their passions, their ambitions, their desires. Vincent was in town, and she had heard nothing from him! True, she had not had many letters of late, but then he had been of course immersed in his election business. She had not expected to hear. And yet, why should he spend his first night in town with these people? Vincent, too, must have got the box. It was evidently his party. The mayor of a provincial town, however many times a millionaire, is not on the lists for first-nights at fashionable theatres in London.

On the stage Mary was conscious that the adventuress was advancing to the footlights murmuring the words, "my husband," and that the curtain was falling on the second act.

She sat with her eyes fixed on her lap. Every nerve in her body was drawn at full tension. It was a relief when the canvas door opened, and one or two men came in. She leaned back in her chair, saying anything, so as not to have to think. The pale-faced boy had slipped again into the chair behind her.

"What do you think I heard about the Higgins' heiress apparent?" he began. "I take such an interest in them, because, you see, I was the first to discover them. You see that man down there, sitting in her pocket? Well, that's Hemming, the man who's just got for Northborough. They say he's going to marry her."

"Is he?" said Mary, and she was astonished to find how natural her voice sounded. After all, she told herself, she knew how it would be on the day of his return from America.

"Yes; isn't it delicious? Why, one might as well be married to a housemaid. But they say he hasn't got a farthing, you know. She'll have twelve thousand a year just to start housekeeping. But the best of it is, I hear the poor devil wants to get out of it, only his worship won't let him off. Stands over him in his chains of office and waves the municipal mace. Says he only got him into the House as a prospective son-in-law. They say she's got a strong Lancashire accent," he concluded in his most malicious and triumphant tone.

"Indeed," said Mary, raising her eyelids, and letting them drop again with a tired gesture. Fortunately no one in the box had heard but herself. Both Lady Jane and Alison were talking to new arrivals. She made an effort—an effort which completely prostrated her next day—to look smiling, calm, imperturbable. Why, the very fabric of society was based on that acquiescent feminine smile. She, like other women before her, must learn her fate with the eyes of the world fixed curiously upon her. If she could only creep away somewhere, hide her face, not see the hideous comedy going on in the box down there, not have to look at the yellow footlights, watch the foolish, inane, unreal comedy on the stage. But she could not leave the theatre without making a scene, having explanations. The curtain rose on the last act.

"Vincent is going to marry Miss Higgins," she said to herself deliberately, as the arch pair of lovers entered quarrelling in a drawing-room set. She tried to realise what this new calamity meant to her, as the comic young gentleman on the stage essayed to appease the arch young lady's wrath by tying an errant shoelace. Vincent and Miss Higgins ... Vincent and Miss Higgins ... living together, always together, husband and wife in all the long, long years to come. For better, for worse, for richer, for poorer, in sickness and in health, till death did them part.... It was with the blurred vision which accompanies mental anguish that Mary saw that the happiness of the sentimental lovers was not to be frustrated, for the adventuress, it transpired, was a bigamist, and was already married. Married! Merciful God! Why Vincent and that girl in the box down below—they, too, were going to be married.

"Dear, you look dreadfully white," said Alison, catching sight of Mary's face. With a fixed, mechanical smile, Mary was thanking Mr. Flower, who was playfully throwing a boa round her shoulders. "I'm afraid you're tired. The play bored one horribly, didn't it? And the theatre's so hot—"

"I'm all right," said Mary, heroically. "It's nothing."

People spoke to her as she went downstairs and along the corridor, and she answered them with pale mauvish lips. Such a charming, pretty piece, wasn't it? Quite an idyl, and so wholesome, after these disgusting plays about heredity,[1] and so on.... It was quite a relief, they said, to get a thoroughly English piece with a happy ending.

And in the pushing crowd at the door her lover almost brushed her elbow as he passed her unwittingly with the Lancashire heiress. The girl, Mary could see, wore the triumphant expression of the underbred young woman who has secured a desirable husband. Mary hardly dared look at Vincent, though every fibre in her body yearned toward him; but as he passed out, with Miss Higgins leaning heavily on his arm, she had a brief vision of a harassed, sheepish, and uneasy face.

"Why, he is unhappy!" she thought, with a pang.

## CHAPTER XVII
## TWO ULTIMATUMS

IN the professional solemnity of the consulting-room, the large, fat face of Dr. Danby looked grave. Tapping his stethoscope, with which he had just made an examination of Mary, he looked her straight in the eyes.

"The fact is, my child, you ought to know the truth. You will not, believe me, be able to do the work you are doing. As a matter of fact, you are very, very far from strong. Nothing dangerous, I admit, but great delicacy," he added thoughtfully, pronouncing the word "delicacy" with a certain unction, as an adjective which applied mostly to charming young women. "None of the vital organs are attacked as yet," he went on, "but there is a terrible want of tone. If I were asked to describe you, I should say you were a bundle of nerves. Slightly anæmic, too," continued the doctor, frowning. "You live too much in London. There is too much strain on the nervous system. You have, you see, an unfortunate previous history. Your father, you must remember, was not able to stand the strain; your poor mother died when she was a mere girl. A mere girl," repeated the great man, shaking his head.

"Well, that, at any rate, I shall not be able to accomplish," said Mary drily. "You know, doctor, that I am nearly twenty-eight."

---

1   A reference to Ibsen's 1881 *Ghosts*, a three-act drama that examines the problems inherent in a slavish devotion to conventional morality, though it is ostensibly a portrait of the ruin wrought by congenital venereal disease in the family of Captain Alving.

"Dear me, dear me—you don't look it." And then he added briskly, taking out a sheet of paper and beginning to write a prescription, "I should like to have all you young ladies living a healthy, out-of-door life, happily married, and with no mental worries. There is something wrong somewhere," he muttered to himself, "with our boasted civilisation. It's all unnatural. Not fit, not fit for girls."

There was a silence. Mary said nothing, but observed, with much interest, a sparrow which was conveying to a nest in the drain-pipe a crust of bread which the servants had thrown out in the yard. Since Vincent's letter—a long, characteristic letter—speaking of new duties and obligations, of personal sacrifices for the cause he had so much at heart, and of his dread of dragging her down "to a life of pecuniary restraints and restricted horizons"—she had almost felt as if she must give up the fight. Her nerves were completely unstrung, but she had never stopped working. In work there was at least forgetfulness.

"Arsenic, iron, and strychnine, with something for the nerves," said the doctor thoughtfully; "and the Volnay[1] I told you of before. There should be a complete change of scene and ideas."

"I'll try the tonic and the burgundy, please," said Mary drearily, as she rose to go. "I cannot leave London now; and I don't see any prospect of doing so. And—and—it isn't exactly serious, dear Dr. Danby?" she continued, looking him, in her turn, straight in the face with her charming eyes.

"My dear child," he said kindly, "life without health and happiness is not worth having. Let me beg you to stop, to take care of yourself, to think of others," he added vaguely.

"I wonder who I've got to think of?" thought Mary, as she went down the steps of the trim Mayfair house. "Jimmie, who will probably marry before he is one-and-twenty? Aunt Julia, at Bournemouth, who thinks I am given over to the Evil One since I've become a journalist. Vincent?"—but here Mary pulled up her thoughts with a jerk. Yet the words "life without health and happiness, very del-i-cate," repeated themselves in her brain, as she made her way toward the Strand, where she had an appointment with the editor of *Illustrations*.

And with this new care pressing upon her, never had the Strand

---

1  An elegant burgundy from the village of Volnay near Meursault, France.

seemed so dreary, so cheaply vicious, as to-day under the hurrying clouds.

"Spesh—shul!—*Globe* piper—*St. James's Gizett*—*Pall Mall*," shouted a newsboy in her ear, at Charing Cross;* and looking down she read, in blue or red letters, spattered and stained with London mud, the posters of the evening newspapers: "The Great Divorce Case. Cross-Examination of the Plaintiff. Unabridged Report. Ladies Ordered Out of Court. Sketches of the Co-Respondents." For the Blaythewaite scandal hung, like a pestilence, over England. Like some foul miasma, it poisoned everything. It met the eye, in columns of close print, at the breakfast-table; it formed the one subject of conversation wherever people met. With hoarse laughs and brutal jests, it was discussed in public houses and at street corners; with tepid, meaning smiles and shrugged shoulders in drawing-rooms and clubs.

And meanwhile, the great tide of humanity swept on. A dray had got across the narrow street, and a procession of loaded omnibuses, whose drivers were bandying oaths and scathing Cockney satire, drew up at the curb. Outside Charing Cross station two girls in tawdry capes were quarrelling and gesticulating, while a man in a round hat, who had just arrived by train, and who appeared to be the cause of the dispute, turned from them both, hailed a hansom, and drove off with a relieved air. A small gaping crowd at once gathered round the wranglers on the pavement. "Run 'em both in," said a raucous voice on the fringe of the crowd; and, indeed, a policeman's helmet was now seen bearing down toward the group. Mary hurried on.

Further on there were sordid little eating-houses displaying a joint of raw meat, a cauliflower, and a plate of oysters; and dark, narrow passages—the entrances to theatres—ornamented with coloured posters of the latest three-act farce. Inexpressibly dreary were the pictures which invited one within: representations of elderly ladies in black silk, falling backward into hip-baths; monster heads of comedians, with flaxen wigs and brick-red complexions, displaying all their teeth in a frightful grin; full-length posters of girls with knowing smiles and abnormally developed limbs: while further on, outside a music-hall, was the picture of a raffish-looking dwarf, who was described with engaging optimism as "screamingly funny."

"Spesh—shul! Extra spesh—shul! The great divorce case! Extraordinary evidence! Cross-examination of Sir Horace Blaythewaite!" shouted a small newsvendor in Mary's ear, as she waited at

Wellington Street* to cross. And all the while, as she hurried along to the office of *Illustrations*, with this new terror of broken health knocking at her brain, she wondered what the abrupt summons could mean which she had received from the editor. Half of the MS. of her novel was in his hands. Could it be possible that he was going to refuse it?

With some trepidation Mary gave her name to her old admirer the small office boy, whom she found casting a supercilious eye over the current number of the paper, while he furtively sucked an acid drop. And in due time she found herself ushered into the editor's private room. Six months of proof-reading, of interviewing incapable artists, of the thousand worries of a newspaper, had not made the manners of the editor of *Illustrations* more gracious.

"Good-day, Miss Erle. Take a chair. Want to talk to you."

"Is it anything," asked Mary, "about the novel?"

"The fact is," said the melancholy looking man, tapping with an irritable looking hand on a pile of manuscript near his desk, which Mary recognised, with some anxiety, as her own, "it won't do at all. It won't do at all."

"It—won't do?" faltered Mary. "Why, I've written it just as you told me. There's a forged will in the first volume, a picnic in the second—"

"Oh, that's all right," interrupted the editor. "But, my dear girl," he added, "you've put the most extraordinary things in this last chapter. Why, there's a young man making love to his friend's wife. I can't put that sort of thing in my paper. The public won't stand it, my dear girl. They want thoroughly healthy reading."

"Do they?" said Mary, who could not help remembering the columns of unedifying matter which had lain on the breakfast-table that morning, nor the newsboys vending the latest details of the great scandal, served red hot, at the street corners. "I thought," she continued quietly, "that the public would take anything—in a newspaper."

For a minute the editor looked perplexed. Then, frowning slightly, he went on: "Not in fiction—not in fiction. Must be fit to go into every parsonage in England. Remember that you write chiefly for healthy English homes."

"But even the people in the country parsonage must occasionally see life as it is—or do they go about with their eyes shut?" ventured Mary quietly.

"Well, we're not going to encourage that sort of thing," he said conclusively, getting up and putting his mouth to the telephone.[1]

"Hullo! Richards! No. Yes, yes, of course. Not got the portrait of Lady Blaythewaite? What? Spoiled? Take another kodak[2] into court, then. Eh? Yes. See that it's a good likeness. All the co-respondents for this week's issue. And see that they're touched up. What? Yes, yes. A couple of pages of drawings."

The editor sat down again. Their eyes met.

"The fact is," he said, looking rather foolish, "novels are—er—well—novels. The British public doesn't expect them to be like life. And if you take my advice, Miss Erle, and cultivate your talents in the right way, you will be able to make a—a—comfortable income. Only there must be a thoroughly breezy, healthy tone."

"Oh, as to breezy," said Mary, in a tired voice, "I never somehow feel like that. I don't know how it is, but I can't help seeing things as they are, and the truth is so supremely attractive."

"But it is just what the public won't stand," repeated the editor. "Now take this chapter back and reconsider it. This young man, now—he isn't a principal character in the story—couldn't you make him her cousin—or her brother!"

"Oh, anything you like," said Mary, taking the manuscript; "but I did like that chapter. I took so much trouble over it. It was a little bit of real observation."

"That's right. And if you don't mind my saying so, there aren't quite enough love scenes between the hero and the heroine. The public like love scenes, and besides, they illustrate so well."

"Is there anything more?" said Mary, trying to force the manuscript into her pocket.

"I should suggest a thoroughly happy ending. The public like happy endings. The novelists are getting so morbid. It's all these French and Russian writers[3] that have done it. It's really difficult now to get a thoroughly breezy book with a wedding at the end.

---

1  Alexander Graham Bell invented the telephone in 1876. England's first government telephone exchange opened at the GPO in 1882.

2  The Kodak hand-held camera was introduced by George Eastman in 1888.

3  A reference to, among others, French novelist Émile Zola (1840-1902), the father of "literary Naturalism" whose grim depictions of the moral poverty of the human condition were often banned in Great Britain, and to Russian novelist Fyodor Dostoyevsky (1821-81), whose dark psychological explorations of the soul of man profoundly influenced the twentieth-century novel.

Take my advice and stick to pretty stories. They're bound to pay best."

"That's what Perry Jackson thinks," said Mary to herself, as she stepped out into the windy Strand. "And he certainly understands—he always did understand—the public."

She walked along with a staring, motley crowd jogging her elbow. The *banal*, the pretty-pretty, the obvious! This was what she was to write—if she wanted to make any money to keep her head above water. And the kindly words of the doctor reiterated themselves in her brain: "All you young ladies ought to be living a healthy, out-door life, happily married, and with no mental worries!" And then, with a kind of obstinate courage, she thought of what she should do to get better. She would try and eat more meat; she would order some burgundy at the stores; she would try and get more out in the open air; and there was the tonic—the arsenic and strychnine—which sometimes, for a week or two, seemed to give her a fresh lease of life. "We've got to be dosed with poisons to make us fit to sit at a desk and write—twaddle."

She had a number of things to order, and it was late when she got out of the stores. The outlines of the long narrow street were growing vague in the twilight. The omnibuses, loaded inside and out, loomed in dark masses against the pink western sky. The aspect of the crowd had changed. Hardly any women were to be seen, and the newsboys, bawling their loudest, were thrusting their wares in the faces of busy lawyers hurrying from the courts. With the passing hours, events, it would seem, had waxed more exciting.

"Spesh-shul! Extry Spesh-shul! Fifth Edition! Sir Horace Blaythewaite in the box! Revolting details! The great divorce case!" shouted the newsboys.

And beneath the cold, unheeding, scudding clouds, the world which writes and buys and sells the news of the evening was pushing, hurrying, and jostling elbows up and down the wind-swept Strand.

## CHAPTER XVIII
## NUMBER TWENTY-SEVEN

THE vast, mud-coloured building loomed out of the fog as the doctor's coachman drew up, with a jerk, under the portico. Against the dark lining of the carriage the fine drawing of a man's profile was visible by the light of a portable lamp. There were irritable folds at the corners of the mouth, a restless look in the keen eyes, as they travelled over the page he was reading. Dr. Dunlop Strange only folded up the medical paper he had been studying as he went up the steps of the Whitechapel Hospital. It was his habit to allow himself no time for vagrant thoughts, so that even to-day, when he was to meet Alison and take her over the hospital along with Mary Erle, even to-day his mind ran on professional matters.

Inside the large bare hall, where a marble statue of the Queen loomed chillily out of the vague half-light, Alison and Mary, the latter carrying a leather note-book, were already awaiting him. Dunlop Strange looked at Alison, taking in every detail of her radiant personality with his swift professional glance. In the after years he always preferred to think of her as he saw her that instant, standing by the white marble statue of the Queen, for never again did she look at him with the same clear, cordial eyes.

The doctor and Alison met as people meet who are more than interested in each other. For some time past she had known that he was devoted to her, and the girl had almost made up her mind, if he asked her, she would accept him. It was a busy, sensible life, that of a doctor's wife, she told herself; and, after all, in her world, one had to marry some day or other. One couldn't permit one's self the luxury of being an old maid, unless one had an income of over five thousand pounds a year. But there was no particular hurry, she said, when well-meaning friends bothered her about it. They were both of a certain age. They both had their own occupations, their own hobbies.

The doctor never took his eyes from her face. To have this woman for his wife would be the crowning act of a brilliantly successful career. He only hesitated to speak until he had received the baronetcy which was in store for him. Not that Alison herself would care; she had none of the usual feminine ambitions; but the doctor was quite aware that it would influence Lady Jane, who had made up her mind that Alison, when she married, should only make, if she could help it, what she called a "sensible match."

They went up a stone staircase, to which a somewhat false air of cheerfulness was imparted by a grass-green painted dado, surmounted by a bright lavender-toned wall, passing a large window giving on a grimy back garden, a garden whose sodden grass plot was closed in by high brown brick walls, and over which hung a heavy, fog-laden sky, etched with sooty branches. On the first landing there was a closed door, and outside an empty stretcher, beside which two hospital porters were waiting. Suddenly the door was pushed ajar, and for an instant there was a vision of anxious, inquisitive faces, lit up by a glare of gas; of a nurse's back, bending forward, and of a surgeon's face, blowing spray on to something that was invisible. Over all an intense silence, broken only by the hoarse whispers of the porters with the stretcher, wondering how long they would have to wait.

"There don't seem to be many students in there," said Alison, in her practical voice.

"No, they don't crowd in here like they do in the other hospitals. We've so many operations, you see. Two or three every afternoon all the year round."

Upstairs, in the Charlotte Ward, the fifty red-quilted beds effaced themselves in the gloom of the winter afternoon. There was a vague odour of medicine, overpowered by that of patent disinfectants. All the beds were alike; there were blue-and-white checked curtains and vallance, a rope by which the patient could pull herself into a sitting posture, a cupboard with food and medicines inside, and a cardboard overhead, on which the number, age, disease, and diet of the patient were all duly inscribed. Yes, the little beds, thought Mary, were curiously alike, and yet on every mattress a different form of pain was being endured.

"Kidney disease, congestion of the lungs, abscess of the liver, peritonitis," said the doctor in an undertone as the two girls passed down the room. A screen was placed round one of the narrow bedsteads.

"What is that for?" whispered Mary.

"Hopeless case," answered the doctor gravely. "It is probably all over by now. We do that to spare the other patients. Death scenes have a bad moral effect."

"And—and how long do they stay there after it's all over?"

"Oh, they are removed to the mortuary at once."

At intervals down the long room, with its shining white boards, blazed large fires, lighting up here and there the bland, unemotional features of a nurse, under her smooth hair and white cap—the sexless features of a woman who has learnt to witness suffering without a sign. Yet they brightened the room, these girls in their lilac cotton gowns and ample aprons, suggesting an out-of-doors where people are healthy and happy, a place where no one was agonising—these nurses, their practical faces, and their strong helpful hands.

On hearing that Dr. Strange was taking some ladies round, Sister Charlotte, the superintendent of the ward, emerged from her private room and hurried forward. The Sister was a long-nosed woman of thirty-five, with bright eyes and a singularly nice manner. The doctor introduced the three ladies to each other, and Sister Charlotte talked, moving forward all the time with a professional look on her bright face. They stopped, now, at every bed. Mary asked questions in an undertone, and Dunlop Strange, whose hospital manner was proverbial, addressed each sick woman in the same tone he would have employed to a duchess. His way with women was one of the things for which he was justly famous. And in this manner the little procession moved somewhat slowly along.

They had come to the end of one line of beds, and were now about to turn up the other end of the room. Sister Charlotte stopped.

"We have a new patient there, doctor," she said briskly. "Number Twenty-seven. A hopeless case of rapid consumption. Poor creature," she whispered to Alison, "she was in a terrible state when she came. I can't tell you. They brought her in from one of the common lodging houses. It seems she tried to commit suicide last summer, on one of those bitterly cold days that we had, but the police fished her out of the canal, and managed to pump back the life into her. That was the beginning of her lung-trouble. Since then she must have sunk very low."

All four stepped up to the foot of the narrow bed. The patient's back was turned to them. She was only a shapeless lump, breathing heavily under the red coverlet. The atmosphere about Number Twenty-seven was unpleasant.

"Don't let's disturb her," said Alison, in a faintly disgusted tone. "Why hadn't they let the wretched woman drown in that muddy canal water, before she could be sucked down in the awful whirlpool of vice. It would have been far better," she said softly to herself.

But there are things written by the great penman we call destiny, which no man's remorse can erase and no woman's tears wash out. Number Twenty-seven tossed over and lay on her back, and the course of two lives was altered.

Number Twenty-seven lay on her back, her vicious face, with its hard mouth and the brownish-pink flush on each cheek-bone, looking sharply emaciated against the whiteness of the pillow. Her fringe, reaching nearly to her eyebrows, was faded and lank; the mouth, with its singularly hard lines, was swollen and livid.

"Oh Alison," whispered Mary, "I know her, although she's terribly changed. I've often seen her, waiting, poor soul, in the Regent's Park, for someone."

Dr. Dunlop Strange bent forward with his searching professional glance. He was famous at diagnosis. He put his hand on her
wrist, and their eyes met. Good God! Could it be? His heart
absolutely stood still. Was this horrible wreck his little girl, the girl
he had taken such a fancy to only a year or two ago? The girl who
had been so fond of him, but who had grown so bad-tempered and
suspicious that he had been obliged to break off all relations with
her. And, merciful God! could it be that this woman—the unsight-
ly corpse, as it were, of his dead pleasure—was going to speak; was
about to spoil the happiness of his whole future life? In all his
forty-five years Dr. Dunlop Strange had never known such an odious moment.

But Number Twenty-seven only laughed—an unmirthful,
coarse, and empty laugh.

"Oh, lord, *are you here?*" she muttered, staring the doctor straight
in the eyes. Then she tossed over.

It was a curious scene. The doctor drew a long breath; he had
grown visibly paler before he spoke. The nurse stared. Alison's eyes
were fixed on the bed quilt. Mary looked perplexed.

"Poor creature! She mistakes me for someone else," he said at
last, in a voice which he tried hard to make natural. "They often
do, just at the last," he added in a lower tone. And then, taking
down the card hung over the bed, on which the patient's age, disease, and diet, as well as the physician's name in charge of the case
were written, he continued in his sympathetic voice:

"Quite right; perfectly right. Dr. Brown, I see, has ordered
everything that could possibly be of use. Sister, look after this case
especially."

Alison roused herself, bent over the patient, saying something
kind, and passed on in a kind of dream. Not an incident of the
strange scene had escaped her. She felt a curious kind of nausea;
perhaps it was the air of the ward. It sounded far-off, the chat and
the talk round the other beds, as they passed up the ward. She felt
an irresistible desire to go back and speak to that poor outcast on
the hospital mattress. They passed to another girl—the battered
leavings of the lust of a great city—and farther on a sallow, bright-
eyed young woman sitting up in bed, who, Sister Charlotte whispered, they must make haste to cure and discharge, as in a month
or two she would become a mother.

"She will become a mother," thought Alison, "the mother, perhaps, of a baby-girl, destined, before she is born, to become like
one of those!"

The face of Number Twenty-seven became an obsession. She must go back and hear her story. Perhaps she could help her, save her, send her out to a farm she knew of at the Cape, where even such as she might begin a new life. People often got well at the Cape when they were far gone in consumption. Mechanically she walked along with the others; through the Jewish wards now, where the sallow faces of dark-eyed Poles and Germans were seen on the narrow pillows, and here and there a handsome, refined face and an elaborate velvet mantle was seen bending over the meagre coverlets.

"These Jewish women are the best looked after in the whole hospital," whispered Sister Charlotte, who had left her own ward and was accompanying the girls. "There are always Jewish ladies here reading to them, inquiring into their cases, seeing after them when they leave."

"Yes? Seeing after them when they leave? That's so sensible," said Alison to the nurse. The doctor and Mary were a little way in front. He was explaining to her an operation which would have to be performed next day on a tiny, pale girl in a cot.

"I should like, Sister Charlotte," she said, trying to make her voice sound indifferent, "to come and see that poor woman— Number Twenty-seven—to-morrow. I have taken an interest in her case. Tell me, where does she come from—what sort of a girl *was* she before—?"

"Oh, she's not a Londoner. Came from Sussex two or three years ago."

"I might," said Alison, "be able to do something for her. I will, if you will let me, come to-morrow."

"You will allow me to drive you both home," said Dr. Dunlop Strange, in his decided way, as they stepped out into the grey mud, the orange gas-lights, and the shuffling crowd of the Whitechapel Road. But there was not much conversation as the carriage rolled westward through the deepening gloom. Mary and the doctor talked spasmodically. Alison hardly spoke.

## CHAPTER XIX
## DUNLOP STRANGE MAKES A MISTAKE

IT was three minutes to eight. Round the marble mantelpiece in the great empty looking drawing-room in Portman Square, a small circle of guests were gathered. Lady Jane was talking. She had been a wit and a beauty in her youth, and with the garrulity of old age, she liked to talk of her triumphs; of her flirtation with Bulwer Lytton,[1] whose waistcoats and whose romances were just then turning the heads of all the women; of the occasion when she snatched a celebrity from Lady Palmerston; that season—nearly half a century ago now—she had interrupted a diplomatic love affair of Princess Lieven's,[2] and, above all, of Disraeli, who, up to the last, had continued to scintillate at her dinner-parties. To-night she was discussing Lord Beaconsfield's cautious affairs of the heart with a little old man, whose parchment face had wrinkled and whose hair had whitened in the service of his country at various minor European courts.

"I always heard, you know, that she was formally engaged to him when her husband was still alive. He went there every day. The thing was accepted."

The wrinkled old man had a senile chuckle, which not infrequently turned into a cough.

"He, he, my dear lady! I know it for a fact. And then there was the other woman. The old lady that used to make appointments with him by the great fountain at the Crystal Palace—"[3]

"And who left him all her money."

"How quite too delicious! Early Victorian scandal," whispered the pale-faced boy to Lady Blaythewaite, who, in her *rôle* of pretty woman, was standing in her favourite swaggering attitude on the hearth-rug, a radiant vision of stolid pink-and-white flesh. "Don't you want to hear it?"

"I don't know who they're talking about," said the pretty woman deliberately. "Does one ever meet these people anywhere—at dinner, or at Sandown?"

---

1  Edward George Earle Lytton, first Baron Lytton (1803-73), was among the more prolific early Victorian novelists. He made a fortune from his flashy "Newgate" novels—adventure stories dealing with criminals recorded in the *Newgate Calendar*—and lived extravagantly as a wit, a dandy, a man of fashion.

2  Princess Dorothea Lieven (1785-1857) was the wife of the Russian ambassador to London (1812-34). She was a brilliant socialite who spent much of her time entertaining the rich and famous in London and Paris.

3  The Crystal Palace was a huge conservatory built for the Great Exhibition of 1851. After the exhibition, the Palace itself was removed from Hyde Park and reconstructed in what is now Crystal Palace Park in Sydenham, south of the Thames. The Palace burned in 1936.

"Oh, they're all dead," sniggered the pale-faced boy, patting the Parma violets in his coat.

"Then why didn't you say so before, you little idiot," announced her ladyship in her rather high voice. She was vaguely afraid of the boy's malicious tongue, but she tolerated him about her because she was more afraid of the spiteful things he would say if she didn't.

"But it's deliciously amusing, Lady Jane's scandal, isn't it?" he continued, with a little wriggle which disposed of the pretty woman's snub. "Can you picture an intrigue in side spring boots, the *coup de foudre*[1] from a spoon-bonnet and a burnous, and white, *blue-white* stockings?"

"No, I can't. They must have looked frumps," replied the lady, with a complacent survey of her Paris frock and her somewhat obvious charms in the huge gilt mirror. It was two months now since the great divorce case; it was considered dull to talk about it any more. The whole affair had remained nebulous. Neither side had been able to obtain a verdict, but most people took the lady's part. Sir Horace was old, ugly, and vicious; she was young, pretty, and "smart." The husband had gone away in his steam yacht to investigate the South Sea Islands, and meanwhile Lady Blythe-waite made a point of being seen everywhere, especially at houses which she would have voted "frumpish" a year ago.

The guests were arriving quickly now. Mr. Bosanquet-Barry, very pink-and-white and important, with something to tell Lady Jane which had to be told in a distant corner, while his hostess tapped him several times playfully with a small carved ivory fan; the Irish Viceroy, over on important business; a well-known beauty without her husband, who was annoyed when she found she was not the last, as she had wished to make an effective entry; Mary, looking pretty in a faint mauve dress; a smart A.D.C. from India,[2] with a crooked line of sunburn across his forehead and a naïve enthusiasm for the two London beauties; and the Attorney-General, famous for his good stories.

"It is my own child," complained Lady Jane to the Viceroy, who had more than once advanced to offer his arm, under the impression that dinner had been announced, "who keeps me waiting for

1 Thunderbolt.
2 *Aide de Camp*, a military officer acting as a secretary or assistant to a superior officer of general rank.

my dinner. Would you believe that that girl of mine spends half her time in a workman's flat, or poking about in those horrible smelly streets in Whitechapel."

"Young ladies," said the Viceroy, frowning, for he was very hungry, "have curious ideas of amusing themselves nowadays."

"In our time, balls and parties were supposed to suffice. But I can't get my child to take a proper interest in society," complained Lady Jane. "I tell her it's absurd. Why, it's such a refuge for a woman in her old age. But it's always the same story. When she is young and pretty, society cares for the woman, but when she is old and—well—repaired, it is of course she who cares for society."

Just then Alison slipped in quietly. "Please forgive me, mother, for being late," she said, in a tired little voice, as she kissed Lady Jane on each plump cheek. "I'm dead tired. I only got home from the hospital at seven."

"Well, you're not the last," said her mother. "Our dear Dunlop Strange hasn't come yet, and he's to take you down."

"Dr. Strange?" said Alison. Her face had become quite white. "I thought he was in Brussels? It was in all the papers that he had been sent for from Laeken."[1]

"So he was. But he'll be back for my dinner to-night. I know, too, he's got an important consultation to-morrow. But we can't wait," said Lady Jane, ringing the bell.

The long procession began to move slowly to the dining-room. Alison went down alone. She took her soup in silence, thankful for the empty chair beside her. Oh, if only something would keep him away to-night. She could not bear it. She was tired, her head ached, her throat felt dry, and she must have caught a chill. A fine drizzle had been falling when she left the Whitechapel Hospital, and nowhere was there a cab to be seen. The long journey home in an omnibus, an omnibus for which she had waited a long time at a corner, had thoroughly tired and chilled her. The conventional voices of the men, the foolish, fixed smiles of the women all around struck her to-night as more than usually puerile. How endless seemed the long procession of fishes and *entrées*, of hocks and clarets! What a foolish superabundance of food.... At one moment, she made up her mind she would get up and slip out of the room. The commonplace voice of Lady Blaythewaite, making the somewhat bald statement that she intended to start for Monte Carlo on

---

1   A district in Brussels, Belgium.

the 28th of the following month, bored and irritated her. On her right hand two people were passionately discussing the way in which red mullet should be cooked. The lady, it would seem, was all for *papillotes*,[1] whereas the gentleman could not endure them without being stuffed and served with port-wine sauce. It was the only moment of the dinner at which the conversation on her right hand had approached any sort of enthusiasm. The wrinkled diplomat, who sat on her mother's left hand, was resuscitating some details of Lola Montez in '48 for her special delectation.[2] The Viceroy was solemnly consuming his dinner. Through the epergnes[3] Alison could hear Mr. Bosanquet-Barry, under the soothing influence of Lady Jane's excellent champagne, airily inciting Mary to write art criticisms for the *Comet*; a fact which Alison was certain he would forget the very next morning. The odour of hot-house flowers, the smell of the meats, the very bouquet of the wines, seemed to overpower her. She had made up her mind to go, when the chair next to her was pulled out, and Dunlop Strange sat down beside her.

It was too late now. She could not leave the room without all London knowing that—

"I'm so sorry. The boat was late getting into Dover, and I've only just got here," said Strange.

"Then I'll let you eat your dinner, doctor," said Alison, making a civil effort, "you must be tired and hungry."

"No, no fish or soup. I'll have what's going," said the doctor to the obsequious butler, who regarded him already as the son-in-law of the house.

"You're a wicked man," cried Lady Jane down the table. "Why didn't you come before? My cook won't forgive you, even if I do."

But Dunlop Strange, as he drank off a glass of champagne and looked round the table, felt tenderly disposed to all the world. He felt, rather than saw, the beautiful profile at his side. He was always

---

1   Fillets of meat or fish cooked in a greased paper wrapper.
2   Lola Montez (1818-61), delicately referred to by her Victorian contemporaries as "La Grande Horizontale," was perhaps the period's greatest *femme fatale*. She was said to have had affairs with the Czar of Russia, Franz Liszt, and Alexandre Dumas *père*, among many others before making her way to California during the gold rush. She died in poverty in New York.
3   Elaborate centerpieces, usually silver or glass and compartmentalized for use as serving dishes.

intensely conscious of Alison's presence. He knew when she was in a room even before he had seen her. No woman that he had ever met had ever attracted him like this one. And in gracefully artificial moments like these Dunlop Strange was happy. The factitious and fleeting emotions which he experienced in society delighted him—emotions heightened by a rare vintage, made memorable by an elaborate dish, accentuated by a fine feminine smile. The half-chaffing, half-caressing tone in which his patients addressed him (for Dunlop Strange was popular with great ladies); the *rôle*, three-parts confessor and one-fourth adorer, which he played with these beautiful victims of the vapours and the megrims, appealed direct-ly to his vanity. He had around him continually in his consulting-room of a morning, during his afternoons spent rapidly driving from one enervating boudoir to another, and at night in society, a voluptuous feminine atmosphere, an atmosphere which had become part of his life, and which he could no more dispense with now than the fine burgundy he was wont to drink at his dinner, the special Havana which assisted the process of digestion after-wards. And there, close beside him, his arm almost touching hers at the crowded dinner-table, sat the woman who was more to him than any other feminine personality—the woman who was to make him one of the most envied men in London.

Alison was speaking now to her neighbour on the right, but Strange was struck, when she turned round, with the hard look on her face. There was an expression in the girl's eyes to-night which he had never seen there, and which he could not quite understand, unless—

"You look tired," he said, in his soft, professional voice. "What have you been doing to-day?"

"I? Oh, I have been at the Whitechapel Hospital. I have been there several times since that day we went with you," she added quietly.

"I wish to Heaven you would not run any such risk! We doc-tors are hardened, you know, but there is always the fear of infec-tion for delicate women."

"I did not," said Alison, "go near the fever ward. I went to see—Sister Charlotte."

Just then Lady Blaythewaite, who was on Strange's left, turned her rather prominent eyes upon him, and for a quarter of an hour Dr. Dunlop Strange was not suffered to waver in his dinner-table devotion, though he was tortured with doubts about Alison—about the girl in the hospital. It was absurd, it was melodramatic, that the girl should have turned up again like a thing in a penny novelette. But with this ugly fact knocking at his brain, he had to lend an attentive ear to the pretty woman's confidences about the Cambridgeshire, and how much ready cash she expected to "land" by her somewhat elaborate transactions. Vaguely, as in a dream, the doctor heard about a dark horse—a certain "Miss Gwendolen"— who had just been scratched, and some foreign admirer, who, it appeared, put Lady Blaythewaite on to various good things. On his other side an animated discussion on the subject of liqueurs was in hand, in which Miss Ives was politely pretending to take an interest. The merits of Kirsch, of Benedictine, of Elixir de Spa, were contended for with some spirit and success, while the pretty woman, joining in, declared herself entirely in favour of green Chartreuse.[1] The subject was beginning to show signs of wear when the doctor turned to Alison:

"And so you went to see Sister Charlotte again? A capital woman. Plenty of common sense—no nonsense about her. The sort of person you can trust."

"I am glad of that," replied Alison quietly, "for she gave me a great deal of information on a subject I am intensely interested in."

"And what," said Strange, with a somewhat uneasy smile, "and what, may I ask, is that?"

"I am interested, doctor, in poor creatures like Number Twenty-seven."

"Ah!" sighed Strange, frowning slightly, as he reached out his hand to the glass of Château Lafite[2] which the butler had just poured carefully out, holding the bottle in its wicker cage like a very treasure lest one drop of the dregs should reach the glass. "Dear Miss Alison, those are terrible cases. They are cankerous evils, eating away the very life of our social system."

Alison looked at him, and there was a royal scorn in her glance. What, he was going to brazen it out, then; to pretend that he knew nothing?

"My dear doctor," she said, very slowly and softly, "you forget

---

1  Continental liqueurs: the first, a brandy, comes from Germany and Switzerland; the second is a sweet liqueur originated by Benedictine monks at Fécamp, France; the third mentioned is from Belgium. The last mentioned, Chartreuse, is usually a bright green liqueur made by the Carthusian monks in Chartreuse, France.
2  The wine of Lafite Castle, in Guienne. In 1755, the Governor of Guienne likened this wine to the discovery of the Fountain of Youth.

that Mr. Lecky[1] maintains that, on the contrary, Number Twenty-seven is the martyr of civilisation.'

"It is a subject," murmured Strange, with a slight movement of the shoulders, "which I must admit I find painful to discuss with young ladies."

"Ah!" said Alison, in her quiet, serious voice, "but then I am not a 'young lady.' I am only a woman, taking a great deal of interest in others of my own sex. The girl, at any rate, seems to be what we are now agreed to call a 'morally deficient person'—one, in fact, who has urgent claims on all men's honour, on all women's pity. Properly trained and protected, she might have been well, happy, and a tolerably useful member of society. Think of it! That woman was younger than I am. If I had only known her earlier, who knows? I might have been her friend; I might have saved her from—"

"Possibly," replied the doctor coolly, "but meanwhile—"

"Meanwhile the girl has succumbed. She died last night."

There was a burst of laughter from each side of the table. The Attorney-General had just told his newest story. Dr. Dunlop Strange was carefully peeling a fine pear as she spoke. In the pause that followed he continued to separate the fruit from its perfumed skin, bending a little, in his short-sighted way, over his Sèvres plate. All his future life, he knew, was involved in her next few words.

"My dear Miss Ives," he said, with something of his consulting-room manner, "pray, don't judge hastily. You have probably only heard half the story. Do you, now, really *know* anything about her?"

"Yes," said Alison abruptly. And, as she looked him straight in the eyes, he knew that she was aware of the whole sordid story.

"I'm not particularly sentimental, as you know," she added; "but I've made up my mind that that poor creature shall be decently buried in the little country churchyard in Sussex, where she used to live. I should like her to rest now, for good. Shall I make the necessary arrangements, or will you," she added, with a shade of irony, "prefer perhaps to do so?"

They were standing up now, for the ladies, gathering up their fans and gloves, were about to leave the room. He looked at her

---

1   William Edward Hartpole Lecky (1838-1903) was an Irish essayist, historian, and politician. Opposing modern Utilitarian economics, he argued that the country's poor should not be ignored, and that the highest acts of virtue are acts of self-sacrifice.

humbly, imploringly, but the beautiful candid eyes were quite hard.

"I—I—perhaps it would be better, on the whole, if you allowed me to see to it."

Nothing more was said. He sat down again when she was gone, staring blankly at the fruit-strewn plates and half-drained glasses, at the tall épergnes and flickering candles. Her crumpled napkin fell across his knee, and, as it fell, he saw, with a shudder a vision of a stiff, silent figure in the hospital mortuary. He could hear the rustle of silk dresses and the sound of feminine voices as the ladies trailed upstairs. And he knew, as he heard them go, that it was all over. Yes, it was all over, for she, at any rate, was not one of those girls who have infinite complaisance for a possible husband.

A man drew up his chair, asked for a light, and began to talk of a bit of scandal that was then enjoying high favour at the clubs. Strange stared at him with haggard eyes, got up, made some excuse, and left the house.

## CHAPTER XX
### ALISON ARRANGES A MATCH

TWO or three days after the dinner in Portman Square, as Mary was trying to impart an air of reality to her "society" article in *The Fan*, a task at which she was busy on three mornings of every month, a pencil note was brought from Alison, dated, to her surprise, from Portman Square.

"Dear little girl," it said, "I'm down with an awful cold—bronchitis, I think. The doctor says I'm not to get up. It's such a nuisance my being seedy, because to-day is Evelina's wedding-day. She's to be married at 2:30. Will you, like a dear, go and see that she's dressed and bring her here to me? And my presents—the tea service and the work basket and the new cot for the baby—see that she has them, won't you?—Yours, ALISON."

"Tell the man," said Mary to the stolid maid of all work, who was waiting, with pendent red hands and slightly open mouth at the door, "that I shall be round in half an hour." There were still another dozen lines to write. The thing must be neatly turned, made acidulous, and sparkling; it took some fifteen minutes of writing and scratching out. Then mechanically she ran her eye once again over the lines, tied up the sheets of MS., and directed it to the editor of *The Fan* before she left the house.

Mary found the bride all dressed and ready when she reached

the flat. Always a silent girl, who accepted things as they came, Evelina seemed to-day paralysed with the excitement of her position. In silence they drove in a four-wheel cab to Portman Square. Lady Jane, with an uneasy look on her plump, worldly face, was issuing from Alison's bedroom when they got upstairs.

"That's so kind of you, my dear Mary. Go in—go in. My poor Alison wishes to see you. And this, no doubt, is the young person she is so interested in. My dear child has such a good heart. You will stay, will you not, while darling Alison is poorly? I have to go to a meeting of the Primrose League—the dear Primrose League. And Mary, my child," she added, as she rustled down the stairs in her ample garments, "kindly ask my maid, as you're near my room, to bring down my bottle of lavender salts; the strong ones with the gold top."

Alison was sitting up in bed, with her head slightly bent forward in a fit of coughing, as they stepped inside. It was in a large, gay-looking bedroom that she lay; a room furnished by Lady Jane in a style which she considered suitable to an unmarried daughter. There were many chintz draperies, patterned with sprawling pink roses; the pillows were trimmed with deep lace, and the ample silk eider-down quilt was of a piercing blue. Little pot-bellied Loves disported themselves on the round looking-glass, and a number of slim gold-and-white chairs were placed about the room. A bronchitis kettle[1] was steaming near the bed, and bright sunshine lay along the counterpane and in patches on the carpet.

"Here she is," said Mary; and Evelina, with loudly creaking boots, stepped, gawky and embarrassed in her finery, to the bedside, her red cheeks and wrists accentuated by the pallor of her soiled white-silk frock. A wreath of stiff kid orange blossoms lay on her wiry, dark hair, from which hung backward a veil of white tulle. One of the thumbs of her white silk gloves had already ripped up. On her ample bosom heaved and fell a gold locket, containing a curl of the baby's hair.

"Kiss me, my dear," whispered Alison; "I hope you are going to be very, very happy. I'm so sorry I can't be at the wedding."

"Oh, Miss Alison," cried the girl, "I'm so sorry you're—you're

---

1  A relative of the modern vaporizer, this device was, according to the *OED*, "a kettle with a long tube and a detachable medicator used for keeping the atmosphere of a room humid and for giving a medicated vapour inhalation to a patient in a case of bronchitis."

not well. Joe and me, we'd both like to put the wedding off till you could come—"

"Don't wait for that, Evelina," said Alison, an anxious look crossing her forehead; "you mustn't wait for that. Mary, you'll go with her to the church, and see that the wedding breakfast—"

"Yes, yes, dear. Don't tire yourself, thinking about it all. How did you catch this dreadful—cold?"

"Waiting for an omnibus in the Mile End Road. You know that night of the dinner here. I had been to the hospital. I must have caught a chill."

"Alison, I'm coming back."

"Oh, yes. Good-bye, my dear Evelina. I wish I could have been with you to-day," she said wistfully; "I hope you'll like the little house; and mind you look after Joe, and keep him steady. Good-bye, good luck!"

And a few minutes later the pink cheeks, the second-hand wedding dress, and the creaking boots were being conveyed in a four-wheeled cab toward matrimonial respectability.

Alison wanted to hear all about it when Mary got back.

"Well, and what did she say?" asked the sick woman.

"She didn't say anything. Brides never do," said Mary.

"And how did Joe behave?"

"As far as I could make out, he was terrified at me, and as I saw that in all probability he would eat nothing as long as I was there, I made an excuse, and left the wedding feast, no doubt to the intense relief of the guests."

"And the baby—my dear fat thing?"

"Oh, the baby," said Mary, "apparently belongs to the new anti-marriage movement. He doesn't approve, it would seem, of any legalising of the bond which unites his father and mother. At any rate, he screamed till he was purple in the face, and had to be removed from the room by a first cousin of his mamma's, a young lady who wore more ostrich feathers than I have ever seen on one human head. And as for poor Evelina," continued Mary, laughing, "I'm afraid, after all the pains you've taken, you haven't developed in her a sense of humour. Otherwise she wouldn't have insisted on being married in a second-hand white silk dress."

"You don't understand," returned Alison; "I think that it shows a certain vague hankering after the ideal—a sort of *élan* toward the unattainable."

"Nonsense! she ought to have been married in a good stout waterproof."

"Oh, thank goodness we're not all sensible. How dull it would be if we were."

"Well, I must say the kid orange blossoms and the reach-me-down wedding dress quite 'made my joy.'"

"You're an unsympathetic beast," said Alison, tossing on her rumpled pillows. "I shouldn't have laughed. I know these people so much better than you do."

Presently she fell into a doze, and Mary sat at the window, trying to read, but with her eyes and thoughts constantly on the bed, where Alison was tossing about in a curiously restless manner.

"Little Mary!" came a voice from the bed presently.

"Yes, dear."

"Promise me that you will never, never do anything to hurt another woman," said the sick girl, running her finger along the pattern on the counterpane. "I don't suppose for an instant you ever would. But there come times in our lives when we can do a great deal of good, or an incalculable amount of harm. If women only used their power in the right way! If we were only united we could lead the world. But we're not," she said, closing her eyes with a tired gesture.

"Yes," said Mary, "our time is dawning—at last. All we modern women are going to help each other, not to hinder. And there's a great deal to do!"

"Yes, it isn't a pretty world," said Alison warmly. "Do you remember the hospital, and that poor girl, Number Twenty-seven?"

"Yes, of course. What makes you think of her?" faltered Mary.

"She's dead, you know. It can't be nice to die in a hospital, can it? The ugly, long ward, those ghastly, twitching faces on the pillows, the students staring at you; then the mortuary and a pauper's funeral."

"Don't talk so, Alison."

"And yet that girl," muttered the sick woman, "was Dunlop Strange's mistress. He made her what she was."

"Oh Alison, are you *sure?*"

Alison nodded.

"I thought at first it might be a got-up story—one hears of such things, you know. But it was true, quite true. She had his photographs, his letters, little things that belonged to him. Mary, that wretched creature was a respectable girl—a shop assistant—when she first saw him. No, it isn't a pretty world!"

"And Dr. Strange? Does he know?"

"I told him that night at the dinner. I was furious. He tried to brave it out, to pretend he knew nothing about her. I hope," she added, while the anxious look deepened on her forehead, "that I shall never have to see him again. You won't," she said excitedly, "let them bring him up here, to me?"

"No, no; of course not."

But the thing seemed like an obsession to the sick girl.

"When did you see her, Mary?" she asked presently. "You seemed to know her when we stopped at that bed."

"I saw her once or twice, in the Regent's Park, waiting about for someone. One day a man came—I only saw his back. Then a long time after I saw her again, one day at the end of July. She waited a long time that day, but he didn't come."

"That was the day they pulled her out of the canal—the slimy, green canal. She got fourteen days for that. The magistrate said it was a painful case, and that he would let her off easily."

"They might have let her drown. It would have been better," replied Mary, gazing into the firelight.

"She never said a word about *him*," said Alison presently, "she never mentioned his name. Lots of girls would have made a scandal, out of revenge. There must have been some good in her. It was only quite at the last."

The November dusk fell early in the spacious bedroom. There was a terrible tension in the air. The very atmosphere seemed charged with feminine emotion, as the two girls, exaggerating, as over-refined women will, the importance of ethical standards of conduct in the great teeming universe, talked on and on in the gathering gloom.

It was dark when Lady Jane returned, bringing, with her large, pink cheeks, her parted hair, her rustling silk clothes, an air at once motherly and mundane into the sick room.

"I shall insist, my darling, on your seeing someone else," she announced in her rather loud but cheery voice. "I can quite understand your not wishing to see our dear Dunlop, for we women," she added with a sigh, "all have our little coquetries. But what objection can you have to seeing Danby? I shall send round at once to Travers Danby."

But the great man, when he finally arrived, preserved an impenetrable mask in the presence of Alison, of her mother, and of Mary. A prolonged consultation with the other doctor resulted in frequent doses of brandy or port wine being ordered, and an admission, just at the hall door, that the case was serious.

Mary went down to the dining-room when the bell rang, leaving Alison's old nurse at the bed-side. Lady Jane's one idea was that Dunlop Strange should be called in.

"If she would only see him," she reiterated for the fifth time, shaking her head tragically when the butler offered her a savoury, "he is so clever with chest complaints, so marvellously, marvellously clever! Why, he cured Kempton—Lord Sandown's eldest son—when he was positively given up by every doctor in London. And they say the poor young man had led a perfectly shocking life."

"Dear Lady Jane," urged Mary, "pray don't insist on it to her. It would be worse than useless—it really would do harm." She had made up her mind to say nothing now about "Number Twenty-seven," and her sordid little tragedy. Lady Jane was kind and charming, but she had retained the prejudices of ladies who were young in the fifties. In all probability she would only call the dead girl some old-fashioned hard names. Certainly she would never comprehend her daughter's extremely modern sympathy for this woman who had drawn her last breath in a hospital ward.

It was settled that Mary should remain all night at the bedside. There were a dozen things to think of: food, medicines, blisters, and emetics if the bronchial tubes became filled up. She ran over carefully in her mind all that she would have to do during the night. Lady Jane said she would lie down in the next room but with the door open, to listen.

Toward ten o'clock, the sick girl sat up, saying she could breathe easier in that position.

"Oh, how I hate being ill," she muttered, clenching her fingers as they lay on the counterpane. "Mary," she continued, while the irritable anxious look deepened on her face—she had to stop—"I feel," she gasped at last, "as if I were choking."

"Dear," said the other girl, whose heart had absolutely stood still, "why don't you lie down?"

"I can't—I can't breathe if I do. Mary, do you think I shall be ill long? I've always hated being ill. There is the personal degradation—one looks odious, one is odious."

"Dear, you will be all right again in a day or two," urged Mary.

"Oh! I don't mean that," she muttered, tossing over. "It doesn't matter; nothing matters, nothing matters," she went on till she fell into an uneasy dose. She was lying like that, with her head lower than her shoulders, when Dr. Danby came again at eleven.

"How long has the patient been in that position?" whispered

the great man. Something in the tone of his voice made her heart stand still.

"She's been lying like that all the time—when she isn't sitting up coughing," faltered the girl.

"Ah! We must keep up the patient's strength in every way. Don't leave her a minute, Miss Erle."

Mary heard the words, but they sounded a long way off.

## CHAPTER XXI
## THE GATE OF SILENCE

"I WILL not, while I have health and strength," said Lady Jane severely at the breakfast table, when the question of a trained nurse was mooted, "consent to have my child nursed by a hireling. It is a mother's duty," she continued, with lofty decision, regarding Mary and her red, tired eyelids somewhat reproachfully. And Lady Jane, to be sure, was convinced that she herself had tended the sick girl through the night. Mary remembered, with something like a smile, that once or twice during that long vigil, her hostess, arrayed in a somewhat short nightdress scantily covered by a pink woolen shawl, had stepped ponderously into the room, upset one or two medicine bottles, and poured some beef-tea into a glass which contained lemonade. Lady Jane had the best intentions, but nature had not cut her out for a sick nurse. She was short-sighted and easily upset, and her natural emotions overcame her so much that twice she retreated in tears, and carried away in her distraction the bottle of medicine which was to be administered every hour.

"No," reiterated the mother, "not while I have health and strength. I shall go to her myself immediately."

The hours passed mournfully enough. There was no improvement during the day. Alison sat up in bed propped up with pillows, while her strength lasted. Her face, which had gradually turned livid, was covered with a clammy perspiration. Every now and again she pushed back the damp strands of hair from her forehead. The choking mucus in the chest was accumulating; she had no longer the strength to pass it away.

"Mary," she whispered once during the morning, "my hands look so horrid. They are swelling—I wonder why?" She pushed one foot from under the bed-clothes. It was quite disfigured already. "Funny it looks," she muttered. "What's his name? the sculptor—the Royal Academician, you know—modelled my foot once. It would be beastly," she continued, staring vacantly at the little swollen foot, while Mary bent down and rearranged the pillows, "to have great fat feet like that. Mary, do you think they will get slim again when I am well?"

"My dear girl, of course, of course."

The sick woman fell into an uneasy doze after that. The doctors' visit brought small comfort. Both bent with anxious faces over the bed. Little could be done but to administer strong restoratives. The two physicians feared some cerebral complication.

"Had the patient," they asked Lady Jane, "recently had any mental shock?"

"Certainly not, certainly not. My poor darling," replied the mother, "was the picture of health and happiness. Impossible that she should have had any trouble of which I am not aware," she announced, with all an old woman's fatuity.

The two doctors glanced at each other and said nothing. Mary detained the elder man downstairs.

"Tell me the truth," she said.

"My dear young lady, I fear there is nothing—absolutely nothing—that can be done. The patient is sinking rapidly. In all probability she will not live through another day. It would be well if you could break it to her poor mother."

Mary stood still for a minute, leaning against the passage wall, as the two doctors closed the door softly. She heard the two carriages roll away—rolling away to other sick rooms, to pronounce, perhaps, another sentence of death before they reached home. It was nothing to them, she remembered; nothing, nothing, nothing. People died every day. Every day people were born. Some had to go, these men of science would say, to make way for others.

"There seems to be no change—for the better," whispered Lady Jane an hour later, as they both stood at the bedside. "She is still asleep, and muttering, my poor darling. If we could only rouse her now. I shall insist on Danby seeing her again," she added feverishly, patting her eyes with a lace handkerchief.

Mary looked at the slight figure in the bed.

"Dear Lady Jane," she said softly, "I don't think we shall ever—be able to rouse her now." It struck her as curiously odd that she should be saying this to the woman near her—this woman that she always pictured at dinner-parties and drums, tapping people with her fan, carrying her bare shoulders and her little stories from drawing-room to drawing-room in the eternal monotony of good society. With a thing so poignant, so human, so pitiful as death, it seemed impossible that this charming lady could ever be associated.

The mother broke down completely, and had to be led away.

Toward four o'clock someone knocked at the door, bringing up letters for Mary. They had been sent round from the lodgings in Bulstrode Street. There were several letters: one from Jimmie, one from her bootmaker, and one she saw, with a curious tight feeling at her heart, was from Vincent and bore a Northborough postmark. Going to the window, she bent forward in the failing light and broke the seal.

*Northborough, Dec. 2nd.*

"MY DEAR MARY: You are perhaps aware that to-morrow is fixed for my marriage, and it is no exaggeration to say that I shall not feel happy when I stand at the altar in the morning unless I have a word of blessing from you, my oldest and most valued friend, on this most auspicious occasion. Although I trust that changed circumstances will not to any great extent separate us, yet I cannot help expressing the hope that such uncommon virtues, intellectual powers, and remarkable perseverance [the word "virtues" had been added as an afterthought, and was squeezed in between "uncommon" and "intellectual"] as are happily yours, may be speedily and justly rewarded.

"Ever your devoted friend,
    "VINCENT HEMMING."

Then she deliberately opened the other letters. There was a small cheque from the editor of *The Fan*; a little note—very affectionate—from Jimmie, requesting the loan of three pounds; and lastly, a bootmaker's bill. Jimmie wanted three pounds to be forwarded immediately. It was annoying—he was always asking for money, in little notes full of the most endearing epithets. Well, there was the cheque from *The Fan*. It was for three guineas—the price of one of her articles—so she could send him a post-office order. As for the bootmaker, he would have to wait. There was something absurd, incongruous about that bootmaker's bill. And yet, after all, one had to pay one's boot bill, even if one's lover was going to be married to-morrow morning.

She felt a curious tightening in her chest, a horrible feeling in her head, as if the brain were pressing against the skull. Something had to be done—to be done at once, she kept saying to herself. Yes, Vincent must be congratulated. It would be undignified to look as if she were considering the matter. Women, she bethought her with a grim smile, should accept their fate with a graceful acquiescence.

And at once Mary made up her mind that she would not write, although there was just time to catch the country post. It would be better to telegraph. She would go herself to the nearest office. Gathering up her letters she crept to the bedside. Alison was asleep. Bending down she kissed the white wrist that lay on the counterpane, and then, telling the maid not to move from the sick room, she threw on her hat and cloak and left the house in the gathering dusk. It was not far to the nearest post office, in Baker Street,★ and once inside she carefully wrote out a post-office order for Jimmie. Then she took a telegraph form and wrote two or three different phrases with the blunt pencil tied to a short piece of string. Finally, when she had scratched out two or three messages, she handed the paper across to the clerk. "I wish you all possible happiness.— Mary," read out the young man in his every-day unemotional voice; and then the girl found herself outside, walking rapidly down Baker Street toward the Regent's Park. "I must walk; I must breathe the open air," she said to herself, "or I shall never be able to sit up again all to-night."

The gates of the Regent's Park were shut, but she walked on, round the outer circle, seeing nothing, for her brain was busy with two overpowering thoughts, the awful struggle with death, the protest against annihilation which was slowly being fought out in that bedroom in Portman Square, and the fact that henceforward she was to walk alone, to fight the battle of life unaided—a moral starveling, whose natural instincts were to be pinched, repressed, and neatly trimmed in conformity with the rules of the higher civilisation. And, to be sure, it was in accordance with the inexorable laws of the higher civilisation that so priceless a boon as a loyal love should weigh as nothing when balanced with a thing which had a nicely ascertained value in the money market.

Pausing on the North Gate bridge,★ she looked down into the dark canal water, on to which the last shivering autumnal leaves were slowly fluttering down. She thought of the girl—of Number Twenty-seven—who had tried to drown herself in those greenish, slimy waters. After all, it was but the open door of the Greek philosophers which she had tried to slip through with uncertain, unsuccessful feet.[1]

---

1  A reference to any number of Greek philosophers—Plato, Pythagoras, Empedocles, among others—who believed in the transmigration of the soul.

The curve of the road outside was all a silvery, shiny grey. Road, sky, and pavement were much the same tone, but the street lamps made an orange sickle of fire, heightened on the other side by the indigo-blueness of the Park, etched with intricate lines of bare stems and branches. The scarlet of a mail-cart flashed past, and afterward, in the solitude of the white road, a shabby, belated mourning carriage. There was a flapping of dingy white scarves as the dyed horses, with lowered heads, moved dejectedly away into the growing dusk, leaving a vision of rusty black clothes and of vague drab faces gazing from the carriage window on to the sombre, naked trees.

Mary shuddered. "I must get back," she thought, and calling a hansom, she was, in ten minutes, mounting the stairs again to the sick room in Portman Square.

Mary hardly dared look when she reached the bedroom again. The sick girl, propped up on pillows, was battling for life with her breath. The distended jugular veins told of the fearful struggle; the lips were livid, her fingers clenched. The beautiful brown eyes were turned on her mother with the look of a dying dog; then her head fell forward, and they laid her lengthwise on the bed.

Alison lay long in a state of somnolence. In the silence of the large bedroom, in which the only other sound was that of the sprightly French clock on the mantelpiece, ticking away the hours, the sick woman's delirious mutterings seemed of fearful importance to the watchers round the bed. What was she saying—she who was never to speak any more to any of them? Long after, Mary remembered the last coherent words she had said: "Will my feet get slim again when I am well?"

The long night began. Alison still lay prone, but the breathing was now stertorous, with a kind of rattle in the throat. Dr. Danby, summoned again by Lady Jane, implored her to be calm, for the end could not be long. But to Mary, during the endless hours of that December night, the end seemed long in coming. It tortured her to see the one human being for whom she cared now in the world, dying that terrible death of suffocation. Toward midnight, the strain on Mary became intense. Alison fell into a doze, and then Mary crept, for a few moments, into the next room and threw open a window. The injustice of life revolted her. Her misery was too poignant for tears. When she was a little child she used to stiffen herself with silent rage when anyone accused or struck her unjustly. The girl felt something of that hardened feeling now. And so Alison, too, was to go. A grim, speechless battle with annihilation was slowly being fought out in that gay, beflowered bedroom, in there.

It was a still winter night, and a great round moon looked over the tops of the tall houses opposite like a white, surprised face. The sounds of the ponderous, buzzing city entered in at the window with the whiff of fresh air; the rattle of cabs and omnibuses; voices of the passers-by; carriages were driving round the square; somebody, two doors off, was giving a dinner-party. On the steps was a little cluster of footmen. Presently the hall door opened, there was a rush of light, and the figures of two ladies, in white cloaks and laces, passed from under the portico. The click of the carriage door was audible, the word "Home!" and the sound of retreating wheels. Presently a couple of men left, lighting their cigars as they went down the steps, and striding off on foot to the sounds of amused laughter. But presently the square was silent. Not a branch stirred. Only the great white moon rose higher in the heavens with her cold, triumphant air.

Mary sank on her knees at the open window, her forehead pressed against the sill.

"Why could it not have been I?" she moaned. "No one wants me, no one cares for me; while Alison—O God! O God! and must I go on living?"

And then she remembered that Death, the great destroyer, had an irony which is all his own. Beautiful noble, helpful lives were crushed, destroyed, annihilated. Death made no more account of them than a schoolboy does of a beetle, on whom, in passing by, he tramps wantonly in a ditch. A minute ago they breathed, and loved, and suffered; another minute in the æons of time, and the insect was a mere blotch of slime, one's passionately loved idol was rotting under the sod. And for a little while, if they were lucky, the idols were remembered, but more often their memories passed away. The burden of sex, the lust of life, the torture of the ideal, the unslaked thirst for immortality, had all been theirs; but always others came to take their places, to suffer the same agonies, to be thrilled, for a brief moment, with the same fears and pleasures. And always the long procession moved on, and on, and on; some fell out, but others jostled forward; the ranks were filled up; there was small time for tears. Yes, forever the great army of humanity moved on, on its strange inexplicable march from a mother's womb to six feet of oozing clay.

The long hours of the night dragged slowly on. In the sick room the only sounds were the ticking of the French clock and the terrible ominous rattle from the lace-trimmed pillows. It was nearing dawn. Restless and hysterical with grief, the mother had run out to write one more vain summons for the doctor. Outside, there were women sobbing on the staircase. Mary sat by the bedside, waiting for the dawn, waiting for the dread inexorable moment. And then, just when there came creeping in behind the blind the wan, drabbish light of the December daybreak—of the morning which Mary remembered with a kind of stunned feeling was to be that of Vincent Hemming's marriage—a strange noise from the pillows made her heart stand still in her body. And suddenly she was aware that there was no sound at all in the sick room but the pert click of the little gilt clock on the mantelpiece ticking, ticking, ticking glibly away.

## CHAPTER XXII
## THE WORLD WAGS ON

FIVE years had passed. All day long the streets had been full of carriages going and coming from Buckingham Palace. The spring sunshine fell on the pink arms, the thin bare shoulders of young girls on the back seats of broughams and closed barouches, which passed swiftly by, leaving a vision of a foam of tulle, an excited young face, a cascade of flowers, or the large complacent bosom of a chaperon. Some of these carriages stopped, toward five o'clock, at Lady Jane Ives' in Portman Square. The drawing-room was already spread with shining satin trains, and heavy with the odour of slightly faded hothouse flowers, before the hostess herself appeared; for Lady Jane was presenting a niece, and had been late in getting away from the Palace. One or two men, vaguely bored, strayed about with uncertain feet among the yards of satin and brocade which covered the floor; and the women in their white gloves and nodding plumes and foolish trains, seemed conscious of their wrinkled throats and faded skins, as they stood, with a somewhat forced smile, receiving the usual compliments.

But very soon Lady Jane appeared, swimming into the room with her large smile, and her ruby velvet train, and having behind her a young girl in white, with puffy pink cheeks and an alarmed air.

"My niece Victoria," she announced to everyone, in her rapid, genial manner. "Presented to-day;[1] my brother's girl, you know.

---

1   The presentation at court, where participants met and were honored by
    the Queen, was the ritual marking the "coming out" into society of
    young girls.

Dear Victoria is so devoted to society; she is going to stay with me. It will be quite charming."

And Mr. Beaufy Flower, with a huge white buttonhole which accentuated the dingy yellow of his skin, and with several tell-tale wrinkles at the corners of his eyes, murmured to Mr. Bosanquet-Barry as he gazed with half-closed lids at the new candidate for society's favours:

"I adore drawing-room teas. One sees so *much* of people, don't you know. And in the daylight too one gets such a good idea of what they're really like," he tittered, turning to where Lady Blaythewaite, in all the superb insolence of her pink-and-white flesh, was standing at the window in the full glare of daylight, the sunlight sparkling on the diamond tiara round her forehead.

"She's got her best 'fender' on," said Mr. Bosanquet-Barry, with rising interest; "by Jove, did you ever see such jewels? And what a skin! She looks like some superb animal."

"Oh, no, she don't," whispered Beaufy, in his acidulous voice; "animals never look depraved. And for my part, I don't admire her so much as all that. Poor Lady Blay is so odiously, blatantly healthy."

The room was nearly full when Mary came up the stairs. A stout lady in green, whose extremities looked extraordinarily large in their white coverings, thrust a bouquet of spiked flowers in her eye as she reached the landing, and then stared, with all the impertinence of a certain kind of British matron, when the girl stepped back annoyed.

"Oh, *dear* Miss Erle," said a shrill voice at the door, "*do* come in. It's such a nice party. I wonder," continued the pale-faced boy, who entertained a good deal himself, "why other people's parties are so much nicer than one's own? I suppose it is because one always knows so many more people at other people's houses!"

"Who's here?" said Mary, who never troubled herself to laugh at his small witticisms.

"All sorts of pretty people. There's Lady Blaythewaite, looking magnificent in yellow," he answered. He always made a point of praising other women when he talked to ladies, in the pleasing hope that it would annoy them. "She never misses going to Court once a year; but really, you know, she's got to! There's the Duchess of Birkenhead, now," he chattered on, "she's only been once since her marriage, you know. But then she needn't, because she's so perfectly, so entirely respectable!" And he disappeared with a delighted little wriggle in the crowd, and a few minutes later Mary saw him pouring his sub-acid compliments into Lady Blaythewaite's ear.

There was some attempt at animation in the rooms now. There were crowds of ladies as well as those who had been to Court, and a hired pianist, making tinkling sounds on a somewhat worn piano, was endeavouring to impart a false air of gaiety to the affair. The words, "the Queen," "the Princess," "heliotrope brocade," "exquisite diamonds," and "fearful crush," were bandied about the room. Someone related a story that a colonial lady of much wealth had been turned away because she had worn tan-coloured gloves, and an ancient legend even found listeners that a *débutante* had fallen over her train while backing from the Royal presence. A woman with pronounced Jewish features, who wore a smart bonnet and a French frock, explained at some length to an indifferent group what had happened when she had been presented last year. And, as she stood talking to Mr. Bosanquet-Barry, who had, as usual, his air of not wishing to be detained, the lady whom Mary remembered in the old days as a player on the harp, had placed a piece of music on the piano, and was singing in an elderly, threadbare voice, and an accent which left much to be desired, something which sounded like: "Allong cueillir lay roas-er,"[1] lifting her eyebrows, standing on tiptoe, and slightly wriggling her shoulders as the song proceeded.

Mary looked round the room. It all seemed foolish enough; the women with their naked, yellow shoulders, their torn veils and faded flowers, the men slipping in and out in their superb frock coats, murmuring scandal of the very people whose hands they had just pressed. And then, too, she could not bear the house since Alison's death. The rooms seemed noisy and yet empty without her. It was the same outwardly, for here were the usual crowd, chattering, smiling, whispering, as they passed in and out. And only she, Mary, seemed to remember. Lady Jane, to be sure, had been immersed in grief for some months after the death, but the next season she had reappeared in mauve and black, and had resumed her round of drums and dinners. All that had happened five years ago. This was the second niece that she had successfully launched in society; the first had made an excellent match, and Lady Jane only hoped, in confidence to all her intimate friends, that Victoria would not think of marrying quite so soon, for it was charming, she said—it made her feel quite young again—to have a girl to take out. She never, she complained, had been able to make her poor

---

1  Let us go and pick the roses.

darling Alison take a proper interest in society; only an eccentric, intermittent one. And people naturally dislike that.

"*Allons cueillir les ro—*"

urged the lady at the piano, but her voice, not being very strong, was inaudible at the end, which was received thankfully, with a decent little murmur of applause.

"Dear Sir Dunlop," cried Lady Jane in her deep, genial tones at the door, "how good of you to find time to drink a dish of tea. Let me introduce to you my niece Victoria. Presented to-day, and so devoted to society. Go in, go in, you will find all your pretty friends in there."

And the face of the fashionable doctor, smooth, smug, successful, was seen here and there chatting in the crowd. If the mouth was still hard, the smile was more insinuating than ever. A voluptuous feminine atmosphere surrounded him as he moved about. Pretty women bent forward to whisper, meeting his eyes with an intimate look, or laying detaining, half-caressing fingers on his arm. He bent down, with the familiar air of a man who is accustomed to the intimacies of the consulting-room. All of these charming ladies had been, were now, or would be, his patients. His reputation had grown apace in the last five years. No one could have the megrims in Belgravia or Mayfair without consulting Sir Dunlop Strange. Reports of his approaching marriage were constantly circulated, but at present, it would seem, there was a barrier in the way. He was understood to be devoted to Lady Blaythewaite. And indeed, as he neared the window where she was still standing, the circle of black coats which surrounded her dissolved, and they stood practically alone, looking out on the square. The lady slowly turned her handsome prominent eyes upon him, and, with a long gaze which took in every detail of her radiant health and beauty, he slipped his nervous, sinewy fingers round her wrist in the shadow of the curtain.

Mary was standing near the door, trying to get a breath of air, when the pale, underbred face of Perry Jackson was seen ascending the stair. She instinctively stepped aside, not knowing whether he would care to speak to her. She heard Lady Jane overwhelm him with pretty phrases, for she was proud of a portrait he had painted of her that year and enjoyed a new celebrity; but Perry Jackson did not come near Mary, and it was with a somewhat forced smile that he returned her greeting. "I have lost my kind little friend," she said to herself with a certain bitterness. And then, as Vincent Hemming was seen coming up the stair, she said to herself with the inconsistency of a woman, "Here, at any rate is someone who cares for me still—a little bit."

The face of Vincent Hemming was that of an irritated, disappointed man. He was, however, as perfectly dressed, as elaborately suave as of old, and he stopped to speak to several dowagers on his way upstairs. It was always half a pleasure, half a pain to her to meet him, and there were times when she felt that the acquiescent feminine smile was a little forced as she talked to him at some crowded party, or called on his wife at Queen's Gate.★

Hemming had made but a brief appearance in the House of Commons, for he had been unseated almost immediately—his agents, it transpired, not having been discreet in the matter of beer; and he had had no opportunity of entering the House since. Meanwhile, Mrs. Vincent Hemming had not made herself popular in London society, and her husband had always a somewhat uneasy air when she was in the same room. Lady Jane Ives, for one, openly snubbed her, and Vincent had arrived at that stage in an unsuccessful marriage when a husband is not offended at being asked out to dinner without his wife. To any other woman but Mary the thing would have been a personal triumph.

"Here is that poor Mr. Hemming that you threw over," whispered Lady Jane to Mary; "I did not ask his impossible wife. I don't know how a man with such delightful outward tastes could marry such a person. If it had only been an American, now. An American or an Australian—and nobody would have minded what she said or did."

And in a few minutes Mary found herself talking, in a conventional voice, of the rain and fine weather, of politics and the Park, with the man who had once been so much to her. Sometimes, indeed, as he took her down to supper, or handed her a cup of tea, with his little formal manner, she wondered how, in those past years, he had been able to make her suffer so. But Mary was beginning to understand that women love most of all the men who have done them an irreparable wrong.

His face looked grey and tired, and it was with a visible effort that he found phrases suitable to be overheard by the nodding plumes, the bare shoulders, and the limp nosegays around.

"You look tired; are you ill?" she said suddenly, in her old sweet manner. For a moment Mary had forgotten.

"No; it is nothing. I am a little out of sorts, I think," he said, avoiding her eyes. Then he added, after a pause, looking straight at the carpet, "You don't know, you can't conceive, what worries I have!"

She said nothing; there was nothing she could say. But he looked miserable, and all her tender, womanly little heart rushed out to him.

"Mayn't I get you a cup of tea?" he said, offering her his arm. They went downstairs There was the usual struggle for a cup, a sugar-basin, a spoon.

"Why mayn't I come and see you sometimes, Mary?" he said, in his voice which meant so much more than the mere words.

"Oh, Vincent! You've put cream in my tea, and I can't bear it," said Mary, with a comical little frown.

"I'm so sorry, and you don't like sugar either. How could I have forgotten it?" said Hemming, wafting it away in his grand manner. "But, Mary," he continued, when he had battled successfully for another cup, "why won't you read me some of your work? I usn't to be a bad critic, though I do little enough myself now. Why can't we see each other, sometimes, like that?"

All the blood left her face. It was horrible, horrible of him to talk so; but he must not even guess that she cared.

"Of course," she said, after a pause, during which they had been pushed apart by the stout lady with the spiky bouquet, who had come downstairs and was forcing her way with a businesslike air to the buffet, "I suppose you can come and be victimised by manu-scripts—if you want to."

"When, Mary?"

"Oh," she added quickly, "not to-morrow. I've got to go to the Strand. But the day after—"

"Aren't you well? Let me look at you," said Hemming, as they went up to the drawing-room again. "Come into the light," he continued in an authoritative tone, when they had reached the drawing-room. "I can't have you getting ill."

There was a movement of departure in the crowd. The mon-strous trains were being caught up, bouquets were seen moving toward the door. The pale-faced boy, slipping in and out, was mur-muring a last impertinence to a pretty woman on her way down-stairs. Lady Blaythewaite's tiara, escorted by the fashionable physi-cian, passed, with superb insolence, through the room. Lady Jane was beginning to look tired, for at seventy, as she said, one wasn't in the first blush of youth; and Miss Victoria, whose puffy cheeks had assumed a purplish hue, announced to everyone, as they made their farewells, that she and her aunt were going to a ball that night, which she expected would be "splendid fun." Mr. Bosanquet-Barry, who approved of Miss Erle as an occasional contributor because he met her in what he called "smart houses," bestowed on her a brief vision of all his gleaming teeth as he squeezed her hand and passed on without a word.

"The day after to-morrow, Mary?" demanded Vincent Hemming, as they stood irresolutely on the door-step among the little crowd of drab-coated footmen. Mary stood silent for a moment, gazing at the stone steps. After all, why should she not see him, her old friend, her father's friend? She felt nervous and unstrung; it would be very sweet to have him there, to talk to him in a sensible way. She would talk to him about his wife, about his little baby girl; she would perhaps be able to make things smoother in that household. Living by herself in lodgings, she never saw any men; there seemed to be no one now whose advice she could ask.

"Yes," she said suddenly, in a high, clear tone, and, as she went down the steps and hurried across the square, she was startled herself by the note of exultation in her voice.

## CHAPTER XXIII
## IN WHICH CIVILISATION TRIUMPHS

ALTHOUGH she had been thinking of Hemming for hours, the sharp, agitated pull of the bell startled Mary as she sat sorting papers at her desk in the little room, crowded with bookshelves, and with a writing-table littered with papers and letters, which she now used as a study, and had made habitable with books and sketches during the six years she had lived there. It had been repapered.

"Mr. Vincent Hemming," said Sarah, opening the door.

He shook hands, without a word. Mary knew instinctively that something was wrong, before he spoke.

"We'll have tea, please, Sarah," she said, and, until the servant brought in the cups and saucers, they sat exchanging commonplaces a little awkwardly. There was a tight feeling in Mary's throat as she looked at Hemming's drawn face and averted eyes. And yet it was good to have him there, all to herself, sitting opposite to her, sipping his tea, on the deep sofa near the window, his brown eyes looking black against the light.

He got up presently, moving restlessly about the little room, examining with curious eyes the place which was Mary's home.

He stopped in front of the old-fashioned writing-table, on which blotting-paper, foolscap, and worn-out pens were scattered. A great odorous bunch of waxen pinkish lilac stood in a jug on the table. On the shelf above the pigeonholes there was a full-length, slightly faded photograph of himself.

"And this is where you work?" he muttered, absently sitting down in the swing chair, and leaning his elbow, with a tired gesture, on the ink-stained desk. "Poor little Mary! Don't you ever paint, now? You used to like it so much."

"I paint very little, to amuse myself, when I get a day or two in the country. Here is a sketch I did last summer," she added, taking a wooden panel from under a pile of papers and holding it a little way off. "It was down there, you know, in that piney, heathery place, where we went before you sailed——"

"I remember," he said gravely.

And then something tightened at her heart as she stood near him, holding out the sketch. It was the very scene she had so often pictured when she lived here waiting for him to come back. Here was the room, lined with book-shelves; the desk, with Vincent half-turned round, while she held her smudgy little painting up for him to see. Only the years had passed away, and he was another woman's husband, the father of another woman's child.

"I remember," he repeated softly, taking the little anæmic hand that hung close to him, and looking at it intently as he held it in his.

"Why Mary, how thin and white you are!" he said, suddenly. "You can't be well. Have you seen Danby?"

"Oh, it's nothing. I'm all right," she answered nervously, pulling away her hand. "I've been working rather hard, that's all. And London never did agree with me."

"You can't stand it, you never could," he muttered. "Do you remember the year you went so much to the museum for your father? I told him it must be stopped. He hadn't noticed how ill you were looking."

"Yes," said Mary, smiling, "father took me away to Torquay.[1] And you came down. What fun we had! I always loved the sea. But I never seem to get there now," she said in her resigned little voice— a voice out of which all joyousness had departed.

---

1  Torquay is a seaside resort town in Devon on the southern coast of England.

"Good Lord!" continued Hemming, scrutinising her face with a swift glance which he turned instantly on the chimney stacks opposite, "you'll be killing yourself, and for what?"

"One works," said Mary, absently, "because one must. And besides," she added, "I'm not a person of wealth and leisure like yourself."

Hemming got up and strode up and down the room, his mouth working nervously at the corners as he answered:

"Heaven knows you needn't reproach me about that. If you knew what my life is, Mary," he blurted out suddenly, his face turning a dark red, "the dreariness, the vulgarity, the commonplace of it."

"You have your—your—wife, your child," she said slowly, her eyes fixed on the empty teacup in her hand, "and I—I have nothing."

"My wife!" he said derisively. "Yes, I have a wife. Someone who sits opposite me at dinner, who pays the bills with her own cheques, who never misses an opportunity of reminding me that I am a failure. I know—I know I'm a failure. Mary, the egotism of a vulgar woman is something that you cannot even conceive of."

"Don't talk like that, don't, don't," implored Mary. "Oh, Vincent, I—it doesn't matter about me," she continued, "but I can't bear to see you unhappy."

She had risen and was standing in front of him, her eyes wet with tears. He took her hands, holding them fast, and bowed his head down, so that his face lay on their joined hands. And in that moment of his humiliation and despair Mary had never loved Vincent Hemming so well.

"My poor, poor dear," she muttered, with a movement of exquisite maternal tenderness, "it will come all right by-and-by. You will try, won't you, to be—nicer—to her?" she added with an effort. "It must be so easy for husband and wife to make it up. And there is the child—"

"The child," he repeated blankly. "A thing three years old. And she is jealous if I even look at the baby. Mary, her jealousy is infernal. I can't live with her, I can't, I can't!"

And then, for a moment, Mary Erle tasted the intoxication of a personal triumph. Vincent did not love his wife; he had come back to her, to her. The years seemed to roll away. In the intimacy of that quiet room it seemed as if time were obliterated; as if nothing had happened. Just as before, in the great empty, dusty drawing-room in Harley Street, where he had first asked her for her love, his passion communicated itself to her. He looked at her, and with a sudden fear she stepped backward, away from him, but he had risen, and his troubled eyes were looking straight into hers.

And once again, just as on that bygone June afternoon, Mary was drawn, in spite of herself, by the mysterious, inexorable bond of the flesh. Youth, the will to live, the imperious demands of human passion for one moment were to have their way.

"Vin—cent," she pleaded, as he held her two wrists like a vice, and then slowly, with a long shudder, she was conscious that arms were enfolding her.

It was good to rest there for a little, to forget, to run an erasing finger over the ugly past, the years of waiting, of disappointment, of unceasing work. To the starved woman it was sweet—so sweet that she stood there, her head bent down, his arms holding her fast.

"Mary, my own little girl. Why won't you look at me? Turn up your face. Let me see your eyes. You belonged to me once, Mary. Look at me, dearest, say you haven't forgotten me altogether? Dear heart, how good it is! No, don't move, don't move, for God's sake! Give me my little bit of happiness," he muttered, as she moaned under his caresses, "we're not hurting anyone, not anyone, Mary."

"No," she cried at last, breaking away from him. She was trembling from head to foot; all the blood in her body seemed to have rushed to her brain. "You're not hurting anyone—but me! You're hurting me—me! You're doing your best to make me a miserable woman."

Hemming flung himself on the sofa, with his head buried in the pillows. From the movement of his shoulders, Mary could see that he was sobbing as she stood at the other end of the little room, supporting herself against the mantelpiece. It was so terrible to see that he, after all, was suffering and through her. He was one of those men whose rather pompous manner surrounds them like a suit of armour; men whom it is difficult to picture breaking down, feeling acutely, bearing their share of the burden of human suffering.

"Vincent," she said softly, crossing over to him, "try and be brave, for—for both our sakes. We—we can't help it now. It's all done with long ago—about you and me. Don't forget that. Don't torture me, for God's sake, dear!"

"Understand me, Mary," he said, uncovering his face, and speaking rapidly, with his eyes fixed on the carpet, "I'm not going back to her. I can't, I won't stand it. I know—I know I'm a failure. I haven't done what she married me for; she has spent her money for nothing, and she lets me know it. I'm going away—anywhere, somewhere I can be quiet and think. The mail train leaves at eight—I shall catch that, and go straight through to Paris. Mary, dear child," he said, drawing her suddenly down beside him on the sofa, "come with me. We know the world, now, you and I. Do you care one jot for its opinion? Is there a human being that will care for more than three weeks whether we go or stay?"

"Whether we go—or stay," repeated Mary. She knew, even as he spoke, that this was the end of everything; that never again, as long as she lived, could they ever be alone together. And all the time she was conscious of the fascination, the odious fascination which belongs to sin.

"Your real wife!" repeated Mary, wonderingly. For the first few seconds, she was not conscious of feeling shocked. For years now, this man had been so constantly in her thoughts, he had represented, in the time of his absence, the one poor joy, the starveling hope in her dreary existence, that she was no more horrified than if her own brain had worded the thought: "His real wife!" But she knew, even as he spoke, that this was the end of everything; that never again, as long as she lived, could they ever be alone together. And all the time she was conscious of the fascination, the odious fascination which belongs to sin.

"Do you know Cattaro?" he continued, taking her thin fingers and entwining them with his. "Cattaro, that little place tucked under the mountains, on the Dalmatian coast?"[1]

"No, I never heard of it," she said.

"We would go there," he whispered, tightening his hold on her. "No one would ever hear of us. No one would know."

"No one would know!" she repeated softly.

"Mary," he went on, "my little girl! Dare to be yourself. Come to me, let us begin a new life, a *real* life, dear. You are above the prejudices of our false civilisation, you are capable of being a true woman, of giving up something for the man you love. In a little while I might be free, and then we could be married. Mary, Mary, don't you really care for me enough for that? Think of it, think of what we are missing? It would not be a selfish life we would lead, Mary. We would work together. You would inspire me to noble things," he added, with a touch of his old manner. "Other women—great women—have been strong enough, single-hearted

---

1   Vincent is trying to get Mary to go away with him to a village on the east coast of the Adriatic Sea in what is now Croatia.

enough, to do as much for the men they loved. Dear heart, think of the years we might spend together."

There was a tense silence. Mary had risen and walked to the window, where she stood fidgeting with the tassel of the blind, and looking down into the street. Those words that she was listening to were the last words of love which she was ever to hear. And she thought, as she stood there, of the irony of life. To her, love had been twice offered: the affection of Perry Jackson, and now the selfish passion of a man who was another woman's husband. After to-day it would all be a blank. And the impotence, the helplessness of woman, struck her with irresistible force. She was the plaything, the sport of Destiny, and Destiny always won the game.

She turned slowly round and faced him, still swinging the tassel of the blind with one hand. Her face was quite white; she looked cold, almost indifferent.

"Vincent," she said, in a grave voice, "I can't do it. I can't, I can't—not even for you! Don't torture me, for God's sake. It is not that I mind what people would say—that's nothing. It isn't that I don't love you. I have always loved you—but it's the other woman—your wife. I can't, I won't, deliberately injure another woman. Think how she would suffer! Oh, the torture of women's lives—the helplessness, the impotence, the emptiness! ... And with all her faults, you chose her; she is the mother of your child. I love your baby, Vincent," she went on after a pause. "I should not like her to grow up and hate me. All we modern women mean to help each other now. We have a bad enough time as it is," she added with a faint smile; "surely we needn't make it worse by our own deliberate acts! We often talked it all over, Alison and I. You don't know the good she did in her life, the help, the sympathy she gave.... You will go away a little, Vincent, and then you will go back. You will go back—to your little daughter?"

The next instant she was gone. He heard her shut and lock her bedroom door, but he sat on and on, hoping she would come back, that she would relent, that she would forgive him.... But no sound came from the little room. He did not know that she had silently left the house.

At last Hemming rang the bell, and Sarah appeared.

"Tell Miss Erle," he said in a harsh, discordant voice, "that I am waiting—to say good-bye."

"Miss Mary went out nearly an hour ago, sir. Didn't you know?"

She was gone, then. It was all over. She had not trusted him.

Eight o'clock struck. He felt wretched, sick, hungry. It was too late now to catch the evening mail, for he had no clothes, and he thought, with a grim smile, that a man couldn't cross the Channel, even if he had been defrauded of his dearest hopes, in a frock coat and a tall hat. Presently he left the house, and wandered along toward Regent Street. He thought he would go to a restaurant and have some dinner; he did not want to meet any of the men at the club.

And afterward, he had an indistinct impression of a dinner at which in his wretchedness he went on ordering half-pints of champagne, of the *couloir* of a music-hall, of rustling gowns, of scarlet smiles, and of someone, very young and rather pretty, who leant upon his arm. It must have been a kind of dream, a sort of madness, he thought afterward, when he had returned, a day or two later, to the decorous solemnity of his home in Queen's Gate.

## CHAPTER XXIV
## THE WOMAN IN THE GLASS

MARY walked rapidly round the Regent's Park. Over yonder, where the sombre trees massed themselves against the pale evening sky, came the sounds and scents of the oncoming summer; children's shrill voices calling to each other near the ornamental water; the tread of sweethearts' feet on the gravel path; the delicate aroma of newly cut grass. All around her were simple human joys. But they were not for her. She had left all that behind her in that little room in Bulstrode Street, where sat the one man in the world that she cared for—the one man, now, who cared for her. There was no one else; there never could be any one else.

But it behooved her henceforward to be sensible—to be strong for both of them. She must never see him again, must above all try and think of Vincent as she used to do, before that afternoon in Harley Street—how many years ago, now?—when he had first made love to her, and asked her to wait for him. How it spoiled everything—this eternal question of sex.... It was almost impossible for a woman to see a man as he really is. And in pursuance of the plan of being sensible, she went deliberately over Hemming's faults. They were obvious enough. He was weak, vacillating; his phrases were absurd. His ambitions, after all, were but vulgar ones, and he had not the will-power to carry out even his most cherished plans. He was all that, and yet he was the only man in the world that she loved. The only man in the world, now, who desired her as a woman.

And yet she must walk on, get as far away from him as possible. Here, at the North Gate, the slim young poplars detached themselves tremblingly against the pinkish sky, while in front of her stretched the long, white Avenue Road, with its square snug houses, holding themselves aloof in their leafy gardens. She would walk on until she came to Hampstead. Up there, there was space, distance; one's horizon opened out. Over the garden walls swayed the waxen, pinkish lilac. The scent struck her like a blow; *that* room, where they had been together, had been filled with the same penetrating, sensuous odour. Pink lilac and foliage made artificial-looking by the yellow light of a gas-lamp; how they always reminded her of Paris! Of Paris, where they were to have been on their way by now.

But she was walking alone, steeling her heart against him, in a road in a London suburb. On each side was the prosperous, orderly, contented life of the middle class, with its placid domesticity, its unemotional joys. From the open window of a long drawing-room came the sound of a young girl's threadlike voice. Upstairs in the nursery the lights were already lowered. The white street was deserted. But suddenly from one of the open gateways appeared a pair of sleek chestnuts. The carriage passed out, and as Mary stood waiting at the curb, a man and a woman's smiling faces were photographed on her brain. A prosperous, middle-aged couple, going out to a placid evening's amusement. Then silence again.

On and on, past the Swiss Cottage, the sleepy Tudor College, up Fitzjohn's Avenue★ with its sham Tudor mansions and its gay little procession of young trees. The girl pushed on, hoping she would tire herself, up the High Street and through a shady road or two, out into the open heath. The after-glow of a crimson sunset still hung in the west. The Surrey Hills were faintly blue, and the heath, with its broken ridges topped with gorse and bracken, swept in superb lines at her feet. The air was very still. Over yonder a mysterious hand had hung a silver sickle in the pale twilight sky.

Mary sank tired on to a seat. But presently two vague figures approached in the growing darkness—the figures of a girl and a young man, working people both, who sat awkwardly down at the other end of the bench, and talked in jerky, constrained whispers. The girl's eyes were bent demurely on her lap, but once, when Mary turned her head in their direction, she could see that the young man's eyes were devouring the face of his shabby little companion with a passionate glance. Something tightened at Mary's throat. Why to-night, of all nights, must she be reminded of what she was giving up? She got up and began to walk rapidly homeward.

"I was not wanted there; I was spoiling their evening," she thought. "I must learn to be discreet."

With some trepidation she rang the bell of her lodgings.

"When did Mr. Hemming go?" she asked.

"About eight o'clock, miss. Will you have some dinner?"

"No, thanks, Sarah. I can't eat anything to-night. I've got one of my headaches."

Mary went straight into the little study and shut the door.

Outwardly nothing was changed. The air was full of his presence. There were the teacups out of which they had drunk; the chair at the writing-table was still half swung round, just as Vincent Hemming had left it. It was here, just at the mantelpiece, that he had taken her into his arms and said all those mad things. She went deliberately over the scene, repeating in her mind everything he had said. On the sofa the cushions were still tumbled where he had sat and sobbed. Ah, for once, she had made *him* suffer! She flung herself down, clenching her fists, with her face against the silken cushions. Her other self revolted against the injustice of human laws. The woman within her cried aloud in the darkness. What had she done that she was always to be sacrificed? Why was she to miss the best that life has to offer? She lay there a long time, miserable, stricken, helpless. Then, going into her bedroom, she began to take off her dress mechanically and to unloosen her hair. Half dressed as she was, she flung herself on the bed. She was tired and footsore with her long walk. For an hour she fell into a fitful sleep.

The night was sultry, but she could hear the flapping of the window-blind, swaying in a light breeze. Mary lay there a long time, every nerve in her body quivering. How long, how long the night was! Would it never end, never be daylight, when she could get up and work again? To work was to forget. If only she could keep strong and not worry too much. She got up presently, weary with lying awake, and lit a couple of candles on the dressing-table. The flapping blind got on her nerves. She had forgotten to wind up her watch, but, from the curious hush in the air, Mary thought it must be nearing dawn. Then she began to pace the room mechanically. Would the night never end?

In the mirror on the dressing-table, she caught sight of herself as she passed. Her fair hair was floating in a kind of halo round her head; her bare arms and shoulders emerged from the whiteness of her bodice. How the eyes looked at her—hauntingly, appealingly—

from out of a pathetic little face. She slipped into the chair at the table, and leaning her face on her hands, looked gravely at the mirror. For a long time now she had had a strange sense of dual individuality. When she looked in the glass a woman looked back at her with reproachful, haunting eyes. And to-night the woman looked at her appealingly. By the soft candle-light the face still looked young. The cheeks were delicately thin, but the lips were those of a girl of eighteen; in the fluffy, fair head the few grey hairs were lost among the pale gold. There was the line of her throat, her beautiful white shoulders, the delicate modelling of her satiny arms. And, as she looked, the woman in the glass softened with a triumphant smile.

"You may torture me, starve me, but you cannot make me unlovable. He loves me!" smiled the woman. "Why, he would ruin himself to-morrow for me. I have only to say one word and his life is mine. What are we two, after all? Two atoms of matter, breathing, living, loving, suffering, for one brief moment on a planet which was once without organic life, and which is slowly grinding on to irreparable decay. A few more drops in the ocean of eternity, and we and our little loves and little hates will be forgotten. A few more drops and mankind itself will have disappeared, and once more a cold, uninhabited globe will continue its monotonous course round the sun. No one can stop the coming of the 'Great Year.' Nature—insolent, triumphant Nature—cares nothing for the individual.... Summer and winter, seedtime and harvest will come and go in the ages to come, but I—*I shall not be here*. Nestlings will crouch, chirruping, under the eaves; there will be dew on the meadow-sweet, sunshine in the orchard; there will be lovers' glances, and the laughter of little children. But for me—*for me*—it *will all be dark*.... But we do have the present moment; let us keep it and hold it. We are alive now. We love each other.... Give him to me! Only a few short years am I here," pleaded the haunting eyes: "I and such as I, tearing our little hands in search of gold, shaking them at the heavens with impotent vengeance. Give him to me, give him to me.... The inexorable years—the years which fade and blight—will pass over us, and then our 'folly' will be forgotten. Why, people in the next generation will shrug their shoulders and say, 'After all, they were only human.' And I," pleaded the woman in the glass, "I shall have lived."

Mary dropped her head on to her arms. The night was mysteriously still. The breeze had dropped, and an uncanny silence hung about the house. The window was shut now, the blind drawn. The two candles on the dressing-table were burning low in their sockets. When she raised her head again, the eyes were no longer triumphant. They were reproachful. "Who am I? Why am I here?" they asked: "To live is to suffer; why do you let me live? Must I go on looking back at you until my eyes are faded, my lashes are grey, until I have run through the gamut of mental and physical pain? I am a living, suffering entity," said the woman in the glass, "in a world of artificial laws; of laws made for man's convenience and pleasure, not for mine. Have I one thing for which I have longed? Have I a human love, have I the hope of immortality, have I even tasted the intoxication of achievement? Human life is but a moment in the æons of time, and yet one little human lifetime contains an eternity of suffering. Why, since you take joy from me, why do you let me live?"

Here, indeed, was a greater temptation than the one from which she had just escaped. She sprang up, horrified, afraid of the haunting eyes.... Was that to be the end?

Pacing the room, Mary fell to thinking of her father; of the kind-eyed enthusiast who, in his younger years at least, had little enough joy, and much toil, who had been blamed and reviled and stoned by the public, and who had worked solely and single-heartedly for Truth's sake.

"To strive, to seek, to find, and not to yield,"[1]

she suddenly said aloud. It was a line she had engraved on her father's tomb at Highgate, a favourite line of his, of that dear worker of whom, even to think, was morally bracing.

"It may be that the gulfs will wash us down,
It may be we shall touch the Happy Isles;
... but something ere I end—
Some work of noble note may yet be done,"

repeated Mary deliberately, as she walked into the little study, pulled up the blind, and raised the sash.[2]

---

1   This line, and the others that Mary here recalls, are from Alfred, Lord Tennyson's (1809-92) dramatic monologue "Ulysses" (1833). If a reader wishes to see hope in the end of the novel, this line seems to indicate Mary's resolve and endurance.
2   In subsequent editions of the novel, the chapter ends here and is followed by the remaining text in a separate chapter.

Outside was the wan light of a wet daybreak. A thin rain flipped her face, cooling her feverish cheeks. The gas-lamps already took on an orange hue, and in the east there flickered a streak of mysterious light. A faint chirruping of birds began, though London still lay mute, but soon the bird-chorus waxed louder, more shrill, more persistent. The terrible night was over. The dawn was at hand.

Mary lit her lamp, and searched about among her papers for the chapter of her novel at which she had been at work yesterday before Vincent came. She had still to do another happy ending, the rapturous finale which the public demanded. She tried to fix her thoughts, but the great bunch of pinkish lilac irritated her with its dominant, sensuous odour. Taking the dripping stalks in her hand she went to the open window, and let them drop gently on the pavement below. And then, there was something else—the large, full-length, faded photograph of Vincent Hemming, which stood just above the pigeonholes on her desk.

Raising the short silk curtain which hid the grate in the summertime, Mary placed the photograph upright in the fire-place, and lit it with a match. Then she sat down on the fur rug, in her dressing-gown, and hunched up, with her chin on her knees, watched the holocaust. There was neither sorrow, love, nor anger in the grey eyes, nothing but a kind of callous curiosity. But the stiff cardboard would not burn. Mary lit it twice with matches, and it caught for a minute, and then went out with a sudden little puff.

"Paper—paper is what I want," she muttered. "I wonder if love-letters burn more ardently than other kinds of paper?" And, going to the table, she unlocked a drawer and took out a thick bundle of letters in thin foreign envelopes; all Vincent's letters during his journey round the world. "It is poetic justice," she thought grimly; "and then—I must keep nothing that will remind me of him— nothing—nothing—nothing!"

So she gathered up all his letters, even the last one, which she had received the day before Alison's death, and laid them under the photograph. Ah! now he burned. First, the boots, then the trousers to the knee, then to the trim waist of the frock coat. But then it went out again, leaving Vincent's head and shoulders still there; Vincent's face, with its slightly superior air, the orchid in the buttonhole. How chilly it had grown! A draught came under the chink of the door, and her bare feet, thrust into bedroom slippers, were deadly cold. Another match. This time it was for good. First the orchid was licked up by the little blue flames, then the chin, the mouth, the eyes. Soon there was only a handful of blackened paper.... Well, it was like that.... The love of lovers was a blaze, a whiff, a vain, fleeting thing. She looked at the little heap of fluttering paper, and saw, with her sane vision, Vincent going back to his wife. Yes, he would go to Paris, and then he would go back to domesticity in Queen's Gate. Next year there would possibly be another child—a boy, perhaps, in whom he would take more interest. He had his wife's fortune, and for sure next time he would secure a safe seat in Parliament. That passionate interview would soon be a mere episode to him.

And when the white daylight came creeping in at the window, Mary took up her pen and began to work.

Late that afternoon a little figure was to be seen toiling up to Highgate Cemetery. Mary had to see the stonemason about the inscription on her father's grave. They had written to say that some of the letters wanted repainting, perhaps recutting. She found the stonemason sitting straddle-legged on a high tomb near, carefully scraping a marble anchor which had become dingy in the course of years. The man clambered down and touched his cap. She remembered him well as a freethinker, and a great admirer of her father's books.

They both looked carefully at the professor's grave. And, to be sure, the line

"To strive, to seek, to find, and not to yield"

was almost illegible. The urn on the top was slightly askew.

"It gets all the wind and the rain, you see, Miss Erle," said the stonemason, gazing critically at his work. "Yer father's tomb, it do stand so 'igh. Almost the 'ighest in the cem'try, I may say. And a sight of rain we do 'ave up here in wintertime. Soaks the clay, it does, and shifts the graves. Look at that angel with the trumpet over there. A bit squiffy, he looks, don't 'e? Some of them tombs 'ave to be repaired constant."

"I want this seen to at once," said Mary.

"It'll be a matter of five pound to do it up properly, Miss," he said, after some consideration, and then he added, in his apologetic workman's voice, "and I shouldn't like, for 'is sake, to skimp the job. Ah! we ain't got many like 'im up 'ere."

When the man had gone, Mary stood for a long time there on the little mound on the top of the hill.

All around her was the joyous activity of springtime. Nature, who never ceases, who never rests, was once again at her work of re-creation. Once again the lilac trees were burgeoning with waxen blossoms. Once again a thrush, somewhere among that great city of sleepers, was swelling its brown throat with an amorous song.[1] The sunset touched her face, her hand, the flush of hawthorn above her head. At her feet, beyond the foreground of spreading trees, lay stretched out a vast ocean of houses, softened, made vague with a silvery veil of smoke, and pricked by endless spires. Here and there a blurred block, a monster hotel, a railway station, rose out of the great sea of dwellings. It was London that lay stretched out at her feet; majestic, awe-inspiring, inexorable, triumphant London.

Standing alone there on the heights, she made a feint as if to grasp the city spread out before her, but the movement ended in a vain gesture, and the radiance of her face was blotted out as she began to plod homeward in the twilight of the suburban road.

## THE END.

---

1 Perhaps believing that her conclusion was not sharply enough defined, Hepworth Dixon added the following portion to subsequent editions: "The air was loaded with the perfume of may; a pair of swifts were circling and swooping against the tender evening sky. And in all this gaiety of a new-born world only she was to have no part. Henceforward she was to stand alone, to fight the dreary battle of life unaided. 'And women live long,' came the ironical thought: 'yes—we live long!'"

# Appendix A: Contemporary Reviews of The Story of a Modern Woman

[The reviews below represent a sampling of the reaction to Ella Hepworth Dixon's novel when it first appeared in the early summer 1894. Though the author is treated favorably, the reactions to her work reveal a Victorian suspicion of anything "New Woman."]

## 1. From W.T. Stead's[1] "The Novel of the Modern Woman" (The Book of the Month) *Review of Reviews* 10 (1894): 64–74

The Novel of the Modern Woman is one of the most notable and significant features of the day. The Modern Woman novel is not merely a novel written by a woman, or a novel written about women, but it is a novel written by a woman about women from the standpoint of Woman. Many women have written novels about their own sex, but they have hitherto considered women either from the general standpoint of society or from the man's standpoint, which comes, in the long run, to pretty much the same thing. For in fiction there has not been, until comparatively recently, any such thing as a distinctively woman's standpoint. The heroines in women's novels, until comparatively recently, were almost invariably mere addenda to the heroes, and important only so far as they contributed to the perfecting or the marring of the said heroes' domestic peace and conjugal felicity. The woman in fiction, especially when the novelist was a woman, has been the ancillary of the man, important only from her position of appendage or complement to the "predominant partner." But in the last year or two the Modern Woman has changed all that. Woman at last has found Woman interesting to herself, and she has studied her, painted her, and analysed her as if she had an independent existence, and even, strange to say, a soul of her own. This astonishing phase of the evolution of the race demands attention and will reward study. It bewilders some, angers others, and interests all.

---

1 Dixon mentions Stead and this review by name in her autobiographical sketches *As I Knew Them* (1930), crediting this piece with helping to establish her as a noteworthy novelist.

Miss Hepworth Dixon, who boldly styles her novel *The Story of a Modern Woman*, portrays two women, both of the modern variety. One of them refuses to marry the man to whom she is engaged after coming upon a cast-off mistress of his left to die in the hospital, after having been flung upon the streets. "She, at any rate," we are told, "was not one of those girls who have infinite complaisances for a possible husband." The result of which was that she broke down and died. The other heroine was not less heroical, although in a different way. When tempted by the man whom she loved, and who loved her all the more because he was married to another, she replied:

"I can't, I won't, deliberately injure another woman. Think how she would suffer! Oh, the torture of women's lives—the helplessness, the impotence, the emptiness!"

"But all we modern women mean to help each other now."

Which is good news that the world will be glad to have confirmed by higher authority than the optimist author of *The Story of a Modern Woman*.

Miss Hepworth Dixon sums up her book's position thus:—

In *The Story of a Modern Woman* I wished to show how hardly our social laws press on women, how, in fact, it is too often the woman who is made, as it were, the moral scapegoat, and who is sent out into the wilderness to expiate the sins of man. "Number Twenty-Seven," ruined and thrown aside by Dunlop Strange, is reduced to the streets and to an ignoble death in a hospital. Mary, jilted by her lover at a time when her chances of marriage are over, is condemned to a long loveless life and a solitary battle with the world. The keynote of the book is the phrase: "All we modern women mean to help each other now. If we were united, we could lead the world." It is a plea for a kind of moral and social trades-unionism among women.

## 2. *The Athenæum* (16 June 1894): 770

The title of Miss Hepworth Dixon's story is unnecessarily forbidding, for her heroine has little in common with the self-assertive, heartless, sexless thing whom various writers have recently brought into fashion, and almost tempted the public to regard, as the typical modern woman. On the contrary, Mary Erle is a gentle and essentially feminine creature, who only took to journalism and a

solitary life in London lodgings owing to the stress of outward circumstances after the death of her father, Prof. Erle. She knew no
inward "call" to forsake home ties and duties in order to lead a
higher life and to get her own way. There is no "modernity" in her.
She meekly accepts her role as a failure in life; gives up drawing
badly; makes what money she can by writing in a second-rate fashion; and loses her lover through his weakness, and her dearest
friend through death, with no touch of wounded vanity or bitterness in her sorrow. There is little "modernity" in such resignation.
Vincent Hemming is a clever outline, and Alison Ives a fairly convincing study of a brilliant young lady with a taste for violent
social contrasts which is decidedly more "up to date" than her
friend's attitude of mind. There is a quiet charm about the character of Mary which would have been heightened if her creator had
treated her with less of the seriousness and copiousness of a biographer. The anecdotes of her childhood might well be spared. It is
an ungraceful habit to refer to any poor heroine as "the girl" so
many times on every page, and really at last suggest maid-of-all
work associations.

### 3. *The Times* (30 June 1894): 19

*Ecce iterum Crispina!*[1] Shall we never have done with the New
Woman? However, it does not appear from Mrs. Hepworth
Dixon's story that the New Woman is so very new. If Mary Erle is
intelligent and good-hearted, why, there have always been intelligent and good-hearted women in the world. If, while yet in her
teens, she feels herself called upon "to make up her mind on the
questions of marriage, of maternity, and education," why, other
young ladies, without doubt, have pondered the same subjects in
times past, although, indeed, they have lacked a sacred bard to analyze their ponderings. No doubt, too, other girls before Mary Erle
have trifled with Rousseau, or, as Mrs. Dixon epigrammatically but
a little obscurely puts it, have "imbibed the Swiss philosopher's diatribes [*sic*] on virtue before they had comprehended what civilized
mankind stigmatizes as vice." All this precocious meditation and
learning ought to have made Mary a phenomenal woman. But she
is not. She is just a brave girl who, when her father, the Professor,

---

1  Behold again Crispina. The reviewer is playing on a line from Roman
   satirist Juvenal's *Satire IV*, "*Ecce iterum Crispinus!*"

dies and leaves her unprovided for, tries, with not too much success, to carry out her own destiny, first as an art student, then as a novelist, and lastly as a scribbler of "personal pars"; who weakly gives her affections to a middle-aged prig, and behaves with more than ordinary vacillation when the prig, after throwing her over for a vulgar and ill-favoured but wealthy woman, begs her to run away with him. What really is the distinctive note of these novels about the New Woman is the very poor figure which man cuts in them. One would imagine that men of honour, sense, and worth had died off altogether instead of growing like blackberries by the wayside. There are many men in this novel, but not one who is not selfish, or a society "dude," or a scandal-monger, or a profligate. What sort of society, one wonders, has the writer moved in who describes a fair, well-bred, modest girl of 21 as finding it troublesome to dispose of "some men who had tired eyes and a dubious smile, and who were fond of starting doubtful topics with a side-long, tentative glance?" Are gentlemen really so scarce, and cads so plentiful? But this vein of writing is only the passing craze of the day; and, after all, Mrs. Dixon shows herself no ineffective satirist of the shams and snobbishness of society. In particular, there is a good deal of truth in her exposure of the catch-penny methods of artists— even members of the Royal Academy—as exemplified in the career of Perry Jackson, A.R.A. In fine, Mrs. Dixon is a smart and clever writer, who will do better when she dissociates herself from the sisterhood who are rending heaven with laments about the "torture, the helplessness, the impotence, and the emptiness of women's lives."

## 4. *The New York Times* (10 June 1894): 27

Not all girls who fall in art, and then try to use journalism as a stepping stone, end by committing suicide. The heroine in *The Story of a Modern Woman* has much the same experiences as Elfrida,[1] but she takes them differently, for she is of different stuff. Mary Erle is a lovable woman, and capable of loving. She is a well-bred

---

1 An allusion to another novel reviewed in the same column. Elfrida is the main character of *A Daughter of To-day* (1894), a novel written by Mrs. Everard Cotes (Sara Jeannette Duncan). Elfrida, a young girl from Sparta, Illinois, moves to Paris and fails as an artist, moves to London and fails as a journalist, and finally commits suicide.

English girl, daughter of a man of science, who leaves her, at his death, with a slender income and a hearty cub of a brother to take care of. Jimmie must go to Oxford, of course. So Mary takes to art. She toils for two years in a preparatory art school and waits patiently for the weak, fickle lover, who has gone to the Orient to get materials for a great work.

When art fails, she goes in for literature, just as Elfrida does, with a purpose quite as noble, if not as flamboyantly expressed. She lives in cheap lodgings and writes a "society article" and stories that are much like stories written by others. Her ambition is slowly crushed out of her as the years pass away. She learns to write what the public wants for bread and butter, and not too much of that. She is still, obscurely, a part of the social life in which she was born, but after the death of her friend, Alison, the rich and beautiful woman who strives, in a practical way, to lessen the sorrows of the poor, she has little interest in that.

After years of disillusion, when she is already beginning to show signs of age, she suffers a cruel temptation. Her false lover, who married a vulgar rich woman, comes to her and urges her to go away with him—to Cattaro, on the Dalmatian coast. But Mary is too strong to succumb, so he goes back to his wife and child, and she resumes her ill-paid toil. Not a cheerful summary, to be sure, but there are brightness and humor, as well as the pathos of blasted hopes, in Ella Hepworth Dixon's novel, and some of the characters are excellently drawn. The condensed narratives of Mary's childhood and youth, in England and Germany, with the episodes of the black cat and Frau Professorin, are delightful.

### 5. *The New York Tribune* (11 October 1894): 8

The moral atmosphere of *The Story of a Modern Woman*, by Ella Hepworth Dixon, is much purer than that of Mr. Monk's book.[1] The heroine, thrown by the death of her father upon her own resources in London, at first goes in for art, and then devotes herself to illustrated journalism and "society reporting," all of which are described in detail, and with a breezy and easy assurance of manner. The real "modern" touch—aside from the discussion of

---

1 Thymol Monk's *An Altar of Earth* (1894) received a condemnatory review in the space preceding this brief review of Hepworth Dixon's novel.

women—is felt when Hemming, who is tired of his rich but vulgar wife, through whose aid he has become an M.P., urges Mary to "rise above the prejudices of our false civilization" and to elope with him. Her refusal of this alluring proposal plunges him into a debauch of forty-eight hours, after which he returns to the "decorous solemnity of his home," while poor Mary tearfully proceeds to complete the arrangements for the inscription on her father's tombstone.

### 6. Thomas Bradfield, "A Dominant Note of Some Recent Fiction," *The Westminster Review* 142 (1894): 537-45

In *The Story of a Modern Woman*, Miss Hepworth Dixon tells us that "Mary, jilted by her lover at a time when her chances of marriage are over, is condemned to a long, loveless life and a solitary battle with the world." Pathetically sad as is the fate of a woman thus hardly treated, quick and true the indignation we feel in sympathy with her position, there is nevertheless something inadequate and disappointing in the novelist's conclusion. A woman deprived of a loving hope for her future is not necessarily condemned to a "long, loveless life," and only in very rare instances to a solitary battle with the world. Such a conception eliminates entirely other consoling and sustaining relations of life, banishes the distressed mind to the limits of its own disappointment, and narrows its energies without allowing it the rays of a deeper hope to assist it to triumph or desolation. There are other interests and attractions in life capable of employing a truly healthy nature and in time animating it to noblest effort. The art critic tells us that, "Rembrandt told all that a golden ray falling through a darkened room awakens in a visionary brain." It would be well if these writers would interpret in a similar manner all that the golden ray of hope is able to awaken in the darkened mind of anguished humanity. The only ideal that will help to solve the problem, or at least determine the lines upon which the attempt may be made with any hope of success, is the odd but ever new and pressing necessity of strenuously subduing instinct to law, by which the spiritual regeneration of each individual, whether male or female, will, as the years deepened, be most definitely assured. The gravest drawback, defect indeed, in the literature that has sprung up about the subject is that it is too personal for the end in view; its inspiration is too local; it has nothing of the privilege of science, of being cosmopolitan in its treatment, and hence the bizarre, confused, and disappointing nature of the manner in which the difficulty is approached. There is too much delineation of passion, too much lingering over unattractive episodes; a too great fondness for delusive sentiment without arriving at any definite principle; and, as we have said, an absence of faith in a Higher Wisdom.

## 7. *The Critic* 681 (9 March 1895): 178

This is an age when books by women about women follow each other in quick succession; when the plain is strewn with wrecks of man's respectability and supremacy; when sanctified women's faces stare pitilessly at him from the heights of angelhood; when he is considered worthy of serious mention only if he can be made to shoulder some crime, recent or of long standing, against womankind; and when, if he is not portrayed as a downright idiot, he is endowed with just enough intelligence to make him the scapegoat for all that is evil in life. It is a state of things to make a sensitive man cut woman's society forever, and betake himself to a purling stream, a fishing-rod and "The Contemplative Man's Recreation."[1] It is a book of this kind that Miss Dixon has produced. We say this without satire and with a sincere appreciation of the seriousness of her attempt to portray life as it appears to her. The story is that of a girl who had a soul and mind, who found the world cruel and destiny against her. It is written from the depths of the author's heart and from a profound conviction of its truthfulness. Mary Erle is the daughter of a distinguished professor who died without leaving a sufficient fortune for the support of his two children. She first tries art and finally drifts into journalism. For neither of these has she any decided gift, but she adopts the latter as a means of support for herself and an indolent brother who must be sent to college. She has two friends—Vincent Hemming, a weak, pompous egoist, and Alison Ives, a beautiful, brilliant girl, a member of the "smart set" "who goes in for" working-girls' clubs and "social betterment." The former friend makes love to Mary and then sails away from England, coming back later to marry a rich wife. Alison Ives dies of a cold caught in a charity hospital, whither she had gone to close the eyes of a victim of the eminent physician she was about to marry.

---

1   Izaak Walton's (1593-1683) *The Compleat Angler; or, The Contemplative Man's Recreation*, a book first published in 1653.

Mary toils on, friendless, dull, drooping, sought and loved only by a little whippersnapper of an artist who guys art and patronizes the British Public, because bad art is the only thing that fetches fame and fortune. In time Vincent Hemming comes back to Mary, having tired of his vulgar wife, and suggests a snug little Dalmatian village. Mary refuses, not because she does not love him, but because she will not deliberately injure another woman, all modern women now being pledged to help each other. Vincent posts off and indulges in an orgy and later returns decorously to his wife's door. Mary goes to the country and puts her father's grave in order. And thus ends the book. It is the record of a life unfulfilled, of a nature beaten and bleeding and crushed—an attempt to portray the battle, lost before it is begun, that woman makes against her two mortal enemies, man and society. Whatever one may think of the truthfulness of Miss Dixon's point of view, he cannot but be impressed with the profound sadness of the story and the tragic earnestness with which it is written. Possessed of a gifted mind, a strong ethical sense, a familiarity with the hollowness of London social life and a special knowledge of the peccadilloes of the smart set, she has faithfully observed and noted the sorrows of the modern woman's existence, and conscientiously nurtured an inherent belief in the injustice of man and his brutality. It is this lack of the sense of proportion that mars Miss Dixon's work. It exhibits itself in her art and in her style as well as in her judgments. The one lacks perspective and is imperfect, because she often fails entirely to convey the impression she tries to create; the other is brilliant, but at times overcrowded with incidental vignettes for whose polished details she has sacrificed the continuity of the narrative and the patience of the reader. Modernity is the quality chiefly discernable in the story, a quality so pronounced and so characteristic of the hour, that it makes George Eliot seem a classic and Olive Schreiner old-fashioned.[1]

---

1   George Eliot (Mary Ann Evans, 1819-1880) was an English novelist known for her novels *Adam Bede* (1859), *The Mill on the Floss* (1860), *Middlemarch* (1868), among others. Olive Schreiner (Olive Emilie Albertina, 1855-1920) was a South African-born author best known for her novel *The Story of an African Farm* (1883).

# Appendix B: 1883 Map of London and Locations Mentioned in the Novel

1. Regent Street
2. To Highgate Slope and Cemetery
3. St. John's Wood
4. London University
5. The Athenæum Club, Pall Mall
6. Harley Street
7. The National Gallery
8. To Mile End Road, East End
9. Mayfair District
10. Whitechapel
11. Bond Street
12a. The Reading Room, British Museum
12b. South Kensington
13. The Royal Academy
14. Kentish Town
15. Portman Square
16. Bulstrode Street
17. The Temple
18. Portland Road
19. Haverstock Hill
20. Fleet Street
21. To Tilbury
22. The Grosvenor Gallery
23. Notting Hill
24. The London Zoological Gardens
25. Waterloo Station
26. The Strand
27. Euston Stations
28. Drury Lane
29. The Regent's Park
30. The Mètropole
31. Kensington High Street; Holland House
32. Charing Cross
33. Wellington Street
34. Baker Street
35. North Gate Bridge
36. Queen's Gate
37. Swiss Cottage; Fitzjohn's Avenue

**London, England, 1883**   1. Regent Street \   2. To Highgate Slope and C
Pall Mall \   6. Harley Street \   7. The National Gallery \   8. To Mile Er
12a. The Reading Room, British Museum \ 12b. South Kensington \ 13. Th
17. The Temple \ 18. Portland Road \ 19. Haverstock Hill \ 20. Fleet St.
24. The London Zoological Gardens \ 25. Waterloo Station \ 26. The Stra
30. The Mètropole \ 31. Kensington High Street; Holland House \ 32. Ch
36. Queen's Gate \ 37. Swiss Cottage; Fitzjohn's Avenue

3. St. John's Wood \ 4. London University \ 5. The Athenæum Club,
st End \ 9. Mayfair District \ 10. Whitechapel \ 11. Bond Street \
ademy \ 14. Kentish Town \ 15. Portman Square \ 16. Bulstrode Street \
To Tilbury \ 22. The Grosvenor Gallery \ 23. Notting Hill \
Euston Stations \ 28. Drury Lane \ 29. The Regent's Park \
\ 33. Wellington Street \ 34. Baker Street \ 35. North Gate Bridge \

# Appendix C: Victorian Fear at the End of the Century: The "New Woman" Debate

[The articles below reveal some of the fundamental issues at the heart of the New Woman debate in life and through literature during the last decade of the nineteenth century. The first two, Sarah Grand's March 1894 article "The New Aspect of the Woman Question"—given credit for being the first to coin the phrase "New Woman"[1]—and Ouida's "The New Woman," a response to Grand's essay written a month later, exemplify the sweeping scope, volatile nature, and strong language of the discussions that were taking place in many journals of the day. The third, an unsigned article from *Cornhill*, oozes sarcasm and bitingly suggests that the "New Woman" has fooled herself into believing that there is more to her mission in life than marrying and raising children. The article, published in October 1894, offers for today's reader a clear indication of the Victorian stereotype of the New Woman as a hard, unfeminine, and anti-maternal creature. Ella Winston's 1896 "The Foibles of the New Woman" is also typical of anti-New Woman rants of the period, listing many of the standard arguments of the anti-suffragists, and making apparent the very real animosity felt by women who opposed the feminist movement. Hugh Stutfield's first article, "Tommyrotics," though it begins as a book review, quickly deteriorates into a diatribe about all things modern, among them the notion of the New Woman and New Woman fiction in general, "Continental decadentism," the "New Hedonism" of novelist Grant Allen, the feminism of novelist Sarah Grand, the plays of Ibsen, and the work of Oscar Wilde. His broad brush of fear and paranoia covers fiction—what he calls erotomaniac novels—and the convention of marriage, sex, and politics. Stutfield's second article, "The Psychology of Feminism," is also, ostensibly, a review of some of the day's fiction and drama, though the article quickly devolves into another of the author's harangues against what he perceived to be the evils of the day.]

---

1 For a discussion of this first recorded use of the phrase "the New Woman," see Ellen Jordan's "The Christening of the New Woman," *Victorian Newsletter* 48 (Spring 1983): 19.

1. **Sarah Grand (Frances Elizabeth McFall) "The New Aspect of the Woman Question,"** *The North American Review* **158 (March 1894): 270–76**

It is amusing as well as interesting to note the pause which the new aspect of the woman question has given to the Bawling Brothers who have hitherto tried to howl down every attempt on the part of our sex to make the world a pleasanter place to live in. That woman should ape man and desire to change places with him was conceivable to him as he stood on the hearth-rug in his lord-and-master-monarch-of-all-I-survey attitude, well inflated with his own conceit; but that she should be content to develop the good material which she finds in herself and be only dissatisfied with the poor quality of that which is being offered to her in man, her mate, must appear to him to be a thing as monstrous as it is unaccountable. "If women don't want to be men, what do they want?" asked the Bawling Brotherhood when the first misgiving of the truth flashed upon them; and then, to reassure themselves, they pointed to a certain sort of woman in proof of the contention that we were all unsexing ourselves.

It would be as rational for us now to declare that men generally are Bawling Brothers or to adopt the hasty conclusion which makes all men out to be fiends on the one hand and all women fools on the other. We have our Shrieking Sisterhood, as the counterpart of the Bawling Brotherhood. The latter consists of two sorts of men. First of all is he who is satisfied with the cow-kind of woman as being most convenient; it is the threat of any strike among his domestic cattle for more consideration that irritates him into loud and angry protests. The other sort of Bawling Brother is he who is under the influence of the scum of our sex, who knows nothing better than women of that class in and out of society, preys upon them or ruins himself for them, takes his whole tone from them, and judges us all by them. Both the cow-woman and the scum-woman are well within the range of the comprehension of the Bawling Brotherhood, but the new woman is a little above him, and he never even thought of looking up to where she has been sitting apart in silent contemplation all these years, thinking and thinking, until at last she solved the problem and proclaimed for herself what was wrong with Home-is-the-Woman's-Sphere, and prescribed the remedy.

What she perceived at the outset was the sudden and violent upheaval of the suffering sex in all parts of the world. Women were awaking from their long apathy, and, as they awoke, like healthy hungry children unable to articulate, they began to whimper for they knew not what. They might have been easily satisfied at that time had not society, like an ill-conditioned and ignorant nurse, instead of finding out what they lacked, shaken them and beaten them and stormed at them until what was once a little wail became convulsive shrieks and roused up the whole human household. Then man, disturbed by the uproar, came upstairs all anger and irritation, and, without waiting to learn what was the matter, added his own old theories to the din, but, finding they did not act rapidly, formed new ones, and made an intolerable nuisance of himself with his opinions and advice. He was in the state of one who cannot comprehend because he has no faculty to perceive the thing in question, and that is why he was so positive. The dimmest perception that you may be mistaken will save you from making an ass of yourself.

We must look upon man's mistakes, however, with some leniency, because we are not blameless in the matter ourselves. We have allowed him to arrange the whole social system and manage or mismanage it all these ages without ever seriously examining his work with a view to considering whether his abilities and his motives were sufficiently good to qualify him for the task. We have listened without a smile to his preachments, about our place in life and all we are good for, on the text that "there is no understanding a woman." We have endured most poignant misery for his sins, and screened him when we should have exposed him and had him punished. We have allowed him to exact all things of us, and have been content to accept the little he grudgingly gave us in return. We have meekly bowed our heads when he called us bad names instead of demanding proofs of the superiority which alone would give him a right to do so. We have listened much edified to man's sermons on the subject of virtue, and have acquiesced uncomplainingly in the convenient arrangement by which this quality has come to be altogether practised for him by us vicariously. We have seen him set up Christ as an example for all men to follow, which argues his belief in the possibility of doing so, and have not only allowed his weakness and hypocrisy in the matter to pass without comment, but, until lately, have not even seen the humor of his pretensions when contrasted with his practices nor held him up to that wholesome ridicule which is a stimulating corrective. Man deprived us of all proper education, and then jeered at us because we had no knowledge. He narrowed our outlook on life so that our view of it should be all distorted, and then declared that our mistaken impression of it proved us to be senseless creatures. He cramped our minds so that there was no room for reason in them, and then made merry at our want of logic. Our divine intuition was not to be controlled by him, but he did his best to damage it by sneering at it as an inferior feminine method of arriving at conclusions; and finally, after having had his own way until he lost his head completely, he set himself up as a sort of a god and required us to worship him, and, to our eternal shame be it said, we did so. The truth has all along been in us, but we have cared more for man than for truth, and so the whole human race has suffered. We have failed of our effect by neglecting our duty here, and have deserved much of the obloquy that was cast upon us. All that is over now, however, and while on the one hand man has shrunk to his true proportions in our estimation, we, on the other, have been expanding to our own; and now we come confidently forward to maintain, not that this or that was "intended," but that there are in ourselves, in both sexes, possibilities hitherto suppressed or abused, which, when properly developed, will supply to either what is lacking in the other.

The man of the future will be better, while the woman will be stronger and wiser. To bring this about is the whole aim and object of the present struggle, and with the discovery of the means lies the solution of the Woman Question. Man, having no conception of himself as imperfect from the woman's point of view, will find this difficult to understand, but we know his weakness, and will be patient with him, and help him with his lesson. It is the woman's place and pride and pleasure to teach the child, and man morally is in his infancy. There have been times when there was a doubt as to whether he was to be raised or woman was to be lowered, but we have turned that corner at last; and now woman holds out a strong hand to the child man, and insists, but with infinite tenderness and pity, upon helping him up.

He must be taught consistency. There are ideals for him which it is to be presumed that he tacitly agrees to accept when he keeps up an expensive establishment to teach them: let him live up to them. Man's faculty for shirking his own responsibility has been carried to such an extent in the past that, rather than be blamed himself when it did not answer to accuse woman, he imputed the whole consequence of his own misery-making peculiarities to God.

But with all his assumption man does not make the most of himself. He has had every advantage of training to increase his insight, for instance, but yet we find him, even at this time of day, unable to perceive that woman has a certain amount of self-respect and practical good sense—enough at all events to enable her to use the proverb about the bird in the hand to her own advantage. She does not in the least intend to sacrifice the privileges she enjoys on the chance of obtaining others, especially of the kind which man seems to think she must aspire to as so much more desirable. Woman may be foolish, but her folly has never been greater than man's conceit, and the one is not more disastrous to the understanding than the other. When a man talks about knowing the world and having lived and that sort of thing, he means something objectionable; in seeing life he generally includes doing wrong; and it is in these respects he is apt to accuse us of wishing to ape him. Of old if a woman ventured to be at all unconventional, man was allowed to slander her with the imputation that she must be abandoned, and he really believed it because with him liberty meant license. He has never accused us of trying to emulate him in any noble, manly quality, because the cultivation of noble qualities has not hitherto been a favorite pursuit of his, not to the extent at least of entering into his calculations and making any perceptible impression on public opinion; and he never, therefore, thought of considering whether it might have attractions for us. The cultivation of noble qualities has been individual rather than general, and the person who practised it is held to be one apart, if not actually eccentric. Man acknowledges that the business of life carried on according to his methods corrodes, and the state of corrosion is a state of decay; and yet he is fatuous enough to imagine that our ambition must be to lie like him for our own benefit in every public capacity. Heaven help the child to perceive with what travail and sorrow we submit to the heavy obligation, when it is forced upon us by our sense of right, of showing him how things ought to be done.

We have been reproached by Ruskin for shutting ourselves up behind park palings and garden walls,[1] regardless of the waste world that moans in misery without, and that has been too much our attitude; but the day of our acquiescence is over. There is that in ourselves which forces us out of our apathy; we have no choice in the matter. When we hear the "Help! help! help!" of the desolate and the oppressed, and still more when we see the awful dumb despair of those who have lost even the hope of help, we must

---

1   Grand refers here to John Ruskin's "Of Queens' Gardens," one of the two 1864 Manchester lectures later published as *Sesame and Lilies* (1865).

respond. This is often inconvenient to man, especially when he has seized upon a defenceless victim whom he would have destroyed had we not come to the rescue; and so, because it is inconvenient to be exposed and thwarted, he snarls about the end of all true womanliness, cants on the subject of the Sphere, and threatens that if we do not sit still at home with cotton-wool in our ears so that we cannot be stirred into having our sympathies aroused by his victims when they shriek, and with shades over our eyes that we may not see him in degradation, we shall be afflicted with short hair, coarse skins, unsymmetrical figures, loud voices, tastelessness in dress, and an unattractive appearance and character generally, and then he will not love us any more or marry us. And this is one of the most amusing of his threats, because he has said and proved on so many occasions that he cannot live without us whatever we are. O man! man! you are a very funny fellow now we know you! But take care. The standard of your pleasure and convenience has already ceased to be our conscience. On one point, however, you may reassure yourself. True womanliness is not in danger, and the sacred duties of wife and mother will be all the more honorably performed when women have a reasonable hope of becoming wives and mothers of *men*. But there is the difficulty. The trouble is not because women are mannish, but because men grow ever more effeminate. Manliness is at a premium now because there is so little of it, and we are accused of aping men in order to conceal the side from which the contrast should evidently be drawn. Man in his manners becomes more and more wanting until we seem to be near the time when there will be nothing left of him but the old Adam, who said, "It wasn't me."

Of course it will be retorted that the past has been improved upon in our day; but that is not a fair comparison. We walk by the electric light: our ancestors had only oil-lamps. We can see what we are doing and where we are going, and should be as much better as we know how to be. But where are our men? Where is the chivalry, the truth, and affection, the earnest purpose, the plain living, high thinking, and noble self-sacrifice that make a man? We look in vain among the bulk of our writers even for appreciation of these qualities. With the younger men all that is usually cultivated is that flippant smartness which is synonymous with cheapness. There is such a want of wit amongst them, too, such a lack of variety, such monotony of threadbare subjects worked to death! Their "comic" papers subsist upon repetitions of those three venerable jests, the mother-in-law, somebody drunk, and an edifying deception successfully practised by an unfaithful husband or wife. As they have nothing true so they have nothing new to give us, nothing either to expand the heart or move us to happy mirth. Their ideas of beauty threaten always to be satisfied with the ballet dancer's legs, pretty things enough in their way, but not worth mentioning as an aid to the moral, intellectual, and physical strength that make a man. They are sadly deficient in imagination, too; that old fallacy to which they cling, that because an evil thing has always been, therefore it must always continue, is as much the result of want of imagination as of the man's trick of evading the responsibility of seeing right done in any matter that does not immediately affect his personal comfort. But there is one thing the younger men are specially good at, and that is giving their opinion; this they do to each other's admiration until they verily believe it to be worth something. Yet they do not even know where we are in the history of the world. One of them only lately, doubtless by way of ingratiating himself with the rest of the Bawling Brotherhood, actually proposed to reintroduce the Acts of the Apostles-of-the-Pavements; he was apparently quite unaware of the fact that the mothers of the English race are too strong to allow themselves to be insulted by the reimposition of another most shocking degradation upon their sex. Let him who is responsible for the economic position which forces women down be punished for the consequence. If any are unaware of cause and effect in that matter, let them read *The Struggle for Life* which the young master wrote in *Wreckage*.[1] As the workingman says with Christ-like compassion: "They wouldn't be there, poor things, if they were not driven to it."

There are upwards of a hundred thousand women in London doomed to damnation by the written law of man if they dare to die, and to infamy for a livelihood if they must live; yet the man at the head of affairs wonders what it is that we with the power are protesting against in the name of our sex. But *is* there any wonder we women wail for the dearth of manliness when we find men from end to end of their rotten social system forever doing the most cowardly deed in their own code, striking at the defenceless woman, especially when she is down?

The Bawling Brotherhood have been seeing reflections of

---

1    "The Struggle for Life" is a bleak story from the collection titled *Wreckage*, published in 1893 by Hubert Crackanthorpe (1870-96). The story portrays a young mother forced by poverty to sell herself to feed her child while her husband spends *his* money on a prostitute across town.

themselves lately which did not flatter them, but their conceit survives, and they cling confidently to the delusion that they are truly all that is admirable, and it is the mirror that is in fault. Mirrors may be either a distorting or a flattering medium, but women do not care to see life any longer in a glass darkly. Let there be light. We suffer in the first shock of it. We shriek in horror at what we discover when it is turned on that which was hidden away in dark corners; but the first principle of good housekeeping is to have no dark corners, and as we recover ourselves we go to work with a will to sweep them out. It is for us to set the human household in order, to see to it that all is clean and sweet and comfortable for the men who are fit to help us to make home in it. We are bound to raise the dust while we are at work, but only those who are in it will suffer any inconvenience from it, and the self-sufficing and self-supporting are not afraid. For the rest it will be all benefits. The Woman Question is the Marriage Question, as shall be shown hereafter.

## 2. From Ouida's (Marie Louise de la Ramée) "The New Woman," *The North American Review* 158 (May 1894): 610–19

It can scarcely be disputed, I think, that in the English language there are conspicuous at the present moment two words which designate two unmitigated bores: The Workingman and the Woman. The Workingman and the Woman, the New Woman, be it remembered, meet us at every page of literature written in the English tongue; and each is convinced that on its own especial W hangs the future of the world. Both he and she want to have their values artificially raised and rated, and a status given to them by favor in lieu of desert. In an age in which persistent clamor is generally crowned by success they have both obtained considerable attention; is it offensive to say much more of it than either deserves? Your contributor avers that the Cow-Woman and the Scum-Woman, man understands, but that the New Woman is above him.[1] The elegance of these appellatives is not calculated to recommend them to readers of either sex; and as a specimen of

---

1   The mention of Cow-Woman and Scum-Woman, as well as the quoted passages sprinkled throughout this article, are references to Sarah Grand's essay "The New Aspect of the Woman Question," to which Ouida's essay is a direct response. Grand's essay precedes this one in Appendix C.

style forces one to hint that the New Woman who, we are told, "has been sitting apart in silent contemplation all these years" might in all these years have studied better models of literary composition. We are farther on told "that the dimmest perception that you may be mistaken, will save you from making an ass of yourself." It appears that even this dimmest perception has never dawned upon the New Woman.

We are farther told that "thinking and thinking" in her solitary sphynx-like contemplation she solved the problem and prescribed the remedy (the remedy to a problem!); but what this remedy was we are not told, nor did the New Woman apparently disclose it to the rest of womankind, since she still hears them in "sudden and violent upheaval" like "children unable to articulate whimpering for they know not what." It is sad to reflect that they might have been "easily satisfied at that time" (at what time?), "but society stormed at them until what was a little wail became convulsive shrieks"; and we are not told why the New Woman who had "the remedy for the problem," did not immediately produce it. We are not told either in what country or at what epoch this startling upheaval of volcanic womanhood took place in which "man merely made himself a nuisance with his opinions and advice," but apparently did quell this wailing and gnashing of teeth since it would seem that he has managed still to remain more masterful than he ought to be.

★ ★ ★ ★ ★

There is something deliciously comical in the idea, thus suggested, that man has only been allowed to "manage or mismanage" the world because woman has graciously refrained from preventing his doing so. But the comic side of this pompous and solemn assertion does not for a moment offer itself to the New Woman sitting aloof and aloft in her solitary meditation on the superiority of her sex. For the New Woman there is no such thing as a joke. She has listened without a smile to her enemy's "preachments"; she has "endured poignant misery for his sins," she has "meekly bowed her head" when he called her bad names; and she has never asked for "any proof of the superiority" which could alone have given him a right to use such naughty expressions. The truth has all along been in the possession of woman; but strange and sad perversity of taste! She has "cared more for man than for truth, and so the whole human race has suffered!"

★ ★ ★ ★ ★

Before me lies an engraving in an illustrated journal of a woman's meeting; whereat a woman is demanding in the name of her sovereign sex the right to vote at political elections. The speaker is middle-aged and plain of feature; she wears an inverted plate on her head tied on with strings under her double-chin; she has balloon-sleeves, a bodice tight to bursting, a waist of ludicrous dimensions in proportion to her portly person; she is gesticulating with one hand, of which all the fingers are stuck out in ungraceful defiance of all artistic laws of gesture. Now, why cannot this orator learn to gesticulate and learn to dress, instead of clamoring for a franchise? She violates in her own person every law, alike of common-sense and artistic fitness, and yet comes forward as a fit and proper person to make laws for others. She is an exact representative of her sex.

Woman, whether new or old, has immense fields of culture untilled, immense areas of influence wholly neglected. She does almost nothing with the resources she possesses, because her whole energy is concentrated on desiring and demanding those she has not. She can write and print anything she chooses; and she scarcely ever takes the pains to acquire correct grammar or elegance of style before wasting ink and paper. She can paint and model any subjects she chooses, but she imprisons herself in men's *atéliers* to endeavor to steal their technique and their methods, and thus loses any originality she might possess. Her influence on children might be so great that through them she would practically rule the future of the world; but she delegates her influence to the vile school boards if she be poor, and if she be rich to governesses and tutors; nor does she in ninety-nine cases out of a hundred ever attempt to educate or control herself into fitness for the personal exercise of such influence. Her precept and example in the treatment of the animal creation[1] might be of infinite use in mitigating the hideous tyranny of humanity over them, but she does little or nothing to this effect; she wears dead birds and the skins of dead creatures; she hunts the hare and shoots the pheasant, she drives and rides with more brutal recklessness than men; she watches with delight the struggles of the dying salmon, of the gralloched deer;[2] she keeps

---

1 Ouida was an ardent anti-vivisectionist and campaigner for animal rights.
2 A disemboweled deer.

her horses standing in the snow and fog for hours with the muscles of their heads and necks tied up in the torture of the bearing rein; when asked to do anything for a stray dog, a lame horse, a poor man's donkey, she is very sorry, but she has so many claims on her already; she never attempts by orders to her household, to her *fournisseurs*,[1] to her dependents, to obtain some degree of mercy in the treatment of sentient creatures and in the methods of their slaughter.

The immense area which lies open to her in private life is almost entirely uncultivated, yet she wants to be admitted into public life. Public life is already overcrowded, verbose, incompetent, fussy, and foolish enough without the addition of her in her sealskin coat with the dead humming bird on her hat. Woman in public life would exaggerate the failings of men, and would not have even their few excellencies. Their legislation would be, as that of men is too often, the offspring of panic and prejudice; and she would not put on the drag of common-sense as man frequently does in public assemblies. There would be little to hope from her humanity, nothing from her liberality; for when she is frightened she is more ferocious than he, and when she has power more merciless.

★ ★ ★ ★ ★

The unfortunate idea that there is no good education without a college curriculum is as injurious as it is erroneous. The college education may have excellencies for men in its *frottement*,[2] its preparation for the world, its rough destruction of personal conceit; but for women it can only be hardening and deforming. If study be delightful to a woman, she will find her way to it as the hart to water brooks. The author of *Aurora Leigh*[3] was not only always at home, but she was an invalid; yet she became a fine classic, and found her path to fame. A college curriculum would have done nothing to improve her rich and beautiful mind; it might have done much to debase it.

The perpetual contact of men with other men may be good for them, but the perpetual contact of women with other women is

---

1 Vendors or suppliers.
2 Literally "rubbing" or "friction," in this case *frottement* means "polishing."
3 Elizabeth Barrett Browning (1806-61) published this "novel in verse" in 1857.

very far from good. The publicity of a college must be odious to a young girl of refined and delicate feeling.

The "Scum-woman" and the "Cow-woman," to quote the elegant phraseology of your contributor, are both of them less of a menace to humankind than the New Woman with her fierce vanity, her undigested knowledge, her over-weening estimate of her own value and her fatal want of all sense of the ridiculous.

When scum comes to the surface it renders a great service to the substance which it leaves behind it; when the cow yields pure nourishment to the young and the suffering, her place is blessed in the realm of nature; but when the New Woman splutters blistering wrath on mankind she is merely odious and baneful.

The error of the New Woman (as of many an old one) lies in speaking of women as the victims of men, and entirely ignoring the frequency with which men are the victims of women. In nine cases out of ten the first to corrupt the youth is the woman. In nine cases out of ten also she becomes corrupt herself because she likes it.

It is all very well to say that prostitutes were at the beginning of their career victims of seduction; but it is not probable and it is not provable. Love of drink and of finery, and a dislike to work, are the more likely motives and origin. It never seems to occur to the accusers of man that women are just as vicious and as lazy as he is in nine cases out of ten, and need no invitation from him to become so.

★ ★ ★ ★ ★

The New Woman reminds me of an agriculturist who, discarding a fine farm of his own, and leaving it to nettles, stones, thistles, and wire-worms, should spend his whole time in demanding neighboring fields which are not his. The New Woman will not even look at the extent of the ground indisputably her own, which she leaves unweeded and untilled.

Not to speak of the entire guidance of childhood, which is certainly already chiefly in the hands of woman (and of which her use does not do her much honor), so long as she goes to see one of her own sex dancing in a lion's den, the lions being meanwhile terrorized by a male brute; so long as she wears dead birds as millinery and dead seals as coats; so long as she goes to races, steeplechases, coursing and pigeon matches; so long as she "walks with the guns"; so long as she goes to see an American lashing horses to death in idiotic contest with velocipedes;[1] so long as she courtesies before princes and emperors who reward the winners of distance-rides; so long as she receives physiologists in her drawing-rooms, and trusts to them in her maladies; so long as she invades literature without culture and art without talent; so long as she orders her court-dress in a hurry; so long as she makes no attempt to interest herself in her servants, in her animals, in the poor slaves of her tradespeople; so long as she shows herself as she does at present without scruple at every brutal and debasing spectacle which is considered fashionable; so longs as she understands nothing of the beauty of meditation, of solitude, of Nature; so long as she is utterly incapable of keeping her sons out of the shambles of modern sport, and lifting her daughters above the pestilent miasma of modern society—so long as she does not, can not, or will not either do, or cause to do, any of these things, she has no possible title or capacity to demand the place or the privilege of man.

### 3. "Character Note: The New Woman," *Cornhill* XXIII, 136 (October 1894): 365–68

"*L'esprit de la plupart des femmes sert plus à fortifier leur folie que leur raison.*"[2]

She is young, of course. She looks older than she really is. And she calls herself a woman. Her mother is content to be called a lady, and is naturally of small account. Novissima's[3] chief characteristic is her unbounded self-satisfaction.

She is dark; and one feels that if she were fair she would be quite a different person. For fairness usually goes with an interest in children, and other gentle weaknesses of which Novissima is conspicuously innocent.

She dresses simply in close-fitting garments, technically known as tailor-made. She wears her elbows well away from her side. It has been hinted that this habit serves to diminish the apparent size of the waist. This may be so. Men do not always understand such things. It certainly adds to a somewhat aggressive air of indepen-

---

1 Early versions of today's bicycles.
2 The wit of most women serves to strengthen their madness more than their reason.
3 (Latin) very new or the latest.

dence which finds its birth in the length of her stride. Novissima strides in (from the hip) where men and angels fear to tread.

In the evening simplicity again marks her dress. Always close-fitting—always manly and wholly simple. Very little jewellery, and close-fitting hair. Which description is perhaps not technical. Her hands are steady and somewhat *en évidence*. Her attitudes are strong and independent, indicative of a self-reliant spirit.

With mild young men she is apt to be crushing. She directs her conversation and her glance above their heads. She has a way of throwing scraps of talk to them in return for their mild platitudes—crumbs from a well-stored intellectual table.

"Pictures—no, I do not care about pictures," she says. "They are all so pretty nowadays."

She has a way of talking of noted men by their surnames *tout court*[1] indicative of a familiarity with them not enjoyed by her hearer. She has a certain number of celebrities whom she marks out for special distinction—obscurity being usually one of their merits.

Prettiness is one of her pet aversions. Novissima is, by the way, not pretty herself. She is white. Pink girls call her sallow. She has a long face, with a discontented mouth, and a nose indicative of intelligence, and too large for feminine beauty as understood by men. Her equanimity, like her complexion, is unassailable. One cannot make her blush. It is the other way round.

In conversation she criticises men and books freely. The military man is the object of her deepest scorn. His intellect, she tells one, is terribly restricted. He never reads—Reads, that is, with a capital. For curates she has a sneaking fondness—a feminine weakness too deeply ingrained to be stamped out in one generation of advancement.

Literary men she tolerates. They have probably read some of the books selected out of the ruck for her approval. But even to these she talks with an air suggestive of the fact that she could tell them a thing or two if she took the trouble. Which no doubt she could.

Novissima's mother is wholly and meekly under Novissima's steady thumb. The respectable lady's attitude is best described as speechless. If she opens her mouth, Novissima closes it for her with a tolerant laugh or a reference to some fictional character with whom the elder lady is fortunately unacquainted.

---

1 Simply or merely.

"Oh, Mother!" she will say, if that relative is mentioned. "Yes; but she is hopelessly behind the times, you know."

That settles Novissima's mother. As for her father—a pleasant, square-built man who is a little deaf—he is not either of much account. Novissima is kind to him as to an animal ignorant of its own strength, requiring management. She describes him as prim, and takes good care, in her jaunty way, that no deleterious fiction comes beneath his gaze.

"He would not understand it, poor old thing!" she explains.

And she is quite right.

Young Calamus,[1] the critic, has had a better education than Novissima's father. He knows half-a-dozen countries, their language and their literature. And *he* does not understand Novissima's fiction.

The world is apt to take Novissima at her own valuation. When she makes a statement—and statements are her strong point—half the people in the room know better, but make the mistake of believing that they must be wrong, because she is so positive. The other half know better also, but are too wise or too lazy to argue.

While on a visit at a great country house Novissima meets young Calamus, of whom she has spoken with an off-hand familiarity for years. The genial hostess, who knows Novissima's standpoint, sends young Calamus down to dinner with her. He is clever enough for anybody, reflects my lady. And Novissima, who is delighted, is more than usually off-hand for the sake of his vanity. Calamus, as it happens, is perfectly indifferent as to what she may be thinking of him.

He is good-natured, and entirely free from self-consciousness. He is the real thing, and not the young man who is going to do something some day. He has begun doing it already. And there is a look in his keen, fair face which suggests that he intends going on.

Novissima's alertness of mind attracts him. Being a man, he is not above the influence of a trim figure and a pair of dark eyes. This is a study, and an entirely pleasant one, for Calamus is about to begin a new novel. He thinks that Novissima will do well for a side character, which is precisely that for which she serves in our daily life. She is not like the rest. But it is the rest that we fall in love with and marry.

Novissima has for the moment forced herself to the front of the stage; but in a few years she will only be a side character. Calamus

---

1  (Latin) a pen.

knows this. He remembers the grim verdict of Dr. Kudos, his junior dean at Cambridge.

"Modern young woman! Yes; interesting development of cheap education; but she proves nothing."

Which is the worst of science. It looks upon us all as specimens, and expects us to prove something.

Novissima is pleased to approve of my lady's judgment in sending her down to dinner with Calamus. She feels that the other girls are a long way below his mental level—that they are wholly unfitted to manufacture conversation of a quality calculated to suit his literary taste.

Calamus happens to be rather a simple-minded young man. He has been everywhere. He has seen most things, and nothing seems to have touched a certain strong purity of thought which he probably acquired in the nursery. Men are thus. They carry heavier moral armour. Outward things affect them little. Novissima, on the other hand, is a little the worse for her reading.

She thinks she knows the style of talk that will suit him, and she is apparently wrong. For Calamus stares about him with speculative grey eyes. His replies are wholly commonplace and somewhat frivolous. Novissima is intensely earnest, and, in her desire to show him the depth of her knowledge, is not always discreet.

She talks of the future of women, of coming generations and woman's influence thereon.

"They had better busy themselves with the beginning of the future generation," says Calamus, in his half-listening way.

"How do you mean?"

"Children," explains Calamus in a single word.

Novissima mentions the name of one or two foreign authors not usually discussed in polite society in their own country, and Calamus frowns. She approaches one or two topics which he refuses to talk about with a simple bluntness.

He is hungry, having been among the turnips all day. He has no intention of treating Novissima to any of those delightfully original ideas which he sells to a foolish public at so much a line.

During the whole visit Novissima and Calamus are considerably thrown together. Gossips say that she runs after him. He is superficially shallow, and refuses to be deep. She is superficially deep, and betrays her shallowness at every turn. He remembers Dr. Kudos, and makes himself very agreeable. She is only a side character. She proves nothing.

Then Calamus packs up his bag and goes back to town. There

he presently marries Edith, according to a long-standing arrangement kept strictly to themselves.

Novissima is rather shocked. She feels, and says, that it is a pity. Edith is a tall girl, with motherly eyes and a clear laugh. She has no notion how clever Calamus is, and would probably care as much for him if he were a fool.

Novissima says that Mr. Calamus has simply thrown away his chance of becoming a great man. She says it, moreover, with all her customary assurance, from the high standpoint of critical disapproval that is hers. And Calamus proceeds to turn out the best work of his life-time, while Edith busies herself with mere household matters, and laughs her clear laugh over a cradle.

There is something wrong somewhere. It cannot, of course, be Novissima, for she is so perfectly sure of herself. Possibly it is Calamus who is wrong. But he is quite happy, and Edith is the same.

It is only Novissima who is not content. Dr. Kudos was right. She proves nothing. She has tried to prove that woman's mission is something higher than the bearing of children and the bringing them up. But she has failed.

### 4. From Ella W. Winston's "Foibles of the New Woman," *Forum* 21 (April 1896): 186–92

When woman revolts against her normal functions and sphere of action, desiring instead to usurp man's prerogatives, she entails upon herself the inevitable penalty of such irregular conduct, and, while losing the womanliness which she apparently scorns, fails to attain the manliness for which she strives. But, unmindful of the frowns of her observers, she is unto herself a perpetual delight, calling herself and her kind by the epithets "new," "awakened," and "superior," and speaking disdainfully of women who differ from her in what, to her judgment, is the all-important question of life—"Shall women vote or not?" To enumerate her foibles is a dangerous task, for what she asserts to-day she will deny to-morrow. She is a stranger to logic, and when consistency was given to mortals the New Woman was conspicuously absent. Her egotism is boundless. She boasts that she has discovered herself, and says it is the greatest discovery of the century. She has christened herself the "new," but when her opponent speaks of her by that name she replies with characteristic contrariety that the New Woman, like the sea-serpent, is largely an imaginary creature. Nevertheless, in the next sentence, she will refer to herself by her favorite cognomen. She has made many strange statements, and one question she often asks is, "What has changed woman's outlook so that she now desires that of which her grandmother did not dream?"

Within the past forty years woman has demanded of man much that he has graciously granted her. She wanted equality with him, and it has been given her in all things for which she is fitted and which will not lower the high standard of womanhood that he desires for her. This she accepts without relinquishing any of the chivalrous attentions which man always bestows upon her. The New Woman tells us that "an ounce of justice is of more value to woman than a ton of chivalry." But, when she obtains her "ounce of justice," she apparently still makes rigorous demands that her "ton of chivalry" be not omitted. Woman asked to work by man's side and on his level; and to-day she has the chance of so doing. The fields of knowledge and opportunity have been opened to her; and she still "desires that of which her grandmother did not dream," because, like an over-indulged child, so long as she is denied one privilege, that privilege she desires above all others. She has decided that without the ballot she can do nothing, for, in her vocabulary, ballot is synonymous with power.

★ ★ ★ ★ ★

The plea which these women make, that they need the ballot for the protection of their homes, is self-contradictory. Has the New Woman never heard that "to teach early is to engrave on marble"? If she would devote some of the time in which she struggles to obtain the ballot to rational reflection on the influence a woman has over the pre-natal life of a child, and would then consider what a mother may do with a plastic human life—say during the first seven years of its existence and before it goes out to be contaminated by the evil influences of the world—she would then find that ballots are not what women need for the protection of their homes. But the faculty of logically reasoning from cause to effect has never been characteristic of the New Woman.

She laments because government is deprived, by lack of equal suffrage, of the "keen moral sense that is native to women as a class." Since all the people in the world are born of women and trained by women, it is difficult to see how government, or anything else, lacks woman's "keen moral sense." Can women make no use of their moral sense without the ballot?

★ ★ ★ ★ ★

"Woman's vote will purify politics." This is her favorite cry. Not long since a prominent equal-suffrage lecturer, while earnestly setting forth this claim, and enlarging on the shameless manner in which men conduct elections, declared that woman's chaste and refined influence was the only thing that could change the present undesirable condition of affairs. She was not ashamed, however, to relate, before the close of her lecture, that, a short time previous, her sister had induced the family's hired man to vote for a certain measure by presenting him, on the eve of election, with a half-dozen new shirts, made by her own hands. The absurdity of this incident reached a climax when it was noticed that, in a large audience of women, few saw anything wrong in female bribery. The fair speaker omitted to inform her audience whether or not this was to be the prevailing mode of political purification, when one half of the burdens of state rest on female shoulders. But, as women never lack expedients, some purifying process, less laborious than shirt-making, may soon be devised.

The New Woman has a mania for reform movements. No sooner does she descry an evil than she immediately moves against it with some sort of an organized force. This is very noble of her—if she have no other duties to perform. It would be more gratifying if her organizations met with greater success; but alas! Her efforts, mighty as they are, usually represent just so much valuable time wasted. The evils remain, and continue to increase. She disdains to inquire into the cause of her numerous failures, and moves serenely on bent upon reforming everything she imagines to be wrong. When she gets the ballot all will be well with the world, and for that day she works and waits. But if the New Woman or any other woman neglects private duties for public works, her reform efforts are not noble, but extremely unworthy of her; for the "duty which lies nearest" is still the most sacred of duties. Possibly the many Mrs. Jellybys of the present day and the undue interest in "Borrioboola-gha"[1] may have something to do with so much being wrong in the average home and with the average individual. When we read of women assembling together, parading streets, and entering saloons to create, as they say, "a public sentiment for temperance," it is but natural to ask, "What are the children of such mothers doing in the meantime?" And it will not be strange if many of them become

---

1   Mrs. Jellyby, a character in Dickens's novel *Bleak House* (1852-53), exercises a "telescopic philanthropy," insisting that her own neglected children provide for the natives of Borrioboola-gha.

drunkards for the coming generation of reformers to struggle with. The New Woman refuses to believe that duty, like charity, begins at home, and cannot see that the most effectual way to keep clean is not to allow dirt to accumulate.

The New Woman professes to believe that all women are good and will use their influence for noble ends—when they are allowed the right of suffrage. This theory is extremely pleasant, if it were only demonstrable; but here, as elsewhere, it is folly to ignore the incontrovertible facts. Woman cannot shirk her responsibility for the sins of the earth. It is easy for her to say that men are bad; that, as a class, they are worse than women. But who trained these bad men? Was it not woman? Herein lies the inconsistency of women—striving for a chance to do good when the opportunity is inherently theirs. It is only when they have neglected to train the saplings aright that the trees are misshapen.

It was the New Woman's earliest, and is her latest, foible that woman is superior to man. Perhaps she is. But the question is not one of superiority or inferiority. There is at bottom of all this talk about women nature's inexorable law. Man is man and woman is woman. That was the order of creation and it must so remain. It is idle to compare the sexes in similar things. It is a question of difference, and the "happiness and perfection of both depend on each asking and receiving from the other what the other only can give."

> "For woman is not undevelopt man,
> But diverse: could we make her as the man,
> Sweet Love were slain: his dearest bond is this,
> Not like to like, but like in difference."[1]

Sentimental and slavish as this may sound to many ears, it is as true as any of the unchanging laws governing the universe, and is the Creator's design for the reproduction and maintenance of the race.

## 5. From Hugh Stutfield's "Tommyrotics," *Blackwood's* (June 1895): 833–45

A most excellent wag—quoted with approval by the grave and sedate *Spectator*—recently described modern fictions as "erotic, neurotic, and Tommyrotic." Judging from certain signs of the times, he might have extended his description to the mental condition in our day of a

---

1 Tennyson's 1847 narrative *The Princess: A Medley* (VII. 3097-3100).

considerable section of civilised mankind. Our restless, dissatisfied, and sadly muddled, much-inquiring generation seems to be smitten with a new malady, which so far bids fair to baffle the doctors. Society, in the limited sense of the word, still dreads the influenza and shudders at the approach of typhoid, but its most dangerous and subtle forces are beyond question "neurotics" and hysteria in their manifold forms.

A wave of unrest is passing over the world. Humanity is beginning to sicken at the daily round, the common task, of ordinary humdrum existence, and is eagerly seeking for new forms of excitement. Hence it is kicking over the traces all round. Revolt is the order of the day. The shadow of an immeasurable, and by no means divine, discontent broods over us all. Everybody is talking and preaching: one is distressed because he cannot solve the riddle of the universe, the why and the wherefore of human existence; another racks his brains to invent brand-new social or political systems which shall make everybody rich, happy, and contented at a bound. It is an age of individual and collective—perhaps I should say, collectivist—fuss, and the last thing that anybody thinks of is settling down to do the work that lies nearest to him. Carlyle is out of fashion, for Israel has taken to stoning her older prophets who exhorted to duty, submission, and suchlike antiquated virtues, and the social anarchist and the New Hedonist bid fair to take their place as teachers of mankind.

★ ★ ★ ★ ★

The physiological excursions of our writers of neuropathic fiction are usually confined to one field—that of sex. Their chief delight seems to be in making their characters discuss matters which would not have been tolerated in the novels of a decade or so ago. Emancipated woman in particular loves to show her independence by dealing freely with the relations of the sexes. Hence all the prating of passion, animalism, "the natural workings of sex," and so forth, with which we are nauseated. Most of the characters in these books seem to be erotomaniacs. Some are "amorous sensitives"; others are apparently sexless, and are at pains to explain this to the reader. Here and there a girl indulges in what would be styled, in another sphere, "straight talks to young men." Those nice heroines of "Iota's"[1] and other writers of the physiologico-pornographic

---

1  Iota, the pen-name for Kathleen Mannington Caffyn, née Hunt (1855-1926), was an Irish-born "New Woman" novelist whose most successful work, *A Yellow Aster* (1894), earned her the scorn of British anti-feminists.

school consort by choice with "unfortunates," or else describe at length their sensations in various interesting phases of their lives. The charming Gallia,[1] in the novel of that name, studies letters on the State Regulation of Vice,[2] and selects her husband on principles which are decidedly startling to the old-fashioned reader. Now this sort of thing may be very high art and wonderful psychology to some people, but to me it is garbage pure and simple, and such dull garbage too. If anybody objects that I have picked out some of the extreme cases, I reply that these are just the books that sell. That morbid and nasty books are written is nothing: their popularity is what is disquieting. I have no wish to pose as a moralist. A book may be shameless and disgusting without being precisely immoral—like the fetid realism of Zola and Mr. George Moore[3]—and the novels I allude to are at any rate thoroughly unhealthy....

★ ★ ★ ★ ★

Some critics are fond of complaining of the lack of humour in the "new" fiction. But what in heaven's name do they expect? In this age of sciolism, or half-knowledge, of smattering and chattering, we are too much occupied in improving our minds to be mirthful. In particular the New Woman, or "the desexualised half-man," as a character in *Discords*[4] unkindly calls her, is a victim of the universal passion for learning and "culture," which, when ill-digested, are apt to cause intellectual dyspepsia. With her head full of all the 'ologies and 'isms, with sex-problems and heredity, and other

---

1   *Gallia* (1895) is a novel written by the "New Woman" novelist Ménie Muriel Dowie (1867-1945). The title character agrees to marry a man she does not love because she feels she may be able to "learn" to love him.

2   Stutfield refers to the Contagious Disease Acts of the 1860s, laws which allowed for the detainment and forced treatment of prostitutes suspected of carrying venereal diseases.

3   Émile Zola (1840-1902) was a French novelist and the father of "literary Naturalism." He was a particular target of the conservative British literary critics. George Moore (1852-1933) was an Anglo-Irish novelist who followed Zola's lead and also fought against the literary censorship of the late nineteenth century. See Moore's article "Literature at Nurse or Circulating Morals" in Appendix F.

4   A novel, written in 1894 by George Egerton, pen-name of Mary Chavelita Bright, née Dunne (1859-1945), one of the most influential "New Woman" novelists.

gleanings from the surgery and the lecture-room, there is no space left for humour, and her novels are for the most part merely pamphlets, sermons, or treatises in disguise. The lady novelist of today resembles the "literary bicyclist" so delightfully satirised by the late Lord Justice Bowen.[1] She covers a vast extent of ground, and sometimes her machine takes her along some sadly muddy roads, where her petticoats—or her knickerbockers—are apt to get soiled.

★ ★ ★ ★ ★

The pathological novel is beyond question a symptom of the mental disease from which civilised mankind is suffering. And if the nerves of humanity at large were in the same state as those of the characters in erotomaniac fiction, ours would be a decaying race indeed.... As far as our decadent lady novelists are concerned, we may console ourselves with the reflection that there is one failing which they certainly do not share with their foreign originals—over-refinement of style. Whatever else may be said of them, they are, as a rule, robustly ungrammatical.

Along with its diseased imaginings—its passion for the abnormal, the morbid, and the unnatural—the anarchical spirit broods over all literature of the decadent and "revolting" type. It is rebellion all along the line. Everybody is to be a law unto himself. The restraints and conventions which civilised mankind have set over their appetites are absurd, and should be dispensed with. Art and morality have nothing to do with one another (twaddle borrowed from the French Parnassians[2]); there is nothing clean but the unclean; wickedness is a myth, and morbid impressionability is the one cardinal virtue....

★ ★ ★ ★ ★

---

1   Charles Bowen (1835-94), Lord Chief Justice of England, was a conservative judge who once said, "Trial by jury itself, instead of being a security to persons who are accused, will be a delusion, a mockery, and a snare."

2   A group of French poets led by Charles-Marie Leconte de Lisle (1818-94) and counting among its members Théophile Gautier (1811-72) and Théodore de Banville (1823-91). Their work in the middle of the century influenced the British Decadents of the 1890s.

It would appear, then, that we are approaching an era of what somebody has called "holy, awful, individual freedom." Life is henceforth to be ordered on the go-as-you-please principle. Novelists and essayists denounce the "disgusting slavery" of wedlock, and minor poets may be heard twittering about free-love and the blessedness of "group-marriages."

★ ★ ★ ★ ★

Mr. Grant Allen is of opinion that "the New Hedonist should take high ground and speak with authority." He should uphold "the moral dignity of his creed" against the "low ideals of narrow and vulgar morality." And his creed is, of course, the old anarchical one which teaches that asceticism and self-sacrifice are not only a bore, but positively disgusting. The one duty of the ego is to itself, and its mission on this sinful earth is to enjoy itself to its utmost capacity. Let us, then, follow Mr. Grant Allen and the erotomaniac authors, and take our appetites for sign-posts, and follow where the passions lead. If they land mankind, as they have in the past, in the moral abysses and abnormalities that cannot be named, what matter if only we find our pleasure? Let us cease to worship the beauty of holiness, and glorify the sexual instinct in its stead. "Everything high and ennobling in our nature," says Mr. Grant Allen, "springs from the sexual instinct." "Its subtle aroma pervades all literature." It does, indeed, and a very unpleasant aroma it is becoming. Let us, therefore, make love as soon and as often as possible, for did not Catullus and Sappho,[1] among others of the ancients, and in these degenerate days good grey Walt Whitman (so Mr. Allen styles that obscene old American twaddler), glorify the gentle passion? "Religion," he says, "is the shadow of which culture is the substance," Christianity in particular being "a religion of Oriental

---

1  Gaius Valerius Catullus (84–54 BC) was a Roman poet who is often considered the greatest writer of Latin lyric verse. Sappho, born around 630 B.C., was one of the great Greek lyric poets and one of the few known female poets of the ancient world. Her works, of which only fragments exist, include wedding songs, poems of friendship, and poetic expressions of homoerotic desire.

fanatics"; and, like his masters the æsthetes, he bids us to look to Hellas for our ideals.[1]

★ ★ ★ ★ ★

The sacredness of the marriage-tie is apparently mere old-fashioned Tory twaddle in the eyes of our *révoltés*, and the grasping dotard of a husband who fondly and selfishly hopes to retain the "monopoly" of the wife of his bosom must learn sounder, because newer, doctrine. Our wives henceforth are to be the partners, of our joys possibly, but of our sorrows only if they so desire it. The lady will take her husband, like her sewing-machine, on approval or on the three-years'-hire system. If he turns out vicious or a bore—or perhaps if he snores unduly—like Ibsen's Nora,[2] she will bang the door and develop her personality apart.... By the way, I never can find any provision made for the case of a virtuous husband who finds himself saddled with a bad wife; but then in "revolting" literature there are no such things as virtuous husbands or bad wives.

★ ★ ★ ★ ★

The *Speaker*, a sober Radical weekly, denounces the "new" prophets and all that pertains to them in language which I, for one, should not venture to use. "For many years past," it says, "Mr. Wilde has been the real leader in this country of the 'new school' in literature—the revolutionary and anarchical school which has forced itself into such prominence in every domain of art." The new criticism, the new fiction, even the new woman, "are all merely creatures of Oscar Wilde's." He is "the father of the whole flock." Surely this is rather strong, the truth being, as I have shown, that they

---

1  Grant Allen (1848-99) was a Canadian-born English novelist whose best-known work, *The Woman Who Did* (1895), is among the sharpest and most critical anti-marriage "New Woman" novels. This section's attack on Allen focuses on his article "The New Hedonism," which was published in *The Fortnightly Review* 55 (1894): 377-92. In it, Allen praises American poet Walt Whitman. The aesthetes mentioned are the Decadent artists of the 1890s such as Walter Pater, Oscar Wilde, Ernest Dowson, and Algernon Swinburne, among others, who—as far as Stutfield was concerned—turned away from Christian morality and looked to the ancient Greeks for their inspiration.

2  A reference to the heroine of *A Doll's House* (1879), Norwegian playwright Henrik Ibsen's best known play.

are all the offspring together of hysteria and Continental decadentism. Nevertheless, the influence of the æsthetic school has been undeniably great during the last decade, and the fact affords much food for melancholy reflection.

★ ★ ★ ★ ★

Hysteria, whether in politics or art, has the same inevitable effect of sapping manliness and making people flabby. To the æsthete and decadent, who worship inaction, all strenuousness is naturally repugnant. The sturdy Radical of former years, whose ideal was independence and a disdain of Governmental petting, is being superseded by the political "degenerate," who preaches the doctrine that all men are equal, when experience proves precisely the opposite, and dislikes the notion of the best man winning in the struggle to live. Individual effort is to be discouraged, while the weak and worthless are to be pampered at the expense of the capable and industrious. State aid is to dispense with the necessity of thrift and self-reliance, for men will be saved from the natural consequences of their own acts. Hence it is that your anarchist or communist is usually an ineffective person who, finding himself worsted in the battle of life, would plunge society into chaos in the hope of bettering himself.

★ ★ ★ ★ ★

Is it the fact that, as many believe, we have fallen on a temporarily sterile time, an age of "mental anæmia" and intellectual exhaustion? The world seems growing weary after the mighty work it has accomplished during this most marvellous of centuries. Perhaps the great Titan, finding his back bending under the too vast orb of his fate, would fain lie down and sleep a while. Be that as it may, in politics we seem to be losing faith in ourselves, and leaning more and more on the State for aid. In literature the effects of brain-exhaustion are certainly apparent. A generation that nourished its early youth on Shakespeare and Scott seems likely to solace its declining years with Ibsen and Sarah Grand,[1] and an

---

1  Henrik Ibsen (1828-1906), was the great Norwegian playwright whose works realistically explored the pain of destructive domestic relationships. Sarah Grand, the pen-name of Frances Elizabeth McFall (1859-1945), was a well known "New Woman" novelist. See Grand's essay "The New Aspect of the Woman Question" (1894) earlier in Appendix C.

epidemic of suicide is to be feared as a result! In no previous age has such a torrent of crazy and offensive drivel been poured forth over Europe—drivel which is not only written, but widely read and admired, and which the new woman and her male coadjutors are now trying to popularise in England.

★ ★ ★ ★ ★

If public opinion should prove powerless to check the growing nuisance, all the poor Philistine can do is to stop his ears and hold his nose until perhaps finally the policeman is called in to his aid. It is always well to dispense with that useful functionary as far as possible, but, if matters go on at the present rate, it may soon become a question whether his services will not again be required. They have proved highly effectual before now, and an occasional prosecution has an amazing moral effect upon the weak-kneed. Above all, it is to be hoped that that much-abused but most necessary official, the Licenser of Plays,[1] will harden his heart and do his duty undeterred by the ridicule heaped upon him by interested persons. Our is a free country, no doubt, but the claim for liberty to disseminate morbid abomination among the public ought not to be entertained for a moment.

Much of the modern spirit of revolt has its origin in the craving for novelty and notoriety that is such a prominent feature of our day. A contempt for conventionalities and a feverish desire to be abreast of the times may be reckoned among the first-fruits of decadentism. Its subtle and all-pervading influence is observable nowadays in the affectations and semi-indecency of fashionable conversation. The social atmosphere is becoming slightly *faisandée*, as Gautier[2] has it. Effeminacy and artificiality of manner are so common that they have almost ceased to appear ridiculous. Table-talk is garnished with the choice flowers of new woman's speech

---

1   The Lord Chamberlain's office—the crown's official Examiner of Plays—licensed, regulated, and censored plays, which had to be submitted for scrutiny before they could be performed anywhere in Great Britain. The office remained intact until the Theatre Act of 1968 took theatrical matters out of its hands.

2   Théophile Gautier (1811-72) was a French poet, novelist, and critic who subscribed wholeheartedly to the importance of *l'art pour l'art* that Walter Pater would champion in England in the 1890s. In this case, *faisandée* means "unwholesome."

or the jargon of our shoddy end-of-the-century Renaissance. In certain sections of society it requires some courage to be merely straightforward and natural. Personally, I esteem it rather a distinction to be commonplace. Affectation is not a mark of wit, nor does the preaching of a novel theory or crack-brained social fad argue the possession of a great intellect. Whence, then, sprang the foolish fear of being natural, the craving to attitudinise in everything? The answer is plain. It was Oscar Wilde who infected us with our dread of the conventional, with the silly straining after originality characteristic of a society that desires above all things to be thought intellectually smart. "To be natural is to be obvious, and to be obvious is to be inartistic"; and the buffoonery of a worldly-wise and cynical charlatan was accepted by many as inspired gospel truth. Truly, they be strange gods before whom modern culture bows down! But let the Philistine take heart of grace. He is not alone in his fight for common-sense and common-decency. That large number of really cultivated people whose instincts are still sound and healthy, who disbelieve in "moral autonomy," but cling to the old ideals of discipline and duty, of manliness and self-reliance in men, and womanliness in women; who sicken at Ibsenism and the problem play, at the putrid eroticism of a literature that is at once hysterical and foul; who, despising the apes and mountebanks of the new culture, refuse to believe that to be "modern" and up-to-date is to have attained to the acme of enlightenment—all these will be on his side.

## 6. From Hugh Stutfield's "The Psychology of Feminism," *Blackwood's* (January 1897): 104-17

The Soul of Woman, its Sphinx-like ambiguities and complexities, its manifold contradictions, its sorrows and joys, its vagrant fancies and never-to-be-satisfied longings, furnish the literary analyst of these days with inexhaustible material. Above all do the sex-problem novelist and the introspective biographer and essayist revel in the theme. Psychology—word more blessed than Mesopotamia—is their never-ending delight; and modern woman, who, if we may believe those who claim to know most about her, is a sort of walking enigma, is their chief subject of investigation. Her ego, that mysterious entity of which she is now only just becoming conscious, is said to remain a *terra incognita* even to herself; but they are determined to explore its inmost recesses. The pioneers of this formidable undertaking must of necessity be women. Man, great, clumsy, comical creature that he is, knows nothing of the inner springs of the modern Eve's complicated nature. He sees everything in her, we are told, without comprehending anything, and the worst of it is that often he cannot even express his ignorance in good English. Man possesses brute force, woman divine influence, and her nature is in closer relation with the infinite than the masculine mind. He is an "utter failure," while her womanhood "almost guarantees to her a knowledge of the eternal verities," which he can only hope partially to attain to through woman.

Obviously, therefore, it is to women writers that we must look for the solution of what is termed the "feminine enigma," and more especially to their more recently published works. It is only lately that woman has really begun to turn herself inside out, as it were, and to put herself into the book.

★ ★ ★ ★ ★

[T]he lady writer has for some years past been busily occupied in baring her soul for our benefit. And not only baring it, but dissecting it, analysing and probing into the innermost crannies of her nature. She is for ever examining her mental self in the looking-glass. Her every thought and impulse, her fleeting whims and fancies, along with the deepest fountains of her feeling, and above all her grievances, are set forth in naked black and white. The monotony of her life, its narrowness of interest, the brutality and selfishness of man, the burden of sex, and the newly awakened consciousness of ill-usage at Nature's hands, form the principal subjects of her complaint; and the chorus of her wailings surges up to heaven in stories, poems, and essays innumerable. Their dominant note is restlessness and discontent with the existing order of things; and that there is some reason in it few will be found to deny. Man has no idea what it feels like to be a woman, but it will not be her fault if he does not soon begin in some degree to understand.

★ ★ ★ ★ ★

There is much that is pathetic in the self-questioning and the cravings of the type of woman depicted in neurotic fiction. There is a note of infinite weariness, a kind of anæmic despondency, in books of the "Keynotes" class;[1] but there is also a note of real pain. No

---

1 *Keynotes* (1893), a collection of stories, is George Egerton's best-known work. It helped to launch the "Keynotes" series of works by other New Woman novelists.

one can read them without seeing that the writers have felt, and felt deeply; but while their dolefulness may command our sympathy, the expression of it in hysterical or squalid stories is not to be encouraged, for it does but add one grain more to the heap of humanity's woes. The sale of these books by thousands is not a healthy sign. People read them because they are interested in them, and the interest arises from the fact that what they read corresponds to something in their own natures. Fru Hansson[1] tells us that when *Keynotes* was published the critics said that the heroines were exceptional types; but the critics, as usual, were wrong. "'Good heavens! How stupid they are!' laughed Mrs. Egerton. Numberless women wrote to her, women whom she did not know, and whose acquaintance she never made. 'We are quite ordinary everyday sort of people,' they said; 'we lead trivial unimportant lives: but there is something in us that vibrates to your touch, for we, too, are such as you describe'." If so many hysterical people really exist, the best advice that can be given them is to try and cultivate a sense of humour and to "bike" in moderation.

One morbid symptom of our social life is certainly fostered and developed by books of the "revolting" type, and that is the mutual suspiciousness of men and women. Fru Hansson remarks that, in spite of the breaking down of many barriers of social intercourse, there never was a time when the sexes stood wider apart than at present; and when man is represented by so many lady novelists as a blackguard or an idiot, or both, sometimes diseased, always a libertine and a bully, one can hardly wonder at the result. There is no doubt that the literature of vituperation and of sex-mania, with its perpetual harping on the miseries of married life, and its public washing of domestic dirty linen, tends to widen the breach between men and women, and to make them more mutually distrustful than ever.

To institute comparisons between the literary pygmies of these days and the giants of the past may possibly provoke a smile. Nevertheless it may be useful, perhaps, *magnis componere parsa*,[2] to see in what qualities we moderns are especially deficient. As far as mere style goes, there are many living writers who are the superi-

---

1 Laura Marholm-Hansson (1854-1928) published *Das Buch der Frauen* (*Modern Woman*), a series of six psychological sketches of famous modern women of various nationalities, in 1896. One of the women profiled is George Egerton.

2 For the sake of comparison.

ors of Scott, to take a single example. This sounds rank heresy, but it is nevertheless true. But in such larger matters as character-drawing, in breadth of sympathy and observation, and, most of all, in their sense of proportion and the atmosphere of restfulness and restraint which envelops their work, the older authors far surpass their successors. Unlike the latter, the great novelists of this century were never morbid or hysterical, and they maintained a dignified reticence in dealing with delicate subjects. The soul of woman was presented by them in less questionable shape. One cannot imagine Diana Vernon,[1] to take one instance that occurs to me, prattling in public about her sexual emotions. Very possibly she may have been filled, like any young person in modern fiction, with "erotic yearnings for fulness of life," but at any rate she had the good taste to keep them to herself. The feebler literary folk of to-day have departed from the wholesome traditions, and have determined to set themselves free from what one of their number, Mr. Grant Allen, calls "the leprous taint of respectability." Not content with the shining examples set them by their great English forerunners, they blindly copy French and Norwegian models, and endeavour to supplement their own lack of talent, and to stimulate the flagging interest of their readers, by concentrating their attention upon whatever is foul and unlovely in life.

I read in the newspapers not long ago that an American lady was fortunate enough to obtain the coveted appointment of Garbage Inspector in the town of Denver, with power to burn and destroy the city refuse; and the thought struck me that it might be well if some enterprising Englishwoman could be found to undertake the post of Literary Garbage Inspector in this country, with authority to relieve the shelves of our circulating libraries of the rubbish under which they groan. I fear, however, the task would be beyond the powers of any single person to accomplish. In the long-run the reading public must always be its own censor of books, with the Press as its most effective auxiliary; and it is the lâches[2] of the Press that are largely responsible for the vulgarisation of our fiction in the past decade. As far as concerns the past year, it may readily be admitted that both the literature and the drama of 1896 have shown a distinct improvement upon those of two or three years ago. The protests of the Philistines have not been altogether in vain. We have seen less of our so-called realists and second-hand Dia-

---

1  The headstrong heroine of Sir Walter Scott's 1817 novel *Rob Roy*.
2  Cowards.

bolists, our fishers for grotesque fantasies in the unclean waters of a diseased imagination. The tide of popular taste is flowing in healthier channels, and the change seems to have affected even that most "modern" of poets, Mr. John Davidson.[1] We thought he belonged to the anarchical school, but the following verse of his "Ballad of a Workman" seems to prove him a convert to the old-fashioned ideas of discipline and self-restraint:—

"Only obedience can be great;
It brings the Golden Age again;
Even to be still, abiding Fate,
Is kingly ministry to men!"

I commend these lines, coming as they do from so unexpected a quarter, to those ladies whose souls are filled with the fret and fury of revolt or the questionings and self-torture of the new psychology. Such sentiments might have emanated from Carlyle himself—so little do they accord with our modern "eleuthero-mania,"[2] or the triumphant doctrine of the ego. We seem to have quitted awhile the seductive society of Baudelaire's *surhomme* or the *Ur-mensch* of Nietzsche,[3] so beloved of the *Keynotes* novelist, and to be listening once more to the voice of the older prophets. I rather fear, however, lest Mr. Davidson may be preaching to deaf ears. Counsels of obedience will be lost upon those watchers for the dawning of the *dies dominæ*[4] who claim, not equality, but admitted supremacy, for their sex. "To be still" is advice no less unpalatable to our neuropaths, male or female, who are so busily occupied in rendering the burden of existence intolerable. It would be well, indeed, if they could be induced to follow it. Both in life and in literature humanity has less need nowadays of mental excitants than of sedatives; and the true prophet of the future will be, not another Ibsen, but one who shall deliver to a disordered world the great gospel of Anti-Fuss.

---

1  Davidson (1857-1909) was a Scottish poet of the realist school, a man whose poems' "dingy urban images" influenced T.S. Eliot.
2  Freedom-mania.
3  French poet Charles Baudelaire's (1821-67) *surhomme*, or superman, was a snobbish aesthete, a dandy, proof of a purposeless existence; German philosopher Friedrich Nietzsche's (1844-1900) *Ur-mensch* or "prehistoric" or "primal" man from whom modern man has descended.
4  Women of the day or new women.

# Appendix D: The New Woman as "Wild Woman": The Exchange between E.L. Linton and Mona Caird

[Eliza Lynn Linton (1822-98), the author of the three "Wild Women" articles excerpted below, was a popular novelist whose career spanned nearly fifty years. From the mid–1860s until the end of her life, she dedicated herself to writing numerous vituperative anti–feminist novels and articles, attacking what she called "the girl of the period" and espousing her philosophy that "[a]ll reforms we have striven for have been granted. Nothing further is now required." Her three articles remain remarkable today for their exposure of Linton's unshaded anger and unwavering bitterness toward the "Women's Rights" movement. Alison Mona Caird (1854-1931) was a successful "New Woman" novelist whose popular and controversial *The Wing of Azrael* (1889) and *The Daughters of Danaus* (1894) helped to stir the "Woman Question" debate. She wrote her powerful response to Linton's attacks against "Wild Women" in May 1892.]

## 1. From Eliza Lynn Linton's "The Wild Women as Politicians," *Nineteenth Century* 30 (July 1891): 79-88

All women are not always lovely, and the wild women never are. As political firebrands and moral insurgents they are specially distasteful, warring as they do against the best traditions, the holiest functions, and the sweetest qualities of their sex. Like certain "sports" which develop hybrid characteristics, these insurgent wild women are in a sense unnatural. They have not "bred true"— not according to the general lines on which the normal woman is constructed. There is in them a curious inversion of sex, which does not necessarily appear in the body, but is evident enough in the mind. Quite as disagreeable as the bearded chin, the bass voice, flat chest, and lean hips of a woman who has physically failed in her rightful development, the unfeminine ways and works of the wild women of politics and morals are even worse for the world in which they live. Their disdain is for the duties and limitations imposed on them by nature, their desire as impossible as that of the moth for the star. Marriage, in its old-fashioned aspect as the union of two lives, they repudiate as a one-sided tyranny; and maternity, for which, after all, women primarily exist, they regard as degradation. Their idea of freedom is their own preponderance, so that they shall do all they wish to do without let or hindrance from outside regulations or the restraints of self-discipline; their idea of morality, that men shall do nothing they choose to disallow. Their grand aim is to directly influence imperial politics, while they, and those men who uphold them, desire to shake off their own peculiar responsibilities.

Such as they are, they attract more attention than perhaps they deserve, for we believe that the great bulk of Englishwomen are absolutely sound at heart, and in no wise tainted with this pernicious craze. Yet, as young people are apt to be caught by declamation, and as false principles know how to present themselves in specious paraphrases, it is not waste of time to treat the preposterous claims put forth by the wild women as if they were really serious—as if this little knot of noisy Mænads[1] did really threaten the stability of society and the well-being of the race.

Be it pleasant or unpleasant, it is none the less an absolute truth— the *raison d'être* of a woman is maternity. For this and this alone nature has differentiated her from man, and built her up cell by cell and organ by organ. The continuance of the race in healthy reproduction, together with the fit nourishment and care of the young after birth, is the ultimate end of woman as such; and whatever tells against these functions, and reduces either her power or her perfectness, is an offence against nature and a wrong done to society. If she chooses to decline her natural office altogether, and to dedicate to other services a life which has no sympathy with the sex of humanity, that comes into her lawful list of preferences and discords. But neither then nor while she is one with the rest, a wife and mother like others, is she free to blaspheme her assigned functions; nor to teach the young to blaspheme them; nor yet to set afoot such undertakings as shall militate against the healthy performance of her first great natural duty and her first great social obligation.

*[margin handwritten: * a woman is born to be a "mother"]*

The cradle lies across the door of the polling-booth and bars the way to the senate. We can conceive of nothing more disastrous to a woman in any stage of maternity, expectant or accomplished, than the heated passions and turmoil of a political contest; for we may put out of court three fallacies—that the vote, if obtained at all, is

---

1 The Mænads, whose name means "frenzied women," were the female attendants of Dionysus (in Rome, Bacchus), the god of wine and revelry.

*[margin note: ~vote should only be for widows + spinsters]*

to be confined to widows and spinsters only; that enfranchised women will content themselves with the vote and not seek after active office; and that they will bring into the world of politics the sweetness and light claimed for them by their adherents, and not, on the contrary, add their own shriller excitement to the men's deeper passions. Nor must we forget that the franchise for women would not simply allow a few well-conducted, well-educated, self-respecting gentlewomen to quietly record their predilection for Liberalism or Conservatism, but would let in the far wider flood of the uneducated, the unrestrained, the irrational and emotional—those who know nothing and imagine all—those whose presence and partisanship on all public questions madden already excited men.

\* \* \* \* \*

By the grace of good luck the question has been shelved for the present session, but the future is ahead. And as, unfortunately, certain of the Conservative party coquet with the woman's vote, believing that they shall thus tap a large Conservative reservoir, we are by no means clear of the danger. What we would wish to do is to convince the young and undetermined that political work is both unwomanly and unnatural; self-destructive and socially hurtful; the sure precursor to the loss of men's personal consideration and to the letting loose the waters of strife; and—what egotism will not regard—the sure precursor to a future regime of redoubled coercion and suppression.

*[margin note: \* need to convince young women — politics is unnatural + self-destructive]*

For, after all, the strong right arm is the *ultima ratio*,[1] and God will have it so; and when men found, as they would, that they were outnumbered, outvoted, and politically nullified, they would have recourse to that ultimate appeal—and the last state of women would be worse than their first.

## 2. From Eliza Lynn Linton's "The Wild Women as Social Insurgents," *Nineteenth Century* 30 (October 1891): 596–605

We must change our ideals. The Desdemonas and Dorotheas, the Enids and Imogens, are all wrong. Milton's Eve is an anachronism,

---

1 The final argument.

so is the Lady, so is Una; so are Christabel and Genevieve.[1] Such women as Panthea and Alcestis, Cornelia and Lucretia,[2] are as much out of date as the chiton and the peplum,[3] the bride's hair parted with a spear, or the worth of a woman reckoned by the flax she spun and thread she wove, by the number of citizens she gave to the State, and the honour that reflected on her through the heroism of her sons. All this is past and done with—effete, rococo, dead. For the *"tacens et placens uxor"*[4] of old-time dreams we must acknowledge now as our Lady of Desire the masterful *domina*[5] of real life—that loud and dictatorial person, insurgent and something more, who suffers no one's opinion to influence her mind, no venerable law hallowed by time, nor custom consecrated by experience, to control her actions. Mistress of herself, the Wild Woman as a social insurgent preaches the "lesson of liberty" broadened into lawlessness and licence. Unconsciously she exemplifies how beauty can degenerate into ugliness, and shows how the once fragrant flower, run to seed, is good for neither food nor ornament.

Her ideal of life for herself is absolute personal independence coupled with supreme power over men. She repudiates the doctrine of individual conformity for the sake of the general good, holding the self-restraint involved as an act of slavishness of which no woman worth her salt would be guilty. She makes between the sexes no dis-

---

1  The figures mentioned here all represent the notion of the suffering but steadfast and loyal woman. Desdemona is the tragic heroine of Shakespeare's *Othello* (1602); Dorothea Brooke is the main figure in George Eliot's novel *Middlemarch* (1871-72); Enid is a heroine in Tennyson's *Idylls of the King* (1859-85); Imogen is the heroine in Shakespeare's *Cymbeline* (1609-10); Milton's Eve is found in *Paradise Lost* (1667); the Lady is from Milton's *Comus* (1637); Una is the heroine in the first book of Edmund Spenser's *The Faerie Queene* (1590-96); Christabel is the main figure in S.T. Coleridge's unfinished *Christabel* (1797-1801; 1816); and Genevieve appears in Coleridge's poem *Love* (1799).

2  The four women mentioned here all represent faith and devotion. Panthea committed suicide after learning that her husband, Abradactus, whom she had urged to become heroic even if it meant dying, had been killed in battle; Cornelia was a revered Roman matron; Alcestis forfeited her life to save her husband, Admentus; Lucretia, raped by Sextus, killed herself rather than live with the shame.

3  The chiton was a tunic and the peplum was a loose outer robe, both worn by women in ancient Greece.

4  A silent and pleasing wife.

5  A dominating woman.

tinctions, moral or aesthetic, nor even personal; but holds that what is lawful to the one is permissible to the other. Why should the world have parcelled out qualities or habits into two different sections, leaving only a few common to both alike? Why, for instance, should men have the fee-simple of courage, and women that of modesty? To men be given the right of the initiative—to women only that of selection? To men the freer indulgence of the senses—to women the chaster discipline of self-denial? The Wild Woman of modern life asks why; and she answers the question in her own way.

★ ★ ★ ★ ★

The Wild Women, in their character, of social insurgents, are bound by none of the conventions which once regulated society. In them we see the odd social phenomenon of the voluntary descent of the higher to the lower forms of ways and works. "Unladylike" is a term that has ceased to be significant. Where "unwomanly" has died out we could scarcely expect this other to survive. The special must needs go with the generic, and we find it so with a vengeance! With other queer inventions the frantic desire of making money has invaded the whole class of Wild Woman; and it does not mitigate their desire that, as things are, they have enough for all reasonable wants. Women who, a few years ago, would not have shaken hands with a dressmaker, still less have sat down to table with her, now open shops and set up in business on their own account—not because they are poor, which would be an honourable and sufficing reason enough, but because they are restless, dissatisfied, insurgent, and like nothing so much as to shock established prejudices and make folk stare. It is such a satire on their inheritance of class distinction, on their superior education—perhaps very superior, stretching out to academical proportions! It is just the kind of topsy-turvydom that pleases them.

★ ★ ★ ★ ★

The spirit of the day is both vagrant and self-advertising, both bold and restless, contemptuous of law and disregarding restraint. We do not suppose that women are intrinsically less virtuous than they were in the time of Hogarth's "Last Stake";[1] but they are more dis-

---

1   William Hogarth's 1758 oil painting "The Lady's Last Stake" portrays a
    woman resisting the attention of a suitor.

satisfied, less occupied, and infinitely less modest. All those old similes about modest violets and chaste lilies, flowers blooming unseen; and roses that "open their glowing bosom" but to one love only—all these are rococo as the Elizabethan ruff or Queen Anne's "laced head." Everyone who has a "gift" must make that gift public, and, so far from wrapping up talents in a napkin, pence are put out to interest, and the world is called on to admire the milling. The enormous amount of inferior work which is thrown on the market in all directions is one of the marvels of the time. Everything is exhibited. If a young lady can draw so far correctly as to give her cow four legs and not five, she sends her sketches to some newspaper, or more boldly transfers them on to a plate or a pot, and exhibits them at some art refuge for the stage below mediocrity.

★ ★ ★ ★ ★

About these Wild Women is always an unpleasant suggestion of the adventuress. Whatever their natural place and lineage, they are of the same family as those hotel heroines who forget to lock the chamber door—those confiding innocents of ripe years, who contract imperfect marriages—those pretty country blossoms who begin life modestly and creditably, and go on to flaunting notoriety and disgrace. One feels that it is only the accident of birth which differences these from those, and determines a certain stability of class.

★ ★ ★ ★ ★

Aggressive, disturbing, officious, unquiet, rebellious to authority and tyrannous to those whom they can subdue, we say emphatically that they are about the most unlovely specimens the sex has yet produced, and between the "purdah-woman"[1] and the modern *homasses*,[2] we, for our own parts, prefer the former. At least the purdah-woman knows how to love. At least she has not forgotten the traditions of modesty as she has been taught them. But what about our half-naked girls and young wives, smoking and drink-

---

1   The behavior that the Muslim faith expects of women may be seen in Purdah, the moral obligation of the woman to live in seclusion, in submission, and with modesty.
2   A "mannish" woman.

ing with the men? Our ramping platform orators? Our unabashed self-advertisers? Our betting women? Our horse-breeders? Our advocates of free love and our contemners of maternal life and domestic duties?

★ ★ ★ ★ ★

Excrescences of the times, products of peace and idleness, of prosperity and overpopulation—would things be better if a great national disaster pruned our superfluities and left us nearer to the essential core of facts? Who knows! Storms shake off the nobler fruit but do not always beat down the ramping weeds. Still, human nature has the trick of pulling itself right in times of stress and strain. Perhaps, if called upon, even our Wild Women would cast off their ugly travesty and become what modesty and virtue designed them to be; and perhaps their male lovers would go back to the ranks of masculine self-respect, and leave off this base subservience to folly which now disfigures and unmans them. *Chi lo sa?*[1] It does no one harm to hope. This hope, then, let us cherish while we can and may.

### 3. From Eliza Lynn Linton's "The Partisans of the Wild Women," *Nineteenth Century* 31 (March 1892): 455–64

To all movements, wise or foolish, flock the two classes of followers —the sincerely convinced and the insincerely affiliated; those who think they are helping to establish the law of righteousness on this earth, and those who see nothing but their own advantage in a general "stramash," when they may pick up some pieces in the scramble. It has always been so, and, pending the arrival of the Millennium, always will be so. Wherefore, following the universal law, we find in the new school of Wild Women both *preux chevaliers*[2] and despicable campfollowers—partisans sincerely believing in the merit of the cause to which they have devoted themselves, and partisans who, with tongue stuck into cheek, believe they can make a good thing for themselves out of it; and who but a fool thinks of aught else?

For the former of these partisans we have only moral respect in spite of strong intellectual deprecation. We think them mistaken,

---

1 Who knows?
2 Valiant knights.

but we know them to be sincere. We question their taste, deplore their sympathies, and wish they could, or would, see farther ahead; but we honour their motives and confess their integrity. Still, how much soever we may respect them as individuals, we cannot shut our eyes to the fact that they are doing their best to bring about one of the greatest social and national disasters that could befall us. Dazzled by the rainbows in the spray, fascinated by that long shining strip in the far distance, they have determined to shoot Niagara for the problematical gain to be found—After. We who do not believe in the wisdom of shooting Niagara, and who foresee the wreck of that After, we would hold them back if we could, as we would hold back dreaming pilots and visionary engine-drivers. All the same for themselves personally, of pure intention and absolute sincerity as they are, we have only moral respect as we say, while opposing them inch by inch on the practical grounds of expediency.

★ ★ ★ ★ ★

For none of those sincerely converted partisans can we find a hard word or a disrespectful thought. We look on them as dupes fatally deluded, or as zealots still more fatally mistaken; but to wish to open their eyes is not to strike them in the face. That may be reserved for the wilfully mischievous who advocate general disorder for their own advantage—the selfish wreckers who, by false lights promising safe harborage, would bring the good ship on to the rocks, for the private gain to be had in the general loss.

★ ★ ★ ★ ★

The one thing they cannot brook is opposition; and the generous allowance of differences is the large grace of God to which they cannot attain. We have only to read their utterances in their chosen organs to judge for ourselves of the small spite, the dishonest interpretation, the reckless assertion and the purely feminine habit of "nagging" which pervades the whole mind and words of these partisans and echoes of the Wild Women of the day.

In politics, in morals, in taste, they are equally examples of what to avoid. Whatever tells against the dignity and integrity of our empire they advocate. They eulogise and uphold the pronounced enemies of our country. They would give the keys of our foreign possessions into the hands of Russia or of France; they brand patriotism as jingoism;

*"Wild women" quest*

and they teach all who will listen to them to break the laws, to despise our national institutions, to ridicule our national traditions, to dishonour our national flag. Cowards to pain, they prefer dishonour to war, and the price they would pay for peace would include the surrender of all that a manly people holds dear. They hate nothing so much as a resolute Government prepared to maintain the English name and prestige at all hazards; and to turn the other cheek to the smiter costs them no effort in foreign policy.

★ ★ ★ ★ ★

In morality they follow on the same track. Their morals are the morals of women, not of men. The grand and heroic virtues of masculine men—like the Stoics say when Stoicism meant self-control and public virtue—these virtues are nowhere with them, while high-falutin' fanfaronnades or noisy declamations bear away the palm. They shrink from all these Stoical virtues, call them cold and hard, materialistic and final; while indiscriminate pity, enthusiastic credulity, spiritual and religious crazes of every kind and description, or impossible philanthropy and the idealisation of masculine chastity, overshadow all the rest. How should it not be so? Affiliated to the Wild Women and their cause, they are themselves like women in all essentials of mind and character.

★ ★ ★ ★ ★

The taste of these partisans is as queer as their morality and as doubtful as their politics. If a woman does anything specially unfeminine and ugly, the hysterical press breaks forth into a hymn of praise which takes away one's breath. A woman who smokes in public and where she is forbidden, who dresses in knickerbockers or a boy's suit, who trails about in tigerskins, who flouts conventional decencies and offends against all the canons of good taste, that woman is pronounced "charming," and the able editor turns on one of his young lions to write her eulogium and celebrate her extravagance.... The less lovely the thing, the more ardently it is celebrated by the men whose main endeavour in this direction is to destroy the old ideals, and to substitute for the beautiful women of history and fiction the swaggering Wild Women of the present craze.

★ ★ ★ ★ ★

Few women are large-minded enough to prefer knowledge to sentiment. The cold light of reason blinds and terrifies them; and things which they do not care to know they would forbid others to learn, if they had the power of the veto. They would confine the area of men's excursions to the limits of their own; and such conditions of the masculine life as they did not care to adopt they would forbid men to practise.

★ ★ ★ ★ ★

Impatient of rebuke, of opposition, of reasonable advice, these partisans, like the Wild Women they champion, show only disrespect to one who runs counter to their craze, no matter how worthy he may be of honour and attention. Let anyone commend to these female runagates quietness, duty, home-staying, and the whole cohort of Wild Women is like an angry beehive which a rough hand has disturbed. They care nothing for home; quietness is abhorrent to them; duty went out with their grandmothers' caps and mittens. They will not hear of differences in virtues, in functions, in duties, in spheres. They do not even honour those of their own sex who do good work quietly, without tomtoms or cowhorns to call attention to their feats. They think them spiritless, and for a very little would brand them as slaves too deeply degraded by slavery to wish for freedom—as squaws whose mission it is to serve the braves and take their leavings with humility. They have lost all respect for the old ideal of womanhood, as they have lost the wish to realise that ideal. They repudiate the charm which gives them influence, and stretch out their hands for the rod of direct power which would turn into a serpent if they had it. And their partisans encourage them with voice and hand, and urge them on to ever fresh outbreaks and more monstrous demands.

The whole thing is an epidemic of vanity and restlessness—a disease as marked as measles or small-pox. Let that be clearly understood. Hereafter this outbreak will stand in history as an instance of national sickness, of moral decadence, of social disorder. Things repeat themselves, and the Revolt of Women has been seen in the world before now. We have no hope of those who are already committed to this subversive movement. It takes courage of a different kind from theirs to acknowledge a mistake. But we may influence some of the younger, hesitating on the brink. Would that they would draw back from the fatal plunge while yet there is time! Would that they could be made to see clearly the folly of their demands and the evil that would come on their attainment! The way of escape is still open to them. In a short time they will have become as hardened as their leaders, and too deeply committed to turn back. Then repentance and restoration will be impossible.

## 4. From Mona Caird's "A Defence of the So-Called 'Wild Women'," *Nineteenth Century* 31 (May 1892): 811-28

The first impulse of women whom Mrs. Lynn Linton calls "wild" is probably to contradict the charges that she makes against them in the course of three ruthless articles, but reflection shows the futility as well as the inconsequence of such a proceeding. After all, those who have lost faith in the old doctrines are not so much concerned to prove themselves, as individuals, wise and estimable, as to lead thinking men and women to consider the nature of popular sentiments with regard to the relation of the sexes, and to ask themselves whether the social fiat which for centuries has forced every woman, whatever be her natural inclinations or powers, into one avocation be really wise or just; whether, in truth, it be in the interests of the race to deprive one half of it of liberty of choice, to select for them their mode of existence, and to prescribe for them their very sentiments.

To the task of opposing the conclusions of Mrs. Lynn Linton her adversaries must bring considerable force and patience, and for this singular reason, that she gives them nothing to answer. One cannot easily reply to strings of accusations against the personal qualities of women who venture to hold views at variance with those at which the world arrived at some happy and infallible epoch in its history. The unbeliever finds himself thrown back upon the simple schoolroom form of discussion, consisting in flat contradiction, persistently repeated until the energies give out. As this method appears undignified and futile, it seems better to let most of the charges pass in silence, commenting only on one or two here and there in passing. It is of no real moment whether Mrs. Lynn Linton's unfavourable impression of the women who differ from her in this matter be just or unjust, the question is simply: are their views nearer or farther from the truth than the doctrines from which they dissent? As regards their personal qualities, it must in fairness be remembered that the position of the advocate of an unpopular cause is a very trying one, the apostles of a new faith are generally driven, by the perpetual fret of opposition and contempt, to some rancour or extravagance; but such conduct merely partakes of the frailty of human nature, and ought not to prejudice a really impartial mind against the views themselves.

\* \* \* \* \*

It would be interesting to make a collection from the writings of Mrs. Lynn Linton of all the terrific charges she has brought against her sex, adding them up in two columns, and placing side by side the numerous couples that contradict each other. At the end of this sad list one might place the simple sentence of defence, "No, we aren't!" and although this would certainly lack the eloquence and literary qualities of Mrs. Lynn Linton's arguments, I deny that it would yield to them in cogency.

There is nothing that is mean, paltry, ungenerous, tasteless, or ridiculous of which the woman who repudiates the ancient doctrines is not capable, according to this lady, unless, indeed, they are such abject fools that they have not the energy to be knaves. The logic is stern: either a woman is a "modest violet, blooming unseen," unquestioning, uncomplaining, a patient producer of children regardless of all costs to herself; suffering "everyone's opinion to influence her mind," and "all venerable laws hallowed by time ... to control her actions"—either this, or a rude masculine creature, stamping over moors with a gun that she may ape the less noble propensities of man; an adventuress who exposes herself to the dangers of travel simply that she may advertise herself in a book on her return, a virago who desires nothing better than to destroy in others the liberty that she so loudly demands for herself There is, according to Mrs. Lynn Linton, no medium between Griselda and a sublimated Frankenstein's monster,[1] which we have all so often heard of and seldom seen. Mrs. Lynn Linton's experience in this respect appears to have been ghastly. This is greatly to be regretted, for it has induced her to divide women roughly into two great classes: the good, beautiful, submissive, charming, noble, and wise on the one hand, and on the other, the bad, ugly, rebellious, ill-mannered, ungenerous, and foolish. The "wild women" are like the plain and wicked elder sisters in a fairy tale, baleful creatures who go about the world doing bad deeds and oppressing innocence as it sits rocking the cradle by the fireside. It seems hard

*women as either one thing or the other*

*—very essentialist; Caird pts. this out.*

---

1   Patient Griselda, the heroine of Chaucer's "The Clerk's Tale," is synonymous with long-suffering fortitude. Frankenstein is the monster in Mary Shelley's 1818 *Frankenstein; or, The Modern Prometheus.*

for the poor elder sisters to be told off to play this dreadful role, amid the hisses of the gallery, and they deserve some sympathy after all, for truly the world offers temptations to evil courses, and innocence at the cradle can be desperately exasperating at times! It has a meek, placid, sneaky, virtuous way of getting what it wants, and making it hot and uncomfortable for unpopular elder sisters. After all, in spite of Mrs. Lynn Linton, there is no more finished tyrant in the world than the meek sweet creature who cares nothing for her "rights," because she knows she can get all she wants by artifice; who makes a weapon of her womanhood, a sword of strength of her weakness, and does not disdain to tyrannise over men to her heart's content by an ungenerous appeal to their chivalry. She is a woman—poor, weak, helpless, and her husband may not call his soul his own! Tears are a stock-in-trade, and nerves a rock of defense. She claims no rights—she can't understand what all this absurd talk is about—she is quite satisfied with things as they are. Personal dignity she has none; it would sadly interfere with her successful methods of insinuating herself through life, in serpentine fashion; she gets what she can as best she may, living by her wits; a mere adventuress, after all, in spite of her unblemished character; appealing to men's passions, frailties, chivalry; often differing from a class of women whose very name she would scarcely mention, in the nature of her surroundings and her supreme sense of respectability, rather than in the essential nature of her position.

But far be it from me to affirm, in simple opposition to Mrs. Lynn Linton, that all women of the old school are of this kind. My object is not merely to bring a counter-charge, but to point to the type which power on the one side and subordination on the other tend to produce. There are thousands, however, of the time-honoured school who never dream of attempting this unconscious retaliation. Many of them neither demand rights nor win their way by artifice. They accept their lot, just as it is, in a literal spirit, being just enough developed to see the meanness of trading upon the chivalry of men, and not enough so to resent being placed in a position which makes them dependent, utterly and hopeless, upon their favour. These women—the most pathetic class of all—have been so well drilled to accept their position without question, that they launch their complaints only at Fate and Nature, if ever they are moved to complain at all. Their conscience and their generosity forbid them to make use of the usual weapons of a dependent race, artifice and flattery; so that they are denied even this redress, which less sensitive women enjoy without stint. These half-developed women respond loyally to the stern demands made upon them by public sentiment; they are martyrs to "duty" in its narrowest sense; they turn a meek ear to society when it addresses homilies to them, inculcating the highest principles, and showering upon them the heaviest responsibilities, without dreaming of bestowing corresponding rights. In short, the women of the old order and the women of the new have faults and virtues each after their own kind, and it is idle to make general affirmations about either class.

It is well, therefore, to check the inherent instinct to contradict when Mrs. Lynn Linton says that women of the new faith are evil and ugly, one must say rather that this is a mere matter of opinion, formed from the impression each person gathers from individual experience, and from the bias with which that experience is met. Let, however, the impression be as unfavourable to the "wild women" as it may, it is neither fair nor philosophic to refuse to consider their claims. The liberal-minded will remember that the claims of a class hitherto subordinate always seem preposterous, and that the more complete has been their exclusion, the more ridiculous will appear their aspirations. Yet this inclination to treat with derision any new demand for liberty stands on a level with the instinct of the street-urchin to jeer at anything to which he is unaccustomed, as for example, any person in foreign garments, though he excel a thousand times in dignity and comeliness the natives of the country.

★ ★ ★ ★ ★

A certain number of rebels are bending all their energies to the removal of this invincible hindrance, and to attain this end they are forced to join more or less in the struggle for a livelihood. It will be a happy day for humanity when a woman can stay in her own home without sacrificing her freedom. Shortsighted is the policy which would keep the wife and mother helpless in the hands of the man whose home she sustains and holds together, which would give her but a meagre share of right to the children which have cost her so much to bear and tend, while burdening her with the fullest responsibility regarding them. To this point I would especially call the attention of that large portion of the community who are convinced of the importance of the fireside and the home, who believe that in every other locality the woman is out of her sphere. Would they not use their influence most wisely, from their own point of view, in seeking to remove some of the heavy penalties that are attached to the enjoyment of home and fireside, and to make them deserve a little better all the sentiment that has been lavished upon them?

It is easy indeed to see the frightful peril to the well-being of the race that lies in the labour of women outside the home; that peril can scarcely be exaggerated; but if women demand the natural human right to take their share of the opportunities, such as they are, which the world has to offer—if they desire the privilege of independence (a privilege denied them, work as they will, within the home), by what right does society refuse their demand? Men are living lives and committing actions day by day which imperil and destroy the well-being of the race; on what principle are women only to be restrained? Why this one-sided sacrifice, this artificial selection of victims for the good of society? The old legends of maidens who were chosen every year and chained to a rock by the shore to propitiate gods or sea-monsters seem not in the least out of date. Sacrifices were performed more frankly in those days, and nobody tried to persuade the victims that it was enjoyable and blessed to be devoured; they did not talk about "woman's sphere" to a maiden chained to the rock within sight of the monster, nor did they tell her that the "true woman" desired no other destiny. They were brutal, but they did not add sickly sentiment to their crime against the individual; they carried out the hideous old doctrine of vicarious sacrifice, which is haunting us like an evil spirit to this day, in all good faith and frankness, and there was no attempt to represent the monster as an engaging beast when you got to know him.

Society has no right to exact these sacrifices; every member of it must stand equal in its sight, if it would claim the name of a free state. On the soil of such a state there must be no arbitrary selection of victims for the general good made from a certain class, or, still worse, from a certain sex. One can imagine the heaven-assaulting howl that would go up were it proposed to deal in this way with a certain body of men; if it were decreed that they should be restricted from seeking their fortunes as might seem good to them, restrained only by the laws that all the rest of the community were called upon to obey. No argument about the welfare of the race would reconcile a nation of free-born men to such a proposal. Yet this is the argument that free-born men do not hesitate to use regarding women.

The attempt to force upon these any sacrifice on the sole ground of their sex, to demand of them a special act of renunciation on that account, gives us an exact analogue of the old tribute to its gods of a nation which chose its victims not by fair hazard from the entire population, but from a class set apart for the cruel purpose. Such actions are subversive of all social life, for the existence of a community depends finally upon its respect for individual rights. Upon these rights society is built; without them, nothing is possible but an aggregation of tyrants and slaves, which does not deserve the name of society, since it is bound together by force, and the union between its members is accidental, not organic. On what rests finally my safety and freedom as a citizen, but on the understanding that if I leave your rights intact you will also respect mine?

But, further, the argument which takes its stand upon the danger to society of the freedom of women, besides being unfair (since it would select a whole sex for the propitiatory victims), is, on its own ground, unsound. True, indeed, is it that if all women were to rush into the labour market and begin to compete with men and with one another, the result would be evil; but it is not true that if they were to be placed on an equality with men in the eye of the law, if in marriage they were free from legal or pecuniary disadvantage, if in society they had no special prejudices to contend with—it is not true in that case that the consequences of this change in their position would be detrimental to the real interests of society. On the contrary, its influence would be for good, and for more good than perhaps any one now dares to believe. And among the many causes of this beneficent result we may number this, that women would be able to choose the work for which they were best suited. We should have fewer governesses who loathed teaching, fewer wives who could do most things better than look after a house, and fewer mothers to whom the training of children was an impossible task. Moreover, society would rejoice in more of that healthy variety among her members which constitutes one of the elements of vitality. There is room for all kinds of women, did we but realise it, and there is certainly no reason why the present movement should sweep away all those of the ancient type in whom Mrs. Lynn Linton takes delight. They have their charm, but it must be acknowledged that, for all their meekness, nothing would please them better than tyrannically to dictate their own mode of life to their sisters. By what charter or authority does the domestic woman (like the person in the train who wants the window up) attempt to restrict within her own limits women who entirely disagree with her in opinion and in temperament?

*its absurd to assume society must have one type of woman*

Granted for a moment that Mrs. Lynn Linton and her followers are justified of Heaven in their views, and that it always was and always will be necessary for women to dedicate themselves wholly to the production of the race, still this truth—if such it be—must be left to demonstrate itself without any tyranny, direct or indirect, from those who realise it, otherwise they violate the condition of social liberty. The history of all persecutions, religious and otherwise, ought to warn us against the danger of allowing the promulgation of the true faith by forcible means, and I include among forcible means all forms of prejudice and sentiment, for often these are far more powerful than legal enactments. Let us not forget the glorious privilege of the citizen of a free state to be in the wrong, and to act upon his error until the torch-bearers of truth shall be able to throw light upon his pathway. That once accomplished, his adherence will be worth having.

The demand that all women shall conform to a certain model of excellence, that they shall be debarred from following the promptings of their powers and instincts, whatsoever be the pretext for the restriction, is the outcome of an illiberal spirit, and ought  to be resisted as all attacks on liberty ought to be resisted. The fact that the attack is made upon liberties which, as yet, are only candidates for existence, is the sole reason why Englishmen do not resent the aggression as they would resent any other interference with personal freedom.

★ ★ ★ ★ ★

If the new movement had no other effect than to rouse women to rebellion against the madness of large families, it would confer a priceless benefit on humanity. Let any reasonable woman expend force that under the old order would have been given to the production of, say, the third, fourth, or fifth child upon work of another kind, and let her also take the rest and enjoyment, whatever her work, that every human being needs. It is certain that the one or two children which such a woman might elect to bear would have cause to be thankful that their mother threw over "the holiest traditions of her sex," and left insane ideas of woman's duties and functions to her grandmothers.

But there are many modern women who in their own way are quite as foolish as those grandmothers, for they are guilty of the madness of trying to live the old domestic life, without modification, while entering upon a larger field of interests, working simultaneously body and brain under conditions of excitement and worry. This insanity, which one might indeed call by a harsher name, will be punished as all overstrain is punished. But the cure for these things is not to immerse women more completely in the cares of domestic life, but to simplify its methods by the aid of a little intelligence and by means which there is not space to discuss here. The present waste of energy in our homes is simply appalling.

★ ★ ★ ★ ★

But there is another consideration in connection with this which Mrs. Lynn Linton overlooks. If the woman is to be asked to surrender so much because she has to produce the succeeding generation, why is the father left altogether out of count? Does his life leave no mark upon his offspring? Or does Mrs. Lynn Linton, perhaps, think that if the mother takes precautions for their welfare to the extent of surrendering her whole existence, the father may be safely left to take no precautions at all?

*very impt!: Linton fails to question the father's role in raising his children*

"The clamour for political rights," this lady says, "is woman's confession of sexual enmity. Gloss it over as we may it comes to this in the end. No woman who loves her husband would usurp his province." Might one not retort: "No man who loves his wife would seek to hamper her freedom or oppose her desires?" But in fact nothing could be more false than the assertion that the new ideals imply sexual enmity. On the contrary, they contemplate a relationship between the sexes which is more close and sympathetic than the world has ever seen.

Friendship between husband and wife on the old terms was almost impossible. Where there is power on the one hand and subordination on the other, whatever the relationship that may arise, it is not likely to be that of friendship. Separate interests and ambitions, minds moving on different planes—all this tended to make strangers of those who had to pass their lives together, hampered eternally by the false sentiment which made it the right of one to command and the duty of the other to obey. But now, for the first time in history, we have come within measurable distance of a union between man and woman as distinguished from a common bondage.

★ ★ ★ ★ ★

The rest of her charges are equally severe, and they induce one to wonder through what unhappy experiences the lady has gone, since she appears never to have encountered a good and generous woman outside the ranks of her own followers—unless it was a born idiot here and there! Even the men who disagree with her are either knaves or fools!

★ ★ ★ ★ ★

It behooves women, above all, to conduct their movement in a quiet, steady, philosophic, and genial spirit; regarding the opposition that they receive, as much as possible, from the point of view of the student rather than of the partisan; realising that in this greatest of all social revolutions they must expect the fiercest resistance; that men in opposing them are neither better nor worse than all human beings of either sex have shown themselves to be as soon as they became possessors of power over their fellows. The noblest cannot stand the test, and of average men and women it makes bullies and tyrants. If this general fact be borne in mind throughout the struggle, it will be easier to avoid the feelings of bitterness and rancour which the sense of injustice creates; it will remind those engaged in the encounter to regard it with calmer eyes, as one would regard the history of past events; it will teach them to be prepared for defeat while hoping for success, and not to be too much dismayed if the change for which they have striven so hard must be delayed until long after they are dead, and all those who would have rejoiced in it are no longer there to see the sun rise over the promised land. It will teach them, too, to realise more strongly than most of us are inclined to do, that men and women are brothers and sisters, bound to stand or fall together; that in trying to raise the position and condition of women, they are serving at least as much the men who are to be their husbands; that, in short—to quote the saying of Hegel—"The master does not become really free till he has liberated his slave."[1]

---

1   Georg F.W. Hegel (1770–1831) was a German philosopher from whose *Phenomenology of the Mind* (1807) this passage is taken.

# Appendix E: Marriage

[The following two essays, written a decade apart by Mona Caird and Ella Hepworth Dixon, two of the best known New Woman novelists, reveal the English woman's changing views on marriage at the end of the nineteenth century. In each one can see many of the issues with which Mary Erle struggles in *The Story of a Modern Woman*.]

## 1. From Mona Caird's "Marriage," *Westminster Review* 130 (August 1888): 186–201

It is not difficult to find people mild and easy-going about religion, and even politics may be regarded with wide-minded tolerance; but broach social subjects, and English men and women at once become alarmed and talk about the foundations of society and the sacredness of the home! Yet the particular form of social life, or of marriage, to which they are so deeply attached, has by no means existed from time immemorial; in fact, modern marriage, with its satellite ideas, only dates as far back as the age of Luther. Of course the institution existed long before, but our particular mode of regarding it can be traced to the era of the Reformation, when commerce, competition, the great bourgeois calls, and that remarkable thing called "Respectability," also began to arise.

★ ★ ★ ★ ★

[I]t is necessary to protest against the careless use of the words "human nature," and especially "woman's nature." History will show us, if anything will, that human nature has an apparently limitless adaptability, and that therefore no conclusion can be built upon special manifestations which may at any time be developed. Such development must be referred to certain conditions, and not be mistaken for the eternal law of being. With regard to "woman's nature," concerning which innumerable contradictory dogmas are held, there is so little really known about it, and its power of development, that all social philosophies are more or less falsified by this universal though sublimely unconscious ignorance.

The difficulties of friendly intercourse between men and women are so great, and the false sentiments induced by our present system so many and so subtle, that it is the hardest thing in the world for either sex to learn the truth concerning the real thoughts and feelings of the other. If they find out what they mutually think about the weather it is as much as can be expected—consistently, that is, with genuine submission to present ordinances. Thinkers, therefore, perforce take no count of the many half-known and less understood ideas and emotions of women, even as these actually exist at the moment, and they make still smaller allowance for potential developments which at the present crisis are almost incalculable. Current phrases of the most shallow kind are taken as if they expressed the whole that is knowable on the subject.

There is in fact no social philosophy, however logical and far-seeing on other points, which does not lapse into incoherence as soon as it touches the subject of women. The thinker abandons the thoughtlaws which he has obeyed until that fatal moment; he forgets every principle of science previously present to his mind, and he suddenly goes back centuries in knowledge and in the consciousness of possibilities, making schoolboy statements, and "babbling of green fields" in a manner that takes away the breath of those who have listened to his former reasoning, and admired his previous delicacies of thought-distinction. Has he been overtaken by some afflicting mental disease? Or does he merely allow himself to hold one subject apart from the circulating currents of his brain, judging it on different principles from those on which he judges every other subject?

★ ★ ★ ★ ★

We chain up a dog to keep watch over our home; we deny him freedom, and in some cases, alas! even sufficient exercise to keep his limbs supple and his body in health. He becomes dull and spiritless, he is miserable and ill-looking, and if by any chance he is let loose, he gets into mischief and runs away. He has not been used to liberty or happiness, and he cannot stand it.

Humane people ask his master: "Why do you keep that dog always chained up?"

"Oh! He is accustomed to it; he is suited for the chain; when we let him loose he runs wild."

So the dog is punished by chaining for the misfortune of having been chained, till death releases him. In the same way we have subjected women for centuries to a restricted life, which called forth one or two forms of domestic activity; we have rigorously excluded (even punished) every other development of power; and we have then insisted that the consequent adaptations of structure, and the violent instincts created by this distorting process, are, by a sort of compound interest, to go on adding to the distortions themselves, and at the same time to go on forming a more and more solid ground for upholding the established system of restriction, and the ideas that accompany it. We chain, because we *have chained*. The dog must not be released, because his nature has adapted itself to the misfortune of captivity.

★ ★ ★ ★ ★

We come then to the conclusion that the present form of marriage—exactly in proportion to its conformity with orthodox ideas—is a vexatious failure. If certain people have made it a success by ignoring those orthodox ideas, such instances afford no argument in favour of the institution as it stands. We are also led to conclude that modern "Respectability" draws its life-blood from the degradation of womanhood in marriage and in prostitution. But what is to be done to remedy these manifold evils? How is marriage to be rescued from a mercenary society, torn from the arms of "Respectability," and established on a footing which will make it no longer an insult to human dignity?

First of all we must set up an ideal, undismayed by what will seem its Utopian impossibility. Every good thing that we enjoy today was once the dream of a "crazy enthusiast" mad enough to believe in the power of ideas and in the power of man to have things as he wills. The ideal marriage then, despite all dangers and difficulties, should be free. So long as love and trust and friendship remain, no bonds are necessary to bind two people together; life apart will be empty and colourless; but whenever these cease the tie becomes false and iniquitous, and no one ought to have power to enforce it. The matter is one in which any interposition, whether of law or of society, is an impertinence. Even the idea of "duty" ought to be excluded from the most perfect marriage, because the intense attraction of one being for another, the intense desire for one another's happiness, would make interchanges of whatever kind the outcome of a feeling so far more passionate than that of duty. It need scarcely be said that there must be a full understanding and acknowledgment of the obvious right of the woman to *possess herself* body and soul, to give or withhold herself body and soul exactly as she wills. The moral right here is so palpable, and its denial implies ideas so low and offensive to human dignity, that no fear of consequences ought to deter us from making this liberty an element of our ideal, in fact its fundamental principle. Without it, no ideal could hold up its head.

★ ★ ★ ★ ★

The economical independence of woman is the first condition of free marriage. She ought not to be tempted to marry, or to remain married, for the sake of bread and butter. But the condition is a very hard one to secure. Our present competitive system, with the daily increasing ferocity of the struggle for existence, is fast reducing itself to an absurdity, woman's labour helping to make the struggle only the fiercer. The problem now offered to the mind and conscience of humanity is to readjust its industrial organization in such a way as to gradually reduce this absurd and useless competition within reasonable limits, and to bring about in its place some form of cooperation, in which no man's interest will depend on the misfortune of his neighbour, but rather on his neighbor's happiness and welfare.

★ ★ ★ ★ ★

The proposed freedom in marriage would of course have to go hand-in-hand with the co-education of the sexes. It is our present absurd interference with the natural civilizing influences of one sex upon the other, that creates half the dangers and difficulties of our social life, and gives colour to the fears of those who would hedge round marriage with a thousand restraints or so-called safeguards, ruinous to happiness, and certainly not productive of a satisfactory social condition. Already the good results of this method of co-education have been proved by experiment in America, but we ought to go farther in this direction than our go ahead cousins have yet gone.

★ ★ ★ ★ ★

The general rise in health, physical and moral, following the improvement in birth, surroundings, and training, would rapidly tell upon the whole state of society. Any one who has observed carefully knows how grateful a response the human organism gives to improved conditions, if only these remain constant. We should have to deal with healthier, better equipped, more reasonable men and women, possessing well-developed minds, and hearts kindly disposed towards their fellow-creatures. Are such people more likely to enter into a union frivolously and ignorantly than are the average men and women of to-day? Surely not. If the number of divorces did not actually decrease there would be the certainty that no couple remained united against their will, and that no lives were sacrificed to a mere convention. With the social changes which would go hand in hand with the changes in the status of marriage, would come inevitably many fresh forms of human power, and thus all sorts of new and stimulating influences would be brought to bear upon society. No man has the right to consider himself educated until he has been under the influence of cultivated women, and the same may be said of women as regards men. Development involves an increase of complexity. It is in all forms of existence, vegetable and animal; it is so in human life. It will be found that men and women as they increase in complexity can enter into a numberless variety of relationships, abandoning no good gift that they now possess, but adding to their powers indefinitely, and thence to their emotions and experiences. The action of the man's nature upon the woman's and of the woman's upon the man's, is now only know in a few instances; there is a whole world yet to explore in this direction, and it is more than probable that the future holds a discovery in the domain of spirit as great as that of Columbus in the domain of matter.

★ ★ ★ ★ ★

We shall begin, slowly but surely, to see the folly of permitting the lines of one sex to pull against and neutralize the workings of the other, to the confusion of our efforts and the checking of our progress. We shall see, in the relations of men and women to one another, the source of all good or of all evil, precisely as those relations are true and noble and equal, or false and low and unjust. With this belief we shall seek to move opinion in all the directions that may bring us to this "consummation devoutly to be wished,"[1] and we look forward steadily, hoping and working for the day when men and women shall be comrades and fellow-workers as well as lovers and husbands and wives, when the rich and many-

---

1   *Hamlet* (III.i.63–4).

sided happiness which they have the power to bestow one on another shall no longer be enjoyed in tantalizing snatches, but shall gladden and give new life to all humanity.

## 2. Ella Hepworth Dixon, "Why Women Are Ceasing to Marry," *Humanitarian* 14 (1899): 392–96

The question has been so often discussed from the strictly utilitarian aspect, that one may be pardoned for taking what, at the first blush, might be considered a somewhat flippant view of an alarming social phenomenon. It has been seriously argued—generally by masculine writers and elderly ladies who find themselves out of sympathy with the modern feminist movement—that women, nowadays, are disposed, from selfish reasons, to shirk the high privileges and duties of maternity and domestic life, to wish to compete with men, and undersell the market from motives of pure vanity, and to have so far unsexed themselves as to have lost the primordial instinct for conjugal life altogether.

Now, that any of these propositions are true can be denied by anyone even superficially acquainted with the modern movement, with those who lead it and with those who follow it. I forget which distinguished writer has said that "every woman, in her heart, hankers after a linen-cupboard," and this delightful aphorism may be truthfully applied, I take it, to every kind of modern woman, except the gypsy class of globe-trotters.

No. The reason why women are ceasing to marry must rather be attributed to a shifting feminine point of view, to a more critical attitude towards their masculine contemporaries. If, of late, they would seem to have shown a disposition to avoid the joys, cares, and responsibilities of the linen cupboard, it is chiefly, I think, because their sense of humour is often as keen as it was once supposed to be blunted. The proper adoring feminine attitude does not, it would seem, come naturally to the present generation, who are apt not so much—in Miltonic phrase—to "see God" in their average suitors as to perceive in these young gentlemen certain of the least endearing qualities of the Anglo-Saxon race; those qualities, it may be whispered, which, though eminently suitable for the making of Empire, are not always entirely appreciated on the domestic hearth. This critical attitude among the women folk is no doubt mostly due to the enormous strides which have been made in feminine education during the last twenty years, though I hasten to add that that education has made them far more tolerant and broadminded, so that the average of domestic felicity will undoubtedly be higher as things progress. Indeed, the famous phrase, "*Tout comprendre, c'est tout pardonner,*"[1] is most applicable of all to the eternal question of the sexes, and the man or woman who has mastered its significance is well on the way to make an ideal partner in marriage.

At present, however, we are in a transition stage, and there is a certain amount of misunderstanding nowadays between the sexes which make marrying and giving in marriage a somewhat hazardous enterprise.

This new and critical attitude on the part of the fair is a thing of quite recent growth. Before, and up to as late as, the mid-Victorian era, the recognised wifely pose was one of blind adoration. Directly a girl married she was supposed to think her husband perfect, unapproachable, wise and beautiful beyond all measure, and of a stupendous understanding. Most of the married ladies in the great mid-Victorian novels looked up to their spouses with admiration tempered by awe. Now that we have educated our womenfolk into a sense of humour—and there is no surer test of breadth of mind—this wifely meekness is no longer possible. Yet, seeing how the old masculine idols are shattered, and the heroes of ladies' novels are no longer Greek gods, or Guardsmen, or even men of blameless life, it is impossible not to sympathise with our masculine contemporaries, *Ces Rois en Exile,*[2] who have lost a crown, and who have not yet made up their minds to swear "Liberty, Equality, Fraternity!" with their feminine critics. It is possible, moreover, that the modern man has begun to see the humorous side of the question also. Occasionally he shows a disposition to step down from his pedestal and even to mix, on equal terms, with his more enlightened feminine friends. No less a modern person, for instance, than Mr. William Archer,[3] has publicly stated that he cannot sit in his stall at the theatre and listen to Katherine's abject speech about "her lord, her king, her governor," at the end of *The Taming of the Shrew.*

"Then vail your stomachs, for it is no boot;
And place your hands below your husband's foot;

---

1   To understand everything is to forgive everything.
2   These kings in exile.
3   Archer (1856-1924) was a dramatist and critic who promoted the plays of Henrik Ibsen (1828-1906).

In token of which duty, if he please,
My hand is ready, may it do him ease."[1]

This was the old idea of marriage. It will be readily seen that we have changed our ideals, and that if it is somewhat of an exaggeration to say that "women are ceasing to marry," it is certain that indiscriminate marrying has, to a certain extent, gone out. In short, *le premier venu*[2] is no longer the successful wooer that he once was. Then, too, this shyness at being caught in the matrimonial net is largely a characteristic of the modern English maiden, for widows, like widowers, usually show an extraordinary eagerness to resume the fetters of the wedded state. Some recent amusing statistics on this subject proved that a man of forty remains a widower for two years only, while his feminine prototype shows even greater eagerness to console herself, for, under the age of thirty-five, she marries again within twenty months.

But we are at present concerned with bachelors and spinsters, of persons, in short, who have still the great experiment to make. It is certain that marriage—and its attendant responsibilities, the bringing up and starting in life of children—is looked upon far more seriously than our immediate forbears were wont to regard it. Elizabeth Barrett Browning (who, as the author of *Aurora Leigh* undoubtedly proclaimed herself one of the earliest of the "new women") was mortally afraid of marriage and did not attempt to conceal the fact from her adoring love. In her recently published letters to Robert Browning, it is amusing to see how—just like any modern woman of 1899—she constantly threatens, that if they do not "get on" when they are married, she will leave him and go to Greece. This question of "going to Greece" becomes one of their principal humorous efforts, but there is just an acid flavour about it that makes one a little doubtful whether the distinguished author of "Pippa Passes" appreciated the lady's constant references to such a contingency. In short, the invalid poetess who had lain for five years on a sofa, and whose knowledge of life must have been largely intuitive, was, in 1846, as timorous of entering on the adventure of marriage as the heroine of any modern problem novel.

The author of the *Sonnets from the Portuguese* was probably alone in her generation. Then, indeed, was the happy-go-lucky time of

---

1   *The Taming of the Shrew* (V.ii.176-79).
2   The first comer.

Dan Cupid.[1] A strictly brought-up young person was not sup-posed to have the only woman's privilege, the privilege of saying "No." She married, as a matter of course, the first young man who offered to settle down, pay taxes, and raise a family, and that fami-ly, unfortunately for her, sometimes assumed alarming proportions. This middle-class recklessness has brought, in this generation, its own Nemesis: an enormous number of young men who are oblig-ed to seek a living in India, Africa, Canada, Australia, and New Zealand; a still larger number of young women who have to stay at home and partly earn their own livelihood.

It is in this way that we have got our young people not only separated by oceans and continents, but curiously afraid of making an experiment which their fathers and mothers entered upon—like the French in the war of 1870—with a light heart. The young girl of to-day, again, has read her *Doll's House*,[2] and is, it may be, firmly resolved to play the part of Nora in the conjugal duologue, and to refuse, in the now classic phrase, to be any man's "squirrel." On his side, the modern young man shows a shrewd tendency to acquire in his wife not so much one of these engaging zoological specimens as a young person who will be able to pay the weekly bills and help him substantially in his career.

All these things, naturally, make for circumspection in marriage, and there are other reasons, chiefly owing to the amazing changes in the social life of women, which have gradually come about dur-ing recent years. Someone has boldly laid it down that it is the bicycle which has finally emancipated women, but it is certain that there are other factors besides the useful and agreeable wheel.

For it is, primarily, the almost complete downfall of Mrs. Grundy[3] that makes the modern spinster's lot, in many respects, an eminently attractive one. Formerly, girls married in order to gain their social liberty; now, they more often remain single to bring about that desirable consummation. If young and pleasing women are permitted by public opinion to go to college, to live alone, to travel, to have a profession, to belong to a club, to give parties, to read and discuss whatsoever seems good to them, and to go to the-

---

1 Dan is a title meaning "sir" or "master" commonly used by old poets.
2 Ibsen's play *A Doll's House* (1879) was first performed in London in 1889.
3 A character in Thomas Morton's 1798 play *Speed the Plough*, Mrs. Grundy became the personification of British prudery.

atres without masculine escort, they have most of the privileges—
and several others thrown in—for which the girl of twenty or thirty years ago was ready to barter herself to the first suitor who
offered himself and the shelter of his name. Then, again, a capable
woman who has begun a career and feels certain of advancement
in it, is often as shy of entangling herself matrimonially as ambitious young men have ever shown themselves under like circumstances. Indeed, the disadvantages of marriage to a woman with a
profession are more obvious than to a man, and it is just this question of maternity, with all its duties and responsibilities, which is,
no doubt, occasionally the cause of many women forswearing the
privileges of the married state. To be quite candid, however, I think
this is very seldom the real cause of a girl's remaining single. Once
her affections are involved, that bundle of nerves and emotions
which we call woman is often capable of all the heroisms, and who
has not numbered among their friends some delicate creature—the
case of Mrs. Oliphant is one in point[1]—who has not only supported, by her own exertions, the children she bore, but the father
of those children?

The modern woman, to be sure, is capable of supporting the
father of her children, if she happens to be fond of that especial
individual, but not (to put an extreme case) of marrying that father
in order to regularise an anomalous position. The most successful
German play of recent times treats, indeed, of this very subject.
Herr Sudermann's Magda,[2] tyrannised over at home, goes out into
the wide world and becomes a famous actress. Meanwhile, during
her Wanderjahre, she has had a lover, a priggish young man whom
she has met in Berlin. Their relations were soon broken off, and the
lover is not even aware that the beautiful young actress has had a
child. On her return home, years after, she meets this man again,
and he offers her marriage, providing their former *liaison* is kept
secret, and the child kept away. Magda indignantly refuses, and goes

---

1   English novelist Mrs. Oliphant's (1828-97) life of domestic difficulties was
    well known among the Victorians. She was left a destitute and pregnant
    widow with two small children when her young husband died in 1859.
    Thereafter, she supported herself and her children—a daughter died in
    1864, and her two sons were miscreants who also predeceased her—by
    writing over one hundred novels.
2   Magda is the central character in German playwright Hermann Suder-
    mann's (1857-1928) drama *Heimat* (1893). Wanderjahre means "years of
    travel."

back to her art, taking her little girl openly with her. The fact of her maternity, she holds, has ennobled her; her marriage with a hypocrite and a coward would degrade her in her own eyes.

This, it is true, may be described as the ultra-modern view of marriage and all that it entails, and it is one which obtains support only among the Teutonic races. The theory that a wedding ceremony mended all and ended all, is one which thoughtful Northern and Western peoples are nowadays inclined to dispute. Formerly, if there were a breath of scandal—sometimes totally unfounded—about two young people, well, you sent for the parson, rung the church-bells, and let the young couple make the best of this rash mating. Whether they were happy or not ever after, sad or merry, prosperous or unfortunate, was no affair of their neighbours. They were married; they had been sacrificed to society's rigorous demand for the outward observance of the proprieties; and if they chafed and fumed, or, finding themselves totally unsuited to each other, broke their spirits or their hearts, why so did other excellent citizens, people whom Robert Louis Stevenson quaintly calls "respectable married people, with umbrellas,"[1] who bound themselves with the same well-nigh indissoluble bonds.

It is just this general doubt of the institution of marriage, joined to that higher ideal of the wedded state with which most educated women seem to be imbued, that makes many people pause on the brink, and, choosing the known evil, remain celibate rather than fly to others that they know not of. It is possible, indeed, that a single woman of altruistic tendencies may argue that, if she is unhappy single, only one person suffers; whereas, if she should marry, and the union turn out disagreeable, probably two people will be made miserable, and, in all probability several people more.

Possibly it was better for the race (if quantity, and not quality, go to the making of a nation) when its feminine half was troubled by no such doubts, but married herself on the faintest provocation, and had no misgivings at rearing a numerous progeny. On the other hand, it would seem certain that if woman continues to cultivate her critical faculties and her sense of humour—to exercise, in short, her feminine prerogative of deliberate choice in the great affair of matrimony—that the standard of human felicity will be steadily raised, and the wedded state will shine forth in a different

---

1 Hepworth Dixon recalls a line from Stevenson's 1881 collection of essays *Virginibus Puerisque*.

light to that in which it stands revealed to many thoughtful persons to-day.

In that golden age, indeed, when the equality of the sexes is reached, it is probable that the shrew, the nagging woman, and the jealous wife will all have become curious specimens of a by-gone era. When a man marries, in short, it is to be hoped that he will no longer "domesticate the 'Recording Angel',"[1] but will welcome to his hearth an agreeable companion, a gracious mistress, and a loyal friend.

---

1   Another passage from Stevenson's *Virginibus Puerisque*.

# Appendix F: Literary Censorship in Victorian England

[By the middle of the nineteenth century, subscription lending libraries dominated the landscape of British fiction. Most of the reading public, finding the price of their favorite novels prohibitive, came to rely heavily on "one-guinea-a-year" subscriptions to lending establishments run by the likes of Charles Mudie and rival William Henry Smith, both very religious, morally conservative men. Mudie and Smith could ruin an author's career by refusing to carry his or her novels, and as a result of their tyranny, many authors chaffed under the yoke of what was perceived to be a fickle and dangerous literary censorship. The articles below all strike a familiar note to those who recall the problems Mary Erle encounters as she attempts to find a publisher for her "realistic" novel.

The first article is by George Moore (1852-1933), who belonged to the Naturalist school of fiction. His novels *A Modern Lover* (1883) and *A Mummer's Wife* (1885) offended some conservative readers and were pulled from Mudie's library. His sales jeopardized, Moore reacted with this scathing and very personal polemic, which he published at his own expense as a pamphlet in 1885. The next three pieces, by Walter Besant, Eliza Lynn Linton, and Thomas Hardy, appeared within one article titled "Candour in Fiction," in early 1890. The three writers, all well known and popular novelists, offer varying opinions on the essence of fiction and the problems of censorship.]

## 1. From George Moore's *Literature at Nurse, or Circulating Morals* (1885)

In an article contributed to the *Pall Mall Gazette* last December [1884], I called attention to the fact that English writers were subject to the censorship of a tradesman who, although doubtless an excellent citizen and a worthy father, was scarcely competent to decide the delicate and difficult artistic questions that authors in their struggles for new ideals might raise: questions that could and should be judged by time alone. I then proceeded to show how, to retain their power, the proprietors of the large circulating libraries exact that books shall be issued at extravagant prices, and be supplied to them at half the published rate, or even less, thus putting it out of the power of the general public to become purchasers, and effectually frustrating the right of the latter to choose for themselves.

The case, so far as I am individually concerned, stands thus: in 1883, I published a novel called *A Modern Lover*. It met with the approval of the entire press; *The Athenæum* and *The Spectator* declared especially that it was not immoral; but Mr. Mudie told me that two ladies in the country had written to him to say that they disapproved of the book, and on that account he could not circulate it. I answered, "You are acting in defiance of the opinion of the press—you are taking a high position indeed, and one from which you will probably be overthrown. I, at least, will have done with you; for I shall find a publisher willing to issue my next book at a purchasable price, and so enable me to appeal direct to the public." Mr. Mudie tried to wheedle, attempted to dissuade me from my rash resolution; he advised me to try another novel in three volumes.

★ ★ ★ ★ ★

Some hold that being the custodian of the national virtue you have by right adopted the now well-known signature [the British Matron] as your *nom de plume*, others insist that the lady in question is your better half (by that is it meant the better half of your nature or the worthy lady who bears your name?), others insist that you yourself are the veritable British Matron. How so strange a belief could have obtained credence I cannot think, nor will I undertake to say if it be your personal appearance, or the constant communication you seem to be in with this mysterious female, or the singularly obtrusive way you both have of forcing your moral and religious beliefs upon the public that has led to this vexatious confusion of sex. It is, however, certain that you are popularly believed to be an old woman; and assuming you to be the British Matron I would suggest, should this pamphlet cause you any annoyance, that you write to *The Times* proving that the books I have quoted from are harmless, and differ nowise from your ordinary circulating morals whereon young ladies are supposed to cut their flirtation teeth. The British Matron has the public by the ear, and her evidence on the subject of impure literature will be as greedily listened to as were her views on painting from the nude. But although I am willing to laugh at you, Mr. Mudie, to speak candidly, I hate you; and I love and am proud of my hate of you. It is the best thing about me. I hate you because you dare question the sacred right of the artist to obey the impulses of his temperament; I hate you because you are the great purveyor of the worthless, the false and the commonplace; I hate you because you are a fetter about the ankles of those who would press forward towards the light of truth; I hate you because you feel not the spirit of scientific inquiry that is bearing our age along; I hate you because you pander to the intellectual sloth of to-day; I hate you because you would mould all ideas to fit the narrow limits in which your own turn; I hate you because you impede the free development of our literature.

★ ★ ★ ★ ★

It has been and will be again advanced that it is impossible to force a man to buy goods if he does not choose to do so: but with every privilege comes a duty. Mr. Mudie possesses a monopoly, and he cannot be allowed to use that monopoly to the detriment of all interests but his own. But even if this were not so, it is no less my right to point out to the public, that the character for strength, virility, and purpose, which our literature has always held, the old literary tradition coming down to us through a long line of glorious ancestors, is being gradually obliterated to suit the commercial views of a narrow-minded tradesman. Instead of being allowed to fight, with and amid, the thoughts and aspirations of men, literature is now rocked to an ignoble rest in the motherly arms of the librarian. That of which he approves is fed with gold; that from which he turns the breast dies like a vagrant's child; while in and out of his voluminous skirts run a motley and monstrous progeny, a callow, a whining, a puking brood of bastard bantlings, a race of Aztecs that disgrace the intelligence of the English nation. Into this nursery none can enter except in baby clothes; and the task of discriminating between a divided skirt and a pair of trousers is performed by the librarian. Deftly his fingers lift skirt and under-skirt, and if the examination prove satisfactory the sometimes decently attired dolls are packed in tin-cornered boxes, and scattered through every drawing-room in the kingdom, to be in rocking-chairs fingered and fondled by the "young person" until she longs for some new fashion in literary frills and furbelows. Mudie is the law we labour after; the suffrage of young women we are supposed to gain: the paradise of the English novelist is in the school-room: he is read there or nowhere. And yet it is certain that never in any age or country have writers been asked to write under such restricted conditions; if the same test by which modern writers are judged were applied to their forefathers, three-fourths of the contents of our libraries would have to be condemned as immoral publications. I don't pretend to judge, but I cannot help thinking that the cultivation of this curiosity is likely to run the nation into literary losses of some magnitude.

★ ★ ★ ★ ★

Genius is a natural production, just as are chickweed and roses; under certain conditions it matures; under others it dies; and the deplorable dearth of talent among the novelists of to-day is owing to the action of the circulating library, which for the last thirty years has been staying the current of ideas, and quietly opposing the development of fresh thought. The poetry, the history, the biographies written in our time will live because they represent the best ideas of our time; but no novel written within the last ten years will live through a generation, because no writer pretends to deal with the moral and religious feeling of his day; and without that no writer will, no writer ever has been able to, invest his work with sufficient vitality to resist twenty years of criticism. When a book is bought it is read because the reader hopes to find an expression of ideas of the existence of which he is already dimly conscious. A literature produced to meet such hopes must of necessity be at once national and pregnant with the thought of the epoch in which it is written. Books, on the contrary, that are sent by the librarian to be returned in a few days, are glanced at with indifference, at most with the vapid curiosity with which we examine the landscape of a strange country seen through a railway-carriage window. The bond of sympathy that should exist between reader and writer is broken—a bond as sacred and as intimate as that which unites the tree to the earth—and those who do not live in communion with the thought of their age are enabled to sell their characterless trash; and a writer who is well known can command as large a sale for a bad book as a good one. The struggle for existence, therefore, no longer exists; the librarian rules the roost; he crows, and every chanticleer pitches his note in the same key. He, not the ladies and gentlemen who place their names on the title-pages, is the author of modern English fiction. He models it, fashions it to suit his purpose, and the artistic individualities of his employés count for as little as that of the makers of the pill-boxes in which are sold certain well-known and mildly purgative medicines. And in accordance with his wishes English fiction now consists of either a sentimental misunderstanding, which is happily cleared up in the end, or of singular escapes over the edges of precipices, and miraculous recoveries of one or more of the senses of which the hero was deprived, until the time has come for the author to bring his tale to a close. The novel of observation, of analysis, exists no longer among us. Why? Because the librarian does not feel as safe in circulating a study of life and manners as a tale concerning a lost will.

To analyze, you must have a subject; a religious or sensual passion is as necessary to the realistic novel as a disease to the physician. The dissection of a healthy subject would not, as a rule, prove interesting, and if the right to probe and comment on humanity's frailties be granted, what becomes of the pretty schoolroom, with its piano tinkling away at the "Maiden's Prayer," and the water-colour drawings representing mill–wheels and Welsh castles? The British mamma is determined that her daughter shall know nothing of life until she is married; at all events, that if she should learn anything, there should be no proof of her knowledge lying about the place—a book would be a proof; consequently the English novel is made so that it will fit in with the "Maiden's Prayer" and the water-mill. And as we are a thoroughly practical nation, the work is done thoroughly; root and branch are swept away, and we begin on a fresh basis, just as if Shakespeare and Ben Jonson had never existed. A novelist may say, "I do not wish to enter into those pretty schoolrooms. I agree with you, my book is not fit reading for young girls; but does this prove that I have written an immoral book?" The librarian answers, "I cater for the masses, and the masses are young unmarried women who are supposed to know but one side of life. I cannot therefore take your book." And so it comes to pass that English literature is sacrificed on the altar of Hymen.[1]

$\star \star \star \star \star$

It is doubtless a terrible thing to advocate the breaking down of the thirty-one and sixpenny safeguards, and to place it in the power of a young girl to buy an immoral book if she chooses to

---

1 Hymen or Hymenaeus was the Greek god of marriage.

do so; but I am afraid it cannot be helped. Important an element as she undoubtedly is in our sociological system, still we must not lose sight of everything but her; and that the nineteenth century should possess a literature characteristic of its nervous, passionate life, I hold is as desirable, and would be as far-reaching in its effects, as the biggest franchise bill ever planned. But even for the alarmed mother I have a word of consolation. For should her daughter, when our novels are sold for half-a-crown in a paper cover, become possessed of one written by a member of the school to which I have the honour to belong, I will vouch that no unfortunate results are the consequence of the reading.

★ ★ ★ ★ ★

All these evils are inherent in the "select" circulating library, but when in addition it sets up a censorship and suppresses works of which it does not approve, it is time to appeal to the public to put an end to such dictatorship, in a very practical way, by withdrawing its support from any library that refuses to supply the books it desires to read.

## 2. Walter Besant, Eliza Lynn Linton, and Thomas Hardy, "Candour in Fiction," *New Review* 2 (January 1890): 6–21

Walter Besant

Fiction, like every other fine art, covers the whole area of life: it is concerned with every passion, every emotion; with every kind of joy and every kind of suffering; with man on a throne or man on a dunghill; with man in purple robes or man in tattered duds. Every conceivable situation of life, every possible phase, every experience: the greatest heights and the lowest depths: the greatest splendours and the blackest miseries: the short-lived Heaven which man and woman sometimes make for themselves; or the Hell of their own devising—all belongs to the art of Fiction. The only thing required of the artist is that his subject shall be adapted to artistic treatment and artistically treated.

This is mere commonplace. But, when questions are raised about narrowness in Art, it is as well to begin by reminding ourselves of the things which lie at the foundation—the things elementary. The world needs to be reminded sometimes that two and two make four. To those who ask why Fiction should be confined within certain bounds, why it should be forbidden to include this or that part of life, the reply is that there are no bounds whatever in the domain of Fiction. She may roam over the whole wide world: she may treat of men and women under any conditions: she may take up any subject. There is but the one condition of artistic fitness. Every artist is free, absolutely free, to exercise his own art in his own way. That is to say, in his own studio and in his own *cénacle*,[1] he is free. It is when he works for exhibition: for the public: for pay or hire: that limitations come in. Then he finds bounds and hedges beyond which, if he chooses to stray, it is at his own peril. These limits are assigned by an authority known as Average Opinion. They may be narrow, because Average Opinion is generally a Philistine. Those who wish to enlarge these boundaries or to remove them altogether must educate and enlarge Average Opinion. In the matter of painting so much has lately been achieved in the enlargement of opinion that those who attempt a similar task in literature may be of good cheer.

He who works for pay must respect the prejudices of his customers: otherwise, he will have few. Some men may be so courageous as to defy these prejudices: others, wiser, may lay themselves out to remove them, if they can. Others, wiser still, will inquire how these prejudices have arisen and what they mean.

Those who demand a wider range for English Fiction desire chiefly, it is understood, a greater freedom in the treatment of Love. Certainly there is no other passion which yields to an artist such boundless possibilities. Without Love, the whole of life is insipid. Without Love, all Art perishes. In Love's escort march all the Emotions: they follow in pairs—each with its opposite. Tenderness with Rage: Truth with Treachery: Joy with Grief. Why should not writers, it is asked, treat of Love in freedom—Love according to the laws of Nature? Love existed before the Church invented a sacrament and called it marriage. The history of mankind is the history of Love. Why restrict those who ask for nothing but a free hand?

Here, however, Average Opinion says, or seems to say: "If you treat of Love, save as Love obedient to the laws of Society, we will have none of you." Average Opinion cannot explain this position.

---

1  Coterie.

Were it more articulate it would be able to give its reasons. It would go on to say, in short: "Modern Society is based upon the unit of the family. The family tie means, absolutely, that the man and the woman are indissolubly united and can only be parted by the shame and disgrace of one or the other. In order to protect the wife and the children, and to keep the family together, we have made stringent laws as to marriage. To make these laws more binding we have allowed the Church to invent for marriage so solemn and sacred a function that most women have come to believe that the Church ceremony constitutes true marriage. The preservation of the family is at the very foundation of our social system. As for the freedom of love which you want to treat in your books, it strikes directly at the family. If men and women are free to rove, there can be no family: if there is no fidelity in marriage, the family drops to pieces. Therefore, we will have none of your literature of free and adulterous Love."

In fact, they will not have it. Average Opinion cannot be resisted. The circulating libraries refuse to distribute such books. They may be sold in certain shops, but not in those where the British Matron buys her books. The railway stalls will not display them. Worse than all, the author becomes liable to a criminal prosecution, which is painful and humiliating. Then those who demand greater freedom cry out upon the world for hypocrisy. "Ye are like," they say, "unto whited sepulchres, which are indeed beautiful outward but are within full of uncleanness. The Press teems daily with proofs, open and manifest, of the existence of free and illegal Love: the very thing of which you will not suffer us to speak has seized upon every rank of society: nay, there has never been a time when the artificial restrictions of social and ecclesiastical law have been obeyed: there has never been any country in which they have been obeyed. You go on prating of social purity. It does not exist. It never has existed. And you think that men's mouths, or women's either, are to be stopped by your prudery and hypocrisy."

Average Opinion is not credited with having much to say in reply. For these charges are partly true, though the exaggerations are indeed enormous. So far as we pretend to social purity as a nation we are indeed hypocrites. But to set up a standard of purity and to advocate it is not hypocrisy. This country, and the remnant still surviving of the New England stock, stand almost alone in the maintenance of such a standard. As for the widespread laxity alleged, it is not true. Certainly, there is a chapter in the lives of many men which they would not willingly publish. But in almost every such case the chapter is closed and is never reopened after the man has contracted the responsibilities of marriage. And as for the women—those above a certain level—*there is never any closed chapter at all in their lives.* When we talk of hypocrisies, let us not forget that the cultured class of British women—a vast and continually increasing class—are entirely to be trusted. Rare, indeed, is it that an Englishman of this class is jealous of his wife: never does he suspect his bride.

These considerations will perhaps explain the attitude of Average Opinion towards the literature of Free Love. Any novelist may write what he pleases: he may make an artistic picture of any materials he chooses; but he will not generally find, if he crosses certain boundaries, that his books will be distributed by Mudie or Smith. It is with him, then, if he desires to treat of things forbidden, a question of money—shall he restrict his pencil or shall he restrict his purse?

There is, however, one more answer to the accusation of narrowness. Is English Fiction narrow? Is the treatment of ungoverned passion absolutely forbidden? Then what of George Eliot, Charles Reade, Wilkie Collins, Nathaniel Hawthorne, Mrs. Gaskell—not to speak of living writers? Can any writer demand greater freedom than has been taken by the authors of *Adam Bede, A Terrible Temptation, Ruth,* or *The Scarlet Letter?*[1] With these examples before him, no one, surely, ought to complain that he is not permitted to treat of Love free and disobedient. The author, however, must recognise

---

1 The authors Besant refers to here all occasionally trod close to the line of acceptable good taste in their works. *Adam Bede* (1859), the first novel by George Eliot (1819-80), offended delicate sensibilities with its portrait of Hetty Sorrel, who becomes pregnant outside of wedlock after being seduced by Arthur Donnithorne and who eventually abandons her new-born, letting the child die. Charles Reade (1814-84) upset critics with virtually all of his novels, often with plot elements involving bigamy, illegitimacy, and other unsavory topics. His portrait of Rhoda Somerset, a disagreeable mistress to Sir Charles, in *A Terrible Temptation* (1871) raised calls for censorship. Wilkie Collins (1824-89) often found himself in hot water with the critics for creating in his novels charismatic villains and sexually attractive villainesses. Elizabeth Gaskell (1810-65) caused a stir with *Ruth* (1852), a novel about a saintly woman who has a child out of wedlock. And Nathaniel Hawthorne (1804-64) also offended some readers of *The Scarlet Letter* (1850) with his sympathetic portrayal of Hester Prynne, a young woman who bears an illegitimate child by her seducer, Arthur Dimmesdale.

in his work the fact that such Love is outside the social pale and is destructive of the very basis of society. He *must*. This is not a law laid down by that great authority, Average Opinion, but by Art herself, who will not allow the creation of impossible figures moving in an unnatural atmosphere. Those writers who yearn to treat of the adulteress and the courtesan because they love to dwell on images of lust are best kept in check by existing discouragements. The modern Elephantis may continue to write in French.

Eliza Lynn Linton

Of all the writers of fiction in Europe or America the English are the most restricted in their choice of subjects. The result is shown in the pitiable poverty of the ordinary novel, the wearisome repetition of the same themes, and the consequent popularity of romances which, not pretending to deal with life as it is, at the least leave no sense of disappointment in their portrayal or of superficiality in their handling. The British Matron is the true censor of the Press, and exerts over fiction the repressive power she has tried to exert over Art. Things as they are—human nature as it is—the conflict always going on between law and passion, the individual and society—she will not have spoken of. She permits certain crimes to be not only described, but dilated on and gloated over. Murder, forgery, lies, and all forms of hate and malevolence she does not object to; but no one must touch the very fringes of uncertificated love under pain of the greater and the lesser excommunication. Hence, the subjects lying to the hand of the British novelist are woefully limited, and the permissible area of the conflict between humanity and society is daily diminishing. Difference of race was a good theme in its time, and the Jew and the Gentile could sigh and weep and struggle through their allotted pages with a fair amount of tragic life-likeness. But now Jew and Gentile run together like two drops of quicksilver, and there are but few Roses of Sharon who would refuse to engraft themselves on an unbelieving stem if that stem stood in an aristocratic garden and they got social rank in return for their modern ducats. The fashion of Ritualism has smoothed the way between the Roman Catholic and the Protestant; and though something more by way of variant is to be made out of Agnosticism and Orthodoxy, still, that theme has been worked so much of late that it will scarcely bear repetition. Politics, too, are so far ameliorated as to be no real obstacle; and Unionists and Home Rulers meet in the pages of a novel, and make a good job of things before the last page is turned. The East End has been a fruitful field in its way; and the sorrows of the poor form the staple of all that smaller kind of literature which is issued by religious and quasi-religious societies. But when taken as a theme by serious fiction writers the British Matron has here again her say, and things have to be depicted ideally with gingerly caution and in white-kid gloves, and by no means with the brutal frankness of Zolaesque truth.[1]

If a writer, disdaining the unwritten law, leaps the barriers set up by Mrs. Grundy[2] and ventures into the forbidden Garden of Roses, he is boycotted by all respectable libraries and the severer kind of booksellers, and his works, though they sell in large numbers, are bought in a manner surreptitiously. Lord Campbell's Act[3] has a wider moral interpretation than even legal power; yet that legal power is strong enough, as more than one insurgent has been made to feel of late.

All this is the outcome of the question: To whom ought Fiction be addressed?—exclusively to the Young Person? or may not men and women, who know life, have their acre to themselves where the *ingénue* has no business to intrude? Must men go without meat because the babes must be fed with milk? Or, because men must have meat, shall the babes be poisoned with food too strong for them to digest? I, for one, am emphatically in favour of specialised literature. Just as we have children's books and medical books, so ought we to have literature fit for the Young Person and literature which gives men and women pictures of life as it is. Had the law which is in favour at the present day been the law of times past we should have lost some of our finest works; and the world would have been so much the poorer in consequence. But would any sane person propose to banish Fielding and Swift and Smollett and

---

1  See note 3, page 147 and note 3, page 225.

2  See note 3, page 263.

3  The "Obscene Publications Act" of 1857 was sponsored by Chancellor and Chief Justice John Campbell, who said it was "intended to apply exclusively to works written for the single purpose of corrupting the morals of youth, and of a nature calculated to shock the common feelings of decency in any well-regulated mind." It made "obscene" publications illegal and, additionally, gave police the power to search premises on which these publications were kept for distribution or sale. The act also enabled customs officers and post office officials to confiscate and destroy consignments of such publications and to prosecute the originators.

Richardson from our libraries, and Bowdlerise all our editions of Shakespeare, and purify the Bible from passages which once were simple everyday facts, that no one was ashamed to discuss, and now are nameless indecencies impossible to be even alluded to, because these are not the fit kind of reading for boys and girls in their teens? With this excessive scrupulosity in fiction we publish the most revolting details in the daily Press; and we let our boys and girls read every paper that comes into the house. If even we debar them from these, with the large amount of uncompanioned liberty they have at the present day, and a penny or even a halfpenny in their pockets, they may sup full of horrors and improprieties, as now the details of some ghastly murder, now those of some highly-coloured divorce suit, sell the papers in the streets and stir up the public imagination. And again, with the new development of education our young Girton girls[1] may study Juvenal and Catullus in the original, and laugh over the plain speaking of the Aristophanes; while French novels, of which the translation lands a man in prison, may be sold by their hundreds in the original language wherein every decently educated girl is a proficient.[2]

The whole thing results from the muddle and the compromise which English morality so delights to make. The British Matron must have a scapegoat whom she sends into the desert laden with a few uncongenial sins, while she keeps all the rest in safe custody in her tents. She must have a whipping-boy for the encouragement of her pupils. In literature this is the seventh commandment in all its forms and ramifications when discussed in the native tongue. Uncandid and also hypocritical, this attitude exposes us as a nation to both ridicule and blame. With a Press so rampantly unmuzzled—with editors of evening papers who go into the most disgusting and minute details of things which are, which have been done, and which, therefore, can be imitated—we fall foul of the writer who takes for his motive the subject of unlawful love,

---

1 Girton College, Cambridge, was established in 1869 as the first residential college for women. The label "Girton Girls" was used derogatorily by those who believed that women had no real right or reason to seek formal higher education.

2 Linton notes the irony of legally censoring translations of salacious works of French authors such as Zola and provocative works of the Roman writers Catullus and Juvenal while at the same time providing young women with the education that would enable them to read the same offensive material in readily available untranslated versions.

though he handles it with scrupulous delicacy and in the broadest manner of indication rather than description. We cut ourselves off from one of the largest and most important areas of that human life we pretend to portray, and we throw the limelight of fancy on crimes which are of comparatively rare occurrence, and which consequently excite but little living sympathy. How many respectable men in England have committed a murder for which they have allowed another man to suffer? How many women have set fire to houses in the hope of burning to death an inconvenient witness of their past folly? Who among us has destroyed a will and so come into money and estates to which we have no right? Which of us is personating a dead man? In whose house is that mad woman kept out of sight to the world? And where do we find the domestic burglar who roams about the passages o'nights, acting the family ghost for nefarious reasons connected with sliding panels and secret treasures? These things are rare in real life, though so prolific as themes of novels. But what is not rare is the "treacherous inclination" which either discounts or overleaps the authorisation of society, or which bravely beats down the rebellious instinct and suffers heart-break rather than social shame.

Truth to human nature and faithful presentation of the realities of human life are one thing; licentiousness of description and plain speaking which is indecent are another. Those who most warmly advocate the view of the first in our fictitious literature, if indeed it is to be taken as a true picture of the world and society, would be most strenuously opposed to the last. Take the greatest master of analytical fiction and the boldest handler of themes we have ever had—Balzac[1]—I do not remember at this moment more than one or two pages which would come under the head of licentiousness. I know him pretty well; but if there are many of this kind I have clean forgotten them. His subjects are another matter. But an English Balzac would be hunted out of social life as well as out of literary existence, and his success would be only of the surreptitious hole-and-corner kind which includes shame as well as secresy— shame to both author and reader alike. The thousand and one lifelike touches which make Balzac's portraits real would be impossible in an English novel. Mrs. Grundy would be up in arms; and all

---

1   French novelist Honoré de Balzac (1799-1850) was respected by the British as a realist with a Dickensian ability to create memorable character and dialogue.

the heads of houses would be incensed, because their young people might be initiated before their time, into certain mysteries of life which should be kept hidden from them. To which objection there is but the repetition of the former argument: Why should these young people be allowed to read books which are not meant for them, when they have more than enough literature of their own?

In olden days, and I should imagine in all well-ordered houses still, the literature which was meant for men was kept on certain prohibited bookshelves of the library, or in the locked bookcase for greater security. The Young Person was warned off these shelves. If her discretion was not to be trusted and her word of honour was only a shaky security, the locked bookcase made all safe. Here the father kept his masculine literature; his translations of certain classical authors; his ethnological and some scientific books; his popular surgical, medical, and anatomical works; perhaps some speculative philosophies of an upsetting tendency; and all the virile work of the last and preceding centuries. To the Young Person we free Jane Austen and Sir Walter Scott, Miss Mitford and Miss Edgeworth, "Eveline," Fenimore Cooper, Marryat, G.P.R. James, and many others in the immediate past, with the largest proportion of the writers of fiction in the present day.[1] If two or three here and there attempted the bow of Ulysses and tried on the mantle of Balzac, his, or more probably her books went into the closed compartment and the Young Person was no whit the worse. And this seems to me a better way all round and a finer kind of safeguarding than the emasculation of all fictitious literature down to the level of boys and girls; and the consequent presentation of human life in stories which are no truer to that human life than so many fairy tales dealing with griffins and flying dragons, good genii and malevolent old witches. The result of our present system of uncandid reticence, of make-believe innocence in one line with impossible villainies in others—the working response made to the demand of the British Matron for fairy tales, not facts—is that, with a few notable exceptions, our fictitious literature is the weakest of all at this present time, the most insincere, the most jejune, the least impressive, and the least tragic. It is wholly wanting in dig-

---

1   The authors mentioned wrote historical novels, novels of manner, domestic novels, novels of community, and relatively tame adventure stories. Linton deems their work safe reading for young women.

nity, in grandeur, in the essential spirit of immortality. Written for the inclusion of the Young Person among its readers, it does not go beyond the schoolgirl standard. It may be charming, as the shy and budding miss is charming; but that smell of bread and butter spoils all quite as much as the smell of the apoplexy spoilt the Archbishop's discourse. Thus we have the queer anomaly of a strong-headed and masculine nation cherishing a feeble, futile, milk-and-water literature—of a truthful and straightforward race accepting the most transparent humbug as pictures of human life. A great king may make himself a hobby-horse for his children to ride on pick-a-back, but a great nation should be candid and truthful in art as well as in life, and mature men and women should not sacrifice truth and common-sense in literature for the sake of the Young Person. The locked bookcase is better.

Thomas Hardy

Even imagination is the slave of stolid circumstance; and the unending flow of inventiveness which finds expression in the literature of Fiction is no exception to the general law. It is conditioned by its surroundings like a river-stream. The varying character and strength of literary creation at different times may, indeed, at first sight seem to be the symptoms of some inherent, arbitrary, and mysterious variation; but if it were possible to compute, as in mechanics, the units of power or faculty, revealed and unrevealed, that exist in the world at stated intervals, an approximately even supply would probably be disclosed. At least there is no valid reason for a contrary supposition. Yet of the inequality in its realisation there can be no question; and the discrepancy would seem to lie in contingencies which, at one period, doom high expression to dumbness and encourage the lower forms, and at another call forth the best in expression and silence triviality.

That something of this is true has indeed been pretty generally admitted in relation to art-products of various other kinds. But when observers and critics remark, as they often do remark, that the great bulk of English fiction of the present day is characterised by its lack of sincerity, they usually omit to trace this serious defect to external, or even eccentric causes. They connect it with an assumption that the attributes of insight, conceptive power, imaginative emotion, are distinctly weaker nowadays than at particular epochs of earlier date. This may or may not be the case to some degree; but, on considering the conditions under which our popular fiction is produced, imaginative deterioration can hardly be deemed the sole or even chief explanation why such an undue proportion of this sort of literature is in England a literature of quackery.

By a sincere school of Fiction we may understand a Fiction that expresses truly the views of life prevalent in its time, by means of a selected chain of action best suited for their exhibition. What are the prevalent views of life just now is a question upon which it is not necessary to enter further than to suggest that the most natural methods of presenting them, the method most in accordance with the views themselves, seems to be by a procedure mainly impassive in its tone and tragic in its developments.

Things move in cycles; dormant principles renew themselves, and exhausted principles are thrust by. There is a revival of the artistic instincts towards great dramatic motives—setting forth that "collision between the individual and the general"—formerly worked out with such force by the Periclean and Elizabethan dramatists, to name no other. More than this, the periodicity which marks the course of taste in civilised countries does not take the form of a true cycle of repetition, but what Comte,[1] in speaking of general progress, happily characters as "a looped orbit": not a movement of revolution but—to use the current word—evolution. Hence, in perceiving that taste is arriving anew at the point of high tragedy, writers are conscious that its revived presentation demands enrichment by further truths—in other words, original treatment: treatment which seeks to show Nature's unconsciousness not of essential laws, but of those laws framed merely as social expedients of humanity, without a basis in the heart of things; treatment which expresses the triumph of the crowd over the hero, of the commonplace majority over the exceptional few.

But originality makes scores of failures for one final success, precisely because its essence is to acknowledge no immediate precursor or guide. It is probably to these inevitable conditions of further acquisition that may be attributed some developments of naturalism in French novelists of the present day, and certain crude results from meritorious attempts in the same direction by intellectual adventurers here and there among our own authors.

Anyhow, conscientious fiction alone it is which can excite a reflective and abiding interest in the minds of thoughtful readers of

---

1   French philosopher Auguste Comte (1798-1857).

mature age, who are weary of puerile inventions and famishing for accuracy; who consider that, in representations of the world, the passions ought to be proportioned as in the world itself. This is the interest which was excited in the minds of the Athenians by their immortal tragedies, and in the minds of Londoners at the first performance of the finer plays of three hundred years ago. They reflect life, revealed life, criticised life. Life being a physiological fact, its honest portrayal must be largely concerned with, for one thing, the relations of the sexes, and the substitution for such catastrophes as favour the false colouring best expressed by the regulation finish that "they married and were happy ever after," of catastrophes based on sexual relationship as it is. To this expansion English society opposes a well-nigh insuperable bar.

The popular vehicles for the introduction of a novel to the public have grown to be, from one cause and another, the magazine and the circulating library; and the object of the magazine and circulating library is not upward advance but lateral advance; to suit themselves to what is called household reading, which means, or is made to mean, the reading either of the majority in a household or of the household collectively. The number of adults, even in a large household, being normally two, and these being the members which, as a rule, have least time on their hands to bestow on current literature, the taste of the majority can hardly be, and seldom is, tempered by the ripe judgment which desires fidelity. However, the immature members of a household often keep an open mind, and they might, and no doubt would, take sincere fiction with the rest but for another condition, almost generally coexistent: which is that adults who would desire true views for, their own reading insist, for a plausible but questionable reason upon false views for the reading of their young people.

As a consequence, the magazine in particular and the circulating library in general do not foster the growth of the novel which reflects and reveals life. They directly tend to exterminate it by monopolising all literary space. Cause and effect were never more clearly conjoined, though commentators upon the result, both French and English, seem seldom if ever to trace their connection. A sincere and comprehensive sequence of the ruling passions, however moral in its ultimate bearings, must not be put on paper as the foundation of imaginative works, which have to claim notice through the above-named channels, though it is extensively welcomed in the form of newspaper reports. That the magazine and library have arrogated to themselves the dispensation of fiction is not the fault of the authors, but of circumstances over which they, as representatives of Grub Street,[1] have no control.

What this practically amounts to is that the patrons of literature—no longer Peers with a taste—acting under the censorship of prudery, rigorously exclude from the pages they regulate subjects that have been made, by general approval of the best judges, the bases of the finest imaginative compositions since literature rose to the dignity of an art. The crash of broken commandments is as necessary an accompaniment to the catastrophe of a tragedy as the noise of drum and cymbals to a triumphal march. But the crash of broken commandments shall not be heard; or, if at all, but gently, like the roaring of Bottom[2]—gently as any sucking dove, or as 'twere any nightingale, lest we should fright the ladies out of their wits. More precisely, an arbitrary proclamation has gone forth that certain picked commandments of the ten shall be preserved intact—to wit, the first, third, and seventh; that the ninth shall be infringed but gingerly; the sixth only as much as necessary; and the remainder alone as much as you please, in a genteel manner.

It is in the self-consciousness engendered by interference with spontaneity, and in aims at a compromise to square with circumstances, that the real secret lies of the charlatanry pervading so much of English fiction. It may be urged that abundance of great and profound novels might be written which should require no compromising, contain not an episode deemed questionable by prudes. This I venture to doubt. In a ramification of the profounder passions the treatment of which makes the great style, something "unsuitable" is sure to arise; and then comes the struggle with the literary conscience. The opening scenes of the would-be great story may, in a rash moment, have been printed in some popular magazine before the remainder is written; as it advances month by month the situations develop, and the writer asks himself, what will his characters do next? What would probably happen to them, given such beginnings? On his life and conscience, though he had not foreseen the thing, only one event could possibly happen, and that therefore he should narrate, as he calls himself a faithful artist. But, though pointing a fine moral, it is just one of those issues which are not to be

1 Originally a street in Moorfields in London, Grub Street became a synonym for hack writers and literary mediocrity after Dr. Johnson described it as a place "much inhabited by writers of small histories, dictionaries, and temporary poems."

2 The bombastic weaver in *A Midsummer-Night's Dream*.

mentioned in respectable magazines and select libraries. The dilemma then confronts him, he must either whip and scourge those characters into doing something contrary to their natures, to produce the spurious effect of their being in harmony with social forms and ordinances, or, by leaving them alone to act as they will, he must bring down the thunders of respectability upon his head, not to say ruin his editor, his publisher, and himself.

What he often does, indeed can scarcely help doing in such a strait, is, belie his literary conscience, do despite to his best imaginative instincts by arranging a *dénouement* which he knows to be indescribably unreal and meretricious, but dear to the Grundyist and subscriber. If the true artist ever weeps it probably is then, when he first discovers the fearful price that he has to pay for the privilege of writing in the English language—no less a price than the complete extinction, in the mind of every mature and penetrating reader, of sympathetic belief in his personages.

To say that few of the old dramatic masterpieces, if newly published as a novel (the form which, experts tell us, they would have taken in modern conditions), would be tolerated in English magazines and libraries is a ludicrous understatement. Fancy a brazen young Shakespeare of our time—*Othello, Hamlet*, or *Anthony and Cleopatra* never having yet appeared—sending up one of those creations in narrative form to the editor of a London magazine, with the author's compliments, and his hope that the story will be found acceptable to the editor's pages; suppose him, further, to have the temerity to ask for the candid remarks of the accomplished editor upon his manuscript. One can imagine the answer that young William would get for his mad supposition of such fitness from any one of the gentlemen who so correctly conduct that branch of the periodical Press.*

Were the objections of the scrupulous limited to a prudent

---

\* It is, indeed, curious to consider what great works of the past the notions of the present day would aim to exclude from circulation, if not from publication, if they were issued as new fiction. In addition to those mentioned, think of the *King Oedipus* of Sophocles, the *Agamemnon* of Æschylus, Milton's *Paradise Lost*. The "unpleasant subjects" of the two first-named compositions, the "unsuitableness" of the next two, would be deemed equalled only by the profanity of the two last; for Milton, as it is hard necessary to remind the reader, handles as his puppets the Christian divinities and fiends quite as freely as the Pagan divinities were handled by the Greek and Latin imaginative authors. [Hardy's note] treatment of the relations of the sexes, or to any view of vice calculated to undermine the essential principles of social order, all honest lovers of literature would be in accord with them. All really true literature directly or indirectly sounds as its refrain the words in *Agamemnon*: "Chant Ælinon, Ælinon! But may the good prevail." But the writer may print the *not* of his broken commandment in capitals of flame; it makes no difference. A question which should be wholly a question of treatment is confusedly regarded as a question of subject.

Why the ancient classic and old English tragedy can be regarded thus deeply, both by young people in their teens and by old people in their moralities, and the modern novel cannot be so regarded; why the honest and uncompromising delineation which makes the old stories and dramas lessons in life must make of the modern novel, following humbly on the same lines, a lesson in iniquity, is to some thinkers a mystery inadequately accounted for by the difference between old and new.

Whether minors should read unvarnished fiction based on the deeper passions, should listen to the eternal verities in the form of narrative, is somewhat a different question from whether the novel ought to be exclusively addressed to those minors. The first consideration is one which must be passed over here; but it will be conceded by most friends of literature that all fiction should not be shackled by conventions concerning budding womanhood, which may be altogether false. It behooves us then to inquire how best to circumvent the present lording of nonage over maturity, and permit the explicit novel to be more generally written.

That the existing magazine and book-lending system will admit of any great modification is scarcely likely. As far as the magazine is concerned it has long been obvious that as a vehicle for fiction dealing with human feeling on a comprehensive scale it is tottering to its fall; and it will probably in the course of time take up openly the position that it already covertly occupies, that of a purveyor of tales for the youth of both sexes, as it assumes that tales for those rather numerous members of society ought to be written.

There remain three courses by which the adult may find deliverance. The first would be a system of publication under which books could be bought and not borrowed, when they would naturally resolve themselves into classes instead of being, as now, made to wear a common livery in style and subject, enforced by their supposed necessities in addressing indiscriminately a general audience.

But it is scarcely likely to be convenient to either authors or publishers that the periodical form of publication for the candid story should be entirely forbidden, and in retaining the old system thus far, yet ensuring that the emancipated serial novel should meet the eyes of those for whom it is intended, the plan of publication as a *feuilleton*[1] in newspapers read mainly by adults might be more generally followed, as in France. In default of this, or co-existent with it, there might be adopted what, upon the whole, would perhaps find more favour than any with those who have artistic interests at heart, and that is, magazines for adults; exclusively for adults, if necessary. As an offshoot there might be at least one magazine for the middle-aged and old.

There is no foretelling; but this (since the magazine form of publication is so firmly rooted) is at least a promising remedy, if English prudery be really, as we hope, only a parental anxiety. There should be no mistaking the matter, no half measures, in the words of Pascal,[2] might then grow to be recognised in the treatment of fiction as in other things, and untrammelled adult opinion on conduct and theology might be axiomatically assumed and dramatically appealed to. Nothing in such literature should for a moment exhibit lax views of that purity of life upon which the well-being of society depends; but the position of man and woman in nature, and the position of belief in the minds of man and woman—things which everybody is thinking but nobody is saying—might be taken up and treated frankly.

---

1 A serial.
2 French philosopher Blaise Pascal (1623-62).

# Select Bibliography

## Works by Ella Hepworth Dixon

*Books*

*My Flirtations*. London: Chatto & Windus, 1892; Philadelphia:
Lippincott, 1893.
*The Story of a Modern Woman*. London: Heinemann, 1894; New
York: Cassell, 1894; Leipzig: Tauchnitz, 1895.
*One Doubtful Hour and Other Side-lights on the Feminine Tempera-
ment*. London: Grant Richards, 1904; Leipzig: Tauchnitz, 1904.

*Periodical Publications*

[This list is incomplete. Hepworth Dixon published stories and
articles, signed and unsigned, in London and New York journals,
newspapers, and magazines during the 1880s and 1890s and the
early 1900s. In particular, she was a contributor to Oscar Wilde's
*Woman's World*, and in the mid-1890s she contributed to *The
Englishwoman*, a monthly of which she was the editor-in-chief.]

"Murder—or Mercy? A Story of To-day," *Woman's World* 1
(1888): 466-69.
"On Cloaks," *Woman's World* 2 (1889): 509-13.
"Women on Horseback," *Woman's World* 2 (1889): 227-33.
"A Garden in the South," *Woman's World* 3 (1890): 247-50.
"A Literary Lover," *Woman's World* 3 (1890): 638-41.
"London in Khaki," *New York Independent* (26 July 1900): 1794-96.
"Why Women Are Ceasing to Marry." *Humanitarian* 14 (1899):
391-96.

*Drama*

*The Toy-Shop of the Heart*. The Playhouse, London. 26 November
1908.

*Autobiography*

*As I Knew Them: Sketches of People I Have Met on the Way*.
London: Hutchinson, 1930.

## Secondary Periodical Material Related to "New Woman" Fiction, 1883–1900

Allen, Grant. "The New Hedonism." *Fortnightly Review* 55 (1 March 1894): 377–92.

———. "Plain Words on the Woman Question." *Fortnightly Review* 46 (1 October 1889): 448–58.

Amos, Sarah. "The Evolution of the Daughters." *Contemporary Review* 65 (April 1894): 515–20.

Arling, Nat. "What is the Role of the 'New Woman?'" *Westminster Review* 150 (June 1898): 576–87.

Barry, William. "The French Decadence." *Quarterly Review* 174, 438 (April 1892): 479–504.

———. "The Strike of a Sex." *Quarterly Review* 179, 358 (October 1894): 289–318.

Beerbohm, Max. "A Defence of Cosmetics." *Yellow Book* 1 (April 1894): 65–82.

Besant, Walter. "Candour in English Fiction." *New Review* 2 (January 1890): 6–9.

Bradfield, Thomas. "A Dominant Note of Some Recent Fiction." *Westminster Review* 142 (November 1894): 537–49.

Caird, Mona. "A Defence of the So-Called 'Wild Women'." *Nineteenth Century* 31 (May 1892): 811–29.

———. "Marriage." *Westminster Review* 130 (August 1888): 186–201.

———. *The Morality of Marriage and Other Essays on the Status and Destiny of Woman.* London: George Redway, 1897.

Crackanthorpe, B.A. "The Revolt of the Daughters." *Nineteenth Century* 35 (January 1894): 23–31.

———. "Sex in Modern Literature." *Nineteenth Century* 37 (April 1895): 607–16.

Eastwood, Mrs. "The New Woman in Fiction and in Fact." *Humanitarian* 5 (1894): 375–79.

Fawcett, Millicent. "The Woman Who Did." *Contemporary Review* 67 (May 1895): 625–31.

Gosse, Edmund. "The Decay of Literary Taste." *North American Review* 161 (July 1895) 109–18.

———. "The Tyranny of the Novel." *National Review* 19 (1892): 163–75.

Grand, Sarah. "The New Aspect of the Woman Question." *North American Review* 158 (March 1894): 270–76.

Hannigan, D.F. "Sex in Fiction." *Westminster Review* 143 (June 1895): 616–25.

Hardy, Thomas. "Candour in English Fiction." *New Review* 2 (January 1890): 15-21.

Harrison, Frederic. "The Emancipation of Women." *Fortnightly Review* 50 (1 October 1891): 437-52.

Hogarth, Janet. "Literary Degenerates." *Fortnightly Review* 57 (1 April 1895): 586-92.

———. "The Monstrous Regiment of Women." *Fortnightly Review* 68 (December 1897): 926-36.

Jeune, May. "The Revolt of the Daughters." *Fortnightly Review* 55 (February 1894): 267-76.

Lang, Andrew. "Realism and Romance." *Contemporary Review* 52 (November 1887): 683-93.

Lee, G.S. "The Sex-Conscious School in Fiction." *New World* (March 1900): 77-84.

Lee, Vernon (Violet Paget). "A Dialogue on Novels." *Contemporary Review* 48 (September 1885): 378-401.

Leppington, Blanche. "The Debrutalisation of Man." *Contemporary Review* 67 (June 1895): 725-43.

Linton, Eliza Lynn. "Candour in English Fiction." *New Review* 2 (January 1890): 10-14.

———. "The Partisans of the Wild Women." *Nineteenth Century* 31 (March 1892): 455-64.

———. "The Wild Women as Politicians." *Nineteenth Century* 30 (July 1891): 79-88.

———. "The Wild Women as Social Insurgents." *Nineteenth Century* 30 (October 1891): 596-605.

"Modern Mannish Maidens." *Blackwood's* 147 (February 1890): 252-64.

Noble, James. "The Fiction of Sexuality." *Contemporary Review* 67 (April 1895): 490-98.

Norman, Henry. "Theories and Practice in Modern Fiction." *Fortnightly Review* 40 (1 December 1883): 870-86.

Oliphant, Margaret. "The Anti-Marriage League." *Blackwood's* 159 (January 1896): 135-49.

Ouida (Marie Louise de la Ramée). "The New Woman." *North American Review* 158 (May 1894): 610-19.

Scott, H.S., and E. Hall. "Character Note: The New Woman." *Cornhill* 70 (October 1894): 365-68.

Slater, Edith. "Men's Women in Fiction." *Westminster Review* 149 (May 1898): 571-77.

Smith, Alys W. Pearsall. "A Reply from the Daughters II." *Nineteenth Century* 35 (March 1894): 443-50.

Stead, W.T. "The Novel of the Modern Woman." *Review of Reviews* 10 (1894): 64–73.

Stutfield, Hugh M. "'Tommyrotics.'" *Blackwood's* 157 (June 1895): 833–45.

———. "The Psychology of Feminism." *Blackwood's* 161 (January 1897): 104–17.

Ward, Mary. "An Appeal Against Female Suffrage." *Nineteenth Century* 25 (June 1889): 781–88.

Winston, Ella W. "Foibles of the New Woman." *Forum* 21 (April 1896): 186–92.

## Recent Secondary Material Related to "New Woman" Fiction

Ardis, Ann. *New Women, New Novels: Feminism and Early Modernism.* New Brunswick, NJ and London: Rutgers UP, 1990.

Basch, Françoise. *Relative Creatures: Victorian Women in Society and the Novel.* New York: Schoken, 1974.

Brake, Laurel. *Subjugated Knowledges: Journalism, Gender and Literature in the Nineteenth Century.* Basingstoke: Macmillan, 1994.

Brandon, Ruth. *The New Women and The Old Men.* London: Secker and Warburg, 1990.

Calder, Jenni. *Women and Marriage in Victorian Fiction.* New York: Oxford UP, 1976.

Cosslett, Tess. *Woman to Woman: Female Friendship in Victorian Fiction.* London: Harvester, 1988.

Cunningham. A.R. "The 'New Woman Fiction' of the 1890s." *Victorian Studies* 17 (December 1973): 177–86.

Cunningham, Gail. *The New Woman in the Victorian Novel.* London and New York: Harper & Row, 1978.

Dowling, Linda. "The Decadent and the New Woman in the 1890s." *Nineteenth Century Fiction* 33 (1979): 434–53.

Fernando, Lloyd. *"New Women" in the Late Victorian Novel.* University Park and London: The Pennsylvania State UP, 1977.

Hollis, Patricia. *Women in Public: The Women's Movement 1850–1900.* London: George Allen and Unwin, 1979.

Flint, Kate. *The Woman Reader: 1837–1914.* Oxford: Clarendon, 1993.

Jackson, Holbrook. *The Eighteen Nineties.* New York: Alfred A. Knopf, 1925.

Jordan, Ellen. "The Christening of the New Woman." *Victorian Newsletter* 48 (Spring 1983): 19.

Kenton, Edna. "A Study of the Old 'New Woman'." *Bookman* 37 (1913): 154–58.

Ledger, Sally. *The New Woman: Fiction and Feminism at the Fin de Siècle.* Manchester and New York: Manchester UP, 1997.

Miller, Jane Eldridge. *Rebel Women: Feminism, Modernism and the Edwardian Novel.* London: Virago, 1994.

Murphy, Patricia. *Time Is of the Essence: Temporality, Gender, and the New Woman.* Albany: State University of New York Press, 2001.

Nelson, Carolyn Cristensen. *British Women Fiction Writers of the 1890s.* New York: Twayne, 1996.

Perkin, Joan. *Victorian Women.* London: John Murray, 1993.

Pykett, Lyn. *The "Improper" Feminine: The Women's Sensation Novel and the New Woman Writing.* London and New York: Routledge, 1992.

———. "Portraits of the Artist as a Young Woman: Representations of the Female Artist in the New Woman Fiction of the 1890s." *Victorian Women Writers and the Woman Question.* Ed. Nicola Diane Thompson. Cambridge: Cambridge UP, 1999. 135–50.

Rubinstein, David. *Before the Suffragettes: Women's Emancipation in the 1890s.* New York: St. Martin's, 1986.

Sanders, Valerie. *Eve's Renegades: Victorian Anti-Feminist Women Novelists.* London: Macmillan, 1996.

Showalter, Elaine. *A Literature of Their Own: British Women Novelists from Brontë to Lessing.* Princeton, NJ: Princeton UP, 1993.

———. *Sexual Anarchy: Gender and Culture at the Fin de Siècle.* New York: Viking Penguin, 1990.

Stetz, Margaret Diane. "New Grub Street and the Woman Writer of the 1890s." *Transforming Genres: New Approaches to British Fiction of the 1890s.* Ed. Nikki Lee Manos and Meri-Jane Rochelson. New York: St. Martin's Press, 1994. 21–45.

———. "Turning Points: Ella Hepworth Dixon" *Turn-of-the-Century Women* 2 (Winter 1984): 2–11.

Stubbs, Patricia. *Women and Fiction: Feminism and the Novel 1880–1920.* Sussex, England: Harvester, 1979.

Swindells, Julia. *Victorian Writing and Working Women: The Other Side of Silence.* Minneapolis: U of Minnesota P, 1985.

Watt, George. *The Fallen Woman in the 19th-Century English Novel.* Totowa, NJ: Barnes & Noble, 1984.

## Additional "New Woman" and Related Fiction, 1883–1900

Allen, Grant. *The Woman Who Did.* London: John Lane, 1895.

Arnold, Ethel. *Platonics*. London: Osgood, McIlvaine, 1894.

Barry, William Frances. *The New Antigone; A Romance*. London and New York: Macmillan, 1887.

——. *The Two Standards*. London: T. Fisher Unwin, 1898.

Beaumont, Mary. *Two New Women and Other Stories*. London: James Clark, 1899.

Benson, E.F. *Dodo*. New York: Appleton, 1893.

Brooke, Emma Frances. *A Superfluous Woman*. New York: Cassell, 1894.

Broughton, Rhoda. *Dear Faustina*. London: Richard Bentley & Son, 1897.

Caird, Mona. *The Daughters of Danaus*. London: Bliss, Sands & Foster, 1894.

——. *The Wing of Azrael*. London: Trübner, 1889.

——. *The Daughters of Danaus*. London: Bliss, Sands, and Foster, 1894.

Cholmondeley, Mary. *Red Pottage*. London: Edward Arnold, 1899.

Cleeve, Lucas. *The Woman Who Wouldn't*. London: Simpkin, Marshall & Co., 1888.

Clifford, Mrs. W.K. *A Flash of Summer: The Story of a Simple Woman's Life*. London: Methuen, 1895.

Crommelin, May. *Dust Before the Wind*. London: Bliss, Sands & Foster, 1894.

Cross, Victoria. *The Woman Who Didn't*. London: John Lane, 1895.

Dalton, Henry Robert S. *Lesbia Newman*. London: George Redway, 1889.

Dowie, Ménie Muriel. *Gallia*. London: Methuen, 1895.

Egerton, George. *Keynotes*. London: John Lane, 1893.

——. *Discords*. London: John Lane, 1894.

Gissing, George. *The Odd Women*. London: Heinemann, 1893.

Grand, Sarah. *A Domestic Experiment*. Edinburgh: Blackwood's, 1891.

——. *Ideala: A Study from Life*. London: E.W. Allen, 1888.

——. *The Heavenly Twins*. London: Heinemann, 1893.

——. *The Beth Book*. London: Heinemann, 1897.

Hardy, Thomas. *Jude the Obscure*. London: Osgood, McIlvaine, 1896.

——. *Tess of the D'Urbervilles*. London: Osgood, McIlvaine, 1891.

Hunt, Violet. *A Hard Woman. A Story in Scenes*. New York: Appleton, 1895.

——. *The Human Interest: A Study in Incompatibilities*. London: Methuen, 1899.

———. *The Maiden's Progress*. New York: Harper, 1894.

———. *The Way of Marriage*. London: Chapman & Hall, 1896.

Iota (Kathleen Mannington Caffyn, née Hunt). *A Comedy in Spasms*. London: Hutchinson, 1895.

———. *A Yellow Aster*. Leipzig: Tauchnitz, 1894.

Schreiner, Olive. *The Story of an African Farm*. London: Chapman & Hall, 1883.

Wotton, Mabel. *A Pretty Radical and Other Stories*. London: David Scott, 1890.